Ashes and Wildflowers

ERIN FAE

Erin Fae

https://erinfaewriting.wordpress.com/

Copyright © 2024 Erin Fae

All rights reserved.

ISBN 9798328102582

Cover by: Krafigs_Creative
Interior formatting & illustrations by: Mariska Maas (Rubre Art)

To all my fellow book goblins.
Prince Lukas and Prince Arenn cannot wait to meet you...

THE FIVE KINGDOMS OF NYTHINIA

CORLIXIR
The Kingdom of Medicine and Healing

DROTHMORE
The Kingdom of Mining and Weaponry

HALLSHIRE
The Kingdom of Farming and Textiles

RYNTOOK
The Kingdom of Fishing and Sea Exploration

DALKING
The Kingdom of Forestry and Construction

PROLOGUE

Young Princess Naria was barely six months old when the Great Blaze burnt through her kingdom. One moment she was dreaming peacefully in her grand fur-lined cradle; the next, smoke was creeping towards her, its wispy fingers weaving through the bars of her bassinet before finally reaching her small sleeping face.

It was her screaming that broke the silence.

"Wha-what is it?" A young man, sleeping beside the baby, stirred under his thick blankets. The bed he slept in was grand and extravagant. Its tall birch frame stretched up to the ceiling while the wood showcased intricate designs of potions and healers, fittingly made for the King and Queen of Corlixir, the kingdom of medicine.

The man groaned at his daughter's cry until he too inhaled a lungful of thick smoke.

"Fire!" He gasped, heaving the blankets away from the

bed. Beside him, still asleep, the Queen twitched as her pale skin was exposed to the chill of night. "Elowen!" The man grasped his wife's shoulders, shaking her frantically.

She began to protest, pressing her face deeper into the sheets, but her annoyance vanished as the heavy stench of smoke reached her nose.

"Great Ancients," she spluttered, forcing herself up and swinging a hand to her face. "What's happening? Where are the guards?" She coughed so forcefully that it echoed off the walls of their palace bedroom.

"We have to go. Now," the King ordered, throwing on a purple silk robe and tossing another to his wife. Elowen hurried to dress herself as she sprinted towards Naria's bassinet. Her feet burned against the hot wooden floor, but she kept moving.

"Shh... Shh," she hushed, wrapping Naria in as many blankets as she could find before lifting the bundle close to her chest. "Don't cry, my angel. Mama's here."

Behind her, the King marched towards their bedroom door. His hand reached for the crystal handle, but the intense heat from the door forced his body to collapse backwards. Like a ragdoll, he fell to the scalding floor.

"Benedict!" the Queen cried, still grasping her daughter as she sprinted to his side.

"Stay away from the door!" he hissed, pushing himself up. "It's too hot. The fire must be right outside."

Elowen stifled a cry and smacked her hand to her mouth. "We're trapped... Oh Great Ancients, save us."

"Someone will come," Benedict asserted, trying his best to remain calm. Rising up from the floor, he furrowed his brow. He'd only owned this bedchamber for two years, and there were no secret passages or hidden doors that he knew of. The only way out of this room was through a door that was red-hot, or through a window barely wide enough for a baby.

Determined, he strode towards the window. It was tall and narrow, with a purple stained-glass pattern that depicted a woman holding an elixir. Along the way, he grabbed a thin iron vase from his bedside. It'd been a gift from another king and in truth he'd never liked it much, but at least now it would serve a purpose.

Without any hesitation, he hurled the vase at the stained glass. Immediately, the window shattered, the ear-splitting noise causing Elowen to scream. Thin shards of glass sliced Benedict's cheek, but he stayed put, even as something wet rolled down his face. Blood or a tear? He wasn't sure.

"It's too high, Bennie, and we won't fit." Elowen rushed over to him, grasping his arm. Her eyes were red and brimming with tears from the smoke.

"We have to try," he insisted as he drew closer to the window. With each step he took, glass crystals crunched beneath him, leaving a trail of red footprints.

Nothing could prepare him for what he was about to see.

Corlixir, his kingdom, his home, lay in ruins. Everywhere he looked, from the Great Libraries to the famous School of Healing, buildings were collapsing in the hungry flames. And there was nothing he could do to stop it. Screams of terror echoed down the streets as his people scattered like leaves in a furious wind. Even the far villages were glowing an orange hue.

In that moment, a breath caught in his throat and it felt like time stood still. There he was, king of a kingdom that was falling to ashes. It was as though the Healing Ancients – the divine beings that formed this land so many centuries ago – had suddenly decided that Corlixir should just cease to exist.

The sound of quiet sobs and glass crunching beside him pulled him harshly back to the tower.

"It's too high, Bennie," Elowen repeated with another forceful cough. The King's heavy gaze then fell from the burning city and to the grass far beneath the window. It was dizzyingly high – at least a hundred foot drop. Even if he and Elowen could squeeze through the stone window opening, no amount of healing would save them after they hit the ground.

"Look!" Elowen gasped, pointing into the distance. Benedict's heart leapt as he noticed movement through the thick trees of the dense forest that bordered their kingdom. He couldn't quite make it out at first, but soon enough, around twenty riders on horseback burst through the treeline, galloping towards the palace.

"They're soldiers from Drothmore, I see the crest," he said, catching sight of the steel-grey cloth that flowed beneath their saddles – steel grey for metal, stone, and swords, Drothmore's main trade.

Elowen used one arm to wave out of the window, the other still clutching Naria, who had quietened against her chest. "Up here! Help us!" she called desperately into the night air.

Leading the riders was a soldier in opulent, gold-decorated armour; his shoulders were broad and his form commanding. With urgency, he pointed towards Elowen and ordered the other soldiers to follow.

"Thank the Ancients, that must be King Ikelos!" Elowen exclaimed. She waved again frantically out of the window.

"Benedict! Elowen!" called the leading soldier as his horse and the other riders neared the palace. "A messenger brought us news of a fire. We came as quickly as we could, and there are more soldiers on the way to evacuate your people."

As the man lifted his gilded visor, the Corlixin King and Queen could clearly see the familiar, rugged face of Ikelos Forgeborn, King of Drothmore.

"We're trapped in here, Ikelos," Benedict called back, his knuckles turning white as he gripped the stone window frame. "You need to save Naria, we'll throw her down to you."

"What?" Elowen gasped, almost choking on both smoke and shock. Horrified, her hands wrapped tighter around the wriggling bundle at her chest. "We are not throwing our baby."

"We have no choice, it's the only way out for her." Benedict turned to stare into his wife's now glossy eyes. He was trying to speak calmly, but his lower lip quivered with each word.

Keep it together, Benedict. For her.

Outside, Ikelos barked orders for his soldiers to enter the palace and find their bedchamber.

"We'll extinguish the flames and get you out," the Drothmore King called up to them after his soldiers hurried off. "No need to throw any babies." He laughed as though Benedict's suggestion was absurd, but his lightheartedness did nothing to calm them. The rising heat in the room was all the pair could focus on.

Despite the chaos, Benedict remained facing his wife. "Listen." His hands clasped her shoulders. "I love you, and I know that you would never let any harm come to our sweet girl, but if we somehow get out through our door, it won't be safe for her. It'll be too hot. What if we collapse from the heat or the smoke? Let Ikelos take her. I trust him. He'll catch her."

But his words did little to slow Elowen's racing heart. Her chest felt heavy as she glanced down at little Naria, who was trying to sleep but the smoke kept waking her. How could she drop her out of a window so high? How could she let her fall into the night? There was no guarantee that Ikelos would catch her. What if he missed? Deep sobs erupted from her chest.

"Let me do it," Benedict offered as he tried to pry the baby away from Elowen's grasp. For a moment, she gripped tighter until an intense wave of heat hit the side of her face. Immediately, the King and Queen reached for each other to avoid stumbling against the wall.

When Elowen could finally open her smoke-filled eyes, she felt her stomach drop as though it had jumped out of the window instead. Their once-grand door had melted away to reveal a blazing wall of fire. It illuminated their bedchamber in a fierce orange glow. And as Elowen stared at the flames, they stared back, stalking closer with every second.

"Please do it now," she whimpered, loosening her grip on the bundle. "I love you so much, my sweet baby girl." Her hand brushed Naria's blonde curls one last time before

Benedict passed her tiny body through the narrow window opening.

"Ikelos!" he announced, biting back a sob. "You need to catch her. Do not let her hit the ground." His words were clear and powerful. A strong warning.

"Forge's Flame," Ikelos muttered, scrambling off his horse. He moved below Naria, his arms outstretched and poised to catch her. Above him, he could see the silhouette of a small baby wrapped in white, a stark contrast to the starry night sky above. She was so small, yet somehow, as her father held her out, she looked almost divine.

"I'm ready!" Ikelos answered, his voice tight.

"My dear girl," Benedict said with a quivering jaw. Elowen hugged his waist, burying her red face in his back. "You will make us so proud. I love you. I—" There was so much more he wanted to say, but another wave of heat, too intense to bear, overcame him. It was so hot; he was certain he felt his blood boil.

Holding back a scream, the King spoke one final time before dropping her into Ikelos's waiting arms.

"You are the next Queen of Corlixir. And you... You will rise like a phoenix from these ashes. We are already so proud of you, our sweet Naria."

And then, she fell.

18 Years Later...

CHAPTER 1

Until that morning, I'd only ever heard about the Steel Palace in stories. Whispers around the village had told me some of the spires were so tall they reached the clouds. Someone else had stopped me to say there's a hidden underground dungeon, where they torture faeries and misbehaving visitors, and that I should always be on my guard.

Seeing it in person, however, was a whole different story.

The spires weren't so tall that they touched the clouds, but they still rose clearly over the trees, dominating the skyline. Colossal steel archways marked the front entrance, and as the horse trotted further down the forest path, pulling our carriage closer, I could just about make out the intricate metal patterns decorating the stained-glass windows.

It was beautiful. Completely majestic. And yet still, the

longer I stared at it, the more I regretted leaving my anxiety powder in my dorm room.

"We're finally almost here! You must be so excited," the young woman sitting across from me chirped like a little bird. She'd arrived with the carriage, introducing herself only a few hours ago and insisting that I'd need her as a travel partner for the 'long' journey. At first, I was unsure, but I'll admit that her bubbly demeanour did help calm my nerves a little.

"Thank you, Lady Raena. Excited is certainly one way to put it," I answered, trying my hardest to match her refined way of speaking.

"Oh please, just Raena. There's no need to be so formal." She swatted a gloved hand towards me. "You know, I was so honoured when the King asked me to help you settle in here. Everyone's been talking about you. The new Princess Naria... Though perhaps we should call you 'Princess Star-ria', considering how popular you're going to be!" She squealed, then reached into her pockets to pluck out a hand fan. "They've even moved my room so that I'm right next to yours, isn't that wonderful?"

I nodded, hiding the sinking feeling in my chest behind a tight smile.

It had only been three days since the letter arrived. Three days since I'd handed the cream-coloured envelope, marked with the Drothmore King's seal, to the village mother, too fearful to open it myself.

"It's the royal summons," she'd told me, peering at the letter through her half-moon spectacles. "The day has finally come, dear child, for our beloved King Ikelos to deliver on his promise. Soon you will depart for the Steel Palace and all that was lost shall be restored."

Later that night, my dormmates and I all huddled around the same candle while we read the letter over and over again. None of us were surprised by the news. After the fire, King Ikelos had moved all the Corlixin survivors, including myself, into a small village tucked deep within the forests of Drothmore. Having been good friends with my parents, he'd promised to keep my people safe until I was old enough to rule them on my own. Then, when I was of age, Corlixir would be rebuilt with myself as queen.

My entire life I'd known this day was coming. I'd longed for the day I could finally take back what was lost, the day I'd be able to repay everyone who'd worked so hard to raise me and taught me everything they knew – to repay them with a kingdom of our own. Still, I couldn't deny the fear that rose in my chest as the carriage glided closer to the mining kingdom's palace.

It was so much bigger than it'd ever been in my daydreams.

"Oh, this is all so exciting. I can hardly breathe!" Raena's babbling tore me from my thoughts. "I'm sure we'll have so much fun together. I've already picked out so many gorgeous dresses for you. And oh! Speaking of gorgeous dresses, the Summer Ball is coming up soon." She grinned, fluttering her hand fan restlessly toward her face. "And with you at my side, a *princess* of all people, I'll have so many suitors lining up to dance with me. It'll be positively enchanting!" She beamed before suddenly stiffening. Quickly, she brought a hand to her face, as a red glow blossomed over her warm brown cheeks. "Forgive me, Your Highness, I'm afraid that sometimes I get so terribly excited, I forget myself." She shook her head. "I meant to say, I know everything there is to know about the Steel Palace, and I'll be sure to assist you here however I can."

Raena dipped her chin in a failing effort to hide her embarrassment.

"It's quite alright," I said with a small laugh. "And please, if we're to be friends, then there's no need for any formalities with me either. Just call me Naria."

In truth, this young woman was hardly my usual type of friend. Her funny upper-class accent and beautiful, lavish gown made her so different from all my friends in the village, but I'd gladly welcome the distraction. Anything to forget about the looming palace that was drawing ever closer.

Raena's blush faded, but she continued flapping the fan a little too intensely, sending curls dancing around her face. "I still can't believe that the King had you hidden away in Honeymeade all this time. It's so far away from... well, everything! You must be so happy to be finally leaving." Her brown eyes sparkled while my heart only sank further into my chest.

"It's certainly overwhelming," I answered honestly.

"I can imagine." Raena nodded, lowering her hand fan to lean closer. "That reminds me, I should fill you in about some of the noble families you'll be meeting. Even if you're a princess, you'll still need to win their favour if you want to make a name for yourself at court." She smiled before eagerly diving into a long explanation of several different families.

I tried my best to listen. I really did. But it was so hard

to stay focused when a dozen questions were racing through my mind. What would King Ikelos be like? Could I ever rule a kingdom? What if my simple clothing offends him? Would he take one look at me, burst into laughter, and order me to return to the forest? With a heavy sigh, I leaned back further into the plush seat of the carriage. The fates of hundreds of people rested upon my shoulders, and there I was, worrying about my gown. Maybe I was already more suited to royal life than I originally thought...

"We're here!" Raena sang, making me flinch as we pulled to a halt. "I can't wait to show you your bedroom. I helped decorate it but you can change anything you want." She charged out of the carriage as I rose cautiously to follow. But the second my slippers hit the stone floor, my jaw almost joined them.

The entrance area was grand, decorated with a layer of opulence like I'd never seen before. Even though this was just an area for carriages and horses, the stone walls were adorned with glistening minerals, perfectly placed to catch the light, with steel veins weaving between them. Gold beams lined the walls, and tapestries hung in the empty spaces – all themed around mining and blacksmithing.

"This way," Raena said, offering her arm to guide me. "The King would've loved to be here to welcome you himself but," something like fear flickered across her face, "you'll understand why soon enough. I've been requested to take you straight to him. Let's not keep him waiting."

If the carriage waiting area was grand, taking Raena's arm and stepping inside the palace was like entering a gold-dusted fairy tale. Together, we walked through countless extravagant hallways, each one proving to be more grandiose than the last. I had no idea there was this much wealth in all the realm. Beside me, my new companion was once again babbling enthusiastically, gossiping about all the dukes, duchesses, and other nobles who also lived here. Every time we'd pass a painting, she'd fill me with stories of who they were, how heavy their coin purse was, and who they had their eye on.

It wasn't long before we turned another gold-beamed corner to reveal a grand carpeted staircase. A gasp slipped by my lips as Raena whispered that this was where the 'most important' court members slept. Suspended from the high ceiling was a stunning chandelier that glittered as it lit up various doors on the top landing, along with the ironclad guards posted outside. Each room probably belonged to some important somebody, although I was hardly excited to meet any of them. Instead, as Raena guided me up the stairs and our footsteps echoed off the cream walls, a knot formed deep inside me. This palace was so grand, it was completely overwhelming. I never thought I'd miss the tiny wooden dorm rooms of home, but in that moment, they were all I could think about.

When we reached the top, Raena paused by a large family portrait and gestured to it with a sweeping arm. "There they are..." She grinned, turning to look at me. "His Royal Majesty King Ikelos, his wife Queen Erissa, and their only son – Prince Lukas Forgeborn."

I shifted my focus to the picture. The King stood proudly in the centre, his arm wrapped tightly around his dainty, blue-eyed wife. To his right, stood a tall boy who looked not much older than me. His dark brown hair waved around his face, perfectly styled beneath a silver crown, and his eyes were a steel-grey colour, just like the walls of his father's palace. Each of them wore a gentle smile in the portrait, but even so, under all their crowns and finery, I couldn't help feeling that they looked sort of... sad.

"He's so handsome, isn't he?" Raena gazed longingly at the prince. Letting my eyes fall over him, I had to agree; he was certainly traditionally handsome. But then again, everyone looks good in portraits.

"I'm sure he has women fawning over him at every ball," I answered matter-of-factly, still studying the portrait. "No doubt he's already picked a suitor – some rich noble probably – like the ones you were telling me about before."

Raena snorted, bringing a gloved hand to her mouth. "Let's get you to the King. There is *much* he needs to tell you."

Without a second's hesitation, she ushered me away from the painting and towards one of the doors lining the corridor. This door was much larger than the rest, and two soldiers stood guard outside, each eyeing us stoically as we neared the King's chambers.

"Princess Naria and Lady Raena to see the King, as requested by His Majesty," Raena announced with volume, although there was a slight quiver in her tone.

After a few silent moments, a gravelly, frail voice sounded from inside the room.

"Let them enter."

As the grand door creaked slowly open, my heart thumped in my ears. And soon enough, I understood exactly why the King had not been waiting to greet me outside.

CHAPTER 2

A strange, stale air filled the King's chambers. It was so heavy and foul-smelling – the sort of smell that conjured up images of neglected bookshelves, damp houses, and what I imagined Death would look like if he was terribly old and covered in a thick layer of dust. The room's cream walls were decorated with gold beams, just like the rest of the palace, though they stood in stark contrast to the harshly-angled darkwood furniture. Across the floors were thick, lush carpets and furs, while a gem-encrusted fireplace with a crackling fire kept the chill from the stone walls at bay.

But it was not the impressive fireplace that first caught my attention. I barely even noticed it at all, because across from the fire, tucked into the largest bed I'd ever seen, was an ancient, dying man.

His skin was deathly pale and seemed to be flaking away

from his wrinkled, withered face. At first, I thought this must be a great-great-grandfather of the King. He had the same sullen brown eyes and ambitious stare as the much younger man in the portrait outside – same broad nose and thin mouth, too. But there was something so odd about the way he appeared, something almost unnatural.

As we approached, my steps just as cautious as Raena's, a loud cough erupted from his chest, sending a small cloud of dust into the air above him. It was then that I understood why this elderly man looked so strange. I'd studied healing long enough with the village elders to know that this was no ordinary ageing.

This was a curse.

"King Ikelos," Raena announced our presence, bowing deeply. Following her lead, I did the same.

Slowly, the old man blinked as loose cobwebs swayed from his eyelashes. "Naria," he wheezed before pausing to cough up another dust cloud. "My dear, you've grown so much. It feels like only last year when I held you in my arms on that dreadful night."

My body stiffened as if the words had bitten me. Of course, I knew all about that *dreadful night*. Not a day had passed in Honeymeade without someone mentioning the fire that had ravaged our kingdom. A few had been fortunate enough to escape before the flames grew out of control, but still, thousands died, along with so much of our kingdom's history. While the village mother had always told me I'd been saved as a baby, I didn't know until I was twelve years old that it was King Ikelos who caught me as I was dropped out of a palace window. A palace! Though

I'll admit, finding out I was a princess didn't change much. How can it when your parents, along with most of your people, are dead and your kingdom is in ashes?

"Elowen and Benedict were such good and loyal rulers," the King carried on, ignoring the dust that seemed to instantly reappear on his chapped lips. "Such good friends. The world hasn't been the same since we lost them." He sighed as his gaze met mine. "Sending you away was for your own good, you know. At first, I thought about keeping you here. Lukas was so young then, too. I could see you becoming good friends. But then I thought about your mother, dear and kind Elowen... She always spoke of how she wanted you to be educated and learn, just as she did, about all of the healing ways of Corlixir. And I knew you wouldn't find that sort of education here. Not unless you can learn about medicine from studying in the mines." He laughed, but it sounded more like rocks tumbling down a cliff, and I fought the urge to wince at the sight of him.

"It wasn't easy to build a village so quickly," he continued, despite his obvious discomfort, "but back then, your people were fighters. We all worked together to build enough houses and schools for the survivors. And while I knew those little wooden buildings wouldn't be the most sturdy, we made sure to choose a location where you would be protected by the giant oak trees. I know it probably never felt like it, but it was all for you, really, and your dear parents. Even the village name came from those little honeybelle flowers that your mother favoured so dearly. I can only hope your time there served you well."

After he finished, I could feel his stare searching mine

for any kind of reaction. There was a hint of guilt in his voice, too. Perhaps he still felt like he hadn't done enough.

"My people and I deeply appreciate everything you have done for us, Your Majesty," I answered, trying my best to sound as regal as a girl could while wearing a dull peasant gown. "And I will be forever grateful that I was allowed to grow up with the rest of my people. Thanks to them, I have a true passion for the medicinal arts, just like my mother did... or so I'm told."

A few beats of silence passed between us before I chewed my lip, considering how best to ask the question that had been on my mind since the moment we'd entered this room.

Bother it. I am a princess, after all.

"Do you know much about the curse that has plagued you?"

King Ikelos chuckled as Raena shot me a look that suggested she wanted the floor to swallow her up. "I don't remember you being this bold when you were just a babe," he said between laughs. "Your father was like this too, you know, straight to the point with everything. Though I'm afraid I cannot tell you much." A thin smile tugged at his lips. "I don't know much about what this curse is or who placed it upon me. But I've already met with some of the best healers in the realm and alas, it seems no one can fix this. All I know is that each day I seem to age faster and faster. With every rising sun, I feel my life slipping away." He cleared his throat, forcing away the dust that had settled on the blankets before him. "Do not worry about me though, child. I was old anyway. And my son is more than ready to take over. Which is precisely why I summoned you, actually. We must discuss the matter of your engagement."

My heart stopped.

Did he just say engagement?

He must've been mistaken, surely. Perhaps his mind was crumbling just as much as his body was. He was supposed to help me rebuild my kingdom, not marry me off to some stranger.

"Engagement?" I questioned, my voice trembling.

A loud laugh rumbled from the King's chest. "Do not look so upset, Naria. I assure you that Lukas is a fine young man, and I have been approached by more mothers and fathers than I can count, all desperate for me to introduce him to their daughters."

"Lukas?" I repeated, feeling my fingers go numb. "You want me to marry your son? But we've never even met."

He shook his head. "Surely you understand that this is common practice for royals? Your mother and father were engaged before they'd ever spoken a word to each other, and what a fine match they turned out to be!" The King beamed, while all I could feel was the colour draining from my cheeks.

"But what if I don't like him, or he doesn't like me?" My voice broke. "I couldn't do that to your son."

"Lukas has already agreed to do what is best for Drothmore, and if you want what's best for Corlixir, then you'll agree to this too." His cracked smile faded. "The truth of it all, Naria, is that your kingdom is still in ruins, and I am dying. When this damned curse first struck, I tried to begin the rebuilding efforts, but without a ruler, there is only so much I can do before I start jeopardising my own kingdom. One king cannot rule his own lands while also seeing to the rebuilding of another. But you and Lukas… If you were to marry, then not only would your safety here be guaranteed, but you could use Drothmore's wealth to rebuild Corlixir when I am gone."

A thin, wiry hand emerged from beneath the white bed sheets and reached for me. Reluctantly, I stepped forward, leaving Raena's side to take the King's frail hand in mine. As soon as we touched, I could feel the curse pulsing through him, sucking away his life essence like a leech. If only there were a way I could help him. All my years learning with the other Corlixins had taught me everything about healing but absolutely nothing about magic.

"Are you sure there is no way to break this curse? You are still young and have so many years left to rule. I don't need to be married to help my kingdom. I can find a way without Lukas. Please, Your Majesty, do not force me to marry someone I do not know, let alone love."

His features darkened, but before he had a chance to respond, a quiet, accented voice chimed from the edge of the room.

"The King needs his rest. It's time for visitors to leave."

I hadn't noticed her before, but near the fireplace, dressed in a long pale-blue robe, was a timid-looking young woman. A blue hood concealed part of her face, and in her delicate hands was a small stone bowl filled with what seemed to be herbal medicine. When neither of us replied, she stepped towards the King, her long robe flowing with each step and again, said, "It's time for visitors to leave."

"Thank you Seraphina," the King grumbled, sending a sharp warning-look her way. His hand clasped mine as he addressed me one final time. "Think about what I said, Naria, and talk to Lukas. He'll make an excellent king someday... And a fine husband."

I bit back the rest of the words I wanted to say as his dusty arm fell onto the bed sheets. From behind me, Lady Raena stepped forward to gently take my other hand. I hadn't noticed, but it'd been clutching my skirt, my fingernails almost piercing through the thin brown fabric.

"It's time to go," she whispered.

I didn't need to be told twice. After dipping my head respectfully, I followed her out of the grand door, leaving the foul-smelling chamber and the dying man inside it.

CHAPTER 3

Raena stayed by my side as we wandered back through the palace. Now that the sun was high in the sky, the corridors were stuffed with finely dressed court members. Each of them eyed us suspiciously as we passed by, and a few even dared to giggle when they turned back to their friends.

"Ignore them," Raena grumbled, leading me down a smaller hallway. "While I love living in the palace, the shallowness of the aristocracy will never cease to surprise me."

Though I'd never considered myself to be a beauty, I didn't think my bare face warranted giggles. With every titter, my cheeks burned a harsher shade of red.

"We'll swap your gown for something more suitable soon. Just wait till you try on the clothes I picked for you. Then we'll see who's laughing," she said with a scoff.

Of course. They were laughing at my dress. I hadn't

changed since we'd arrived, and I was still wearing the plain beige gown, typical for girls in my village. There was nothing really flattering about it, with its long sleeves and dull fabric skirt – hardly a gown fit for a princess. Shame crept over me as my arms hugged my chest. If only there was some kind of elixir I could mix up to turn invisible; I'd down it in a heartbeat.

We passed through several more stone-walled hallways riddled with tittering court members until Raena eventually led me towards a huge archway.

"If we cut through this banquet hall, we'll get to your room much faster." She had to raise her voice to be heard over the raucous laughter and cheering from within the hall. The nerves must've been showing on my face because, before we stepped inside, she squeezed my hand reassuringly. "Just stay close to me and try to keep quiet. They're running a duelling club today, so as long as you keep your head down, everyone will be too busy cheering on the fighters to notice you."

I nodded. Truthfully, her words did little to steady my rocking stomach, but before I could insist we take another route, she tugged my arm towards the hall.

The banquet hall was overflowing with dozens upon dozens of people. Far too many people. Some were finely dressed, thickly perfumed nobles, clinking golden goblets and chattering amongst themselves. Others were plainly dressed servants or catering staff, confidently flitting between the groups of nobility, refilling empty goblets and sweeping away any finished plates.

If it weren't for Raena's grounding hand as she guided

me around the long tables, I'd probably scream and hope the tiled floor gobbled me up. I'd never really understood why, but for as long as I could remember, bustling rooms would always make me feel like the whole world was caving in on me. Each unexpected noise and sudden movement would feel like a dozen talons scraping under my skin. The only way to make the panic stop would be to hide somewhere quiet and dark, or to force my mind to focus on something predictable and repetitive. Since hiding under a banquet table and clamping my hands over my ears wasn't an option right now, I let my free hand draw subtle circles against my skirt.

Round and round and round and round. Until the jarring laughter wasn't so jarring anymore.

"Duellists, prepare!" someone bellowed from across the hall, causing me to flinch and jerk my chin towards the sound. Around us, the chatter gradually faded as the crowd's attention shifted to the centre of the room. All eyes were now on two young men, both standing poised and ready to fight on an empty banquet table. Each was dressed in lightweight athletic tunics, with narrow black masks partially covering their faces, and in each duellist's right hand was a thin wooden practice sword. Despite the harmless nature of their blades, the sheer determination in their glares could've turned those swords into deadly weapons. And as a healer, I couldn't help but scowl at the sight of it.

"Let the duel commence!" the same voice bellowed again. Then, with a swift beat of a drum, the duellists leapt into action, their weapons clashing together hard.

Suddenly, my feet were rooted to the ground. Raena's

hand tugged at mine, but I was too fixated on the scene to let her pull me away. It was a flurry of motion, a ballet of combat. The leftmost duellist, slightly shorter and with thick blonde curls, appeared to float across the table as he parried his attacker's swings. The other, taller and with dark brown waves, struck fiercely and repeatedly, each swing meeting his opponent's sword with a satisfying clack.

As their fight continued, the taller one seemed to grow frustrated. Even with my utter lack of combat experience, I could tell his attacks were becoming sloppy. They were too powered by emotion, and each swing became more and more careless. Seeming to sense this too, the shorter one moved to attack, then abruptly changed his stance, twisting his body to strike at the taller duellist's knees. With a gasp from the crowd, the taller one was knocked backwards, his body thrown down and his head whacking against the wooden banquet table with an uncomfortably loud thud.

I winced. That didn't sound like a healthy fall.

Worried murmurs rippled through the audience as the shorter one lowered his sword. He leaned down, clearly intending to help the other duellist up, but before he could, the fallen man kicked out his legs and sent his opponent flying. The crowd roared. It appeared the fight wasn't over yet.

The taller duellist leapt to his feet, swaying a little before marching over to the shorter man who was now sprawled across the banquet table.

"Yield," he spat, looming over his fallen opponent and pointing his sword towards his neck.

"You cheated," the shorter one accused, "you were down and—"

"And now I'm up," he cut him off, bringing the blade closer to his neck, "and now you're on the table under my sword, so yield."

The shorter man looked like he wanted to protest, but then something flashed across his face – recognition, perhaps? Both fighters were masked, but it's possible he knew his voice. Before I had a chance to ponder more, the taller duellist swayed again.

'Possible mindjarring,' a voice within me announced. *'The patient is irritated and has trouble balancing after a head injury.'*

Memories of a past lesson on mindjarring flooded my thoughts. Our teacher, one of the village elders, had used a jar of pickled vegetables to mimic the mind within a skull. She violently shook the jar to show how a sudden impact can jostle the mind, causing head pain, dizziness, confusion, and in severe cases – a loss of consciousness. Failure to treat could lead to chronic head pain and irritability, and she'd insisted it was imperative that someone who is mindjarred should seek immediate medical attention.

Immediate medical attention.

My heart caught in my throat. So much for keeping my head down. Without hesitating, I shoved through the crowds.

"Naria, what are you doing? Come back!" Raena hissed, but it was too late to try to stop me. I'd already disappeared into the mob.

"Please let me pass!" I called out with all the importance I could muster. "I'm a healer. I need to attend to the duellists." Confused mumbles echoed around me, but eventually, the crowd surrounding the main table stepped aside. As soon as the path cleared, I raced towards the fighters.

"What is the meaning of this? Who are you?" The taller duellist shifted his attention to me, keeping the tip of his sword pointed at the fallen man.

"You might be mindjarred, so I need to examine you." I swung my leg onto the table and heard him scoff as I heaved myself up.

"Might be what?" He shook his head. "This is absurd. Get back to the floor, *servant*, the duel isn't over."

Ignoring his complaints, I marched towards him. "I'm not a servant, I'm a healer," I replied, but he was so tall it was difficult to maintain my serious facade. "Now, please remove your mask. I need to check your vision."

The duellist watched me suspiciously until eventually he threw his wooden sword to the side, letting it clatter against the table. Then, he slipped off the black mask, sending shocked murmurs ringing through the crowd. My heart fluttered for a second. While I'll admit his face was certainly very nice to look at, maybe even a little familiar, I didn't let my focus slip from the task at hand.

"Follow my finger with your eyes, please," I instructed, raising my finger up to his face. Slowly, I swished it from side to side. Thankfully, his grey irises followed my hand without any obvious difficulty. "That's good," I commented, while the young man raised an eyebrow. "You're not mindjarred, but I should still check for any swelling." My fingers reached for his head, and as I felt around gently for where the impact was, I tried to ignore how soft his dark brown hair was, or how it smelled like summer fruits. While I worked, outraged whispers sounded from the crowd, and for a moment, I caught a brief glimpse of Raena.

Horrified would not even begin to describe her expression.

Who was this duellist? Was he perhaps a well-known knight? Was that why he looked so familiar? I searched his face again as I continued feeling for any swelling. His eyes were a smooth, smoky grey – so similar to the King's own eyes.

My heart sank. I knew this face. Of course, I did. I'd seen it less than an hour ago, standing beside the King in the grand portrait above the stairs.

"Well, *healer*, am I going to die? Or do you wish to just continue playing with my hair?" The prince's words were laced with sarcasm as my hands quickly fell away from him.

"No." I swallowed. "I apologise for interrupting your duel. There's no swelling, so you'll be fine. Now please excuse me... Your Highness." Quickly, I stepped back and went to jump down off the table. But before I could take another step, a cold hand clamped around my wrist.

"Who are you?" He spoke in a low tone, pulling me closer.

There was no point in hiding it. He'd find out soon enough anyway. So, with a shaking voice, I replied, "My name is Naria."

"Naria?" he repeated, surprise parting his lips. "You're the Corlixin Princess?"

I nodded, still very aware of his hand gripping my wrist.

"You're certainly not how I expected."

I wasn't sure how to respond to that, so I let a silence fall between us. Then, when I tried to slip my hand free, his grip around my wrist only tightened.

"You'll come to the royal dining room for dinner tonight," he ordered. "There is much we need to discuss. And we must be properly acquainted, especially since my father has decided that you are my new fiancée."

Gasps echoed throughout the hall.

Fiancée...

The word sounded so foreign, and thanks to the prince, if our engagement wasn't common knowledge before, it was now.

"I'll see you tonight then." I dipped my head, trying my hardest to avoid his gaze as I felt it stalk over my trembling body.

"Nervous little thing, aren't you?" An almost devious smile tugged at his lips. "But you were so confident before, when you were playing healer." A few of our onlookers sneered with laughter, sending a rosy blush blooming over my cheeks.

I should've held back. I should've just bitten my tongue and stared him down until eventually he released my wrist, but with my heart pounding and the cruel tittering seeming to come at me from every direction, I couldn't stop myself.

"I apologise again for interrupting your duel." My tone was cold as I tilted my chin up to meet his amused grin. "But might I suggest that perhaps next time you practise your duelling technique a little more before you embarrass yourself in front of all these people. It is much easier for a healer to fix a bruised head than a bruised ego, *Your Highness*." I dipped my head with a sarcastic curtsy.

No one dared to pierce the deafening silence that followed. The prince dropped my wrist as though it burned, and the wicked smile that only moments ago covered his face had given way to a darkened anger.

"I'll see you at dinner, fiancée." He scowled before whirling away to face his opponent. "You!" He jabbed his finger towards the man still sprawled across the banquet table. "Get up. We're not finished yet."

I hadn't noticed Raena slipping through the surrounding crowd until she tugged on the hem of my skirts, beckoning me down from the table. "Can I at least show you to your chamber before you start any more arguments with members of the *royal family*?" she hissed with a disappointed head shake.

Technically, it was his comment that started it, but I didn't feel like arguing over the small details. Jumping down from the table, I quickly followed her out of the hall, the furious sounds of wooden swords clashing together growing quieter with every step.

CHAPTER 4

Whoever picked out this room for me must've thought I was in dire need of exercise. I'd never panted and scowled so much in my life as we climbed what seemed to be an endless spiral staircase near the far side of the palace. Even Raena, who must be used to scaling these white marble stairs, was definitely beginning to slow in her heavy ruffled gown.

"We're almost there, I promise," she called out between deep breaths. "It'll be worth it once we get to the top. You'll see."

After it felt like we'd climbed higher than the Drothmore Mountains, we finally reached the curved roof of the tower. Raena guided me away from the steps and down a small corridor, until we stopped outside an arched white door. From a few steps away, the door didn't seem to be anything spectacular, but when I peered closer, a soft gasp tumbled from my lips. Hundreds of small carvings of healers and potion mixers decorated the panelling of the wood. Weaving around them were vines, trees, and quaint little buildings, each one delicately etched into the door. I lifted my hand to let my fingers run over them, feeling every perfectly sanded bump and dip in the design.

"It's beautiful," I sighed.

"The King had it commissioned specially from expert wood carvers in Dalking." Raena grinned, bringing out her hand fan to flutter it against her face. "He wanted it to remind you of home."

Home. I wasn't sure if she meant Corlixir or Honeymeade, since neither truly felt like home to me.

"If you like this..." Her smile grew as she snapped the fan shut, then pointed it towards the door. "You should see what it's like inside."

After Raena twisted the golden doorknob, my heart nearly did a somersault. Behind the arched door was the prettiest room I'd ever seen. With its ornate decorations and soft lavender rugs, it looked so different from the rest of the palace, as though it'd been plucked straight from the pages of a fairy tale. The walls were a crisp white with wooden beams that reached up to the domed ceiling, while in the centre of the room was a curved four-poster bed. From the top of the bed frame, thin birch branches weaved all the way down to the bright wooden floors, creating intricate patterns on the walls. Even the little dressers and tables were delicately made and covered in tiny decorative flowers – so completely different from the harsher, more practical-looking furniture I'd seen dotted around the palace.

"The King did all this for me?" I gasped as I stepped further inside, twisting my body to try and take it all in.

"Well... I helped with a lot of the design," Raena chuckled. "I'm not from Drothmore so I never really understood the mining look." She fluttered her hand fan again. "I thought this would be a bit more... appropriate."

"I love it," I breathed. Beneath me, my skirts twirled as I continued to soak up every inch of the magnificent room. "I don't know how I'll ever sleep here though. It's so big and I've never slept in a room on my own before."

"How bizarre," Raena quipped. "I could never share a room with someone else... Unless that someone else was a he and *he* was very, very handsome." She squeaked with laughter, then pointed her fan towards another door a few metres away from the bed. "My room is just through there, so I'll hear you if you shout out for me. And the servants will always come if you call them too."

"Servants?" My eyes widened.

Raena tilted her head before replying casually, "Of course. You'll have at least three or so to come in and help you dress in the mornings. Oh, and they also help with bathing."

My nose scrunched at the thought. "I don't need help to bathe."

"You never *need* it," she said with a playful smile, "but it is certainly lovely to have someone massage oils into your hair while you just lie back and relax in the bubbles." A giggle burst from her throat, and in that moment, all I could think of was just how far I was from my simple village in the woods.

Raena then showed me to the wardrobe, proudly lifting

each dress to describe exactly why she'd purchased it and marvelling at how much they cost. We were rarely given money in Honeymeade, and even when we were, it would only ever be a few coins to spend at the local markets. Still, in my entire life I didn't think I'd spent as much as the price of even one of these dresses. Every time she pulled out another gown, I found myself gawking more and more at the absurd numbers.

"And this one," she began, tugging on the skirt of a lilac off-the-shoulder gown, "would be perfect for dinner tonight, don't you agree?" She lifted it off the rail to present it to me, beaming as if she'd stitched it herself. "Apparently purple was always the preferred colour in Corlixir. When I saw this in the dressmakers, I knew you simply *had* to have it."

My fingers reached out to brush against the soft fabric. "It's so lovely, thank you," I told her honestly, just as I'd said with every other dress.

"I'll call the servants. They'll help you get ready." Raena laid the gown gently on the bed before drifting back over to where I was standing. "We'll have to do something about your hair too." She reached for the thin blonde strand that was resting on my shoulder. "You may already be the prince's fiancée, but you can still make an effort to impress him. And after how today's introductions went, you really ought to try impressing him," she added with a chuckle. "You've had a stressful day. As long as you apologise, I'm sure he'll understand."

I wanted to pull a face. If anything, *he* should be the one apologising. Still, I held my tongue. It wasn't Raena's fault that the prince had such an oversized ego.

A few moments after my new friend had disappeared down the hallway, a small group of servants swooped in to begin dressing me. They worked surprisingly quickly to help remove my dress and swap it for the gown Raena had selected. I tried to make conversation with one of them as she was lacing up my corset, but the girl was quickly shushed by an older servant the moment she opened her mouth to reply. Perhaps this was really the life of a princess – always surrounded by people, yet somehow still alone.

Once they had finished, I was brought to a large birch vanity so they could begin fixing my hair. As the light blonde mess on my head was brushed out, I let my gaze drift down at the dress now sitting comfortably against my skin. It hugged my figure like nothing I'd ever worn before. I hardly recognised the stranger in the mirror as the busy ladies behind me pinned up parts of my hair, leaving the rest down with its natural wave. One of them stepped forward when my hair was nearly finished to apply a rouge colour to my lips and cheeks. Just as I was beginning to feel more like a doll than myself, Raena stepped into the room once again.

"Oh, you look wonderful!" She grinned, clapping her hands together. "You've done a brilliant job, ladies. Thank you." The three servants dipped their heads before hastily leaving my new bedchamber, disappearing just as quickly as they'd arrived. "I'm here to take you to dinner," Raena announced. "Are you ready?"

Physically? *Yes.* Mentally? *Absolutely not.*

Slowly, I nodded.

The thought of meeting Lukas again made me feel queasy. Of course I couldn't deny that his looks were charming;

but still, after our last conversation, any butterflies that might have fluttered around in my stomach had long since drowned in a deep sea of nerves.

"Let's not keep your future husband waiting," Raena said with a smile, extending her arm for me to take.

CHAPTER 5

The endless stairs felt so much shorter on the way down, and it wasn't long before we arrived at the private dining room reserved for royals. Upon reaching the great wooden doors that marked the entrance, Raena bid her goodbyes and wished me luck with a final squeeze of my hand.

I held my breath as the guards heaved open the tall wooden doors. The pink ruffles of Raena's gown had long since disappeared down the hallway, leaving me alone with my thoughts and each one was far too heavy with dread. Swallowing thickly, I paused for a moment. Then, without giving myself any more chances to change my mind, I stepped into the room.

Despite the grand entrance, the royal dining room was much smaller and far more intimate than I was expecting. The walls were painted a warm shade of cream and decorated with gilded portraits, while several large arched windows bathed the room in the glow of the evening sun. In the centre of the room was a long wooden table, covered with a pristine white tablecloth. And sitting at the head of that otherwise empty table, leaning back rather comfortably in his chair, was a familiar young man. This morning's athletic tunic had been replaced by a loose ivory dress shirt that fit tightly around his wrists, and resting perfectly upon the dark waves of his hair was a shining silver crown.

I could feel the prince's eyes on me immediately as I entered the room. His fingers, which were drumming softly away against the table, paused as he cast a slow, sweeping look over my gown. Once he was satisfied, he rose from his seat and tipped his chin in respect. Not wanting to offend, I returned his greeting with a small curtsy.

"I see the servants have worked their magic." He spoke first, meeting my gaze.

"Was that supposed to be a compliment?" I asked bluntly.

He raised an eyebrow. "In a way." Then he gestured to the seat beside him. "Please, join me."

'*No thank you*,' was what I probably should have said. But instead, I ignored him and moved to pull out the chair at the opposite end of the table, making no effort to hide the deafeningly loud noise as it scraped along the wooden floor. Without waiting for him to object, I plopped myself down into the chair and turned my head towards the nearest window. Though I could still feel him studying me, even as my gaze drifted over the distant mountains.

"I feel like I have offended you," he said indifferently, before taking a seat in a much more graceful manner at his end of the table. "How about we start again?"

Tentatively, I returned my focus to him as he reached for a spiced bread roll that was resting on a silver platter.

"You look ravishing in that dress, Naria," he breathed before taking a bite.

Unwanted heat flooded my cheeks, flushing them red. There was something so dark and enticing about the way he said my name. It was as though each vowel danced off his full lips. No one had ever said it like that before...

Clenching my jaw, I caught myself before I could tumble any further. I barely knew him, and the little I did know was violent and saw no issue with embarrassing me in front of more than a dozen of his sneering friends. It would take a lot more than a nice compliment to sweep me off my feet.

Taking a breath, I reached for my wine goblet. "So, what's it like being a prince?" I asked, desperate to hear anything other than the pounding of my own heart in my ears.

Lukas shrugged. "There are good days and bad days."

"And what would be a good day?" I took a sip.

"Well..." He pondered for a moment, resting his chin on his palm. "I suppose this morning was quite a good day... waking up to a knock on the door, being told that I'd finally get to meet my *mysterious* fiancée, and that the carriage had already been sent to fetch her."

Something mischievous danced across his features. I opened my mouth to respond, but his voice cut me off. "Then again, when I came back to bed, Giselle wasn't best pleased with the news." My entire body stiffened. He was handsome and a prince, so of course he already had a lover. "Lady Vivian wasn't too happy either at breakfast, when I told her that you were on your way," he added, a half-smile tugging at his jaw.

So much for good first impressions.

Biting back the urge to launch my silver goblet at his head, I continued, "A busy morning for you then."

"Indeed," the prince chuckled, tearing off a piece of bread and tossing it into his mouth.

A line of servants appeared from behind me then, each carrying plates filled with various delicacies. They placed them down gently on the table between us, and when the delicious smells hit my nose, it was a struggle not to gasp.

Meals in the village had never been anything special. We'd usually have some kind of plain meat or potato dish, and we'd be lucky if it was even warm. This feast, however, was like nothing I'd ever seen before. Rows of different meats, fish, and pastries covered the table, and my eyes widened as they darted from platter to platter, unable to decide where to begin. There were fruits and vegetables I couldn't even name, stirred into colourful sauces and pasta dishes.

As I took it all in, I could still feel Lukas's judgmental stare burning into me, but I didn't care anymore. I would marry him and he could have a thousand lovers if it meant I would get to eat a feast like this every day.

"Did they not feed you where you come from?" He glared across the table.

"Not with food like this," I sighed, my mouth watering.

Neither of us spoke for a while as I spooned as much as I could fit onto my too-small dinner plate. I tried pieces of everything, each mouthful tasting more divine than the last.

When I was finally too full to eat another bite, I lowered

my fork and forced my attention away from the food. Across the table, Lukas was staring with a look of disgust plastered across his face.

"Remind me to ask my father to organise you some etiquette lessons," he scoffed.

It took everything in me to not pull a face of disgust straight back at him.

"The food was excellent," I said with a smile, dismissing his comment. "Do we need to help clean up?" I reached for the plate in front of me, rising out of my seat.

Suddenly, the prince burst into a fit of laughter just as a servant swooped in to snatch the plate out of my hands.

"Sit down, Naria," Lukas called up to me, still chuckling. "You know, I was astounded when my father told me my future bride had been living all this time in Honeymeade… Honeymeade! Of all the hovels in the realm!" His head fell into his hands while his shoulders shook with vicious laughter. "Still, I thought, 'forest princess or not, they must've taught you something about class.' But no, you're really quite common, aren't you?" Once he was finally able to contain himself, he leaned forward in his seat. "I wonder what other dirty things your common friends have taught you. I suppose I'll find out once we're married." He took a sip from his wine goblet.

"You're disgusting." I scowled, hands clenched at my sides.

"Now, now, fiancée. Let's not fight." He lifted a finger up and wagged it from side to side before tapping it against the goblet in his hand. "Let's speak of more pressing things. You must tell me of your plans once you become Queen." He extended an arm, gesturing for me to take a seat again.

Still scowling, I lowered myself to sit. "My only plan is to rebuild my kingdom," I began in a serious tone. "I'm sure you are aware of the many refugees living in the forest village your father built. I want... I need to see them returning home to a rebuilt city."

Lukas smiled deviously. "Ah... So you wish to rebuild Corlixir?"

"Why wouldn't I?" I answered, confused that he would even ask. "That is why your father wishes for us to be married, isn't it? Since he can no longer fulfil his promise? As Queen, and with Drothmore's help, I can focus on restoring my kingdom while you can focus on yours."

"Any promises of my father shall be of no concern once I am King," Lukas shot back in a low tone. "Since it is his dying wish for us to marry, I will grant him that, but I refuse to entertain any of this rebuilding the fifth kingdom nonsense—"

"What are you talking about?" I cut him off, suddenly feeling quite queasy. "To not help Corlixir is simply not an option. Our parents were allies, and Drothmore has always promised my people that when I was of age, my kingdom would be restored."

"You are forgetting who holds the power here, forest princess." He leaned forward, his steel gaze meeting mine. "One of us is set to inherit the wealthiest and most powerful kingdom in the realm, and the other is just a little girl in a nice dress that my father paid for."

Letting his words sit for a few moments, he then settled back into his chair. "Besides, if you are off rebuilding Corlixir, who will be around to plan the festivals and monitor our relationships with the rest of the court? Not to mention, you will need to spend time with my heirs." At those words, something bristled deep inside me. "We must present a united front. My kingdom needs a loyal queen, so you need to be here, in Drothmore. Let Corlixir fight its own battles. You may be their last princess, but once we are married you'll answer only to me... as my doting obedient wife." A smirk snaked its way onto his face, and for a moment, I almost couldn't breathe – I couldn't believe what I was hearing.

"What can you possibly even mean by any of that? How can it fight its own battles when there is nothing left of it to fight?" I gripped the wooden table, my knuckles turning white.

"Well then, that makes things an awful lot easier, if you think about it," Lukas carried on, swirling the wine goblet in his hand. "The kingdom is dead, and we should let it stay that way. One less potential enemy to worry about. From what I've read, Corlixir never contributed much to the realm. Perhaps if they'd spent less time researching useless cures, they would've been better defended against the Great Blaze."

I wanted to scream. I wanted to pick up my goblet and hurl it across the room. I wanted him to suffer and understand what it was like to grow up in a hastily-built village, where every day you are told about your 'real home' as if one day you'll get to see it, but deep down, you fear that day will never come. I wanted to say something, anything. But instead, I found myself sitting there like an idiot – open-mouthed and frozen solid.

"Don't you agree?" he taunted with a grin.

Before I could do something I knew I would regret, I bolted up from my seat, letting the wooden chair once again loudly scrape against the floor. Lukas said nothing while I marched over to the exit, but I could feel his cold stare piercing into my back right up until the door slammed shut behind me.

On the journey back to my room, several thoughts bounced around my head, each one sounding clearer and clearer with every step against the palace's stone floor:

I would not be planning any parties, and I would not be having 'his heirs'.

My kingdom will be rebuilt, and I would do it without any help from him.

And finally, I would not under any circumstances, or ever in a *million years*, be marrying that stuck-up pig of a prince.

CHAPTER 6

I hardly slept that night. In fact, it was only as the birds began to sing outside and morning light crept into the room that I was finally able to drift off at all.

That was until I awoke hours later, confronted with Raena's concerned face as she shook my shoulder, rattling the sleep out of me enough to force my tired eyes open.

"Thank the Oceans!" she cried, bringing a hand to her chest. "The servants came to fetch me. No one could wake you. They thought you might've been dead!"

I blinked a few times. It took a moment to recall where I was.

Then I saw the lilac gown still hanging from the back of the chair, exactly where I'd thrown it last night, and all the memories came flooding back. This was my life now: the last Princess of Corlixir, soon to be the bride of the Crown Prince of Drothmore, or as he had so bluntly put it – his doting obedient wife.

Ugh.

The mere thought of it all made me want to roll over, pull a blanket over my face, and sleep for the rest of the year.

"Was dinner last night really *that* good? I bet you couldn't sleep from all the excitement!" Raena trilled. She brought out her hand fan and fluttered it against her pretty highborn face. "Or is there something else you're not telling me? Did the prince come back here last night and that's why you're so tired?" Her eyes darted from side to side. "Naria, you devious thing. You're not even married yet." She swatted her fan at my shoulder, giggling playfully.

"Nothing happened after dinner," I grunted. Intricate floral bed sheets fell away from my nightgown as I pushed myself up and leaned against a pillow. "Lukas and I spoke. And then we ate. And then I decided that I am absolutely not marrying him."

Raena's cheerful mood dropped like a stone in a pond.

"What?" she gasped. "Why ever not?"

"Have you even spoken to him?" I retorted, whipping my head to meet her gaze. "He's a complete pig! He insulted my background, admitted to having at least two lovers, said that once we were married he would practically own me, and finally, to top it off, he told me that he has absolutely no intention of ever rebuilding Corlixir and would actively try to prevent me from doing so if I tried. How am I supposed to want to marry him, Raena?"

Guilt overcame me the second my shouting ceased, and I knew immediately I should've apologised for my outburst. But when I went to speak, all that came out were heavy sobs and gasps. This was all too much. Somehow, in less than a day here, I had already failed my people. The only way for me to rebuild Corlixir was to gain power through an alliance with another kingdom. The only person who could offer me that alliance seemed to have no interest in helping me at all. My lower lip trembled. I never wanted to see Lukas's smug face again.

If only there were some other way to find help.

Beside me, Raena lowered herself and pressed a hand gently against my shoulder. "I'm so sorry, Naria. This is all my fault," she said quietly.

I glanced up at her, shaking my head. "Don't be silly." My crying slowed to a softer sniffle. "It's not your fault that the prince is a heartless brat."

"I should've warned you, though." Raena chewed her lip. "He's been like this for a while now, but I thought that since you're his fiancée, he would at least be cordial... I suppose not." She pressed her fingers into her temples. "Lukas has always been cold, but ever since the King was cursed, he's been particularly... challenging. There's only a handful of court ladies he hasn't taken to his chambers yet, myself being one of them. I didn't want to believe it, but I'm certain that's why I was chosen to help you settle in here." She scrunched up her nose. "It would have been terribly awkward for you otherwise."

A frustrated sigh rolled off my chest. Of all the princes in the realm... Why did mine have to be such a monster?

"I can't marry him, Raena," I groaned. "I just can't do it."

Raena leaned closer, rubbing a reassuring hand on my back. "Sometimes we have to do things that don't feel right to us, for the sake of our people. You never know what the future holds. There's still a chance that the prince may change his mind about Corlixir. I know he seems unreasonable right now, but you didn't see him before the curse. Every day he grieves for his father's suffering. Perhaps you can help him through it? He might be more sympathetic to your cause once he has accepted the loss."

I hated how sensible she sounded. Why couldn't Raena be his fiancée instead of me? The very thought of being around Lukas made me feel queasy. What would my parents think if they knew I was being this selfish?

Tears stung in the corners of my eyes.

"I need to show you something," Raena said, reaching for my hand.

I let her guide me out of bed and towards a wide window. As we passed the vanity, I caught sight of my tear-stained face and puffy features. I was certainly in a sorry state. Maybe Lukas would call off the engagement himself if I showed up to every dinner looking like this.

When we reached the window, Raena pointed to something in the distance. I drew closer, letting my nose brush against the glass. A gasp flew from my lips the moment I realised just what she was pointing at.

"This is why the King insisted on your room being so high up in this tower," Raena explained in a soothing voice.

Far off in the distance, over a dense forest and several grassy hills, I could just about see the tips of a ruined lavender-coloured palace. Most of the spires and high walls had crumbled away, but a few were left standing proud against the skyline. While living in Honeymeade, we'd never been allowed to venture out and see the ruins of our kingdom. They told us it was because they wanted us to remember Corlixir as it was depicted in the history books, when it was thriving and at its greatest. But now, seeing the remnants before me like this, I felt nothing but power and strength pulsing through my veins. That was *my* kingdom. The refugees were *my* people to protect. And I had to protect them. Even if it meant marrying Lukas and doing everything in my power to change his mind.

"That," Raena said, her finger pressing against the glass, "is why you're here. Don't forget it."

The tears had stopped, leaving my vision crystal clear. "I understand now," I said quietly.

Leaning against the window, Raena sighed. "It's certainly frustrating how Lukas is being so uncooperative, though. I suppose it's because he knows you don't have a choice. He can be as monstrous as he likes and you'll still have to marry him. He knows—"

"Wait," I interrupted, my heart racing. "Are you sure that I don't have a choice?" It was as though someone had just ignited a fire in my mind. How had I not thought of this before?

"What do you mean?" Raena asked as she just blinked at me, confused. "Even if you're a princess, that doesn't mean you have enough money to fund what you need. If you want to rebuild your kingdom, then surely you'll need Lukas's help to do it?"

"Yes..." I pondered out loud. "But why does it have to be him?" My stomach dropped with the realisation. "There are three other kingdoms. And surely one of them has someone else I could marry. It doesn't even need to be someone of royal blood. I just need someone powerful, someone who could influence their ruler to provide the funds."

Raena's mouth fell open. "You could find another suitor!" She gasped and brought up her hand fan, flapping it nervously. "But... you know, the prince would hate that."

"It would serve him right," I spat. "And perhaps if he thought he had competition, maybe he might try being a bit more agreeable with me."

"Or he'll just exile you..."

I shot Raena a look.

"Just teasing." She grimaced, though her fan was flapping more intensely than before. "There's a book in the library with details of all the other noble families. I had to study it once for a lesson, and it was *terribly boring*, but it would at least tell you who is eligible to be married."

"That's perfect, let's go and find it now!" I declared.

Spinning on my heels, I charged towards the door. But before I could reach it, I was jerked backwards by Raena's hand grabbing my wrist. She gestured at my tear-stained nightgown, shaking her head disapprovingly.

"You're not going anywhere until you get dressed. And please, before you decide who your new fiancé should be, let's have the servants bring you some breakfast."

My traitorous stomach growled in approval as I scowled. "I suppose my future husband will just have to wait."

CHAPTER 7

"The library is awfully dull, and you *will* get dust all over your skirts, so please, let's not stay there for too long," Raena complained as we passed by countless crowds of gossiping court members on our way to the palace library. "Oh, and there are bookkeepers too, who just sort of *linger* between the bookshelves. You think you're alone, and then suddenly one will pop up behind you to ask about what you're reading. It's so unnerving." She shuddered.

I tried my best to listen to her as we stepped through the hallways, but all I could think about was how every noble's attention seemed to be fixed on me. They eyed me like I was a piece of fresh meat and they were wild bears during the hungry months of winter. It wasn't so bad when they just stared, but when they turned to their friends to whisper and giggle... I just wanted the walls to cave in around me.

"Here it is!" Raena announced as we reached the iron archway that led into the library. "Let's make this quick, though. This dress is new, and I'd like to at least get a few days of use out of it," she huffed, picking up the skirts of her apricot ruffled gown.

We made our way down a small set of stairs and into a vast underground room lit by candles. Rows upon rows of bookshelves stretched back as far as I could see. Raena was right about the dust, too. I had to cover my mouth to stifle a loud cough from echoing off the sandstone walls. Dotted around the room were various people dressed in long, formal-looking robes, with their noses buried into books. A few glanced up at us as we entered, watching us suspiciously.

"Ignore them," Raena hissed to me. "They're more stuck up than the nobles outside."

My eyebrows shot up at her comment, but before I had a chance to respond, she took my arm and led me over to a dusty wooden desk, illuminated by several ornate candelabras. In the centre of the desk was a seemingly ancient tome opened to a page listing new births in the realm. Beside the book, resting in an inkpot was a white feathered quill, clearly used recently as the ink on the page was still glistening in the candlelight.

"Everything you need will be in this old thing." Raena smiled, patting its yellowed pages. "Every birth of every highborn who ever was is written here, including yours."

I reached forward and flicked through the book, being careful not to smear the fresh ink on the page where it was left open. It didn't take long to find the section with my name and the details of my birth.

> *Princess Naria Alderbrook of Corlixir*
> *Born the 2^d of Midspring, Year 1329*
> *Daughter of King Benedict and Queen Elowen Alderbrook of Corlixir*

My fingers stroked the black ink where my parents' names were. I had no idea I had a last name. None of us in the village did. There weren't enough of us Corlixins left to even need them.

Alderbrook.

I wondered if it meant anything, or if it was just another thing I would lose if I married Lukas.

"Prince Lukas is a few pages before you," Raena said, pulling me from my thoughts. She flicked through more aged pages and pointed to another section similar to mine.

> *Prince Lukas Forgeborn of Drothmore*
> *Born the 28th of Latesummer, Year 1327*
> *Son of King Ikelos and Queen Erissa Forgeborn of Drothmore*

"We should search around here if you want to find another noble to marry," she suggested, waving her finger over the page. "I know a lot about the different powerful families across the realm, so together we should be able to figure out if any are worth pursuing."

Relief washed over me as I scoured all the different names. "Thank you," I said, reaching for her hand, "for helping with this. And for everything else you've done for me."

Raena blinked a few times, her deep brown eyes reflecting the candlelight. "Anything to help a new friend." She squeezed my hand. "Oh, but I am expecting that once you become a queen, you'll help me find a good suitor too. I'm very picky though. He must be kind, and handsome, terribly rich too, and oh! He must allocate an entire section of his estate just to house my gowns." She whipped open her hand fan and fluttered it dreamily against her face. "So yes, it might take quite a few dusty library sessions to find him." We both chuckled before returning to the book to begin searching.

"This is absolutely hopeless," Raena sighed, letting her head crash against the desk. Hours had passed. In the time we'd been searching, a few bookkeepers had wandered over, offering plush chairs for us to sit on while we read, and some even asked if they could help. A quick look from Raena, however, had sent them scurrying away, though we did accept the chairs.

I sighed too and rested my chin on my open palm. "There are so many people here but none of them could I ever consider. They're all either married already or not rich enough."

"Now you see my predicament," Raena grumbled, her face still smushed against the wooden desk.

I stifled a laugh. While there were *a few* unmarried options, Raena didn't know enough about their family histories to be able to confirm if they'd be sympathetic to my cause. In Honeymeade, everyone was so enamoured with the idea of Corlixir rising again. But here, it seemed that everyone had better things to worry about – like what they would wear to any upcoming balls or which sort of exotic bird they should have for dinner.

"I'm going to look for another book," I decided, pushing myself up from the desk.

Raena grunted. "Why? All the information about the nobility is here."

"I'm not giving up just yet. There has to be something else that can help."

Raena gestured vaguely at some distant bookshelves against the back wall. "I know there are some books about the different families down there. You might find something useful."

I nodded and made my way over, leaving my companion to sulk at the desk.

The air in the far corner of the library was much cooler than where we had been sitting. There were also fewer candles, which made it difficult to read the thin gold writing of the book titles. I ran my fingers down the spine of each book, trying my best to make sense of the titles, but I found myself pausing when my hand brushed against a book that seemed different to the others. The cover was lavender, just like the spires of my parents' palace, and there was something unusual about the texture.

I drew closer. Oddly, there was no writing on the spine, and when I went to pull the book from the shelf, it wouldn't budge. No matter how hard I tugged, there was no movement at all.

Frustrated, I brought up both hands, jammed my fingers

against the book cover, and used all my strength to heave. Finally, the book shifted as a loud click sounded through the walls. I almost yelped as the bookshelf swung towards me, but instead of crashing to the floor, it swung to the side to reveal a dimly lit passageway.

"It's not polite to poke your nose in places you don't belong, Princess."

My whole body flinched as I whipped around. A few feet away, a hooded woman was leaning against a bookshelf, quietly observing me. She stepped closer, her face gradually being illuminated by the candlelight until, when she was just a few steps away, I could finally make out her features properly. It didn't take me long to recognise that familiar pinched nose and thin mouth.

"Seraphina?" I breathed. "You're that healer, from the King's chambers?"

She dipped her head for a moment. "That is I. And you are Naria... Princess Naria from that little village in the woods. Soon to be Queen of Drothmore, I hear."

"Not if I can help it."

"Oh?" A smile crept up the side of her mouth. "You don't want to marry the prince? With his current reputation, I can't say I blame you." She laughed quietly before raising an eyebrow. "Although that doesn't explain why you were about to enter the forbidden library."

"Forbidden library?" I blurted out, then shook my head. "It was an accident," I admitted, brushing a stray curl away from my face. "Lukas isn't interested in helping with my... predicament. So, I came here with a friend to try and find someone else who could. I was looking through these books because I thought there might be information about any powerful families who were allied with my kingdom. And then... Well, then I found this door." I looked back at the open passageway. It was so dark inside, and the air pouring out felt strange and ominously heavy.

"How intriguing," Seraphina mused. "I wonder, Naria, do you know anything about the Dark Kingdoms?"

The Dark Kingdoms?

"The what?" I blinked at her, my confusion only widening Seraphina's smile.

"The three kingdoms that house the faeries, the merfolk, and the goblins," she explained, leaning closer and dropping her voice to a whisper.

"Oh." I paused. We'd studied magical beings during our lessons in the village, but only very briefly. We were taught that you'd have to venture far into the mountains beyond Drothmore to find goblins, while merfolk could sometimes be spotted diving in and out of the waves off the coasts of Ryntook. Our lessons on faeries, however, were even more vague. When it came to the fae we were taught only two things.

One, that they exist.

Two, that you should never *ever* go out searching for one. We may both share the same realm, but faeries are fickle, selfish creatures, incapable of feeling any human emotions, and would happily murder an entire household for a mere pretty crystal.

"Why are you telling me this?" I questioned her suspiciously. "Magical beings just roam the lands and seas like beasts. Even if they had kingdoms, and they could help, they'd never want to help me. I don't have anything to offer."

Seraphina's blue eyes glistened. "Have you ever met a faery?"

"No." I shuddered at the thought.

"Perhaps if you did, you would realise they're not so beastlike after all." She gestured at the dark passageway behind me. "I'd like to show you something, if you have some time to spare from your book hunting."

Fear twitched inside my stomach and I glanced from the hallway back to Seraphina.

"Is it safe?" I asked in a quiet voice.

Seraphina chuckled and began to head into the darkness. "You won't find any goblins or ghouls down here, Naria. Only the truth, which, for you, might be even scarier." Her voice faded as I heard her descending a set of stairs.

I shouldn't have done it. I should've stayed where it was safe and definitely human. But my own curiosity lured me into that passageway before I even had a chance to change my mind. So, I stepped forward. Behind me, the bookshelf swung shut, plunging me into complete darkness. My heart pounded in the silence until I heard footsteps again, and Seraphina appeared with a small candle clutched in her hand.

"This way." She smiled, beckoning me further inside.

We descended a set of stairs until we reached another doorway. A mysterious golden light spilled from the room ahead and onto the black tiled floor. As we entered, my mouth fell open. The room itself wasn't anything spectacular – just a small, normal-looking space with black bookshelves covering the walls from floor to ceiling. The wonder came from the books themselves. They were all so brightly illuminated in colours I'd never seen before, and anything but normal. Some of them shivered where they rested, and a few even sang quiet songs from their shelves. It was as though they were alive and buzzing with the excitement of finally seeing some readers.

"Is this magic?" I gasped, trying to take in every inch of the small room.

"Of course," Seraphina said casually. "But that's not why I brought you here." She moved over to a shelf and lifted a huge purple book that appeared to chuckle as she grabbed it. "This is the book that details all of the faery nobility." She lugged the book over to a table and with a heavy thud, dropped it onto the wood. "You'll find, in here, that the Faery King and Queen have a son who's only a few years older than you, and he's unmarried." Something flickered across her sharp features as she leafed through the pages, the book still giggling quietly to itself.

"I can't make an alliance with a faery, let alone marry one." My nose wrinkled at the thought. "Faeries and humans just don't mix." I shook my head frantically.

"You believe too many of the lies you've been told," Seraphina sighed, continuing to turn the book's giggling pages. "Your parents maintained good relations with the faery court. Where do you think your mages got their magic from?"

Mages? While I'd never met one, I'd been told by my teachers that they existed in Corlixir prior to the Great Blaze. They were ordinary humans who had the not-so-ordinary ability to cast magic. But just thinking that a Corlixin had anything to do with the faeries made my head spin. This was all made up. It had to be.

"All mages are descendants of the fae," Seraphina

explained. "Mostly human, with just a trace of faery blood running through their veins. For a time, Corlixir served almost like a bridge between the dark kingdoms and the human realm. Faeries wandered the streets of your kingdom as freely as we humans did." She paused as she ran her fingers down one of the pages.

"How do you know this to be true?" I asked, my eyebrows knitting together. In the golden light of the room, I could see Seraphina clearly. Even with her hood still up, I knew for certain she must've been no older than eighteen. Her blonde hair hung in ringlets around her youthful face. The Great Blaze would've been when she was just a baby.

"We're so alike," Seraphina said, meeting my stare. "I lost my parents when I was just a baby, too. But the family who took me in – they never hid the truth. Despite what King Ikelos wants everyone to believe, the faeries are not villainous fiends waiting in the woods to trap innocent children. They have their own culture, just like us, and I know they would be willing to help your cause. If Corlixir could be rebuilt, perhaps so too could the bridge between our worlds."

She spoke with such light in her voice, such hope. But I couldn't believe her. I didn't want to. Faeries were evil demonic creatures. I still vividly remembered the lesson from less than a year ago when they showed us a portrait of a captured faery and all but a couple of the braver students screamed. One girl had to take the rest of the day off, sick from her fright. I could still see the portrait clearly in my mind: a horrible, gnarled, blue-skinned wraith of a thing.

And then, why did she mention King Ikelos? Drothmore has been a firm ally of my kingdom since before my parents were born. What did he have to do with any of this?

"This is all wrong," I breathed, stepping back.

"Princess Naria, please you must—" The hooded woman looked as if she wanted to say more, but then something stopped her. In the distance, I could hear a faint shouting. We both turned to the doorway.

"Naria!" The shout echoed again. It was a girl's voice, and getting closer.

Gently, Seraphina pushed me towards the stairs. "You should leave now," she said, guiding me out of the room. "Forget about our conversation and marry Prince Lukas if you so desire. But if you ever change your mind and want to take a leap of faith for the good of your kingdom, and the realm, you know where to look." She waved her hand at the hidden library behind us.

I nodded, my teeth catching on my lower lip.

Before long, as if nothing had ever happened, I was back in the palace library with the hidden doorway clicking shut behind me. The blue-hooded healer hurried off just as Raena rounded a corner, but she wasn't alone. A young man, slightly timid-looking and dressed in a servant's tunic, stood beside her.

"Where have you been? We searched all over the library for you. Your dress is filthy!" Raena gasped, rushing to slap some of the dust off my skirts.

"I was right here," I told her, silently begging they didn't notice my lie. "There's so many interesting books here. I must've not heard you looking." The nervous smile stuck to my face as I pivoted towards the young man. "Who is this?"

With each word, his voice quivered. "Princess Naria?"

I nodded.

"My name is Ryan. I've been sent by Prince Lukas to fetch you. He wishes to speak with you immediately."

It was a struggle not to groan. But since the boy in front of me was clearly so terrified, I tried my best to answer in a way that would not frighten him more. "Thank you for coming all this way to find me, Sir Ryan, but please tell His Highness that I am quite busy right now and I do not wish to be disturbed."

At my response, the servant's face paled.

"Naria..." Raena hissed with a forced smile. She drew closer then tugged my ear to her lips, warning me in a low whisper, "I know you do not wish to marry him, but it is not proper to ignore the Crown Prince's orders."

"P-please Your Highness," the servant stuttered, looking close to fainting. "I'm sure it won't take long. I believe he only wishes to walk with you in the grounds."

Raena stared up at me with a pleading expression. She didn't say it, but I knew she meant for me to go – not just for my sake, but for the sake of this poor servant.

"Fine," I grumbled as Ryan looked as though he might burst with happiness. "Please take me to him."

CHAPTER 8

The palace grounds looked absolutely spectacular under the relentless heat of the Latesummer sun. I'd never seen so many different types of flowers and blooming shrubs, all neatly trimmed into ornate miniature gardens. Dozens of gardeners bustled about, pruning hedges and picking up after the crowds of nobles who were promenading their latest waistcoats or elaborate gowns in the sunshine. Were it not for the rushing servant at my side, I could've spent hours out here, exploring every inch of this vast place.

When we finally reached the prince, it took everything in my power to not storm straight back to the palace and lock myself forever inside my tower bedroom. We'd arrived at a little secluded rose garden, tucked far from the entrance of the palace grounds. Some of the rose shrubs had been shaped into angelic figures, while others formed arches over elegantly crafted iron benches. Near the back of the garden, Prince Lukas lounged on one of those lovely iron benches. And as my gaze caught his, I thought about how this perhaps might've been quite a romantic encounter, had it not been for the giggling copper-haired beauty that was perched upon his lap.

I wanted to be sick on the grass.

"Fiancée!" Lukas exclaimed with a grin as Ryan continued ushering me closer to the prince and his 'companion'. "Please, join us. You must tell me, how are you liking my gardens?"

As the young woman on his lap caught my eye, her pretty face instantly soured. I expected her to say something, perhaps even mutter an apology, but instead, she chose to lean further into Lukas's chest, nuzzling his white tunic.

"The gardens are indeed beautiful," I said calmly, after forcing my attention away from the limpet. "But as much as I'd love to stay and chat, I was actually quite busy. So, if you'll excuse me—"

"Busy?" Lukas cut in. "I didn't see you at breakfast, or lunch for that matter. What could possibly be so important?"

The copper-haired girl tittered. "Rolling in cobwebs, perhaps?" She shot a sly glance at my skirts and grimaced. Unfortunately, Raena wasn't exaggerating about the dust problem in the library.

Ignoring her, I answered flatly, "I had breakfast delivered to my room. And as for lunch, I was with Lady Raena. Now, if you'll excuse me."

"Wait." Lukas leaned forward, causing the copper-haired girl to shriek as she nearly fell from his lap. He scowled at her, then gestured dismissively for her to stand. "Leave us, Giselle."

The young woman hurried to her feet and gave Lukas a curt nod. There was no denying the fury that burned across her face as she stalked away. I'd have to ask Raena about her later.

"You know, if you are to be Queen, you'll need to leave your room and engage with the court." Lukas rose from the ornate bench. He was so tall as he stared down at me, his dark brown hair glinting in the sunlight. "I know my mother is not the best example, but I refuse to let you follow her behaviour."

"Well, fortunately for you, I have no intention of becoming your queen." I tilted my chin up to meet his fierce gaze. "So perhaps you can go and say all this to Giselle, or whichever other lady is unlucky enough to become your bride." My skirts twirled as I began to turn away, but he quickly seized my wrist, gripping it tightly.

"Let. Go." My voice was deathly calm.

"You would do well to remember your place, forest princess." He matched my tone, keeping a firm grip on me. "You're lucky that I am a patient man."

"Patient?" I scoffed. "Just how long did you wait here for me before summoning another lady to keep you company?"

His lips curled into a devious smile. "Jealous, fiancée?"

"Don't flatter yourself." I scowled. "I only ask that next time, you keep your playthings in your chambers. It's already bad enough that the entire palace knows we are engaged. I'd rather not deal with any pitiful stares, too."

"You know, it is not my fault that it took my servant almost half a day to find you." He tugged my wrist closer to study my dust-covered fingers, his thumb sweeping gently over my palm. "I told him to visit the tower first. Although, perhaps I should've sent him to search the stables instead." He lowered my wrist. "Giselle just so happened to be walking by and we struck up a conversation. Besides, as Crown Prince, am I really not allowed to indulge in the pleasures of my own court?" His cruel smile felt like a dagger plunging into my chest. So I smiled too, except my smile was sweeter than candied plums.

"Oh please, indulge all you like." I dipped my head in a mockingly innocent way. "Of course, we royals should never be deprived of our pleasures." My lips then drew closer to his ear as I giggled in a way that mimicked Raena's when she had once spotted a handsome guard. "And if we're speaking candidly, now that I'm here, there are a few highborns I've been eager to catch alone myself... Oh, and don't even get me started on the guards; some of them could be angels!" I squealed playfully. Of course, this was all a lie. There was no one, noble or common, who had ever caught my eye here, but it would take one look at Lukas's furious face to see that clearly he hadn't realised that.

"That's absurd," he growled. "Queens can't have lovers."

How predictably hypocritical.

"Oh, that's a shame, Sir Curtis will be very disappointed when I share the news." I pouted with a dramatic tilt of my head. "Though, I suppose it's a good thing I still have no intention of becoming *your* queen. So perhaps there is hope for dear Curty and I after all."

I prayed that there wasn't actually some poor soul named Sir Curtis within this palace. Judging by the murderous look that darkened over Lukas's face, even if 'Curty' did exist, he wouldn't be alive for much longer.

"What are you talking about?" he demanded. "Who is... Enough of this!" His voice hardened, and he drew closer until I could feel his breath on my lips. "You shall not have lovers. I forbid it. And besides, once we are married, you will have no choice but to ascend the throne. So stop with this nonsense about not being Queen."

"*If* we are married," I hissed. "You have made it perfectly clear that you have no intention of helping me rebuild my kingdom and," I gestured to where Giselle had sauntered off to, "you clearly have more than enough ladies who would gladly take my place." Lukas's grip on my wrist finally loosened as I let my arm fall away, but I didn't step back. "You are not the only man in this realm with power, Lukas." I reminded him, our bodies only inches apart. "I will find someone else who can help, and I pray to the Ancients that I find him soon, so I don't need to deal with you or your silly court any longer than I have to."

"Do not be like this, Naria," he started, but I had already turned to leave the rose garden. "You will regret this!"

"Maybe I will," I snapped over my shoulder. "Or maybe I will find another prince to marry. Maybe one who actually has some empathy."

Perhaps I shouldn't have said those exact words, but in that moment, all I could see was red – and it was certainly not the deep crimson of the roses. Even Ryan didn't dare to stop me as I stormed out of the garden and back towards the palace. I needed some space away from everyone, desperately. With every second that passed, I felt less and less like a princess and more like a hopelessly lost child. I couldn't stay here, in this palace, but I had no way of returning to Honeymeade. And I was sure, even if I did find a way back, that they would return me immediately to the palace and straight into Lukas's lap.

This palace was the grandest prison anyone could ever call a home.

CHAPTER 9

My hands were balled into tight fists as I stomped back through the palace. Gaggles of babbling nobles clogged up the hallways like mud in a stream, but I shoved past them without a second thought. It'd only been five minutes since my exchange with the prince in the gardens, and yet the longer I thought about it, the more I wanted to force my fists through each one of the gaudy portraits on the walls. How dare he humiliate me in that way?

Perhaps I should find a 'Curty'. I'd find the handsomest guard and parade him around the grounds, too. We'd see how much the prince appreciated that. I'd make sure he was taller, with nicer hair, and eyes that reminded me of a forest in the golden afternoon sun. If I kissed him, perhaps Lukas would throw a fit so hysterical it would knock his crown off. That would be glorious. And I'd make sure to do it in front of all of his pompous friends. News of his tantrum would spread through the Steel Palace like a wildfire.

I veered around another gold-beamed corner, then stopped suddenly – confusion washing away the storm of anger in my mind. I was certain I'd been down this corridor already. Those particular metal beams seemed suspiciously familiar. But I didn't recognise the portraits that lined the walls. Or did I? They all had the same ornate frames and their subjects all had the same pouty, solemn look.

Pacing down the hallway, I kept my head held high as I passed more servants and guards. If I could just at least find my way to the royal dining hall, then maybe I would start to make sense of this all.

"Please settle down, my lady!" a flustered woman's voice echoed from a nearby passageway, followed by a low, wailing cry. "You'll hurt yourself if you keep thrashing like that. It's not safe for you to be out here."

"Stay back, you foul wretch!" someone else snarled, but they sounded so afraid – more like a wounded animal than a woman. I knew I should've stuck to my path and continued on my way back through the palace, but curiosity got the better of me. Quickly, and without any more doubt, I darted down the corridor, following the sounds of their heated conversation.

"I said stay back!" the same woman yelped again.

My skirts whirled as I rounded another corner. Then, just as I burst into another grand hallway, my racing legs froze. Several servants surrounded a trembling woman as she cowered with her back pressed against an arched window. Her long, wispy hair was whiter than frost, and her thin, skeleton-like body was barely covered in an ivory nightgown. There was something almost inhuman about her face, too. Her cheeks were hollow, and her pale irises appeared to mimic glass – such unbearably fragile glass.

"Please, my lady," one of the servants closest to her began. She held out her palms in a soothing manner. "Please let us take you back to your chambers. We don't want to upset His Majesty by having you wandering the palace again."

The trembling woman scowled, then spat on the floor. "Come closer, wretch, and I'll show you what I think of *His Majesty*," she growled.

It didn't surprise me that the King had enemies – I was sure all kings did. But why did he keep this one tucked away in his palace, attended by servants and dressed in an expensive lace-trimmed nightgown?

"Elowen?"

I bristled at the sound of my mother's name. Snapping my attention to the scene, I noticed the trembling woman's glassy eyes had locked onto me. As she stared, the servants whipped their heads around to where I was standing. Suddenly, I felt barely inches tall as their glares pierced into me like a dozen loosed arrows.

"You shouldn't be here, my lady," someone, I'm assuming the head servant, addressed me sharply.

"Sorry, I—" I stammered. Then, as if realising what had just been said, I glanced back at the woman by the window. "Wait... How do you know my mother's name?"

"Your mother?" the woman repeated, looking more confused than afraid now. "No, no, my dear, look at you. Are you not well? You *are* Elowen." She pushed herself away from the wall and moved towards me, the servants stepping aside to let her pass. I shivered as she stopped only inches from my face. There was something so cold about her. "Do you not remember?" She grinned eagerly. "We used to run along the beach together. You and I... I'd tie seashells in your hair, just like my sisters did for me." She curled her fingers around a blonde ringlet that hung by my face. "Such pretty, pretty hair."

Behind her, a servant stepped forward. "My lady I really must insist—"

"I'm sorry," I went on, taking no notice of our audience, "but I'm really not Elowen. My name is Naria. Elowen is my mother. Were the two of you friends?"

"Naria," the woman echoed. She ignored my question as she let the name rest on her pale tongue. "Elowen's little girl. I'm so sorry... I'm tired. So very tired. And I fear I am seeing things. Elowen is dead." The words made my heart ache. "So dead. Very dead. So very, very dead," she muttered mindlessly to herself.

"Come, my lady. Let's get you back to your chambers now." The servant who stepped forward gently took the woman's wrist.

"So tired, but I cannot rest," she muttered again. "Elowen is dead, so I cannot rest."

"Wait," I said, calling after her. "Did my mother help you before? She was a healer. Did she give you medicine?"

A wisp of recognition drifted across the woman's hollow face. "Yes..." she replied breathily. "Dear Elowen would give me powder to help me sleep after... after..." Her words trailed off into several sharp intakes of breath.

"Damn the realm, it's happening again," the head servant panicked. "Quick, girls, let's get her back to bed!"

The servants flew into motion to manoeuvre the woman, who was now struggling to breathe through deep, unwavering sobs. She was in such a state, her pale cheeks now red and puffy from the overwhelming panic. I tried to reach forward and comfort her, but the servants brushed my hands away. It was so hard to hold back my own tears. I had felt raw, consuming panic like this many times before. Thankfully, I'd always had my friends to support me, but here, this poor woman only had the rough hands of servants who spared her little sympathy as they dragged her away.

"Wait!" I cried out again. "What is your name? I can make you the same powder. I know the recipe. I just need to know where to find you. Let me help you, like my mother did. Like Elowen did."

After a few moments of resisting the servants' manhandling, the woman's gasps slowed enough to allow her to share her name. "Erissa," she finally answered.

Something stirred within me. The name sounded so familiar... Why?

Then her lower lip trembled as she spoke through gritted teeth. "Have your servant deliver the powder to Erissa. Specifically, Queen Erissa of this damned kingdom."

Queen Erissa? This hollow wisp of a woman was Queen Erissa? My jaw hit the floor.

"Tell no one of what you saw here, Your Highness," the servant gripping the trembling queen's arm warned. "The King will have all our heads if word of his wife's condition spreads around the palace."

"How long has she been like this?" I asked. I'd never treated mental wounds like this before, but perhaps there was something I could do to help.

The servant just shook her head. "Too long for any of your Corlixin potions to make a difference now. The best thing for her is bed rest."

"Bed rest..." I repeated. "Then let me help with that. I'll deliver the sleeping powder tomorrow. I can find the flowers I need in the palace grounds, and everything else is in my bedchamber. To make a batch won't take long at all."

Erissa stared up at me, rivers of glassy tears streaming down her cheeks. "Thank you, dear child. There is kindness in this damned place after all."

The head servant flashed me one last pitiful look before hauling the Queen away.

CHAPTER 10

A week later, I awoke to the harsh morning light in my bedchamber, still laced up in yesterday's uncomfortable gown. Beside me, Raena was sprawled out across my bed, also wearing the same silver ruffled gown as yesterday, but clutched in her hand was a silver chess piece. Our game last night must've continued for a little too long, with neither of us allowing the other to win. For a highborn girl who insisted she'd spent her whole life preparing only to please her future husband, she was surprisingly good at chess.

Our late-night games were also useful for another purpose. They served as an excellent distraction from my current predicament. Dinners with Lukas had become terribly awkward after our exchange in the gardens. Thankfully, most nights he didn't show up at all, choosing instead to take dinner alone in his chambers. However, on the few nights that I was unfortunately graced with his princely presence, we'd spend the entire meal sitting in silence while he scowled at me across the table. I'll admit, I didn't even realise it was possible to scowl while eating, but apparently Lukas had mastered that skill.

Deciding to leave Raena to sleep, I wandered absent-mindedly to the window. My gaze drifted from the purple spires of Corlixir and over to the vast forests. Somewhere, hidden within the trees, was the village where I'd grown up, and perhaps hidden more deeply, was the faery kingdom.

I shuddered just thinking about it. Seraphina had insisted I'd been lied to about the true nature of the fae, but still, I couldn't get that twisted, blue faery from the portrait out of my head. Even if the faeries could form some kind of alliance with me, could I even bear to be in the same room with one long enough to sign a contract?

My attention was pulled away from the window by a shuffling sound behind me. Turning to face the noise, I was greeted by a half-asleep Raena, rubbing her eyes while desperately trying to smooth out the crinkles in her dress.

"Goodness, look at the state of us!" she complained as she caught sight of her tangled hair in the vanity mirror. "The servants will need at least a few hours to fix all this," she tsked, pushing herself up from the bed.

"Sorry for keeping you up so late," I apologised, wincing at the chess board.

"Nonsense." Raena shot me her usual cheery smile. "At least I was finally able to beat you!"

"Oh, I didn't realise you—"

My mouth clamped shut as Raena furrowed her brow in mock anger.

"Nevermind." I shook my head as we both chuckled. It was so lovely to have a friend here, and after we'd spent so much time together over the past few days, I felt like I could tell her anything. Even something that perhaps I should've kept to myself.

"Can I ask you something, Raena?" I started while moving towards her. My skirts bunched up uncomfortably as I perched on the end of the bed. Someday I'd figure out how to navigate the world in these extravagant dresses.

"Of course," she replied, taking a seat next to me and effortlessly smoothing her gown.

"What do you know about faeries?" I asked.

By the way her body tensed, I could tell the question had caught her off guard.

"Faeries..." she murmured quietly. "My family never really spoke of them, but I know they exist, or at least they used to. I've never seen one in the flesh. Why do you ask? Do you think there's one here in the palace?" She glanced around nervously.

So she'd heard the stories too...

Quickly, I shook my head. "I don't think so."

A brief silence fell between us as Raena continued to study my blank expression, her lips thinning until eventually she slipped. "What aren't you telling me?"

"Nothing," I said, perhaps a bit too eagerly.

Raena tilted her head back with playful laughter. "Come on, you wouldn't just ask me about faeries without a good reason. Did you perhaps encounter one in the garden? Is that why the prince was so angry? Was he jealous?"

A breath caught in my throat.

"Why would he be jealous?" I wanted to laugh at the absurdity of her question. "Faeries are hideous creatures. And while Lukas and I may have our differences, I can't imagine a world where he'd ever be jealous of one of them."

Raena just blinked, seemingly confused. "But faeries are supposed to be beautiful, aren't they?" My eyebrows shot up. "Again, I've never seen one, but all the books in my family's manor describe them as looking like gods. Apparently, they use magic to just wish away their flaws." Her chin fell into her hand as she stared at my vanity, gazing into the mirror longingly. "I wish I could do that with my nose."

"Don't say that. You have a beautiful nose."

Raena acted as though I hadn't said a word, continuing to squish her perfect nose with her fingertips.

Visions of that gnarled, blue faery flooded my mind. They'd definitely told us with certainty that this is what faeries looked like. I remembered the lesson clearly. It all started when a girl from my dormitory bought a seemingly innocent storybook at the market. She didn't realise it at the time, but it was a love story between a faery and a human. Of course, a few hours after she'd read it, the teachers snatched it away and tossed it into the fire. The very next day, they brought out the portrait, and it'd been that same poor girl who had run back to our room, in tears of pure fright. Raena was probably just swept up in all the fairy tales. Faeries weren't beautiful or godlike; they were terrifying, wicked creatures. They had to be.

You believe too many of the lies you've been told.

Seraphina's words echoed in my head.

"Are you alright, Naria?" Raena asked, tapping me on

the shoulder.

"I... I'm not sure," I answered as my hands gripped the fabric of my skirt. "I found something the other day in the library. Something I wasn't supposed to find."

Raena tilted her head. "What was it?"

"I..." I wanted to explain, but then I stopped myself. Instead, I reached for her open palm and began to rise off the bed. "Let me show you."

CHAPTER 11

Of course, Raena did not immediately agree to come to the forbidden library. First, she insisted that we call the servants to help us bathe and get changed into new dresses, making sure I understood that to be seen in the same outfit twice would mark the death of any highborn's social life. For me, she picked out a long red gown, and for herself, she chose a gown draped in ruffled midnight blue fabric – apparently, these were the best choices for hiding all the dust we would be 'swimming through' during our second visit to the library. Then, she ordered a guard to fetch a platter of fruit for us to feast on while the servants fixed our hair. And as much as I hated to admit it, I found myself starting to enjoy all the preening. It really helped to clear my mind, even if the bliss only ever lasted a few minutes.

By the time we were finally ready to go, the sun was

already high in the sky, and the halls of the palace were crawling with eagle-eyed, judgmental court members. As we walked through the hallways, I found myself very grateful for Raena's fashion advice. For once, the number of approving looks I received far outweighed the distasteful ones.

It didn't take long before we were back in the dimly lit library, where I hurriedly guided Raena towards the back corner. My fingers skimmed over the book spines just as they did before until, eventually, they paused on the spine of that same stiff purple book. Bringing both hands up again, I tugged.

Click.

I could hear Raena gasp beside me as the bookshelf door swung open.

"I knew this palace would have secrets," she stammered, "but I never thought there would be anything here, in this old place…"

Meeting her gaze, I spoke in a serious tone. "Promise me that you won't tell anyone about *anything* that you see here?"

She nodded, albeit reluctantly, and then without any more hesitation, we descended together into the darkness of the corridor. For the entire walk, Raena gripped my arm with more strength than you'd think possible for a young girl in a ruffled gown. From the way she was shuddering, I was certain she believed that if she were to let go, she would be lost here forever. Eventually, we reached the set of stairs that led to the secret room. I guided her down, but as we neared the bottom, I felt Raena almost leap out of her skin as a voice called to us from beyond the shadows.

"Who goes there?" It was a timid woman's voice. Instantly, I recognised her subtle accent.

"Seraphina?" I called back. "It's just me and... a friend."

We veered into the open doorway to see Seraphina, partially hidden by her familiar blue hood, alone amidst the tall bookshelves. Except it didn't sound like she was alone. All along the walls, books babbled and rocked as though they were excited to greet us. And beside me, Raena struggled to stay standing while taking in the shocking sight of it all.

"It's good to see you again, Princess." Seraphina smiled, closing the brown leather book she was reading. It appeared to sigh dramatically as her hand slid down the dusty cover.

"What... is all this?" Raena breathed, her gaze frantically darting from one book to the next.

Seraphina rose from her plush armchair and stalked towards us. "Who is your friend?" she asked, her bell-like voice chiming with suspicion.

"Oh yes, sorry. This is Lady Raena." Gently, I pried the quivering girl's hand from my sleeve. "I brought her here to help me decide what to make of all this." Although, based on how she was coping with the babbling books, maybe this wasn't such a good idea after all.

"So you are considering approaching the fae?" Seraphina mused, a smile tugging at the corner of her thin lips. "I knew you'd come back. You struck me as the curious sort."

"I want to know more about the prince," I said, dismissing her comment. "You said that he's unmarried. What is he like?"

Beside me, Raena spluttered as she choked on a breath. "I'm sorry, but... Naria, tell me you did not bring me down here just to say you're considering marrying a faery instead of Lukas? I know I said that they can be beautiful, but how can they possibly help with your kingdom?" She lowered her voice, ignoring Seraphina's impatient gaze. "If you just want to marry someone beautiful, there are many lovely guards I can introduce you to."

"Foolish girl," the healer snarled.

My friend's attention whipped to her, but before she had a chance to snap back, I held my hand out to separate them. "It's alright, Raena. Please trust me on this. I won't take any risks without knowing what I'm getting into... Which is why I'm here." My gaze returned to the hooded woman. "Please can you tell me more about the prince? Do you think he would be willing to help my kingdom?"

I saw it then. That slight grin that slithered over her cheeks like a thin snake. And then I felt it too, in the pit of my stomach. It was like something deep inside me was trying to say this was a very bad idea.

"I've never met him in person," Seraphina began, moving over to the tall, looming bookshelves. "But from what I've read of both your families' histories, I'd be very surprised if he didn't want to help you." She reached up to retrieve that same violet giggling book that she'd found before. "Your parents were good friends with the Faery King and Queen, you know. Many of the healing powders we use today originated from the crystals found by your parents who searched the faery caverns. And the fae were able to learn more about the origins of their own magic with your kingdom's advanced medical knowledge. Together, they achieved so much."

She carried the book over, letting it land with a soft

thud on the table in front of us. Its pages resumed their quiet laughter as Seraphina leafed through.

"But I don't understand," I wondered out loud. "If what you're saying is true, and my parents formed such strong relations with the fae, why is there so much distrust towards them now? What changed after the fire?"

The healer just shook her head as she continued leafing through the book. "Many things changed after the fire, dear princess... Although I suppose the reason why there are no faeries wandering around the Steel Palace, is mostly down to jealousy. Maybe even fear too." She paused her reading to glance up at us. "I'm sure you've been told before that with magic, one faery could easily overpower several humans. It wouldn't be hard to believe that the only reason the entire realm is not ruled by fae is because humans outnumber faeries tenfold. Apparently, there were an awful lot of people who didn't appreciate how much power Corlixir was giving to the fae – many of those, were the rulers of our great kingdoms."

"But what about my teachers and the village elders?" I persisted, moving closer. "They would've lived in Corlixir with the fae. Some of them were even researchers who I know worked alongside my parents, and yet they always insisted that we stay away from the faeries. Why?"

"You grew up with your fellow Corlixins in Honeymeade, correct?"

I nodded.

"Honeymeade belongs to Drothmore. Therefore, the King can impose whatever sort of curriculum he likes upon the young and highly impressionable children of Corlixir. Even if what he's insisting you learn is completely incorrect."

"That can't be true," Raena cut in. "King Ikelos would never do that. He's a good king!"

"Is he?" Seraphina shot back with a frown. "Good king or not, never underestimate how far a man would go to keep away a potential threat to his throne, or his family." Her last few words were heavy, as though there was a lot more to this story than she was willing to share right now. But I didn't press, I already had so much else to think about. After hearing all of this my mind was such a mess. Next to me, Raena remained silent, and I wondered if the inside of her head was equally as scrambled. No doubt whatever happened here next, she would still spend the next hour scolding me when we returned to the tower. And I wouldn't blame her. Talks like this within the walls of Drothmore's palace were bordering on treasonous. If only the King knew about this conversation happening in his hidden library...

"I must say though." Seraphina's chiming voice interrupted my thoughts. "You came to me at the perfect time." Her finger hovered over one of the book's pages. "It says here that in only a few weeks, the faery royal family are hosting a grand ball where the crown prince will choose his bride. Didn't you tell me you were looking for another prince?"

"How convenient..." Raena huffed. "We should go, Naria. I don't trust any of this."

"Wait," I said quietly, causing both Seraphina's and Raena's attention to snap to me. "How certain are you that they would help me rebuild my kingdom?"

"I would bet my life on it," Seraphina answered, and for some strange reason, I couldn't help but feel she was telling the truth. "Even if the prince already has a bride in mind, for the greater good of both of your kingdoms, it would be such a wasted opportunity for you to not at least form some kind of alliance."

Raena's mouth fell open. "Naria, please don't actually consider this."

"I don't know if I have a choice," I said back to her. "If Lukas is not interested in helping me and there are no other options for me here, then speaking with the faeries may be the only way for Corlixir to ever be restored to what it once was."

"But there are other options," Raena snapped back. "There has to be. We just haven't found them yet. And there's still a chance that Lukas might change his mind about helping you with your kingdom. You've known each other for barely a week. Just give it more time."

Across the table, Seraphina chuckled. "Maybe, might, a chance... Tell me, Naria, would you happily leave the fate of your kingdom up to chance? Would you marry the Prince of Drothmore because maybe he will help your people... someday?"

She was right. My people needed certainty, and if Lukas couldn't provide that, then maybe the fae would? But could I really trust Seraphina? Raena had a fair point when she said this was all very convenient. What if this was all some horrid trap and, like a fool, I was walking right into it?

My head was spinning.

"I just – I don't know," I replied honestly.

The healer's finger lazily traced the page she was reading before asking in a cool tone, "How about this then... Do you know where to find the faery kingdom?"

Both Raena and I said nothing, staring blankly.

"This library has taught me a lot about the fae," Seraphina started. "Apparently, many of their magic rituals require crystals that can only be found in cave systems hidden deep underground. Which means that for centuries now, the faeries have resided in the ground beneath us. They call their kingdom Faelenna, and it is said to be so vast that it spans from the mountains to the coasts."

"They live underground?" I remarked. "How is that even possible?"

"They must be terribly filthy all the time," Raena added, wrinkling her nose in disgust.

Seraphina eyed her with another harsh frown. "I would suspect that considering they have a court and a royal family, that they do not just dig around in the dirt all day like beasts." She then turned to me. "I've heard there is an entrance to it, hidden away in Drothmore's forests, about an hour's ride from here. If you're convinced that I am lying about all this, I suggest you try talking to them yourselves."

"Absolutely not!" Raena spat.

I wanted to speak, but no words came out. Inside my mind, a thousand thoughts were racing and swirling like a wild hurricane. What if Seraphina was telling the truth? What if the fae were the best hope for Corlixir? But what if she was lying?

Eventually, I sighed and brought my hand up to my face, letting the smooth part of my nail brush against my lip. "I'll go," I said, without even realising I'd spoken.

"What?" Raena spluttered.

"I'll just go and speak with them," I explained. "If there's even a chance that they can help my people, then I need to at least try."

Raena shook her head with a furious scowl. "This is so foolish. You could *die*, Naria. What if something happens to you? You'll be in the middle of a forest. There won't be any guards to protect you!"

"Then let's bring some with us. Surely there must be a few guards you trust to keep us safe."

She snorted. "Us? Tell me you do not expect me to come along for this death mission."

"Please, Raena." My lower lip trembled. "I can't do this alone, and you're the only person here I trust." We'd been friends for barely more than a week, but already she'd helped me through so much. I wasn't lying when I said I needed her there with me.

Her lips parted as though she wanted to protest, but all that came out was a heavy sigh. And after a few long seconds, she grumbled, "I do have some friends in the garrison. I'm sure I could convince them to come with us, even if only to accompany us through the forest... But, you need to promise me something." She took my hands, her brown eyes staring deep into mine. "If there's even a chance of any danger, anything at all that might hurt either of us, we leave immediately and we don't turn back."

I swallowed thickly, then nodded. It was decided.

Across the table, Seraphina was dipping a feathered quill into some ink. I hadn't noticed, but during our conversation, she'd been scribbling something onto a faded scrap of parchment.

"These are directions," she explained, continuing to write hurriedly.

"You're not coming with us?" I asked.

She shook her head. "My place is here, with the King. And as much as I don't agree with some of his decisions, I have been hired as a healer and I will never refuse to give someone care, no matter how undeserving they may be."

Respect blossomed in my chest. I understood very well the pledge that healers take once they begin practising. They always strive to protect, no matter when, no matter who. Even when the 'who' was someone you couldn't stand.

Seraphina passed the note towards us, and I accepted it while trying to force down the fear rising in my throat.

"Stay safe in the forests, Naria. Since you are the Princess of Corlixir, the fae should not harm you, but I cannot speak for the wolves."

As she spoke, I shuddered.

"You're *really* making me want to change my mind," Raena complained, but before she could say any more, I ushered her towards the door.

"Thank you for this, Seraphina," I called back for a final time as we turned to leave.

"You do not need to thank me, Princess Naria. I shall pray every night to your Ancients that Corlixir will rise again." The healer dipped her head in parting. "Like a phoenix from the ashes."

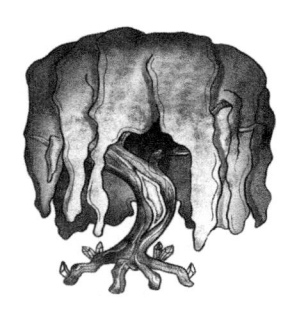

CHAPTER 12

Despite Raena's natural charm, it took a few days before she was able to convince enough of her guard friends to accompany us into the forest. Thankfully, none of them ran straight to the King after hearing of our plans. There's nothing like the weight of a heavy coin purse and the fluttering eyelashes of a pretty noble to keep someone's lips sealed.

While she was busy, I spent most of my time flitting between the forbidden library and my bedchamber, trying to learn as much about the faeries as possible while also staying far away from Lukas. A few times, his servants accosted me while walking through the halls to let me know that the prince was desperate to see me. Every time, I made some sorry excuse.

I had, of course, been very poorly that week. Far too ill to speak to His Royal Highness. And we wouldn't want him to catch anything... Some sneezes and a few fake coughs every time I passed his manservant seemed to be enough to keep the prince and his servants at bay.

When it was finally time to leave, Raena led me through the palace grounds and towards the stables. She'd organised for two of her trusted guards to meet us there at midnight. Nerves fluttered in my stomach like little butterflies as we approached the thick stone outbuilding. We were wearing thin black cloaks, both to conceal our identities and to hide our more 'practical' travelling dresses. While a low-cut silk gown wouldn't be my personal idea of practical, Raena insisted they were the best option for our little venture through the woods. That, and the fact she'd made it very clear she wouldn't let us be seen dead in breeches.

Inside the stables, two guards dipped their heads in respect as we passed through the open doorway. One, broad-shouldered with cropped black hair, busied himself fastening a saddle to a horse in a stall, while the other, a taller man with golden hair, stood much closer, leaning against a wooden pillar and sharpening a broadsword.

"Your Highness," the one who was holding a sword greeted me. He then turned to my companion, a flicker of something I wasn't expecting flashing briefly across his sharp features. "Lady Raena."

"Thank you for meeting us," she replied, lifting her hood and letting it drop to her shoulders. "And thank you for agreeing to help. Naria has been so desperate to add those pesky mushrooms to her medicine collection, but unfortunately there's only one place in the woods you can find them."

I raised an eyebrow.

So she hadn't told them what we were really doing... It made sense. Our plan was arguably treason. And if any of the guards did let the information trickle back to the King, while I'm sure we would still be punished for our reckless behaviour, if he believed we were only picking mushrooms, it wouldn't be anything too severe. Hopefully. As I pondered the dozen different ways we might be executed, I felt Raena reach for my hand, giving it a reassuring tug.

Oh Ancients, I hope we can trust these guards.

The golden-haired guard then sheathed his sword and stepped forward, the dim light of the stables casting shadows across his tanned face. He was young, maybe a few years older than Raena and me, and wearing a simple dark tunic that left his toned forearms exposed.

"We've prepared the horses," he said in a low voice. "I know Lady Raena can ride, but what about you, Your Highness?"

My stomach dropped as Raena chuckled. "Don't be silly, of course she can ride! What kind of princess doesn't ride horses?" She glanced at me, the smile slowly slipping from her face when she noticed my expression. "Naria... Tell me you *can* ride a horse."

"I – uhh."

There was really no need for any horses in my village. Even if I'd had enough coin for one, everywhere I needed to go was close enough to walk to, and even the Drothmore markets were only a half-hour stroll away. Still, by the way Raena was gawking at me, anyone would've believed I'd just stabbed the King.

I shook my head, embarrassment burning on my cheeks.

"It's alright," the other guard, who'd been fastening the buckles on a horse's saddle, called over to us. He stepped out of the wooden stable stall, and I noticed his short dark hair was thick and curled, just like Raena's. "We can go slowly, and I can lead your horse. All you have to do is try not to fall off." He flashed me a playful grin.

"I'm sure you'll learn quickly," Raena said quietly, patting my back.

We'd been travelling through the dense forest for what felt like the entire night, but judging by the moon's position in the murky sky, it must've been no more than an hour. The horse beneath me continued trudging along, and with each step it took, I had to tense my thighs and grip the saddle tightly to not fall off. Up ahead, Raena made it look so easy. Her body bobbed along smoothly with the horse's rhythm. And despite her earlier reluctance, even she didn't seem too afraid of the endless woods surrounding us. Meanwhile, I tried not to stare for too long into the darkness between the trees, in fear that something blue and gnarled might be staring back.

"Not much further now," Raena called back to me. She held the parchment in her delicate hands and occasionally shouted out directions to the guards riding beside us. They'd been mostly silent for the journey, speaking only near the beginning to give us their names.

Erik, the golden-haired, tan-skinned guard, rode alongside Raena. A few times she'd tried, pointlessly, to strike up conversation with him, but he would only ever give gruff, one-word answers or remind her that the wolves were always listening. The other guard, with darker hair and warm brown skin, was named Theo. He seemed much more cheerful than Erik as he kept hold of the reins of my horse, leading it to follow his own deep brown mount. Still, he constantly scanned the treeline, watching for wolves or maybe something else. I didn't want to ask what.

Raena's horse whinnied and snorted as she brought it to a halt near a huge forest clearing. In the centre, illuminated by the moonlight, was an unnaturally large willow tree. The tree towered over the rest of the forest, and yet its branches hung low, almost touching the ground. Surrounding the willow was a wide halo of tall grass that swayed gently in the nighttime breeze. Had I not known our true reason for being here, the oddly tranquil scene might've relaxed me.

"This must be it," announced Raena as she swung her legs off her horse.

"I don't see any mushrooms," Erik grumbled.

"They're probably hidden in the tall grass." Raena moved towards my horse and extended a hand to help me down. "Or under that big willow." She gave me a knowing look.

Ungracefully, I leaned against the horse as I slipped down its side, almost crashing into Raena.

"Want us to help you find them?" Theo offered, trying his best to steady my horse as I dismounted.

I quickly shook my head. "No need. Raena and I will be fine."

"Will we?" Raena's voice quivered.

"Just trust me," I whispered to her, although I wasn't quite certain that I trusted myself. Turning back to the guards, I instructed with rapidly fading confidence, "Please just wait with the horses. We might be gone a few hours, but we'll be sure to return long before dawn."

"A few hours?" Erik said, his lips thinning. "These must be some special mushrooms..."

"Very special," I lied. "There's a very specific way we have to locate them, and then to pick them is very—"

"Oh, be quiet," Raena groaned, dragging me away by my arm. "We'll return as soon as we can," she called over her shoulder as Theo waved us off with a confused chuckle.

"What were you thinking?" she hissed at me when we were more than a few metres away. "It's so obvious you're lying."

"You're the one who brought up mushrooms," I reminded her. Together, we began wading through the long grass, heading towards the grand willow.

"What else should I have said? I couldn't exactly wander up to the King's guards and ask them to join us on our jaunt to the faery kingdom. If they didn't just assume I was mad, they'd go straight to the King, and then we'd both end up in shackles."

"I thought you trusted them?"

She sighed. "I do, but they've still pledged loyalty to the King. It's one thing for a guard to sneak you out to a tavern, but to a place like this?"

"You sneak out to taverns?" I teased. "With guards?"

"I never said that." Her cheeks glowed a rosy red.

"I can't believe you." I brought a hand to my face to stifle a laugh. "Gentle Lady Raena sneaking out to taverns with the palace guards. It's scandalous... You must bring me along next time."

We both erupted into giggles, though our laughter promptly faded the moment we realised we'd reached the willow tree.

"What now?" Raena asked, drawing her cloak closer to her chest.

"From what I've read, there should be an opening somewhere in the tree trunk." I reached forward to part some of the willow leaves, then peered towards the centre. "This way."

She followed closely behind as I pushed through the leaves. It was so dark under the willow canopy, but I kept forcing my way through, treading carefully to avoid the uneven ground. Eventually, my hand hit something hard and bark-like, and I felt a strange sensation pulse through me. *This must be it.* I continued padding my hand against the tree trunk, trying to feel for a door or some kind of opening.

"Have you found the way in?" Raena whispered.

"Not yet," I called back.

But then I felt it.

Beneath my hand, the bark seemed to shift and change until eventually it parted, the hole growing wider and wider. A faint violet light seeped out of the hole, until I could see my hands again and clearly make out the features on Raena's concerned face.

"Blessed Oceans..." she breathed as the hole morphed into a small archway. Just beyond the arch, a long hallway stretched out in front of us. Violet orbs lined its packed dirt walls as the corridor seemed to slope directly into the ground, and at the end of the hall, a small spiral staircase descended into the unknown.

"I think I found the entrance," I said, my heart thrumming

in my chest. Now the doorway was wide open, I could feel something strange mixed in with the air that was pouring out. It smelled like sugar and fresh spring blossoms, while the feeling of it against my skin sent a warmth rushing down my spine.

Magic, perhaps? I didn't know. Whatever it was, it made my fingers tingle.

"After you," Raena offered quietly, gesturing towards the hallway. Her hands were shaking, but when I went to comfort her, I realised mine were too.

"Let's do it at the same time," I suggested, intertwining my trembling fingers with hers. She gulped, her gaze fixed on the passageway before us. The violet light spilling from it made her brown eyes shimmer like gemstones.

"For Corlixir," I breathed, as we stepped together under the willow archway and into the kingdom of the fae.

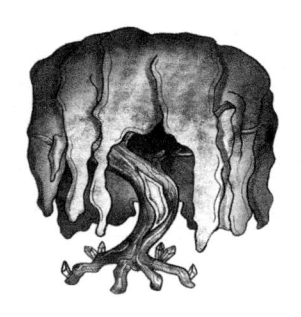

CHAPTER 13

The air changed again as soon as we passed under the archway, wrapping around us like a silk veil. I'd never felt anything like it before. Like a soft caress, it tickled every part of my body. Even the dirt walls seemed to hum with life as we made our way down the hallway lit by violet orbs.

"Can you smell that?" I asked Raena in a hushed voice. The scent of spring blossoms was thick in the air around us. I could practically taste the power radiating off this place.

"I don't smell anything," she replied, her voice equally quiet, "but this place certainly scares me."

We carried on until we reached the archway before the spiral staircase. Each step seemed to be moulded from the roots of the willow, but it was too narrow to walk down together so Raena *courageously* let me lead the way. As we descended, I could hear a faint voice talking beneath us, and then another that replied to the first voice with a deep, rumbling chuckle.

Just as we reached the final steps and the doorway to lead us out of this tower, the faint voices quietened. Then, I heard a sudden hiss of panic and the clattering of swords.

"Who goes there?" a male voice squeaked.

Carefully, we stepped out under the archway, and I raised my empty palms as a sign of innocence. Before us, was another much grander corridor. These dirt walls were lined with dark wooden beams, and violet orbs suspended from golden chains lit the hallway. At the end of the corridor were two men that appeared to be guarding a large round door.

At least I thought they were men.

The longer I looked, the more I realised just how inhuman they were. Their cheekbones were sharp and the tips of their ears extended into long points. Even their eyes seemed strange, as their irises glowed with an unnatural purple hue. And while they didn't seem much taller than each of us, their limbs were longer and more fluid. It didn't take me long to realise why they looked so... inhuman. It's because they weren't human at all. These were faeries. Angry faeries whose faces began to drain of colour as they pointed their swords towards us.

"Humans!" they growled.

"We come in peace," I shouted, keeping my arms raised. Raena quickly mirrored my action, stepping towards me and lifting her palms too. "My name is Princess Naria Alderbrook of Corlixir, and my companion is Lady Raena of Ryntook." I swallowed down the trembling in my voice. "We have come to request an audience with the Faery King and Queen."

The two guards' mouths swung open as though they were completely dumbfounded. Then, their heads whipped back and forth as they exchanged looks at each other, and then back to me.

"No one is supposed to come down here," one of them hissed to the other, "especially not humans!"

"Shh." The other grabbed the head of his partner, yanking it close to whisper something into his long ear. After a few moments of frantic hissing and whispering, their heads popped back up, and one of them stalked towards us, aiming his sword out in front of him.

"If you are a princess," he sneered in a grating voice, "then prove it."

A cold knot formed in my throat. "I... I have no proof."

"Why are you really here?" he pressed, lowering his sword to the hem of my skirt. "Are you hiding any weapons under this pretty dress? I can't believe the humans would send two puny girls to try to assassinate our king. How weak do they think we are?" The pair of them snickered as the nearer one used the tip of his sword to lift my skirt.

"Stop that!" Raena cried, and suddenly she dropped her hands to tug something sharp out of her boot. It glinted in the violet light as she held it out towards the guard.

An iron dagger. My heart sank.

"You are assassins!" the guard yelped, staggering backwards. "Get them!" he barked at his companion, who almost dropped his sword in shock.

"Run!" I all but screamed, grabbing Raena's hand and pulling her into a sprint. We charged towards the round door, the dagger still locked in her grasp. "Please be unlocked.

Please be unlocked," I pleaded as the huge door came closer and closer.

Thankfully, the divine beings must've been smiling down on us that night, because as soon as my palms crashed against the door, it swung open to reveal a bustling night market town. Rows of stalls and carts, each one crammed full of exotic treasures, lined a winding cobblestone path. Behind them, tall, oddly-built terraced houses stood watch over the busy street, the flickering lights from the windows casting a warm glow on the people below.

That's if you could consider *them* to be people.

Flitting between the stalls, laughing and bartering with the market sellers, were dozens upon dozens of long-limbed faeries. They moved so gracefully, like fish in a stream as the unusual fabrics of their clothing shimmered in the light. Their complexions were strange, too, their skin tones ranging in every colour from natural hues to bright pastels. And while some of them were blue, none of them had the horrid, gnarled look of that 'faery' in the portrait.

I could've spent hours taking it all in. But unfortunately, with the sounds of clinking armour rapidly approaching behind us, we had no time to marvel.

With a quick breath, I charged into the crowds, Raena following closely behind. Either side of us, faeries leapt out of the way, some yelping upon noticing our human faces and then Raena's weapon.

"Hide that dagger!" I hissed.

Raena didn't dare argue. Within seconds, it was concealed behind her cloak.

"Why do you even have that?" I demanded, plunging

deeper into the market crowds. Apologies bubbled out of my throat as our bodies bumped into so many innocent faeries.

"Why do you think? We couldn't just come here without any sort of protection!" Raena shot back, struggling to keep up.

"We would've been fine if you hadn't overreacted!"

"Me? Overreacting? He was about to lift up your skirts! I'm surprised you didn't smack him yourself."

Behind us, the guards' furious shouts sliced through the market noise. "After them!" one barked. "Assassins! Human assassins!"

In the distance, a deafeningly loud horn sounded. It echoed across the streets, the shocking volume causing the faeries around us to clasp their hands over their pointed ears.

"We have to get out of here," I said, not wanting to wait and find out what the siren meant for us. Chest burning, I raced through the crowds, Raena sprinting alongside me. Together, we moved with such urgency that I didn't even stop to apologise as we sent a faery man crashing into a barrel of strange fruit. Golden berries tumbled down the cobbled path as we struggled to keep on our feet.

After a few more panicked minutes, we both skidded to a halt. The market stalls had disappeared and before us was a crossroad.

"This way!" I grabbed Raena's hand and pulled her to the right, not daring to stop and think about it. Tall houses flew past us as we kept panting and running down the long winding road. From the fading sound of their steps against the stone, the two guards behind us appeared to slow. And for a moment, I thought we might actually escape. That was until, up ahead, I heard the sound of at least twenty more footsteps, and then fifty, and then at least a hundred – all charging towards us.

Suddenly, a small army of guards, their swords and spears drawn, marched down the street. When I went to whirl around and pull Raena back the way we came, another few squads came bounding over from the opposite direction.

We were completely surrounded. Every possible path was blocked.

"Oh Oceans..." Raena squealed. "This is it."

"Stay calm. Seraphina promised they wouldn't harm us." Although I struggled to believe her with the faery guards prowling closer and closer, gaining on us until I could see our panicked faces reflecting in their silver armour. My eyes squeezed shut. The heavy footsteps and clanging metal was almost louder than the pounding heartbeat in my ears. Maybe death wouldn't be so bad... Perhaps my parents would be waiting for me.

And then, there was a short deathly silence until a male voice cut through the heavy air.

"My my... What do we have here?"

Slowly, my eyes fluttered open, and as the darkness faded from my vision, I could see the tall, imposing figure of a dark-haired faery standing just metres away. He wasn't wearing any armour, only a well-fitted black shirt and matching breeches. Across his chest, the black fabric of his tunic appeared to mimic scales, or perhaps leaves, each one held together by thin silver thread. These clothes were much finer than those worn by the faeries in the markets, and resting upon his head, cushioned by the thick black waves of his hair, was a smooth silver circlet.

His gaze felt hot against my skin as I remained rooted in place. I didn't know how faery ageing worked, or if they even could age, but judging by his clear pale face, he appeared no older than twenty. His irises were a fiery amber, while his jawline could cut through steel like the edge of a thorn. And yet, despite the inhuman sharpness of his faery-like features, that perfect face could probably break more hearts than there were stars in the sky.

"Your Highness," one of the guards surrounding us announced with a bow. My heart leapt. So this was the prince? "These girls were apprehended at the gate. One of them has a dagger." He shuffled in place nervously. "Apparently, they're assassins sent by the humans." A murmur of fear rippled through the crowd of guards.

"That is not true!" I blurted out.

The prince smiled, a subtle darkness flickering across his lips. "Two human girls, and one with a dagger, just so happen to wander into Faelenna." His voice lowered. "My dear, if you are not an assassin, then why are you here?"

"I..." I glanced around as the guards edged closer. "My name is Princess Naria. I am here to request an audience with the Faery King and Queen." Another murmur rippled through the guards, this time one of disbelief.

"A princess? How intriguing," he mused, his smile widening. "Tell me, *Princess*, what news do you bring that is important enough to disturb my parents?"

I tried to steady my beating heart as I answered, "I have come to propose the idea of some kind of alliance. My own mother and father were King and Queen of Corlixir." The last few words seemed to send the guards into a gasping frenzy.

"Corlixir?" The prince's eyebrows shot up, and he raised a hand to silence the guards. "Corlixir was destroyed, burnt down to ashes by the Great Blaze all those years ago." He stalked closer, trailing long sweeping looks down my body as he began to pace around me in a small circle. "But how do we know that you speak the truth?" He leaned in, dropping his voice to a whisper. "How can you prove that you were not just sent here to drag your friend's dagger through the heart of the King?"

Had Raena not been such a trembling mess beside me, I would've been resisting the urge to murder her.

"I assure you, Your Highness," I began, gulping down the fear that had risen in my chest, "whatever happened with those two guards, was a complete misunderstanding. We come here in peace."

"You certainly made quite a peaceful entrance," the prince chuckled darkly as he returned to his original position. "But very well, *Princess*, I will take you to speak with my parents."

"Oh, thank you tha—"

"Although," the prince silenced my gratitude by raising his hand again, "I will need to verify your identity first, to make sure you are really who you claim to be." For a brief second, something almost threatening flashed across his face, but I brushed any fear aside, along with all the other unwanted feelings this encounter was stirring up inside me.

"Of course," I accepted.

The prince's attention then snapped to a young green-skinned faery guard. "You," he barked.

The guard straightened. "Y-yes, sire?"

"Search her." The prince aimed a slender finger towards Raena, who quivered where she stood.

"This is quite improper!" I protested. But my complaints were completely ignored as the guard marched over and roughly patted Raena down. It didn't take him long to extract the dagger from her cloak, slipping it into his belt.

"Want me to do that one too?" the green-skinned guard huffed, nodding in my direction.

The prince shook his head. "Take the one with the dagger to the palace dungeon. Put her in the block with the other important prisoners. You know where."

The guard nodded and grabbed Raena, twisting her arms behind her back. She shrieked and kicked her legs wildly as he began to wrestle her away.

"Stop! Let her go!" I rushed to stop him, but before I could intervene, the prince was behind me, grabbing and twisting my own wrists just as the other guard had done to Raena.

"Don't try anything foolish now, *Princess*." He pulled me against his hard chest until I could feel the warmth of his body on my back, his breath teasing my ear. "You and your violent friend will be reunited once we've had our little chat…"

"Let her go, please," I begged him.

My captor ignored my pleading, holding both my wrists with one moonlight-pale hand and using the other to run his slender fingers down my cheek. In that moment,

I feared that perhaps I had left the cold, steel-eyed Prince of Drothmore for someone far more dangerous. Someone who saw no issue with manhandling a princess and her companion in the middle of the street.

"It is normally frowned upon for a royal to beg, but on you... it is quite becoming, assuming you are even a royal," he taunted in a low voice, letting his fingers trail down my chin and neck. They paused just before my collarbone, then followed the curve of my left shoulder. "I've never seen a human before. Are they all as pretty as you?"

"Please, just let her go." I tried my hardest to ignore the way my cheeks heated as I felt his lips brush my ear.

"You'll see her soon enough," he murmured, "but for now, pretty assassin, you'll come with me."

Suddenly, a tingling sensation sprouted in my toes and crept slowly up my wobbling legs. It carried a strange warmth that seemed to lull each of my muscles into a heavy, forced sleep. As the tingling hit my knees, they buckled, but before I could collapse onto the cobbled floor, a pair of strong arms caught me under my shoulders. With each passing second, my body felt weaker, more fluid, as stars fizzled in the corners of my vision. The last thing I remembered before darkness overtook me completely was the faery prince's taunting smile as I was swept up into his arms.

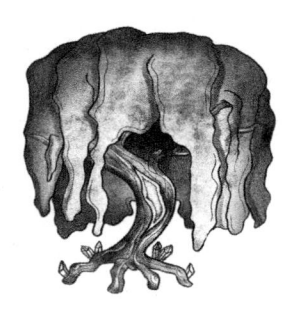

CHAPTER 14

Awareness slowly trickled into my senses as the scent of flowers hit me first. The sweet smell overwhelmed my nose and reminded me of jasmine and the spring blossoms that grew in the groves near my old school.

Then, mysterious colours and shapes swirled into my vision, blurry at first, but with every second that passed, they became more and more clear. Glowing violet orbs, flaming amber eyes, Raena's strained face as she was torn away. Suddenly, my eyes sprung open, and a loud gasp escaped my throat.

I was no longer in the cobbled faery street.

"The sleeping beauty awakens," a low, masculine voice sounded from nearby.

My head whipped around. I was lying down, sprawled across what felt like a giant silk bed. Above me, thick tree roots weaved through a dark burgundy ceiling as though this room was built beneath a large willow tree.

A large willow tree...

It was then that the memories came flooding back – the forest clearing, the hidden archway, the guards, *the prince*. Panicking, I hurried to push myself up, but a soft clinking sound stopped me as I realised my hands were suspended above my head, chained to the wooden bed frame.

"I would apologise for the restraints, but your friend did have a dagger." The voice spoke again. This time, I realised who it was coming from.

Twisting my body, I was able to sit up on the giant bed, my wrists remaining fixed to the bed frame behind me. At the foot of the bed, lounging in an ornate wooden chair, was the dark-haired faery prince. My breath caught as I saw him. In the harsh light of the bedchamber, I could finally take in his sharp features and long, pointed ears. Though it didn't take long for a smile to creep across his face as he noticed me staring.

"Like what you see?" he teased.

Oh Ancients, he's even more insufferable than Lukas.

"Why am I here?" I demanded, ignoring his question.

The prince grinned. "So I can assess if you really are the true Princess of Corlixir, or if you are simply a very beautiful assassin. Although I'm betting on the latter." He winked.

"Well, I'm sorry to disappoint you." Tearing my gaze away, I focused on the cold metal around my wrists. I tugged at them, testing their strength. "Do you interrogate all your prisoners like this?" I complained, realising that I wasn't getting out of these without a key.

"Only the pretty ones who claim to be a princess." His candid response made my cheeks feel warm.

Beside him on a small wooden table was a white goblet encrusted with violet jewels. Moving out of his seat, he scooped up the goblet and slowly made his way over to me, his footsteps echoing across the smooth quartz floor.

"In my hand is a truth serum," he explained. "Once you take a sip, you will be compelled to speak only the truth for the next few minutes." He lowered his tall frame and took a seat on the bed, his back only inches from my thighs.

I eyed the goblet suspiciously. "How do I know it's not poison?"

A laugh rumbled from his chest. "It would be very foolish of me to poison the Princess of Corlixir now, wouldn't it? Especially since, if you are telling the truth – which I very much doubt you are – my mother and father would be eager to meet you."

"And I, them," I reminded him.

"I must admit you are playing your role beautifully." He pushed the goblet towards my lips. "But please, enough with the theatrics. You must drink this so I can find out who you really are."

My jaw clenched as my lips remained sealed.

"Drink, pretty assassin," he ordered again, but this time, something strange happened. His words seemed to echo in my mind as my eyelids lowered. "Drink..." he pressured once more, and then, without even wanting to, my own lips betrayed me as the honey-flavoured liquid pooled in my throat.

After a few seconds, he drew the goblet away, and I coughed, clarity flooding my mind.

"What was that?" I spluttered.

"Compulsion." Another smirk crept over his face. "It's a rare gift, but everyone in my family can do it." A soft thud sounded as he placed the goblet on the bedside table. "Now," he mused, drawing closer, "tell me your name."

"My name is Naria Alderbrook." I gasped as the words spilled out of me without any effort at all.

"Intriguing..." The prince swept a suspicious gaze over me. "But I suppose you could still have the same name as her... How about this, tell me why you're here?"

Once again, the words tumbled out of me. "I am here because I absolutely cannot stand to marry Prince Lukas. King Ikelos seems to think it is best for my kingdom, and the prince is certainly handsome, but he has absolutely no manners or respect for me. He saw no issue with parading his lovers around the palace and told me very matter-of-factly that he has no intention of letting me rebuild Corlixir, and would probably rather all my people leave Honeymeade and find homes in other kingdoms." My chest felt heavy as I spoke, but I couldn't stop. The traitorous words kept tumbling out. "I met someone in the library, a healer, she told me about this place and how the fae had good connections with Corlixir. I thought I might be able to find another suitor here, or at least form some kind of alliance to help rebuild my kingdom. Then there would be no need for me to marry Lukas. I could save my kingdom and I'd never have to see his smug face again."

The faery prince just stared with an open mouth, as if he couldn't quite believe what he was hearing. "You really are her?" he breathed.

I nodded, my lower lip trembling.

"What do you know of the night of the fire? How did you escape?"

I tried so desperately to keep my jaw clamped shut. Answering his questions in this way felt like such an invasion into my mind. But of course, even with my teeth biting down my tongue, the reply still forced its way through. "I don't remember exactly." A hot tear rolled down my cheek. "I was only a baby. But I was told by the village mother that King Ikelos saved me that night and took me to Drothmore. He caught me after my parents dropped me out of their window." I tried to pause and chew my lip, but the words wouldn't stop. "Apparently their screams rang through the entire kingdom after King Ikelos took me away and the... the fire consumed them." The last words pierced my chest like a dagger.

When I was a child, I used to spend hours lying awake wondering about my family. I liked to imagine, as morbid as it sounds, that they passed away peacefully in their sleep from the thick smoke of the Great Blaze. Or perhaps the fire took them cleanly and quickly without too much pain. To know how they really died made everything feel so much worse. Some days, I wished the village mother had never told me anything at all.

Silence filled the room as the prince's gaze remained fixed on me. His taunting smile had faded into a look of pity. I hated that. Let me feel sad, let me mourn for them, but do not make me feel helpless.

Eventually, he straightened, clearing his throat as he reached into a pocket by this thigh. A small silver key appeared in his palm.

"I once again apologise for the restraints, Your Highness." His tone was different now. He spoke with a new air of respect. "And I apologise for not believing your story when you first came to us. I hope you can understand that the circumstances of your arrival were... unique." He leaned forward to reach for the cold metal rings around my wrists. As he searched for the keyhole, his hands brushed mine, sending something fluttering in my chest. He was so close that I could see the muscles in his neck. The smell of wildflowers with cinnamon undertones crept into my nose, and I noticed my bodice felt unusually tight. Perhaps this was just the truth serum wearing off.

Eventually, with a soft click, the restraints fell away, and I lowered my hands to massage my tingling wrists. The prince remained leaning forward until, without any warning, he carefully took one of my hands and pressed the back of it to his lips. After planting a soft kiss on my skin, he lowered my hand then met my confused gaze.

"I realise that we haven't been formally introduced." Another smile tugged at his lips. "My name is Prince Arenn Dalsidian of Faelenna, but please, just call me Arenn." He returned my hand gently to the silk bed sheets. "It's so good to meet you, Naria... I trust it's acceptable for me to call you that?"

I nodded slowly as unease settled in my stomach. This was so far from how I imagined meeting the prince would be. A small part of me wondered how Lukas would feel if he knew I was here right now – with my face inches away from a beautiful amber-eyed faery. I blinked, casting the thought aside. It didn't matter what he thought, and if this night went well, I might never have to think of him again.

"I would like to speak with the Faery King and Queen as soon as possible," I requested while trying to steady my shaking breath. "I also need Lady Raena to be released. She is innocent. I had no idea she brought a dagger, but you must believe me when I say that I trust the dagger was only for our protection."

The prince straightened and nodded once. "She will be released immediately. I will have a guard escort her to the throne room." He rose from the bed, turning to extend a hand out to me. "In the meantime, I'll take you to the King and Queen. I'm sure they'll be delighted to meet you." Excitement flashed across his sharp features.

"Thank you," I said as I carefully accepted his hand.

The moment I stepped out of the silk bed, my legs wobbled beneath me, and suddenly the room began to spin. Quickly, Arenn slipped an arm around my waist, steadying me before I could fall. A soft gasp leapt from my throat as his hand pressed against my lower back. No one had ever touched me in that way before. The feeling made my cheeks burn redder than roses.

"Sorry," I whispered, resting my palm against his chest to support myself.

"You needn't apologise." His arm remained firmly around my waist as he continued to hold me. "It's most likely from the spell I used to bring you here. Though I must insist, had I known you were a princess, I can assure you I would've taken you straight to the King and Queen."

"It's not your fault. We should've come more prepared. This was actually quite a rushed decision," I said, pressing a hand to my forehead in an attempt to ease the dizziness.

"Of course. You'll have to tell me all about this foolish human prince that you ran away from," he replied with a curious smile.

"I'm afraid he's far from foolish," I sighed, closing my eyes to stop the room swirling around me. "Just incredibly arrogant."

"Arrogant or not," the prince shot back in a teasing tone, "he'd have to be foolish to let someone as pretty as you slip away from his palace in the middle of the night."

My cheeks burned once more as I opened my eyes to glance up at him. When standing beside me, he was at least a head taller than I was. "You're quite the charmer," I commented with a shy smile. "Am I to discover that you also have several lovers that you parade around the streets here?"

Arenn grinned, showing a line of perfect white teeth. "If I did, would you still want to form an alliance with my family? Or would you run to the next kingdom? Perhaps to the goblins? Though I've heard they can be a little beastly and they're quite... well... small."

A laugh bubbled in my throat. "I'd gladly marry the smallest goblin if I could trust him to be loyal to myself and my kingdom."

"How intriguing," he mused playfully. "But please, I request that while I am courting you, you don't let anyone catch you sneaking off with any goblins. It would certainly ruin my reputation."

"So you plan on courting me?" I retorted, heart fluttering in my chest.

He leaned closer and in a low voice said, "You are a mysterious human princess... I would be a very foolish prince not to."

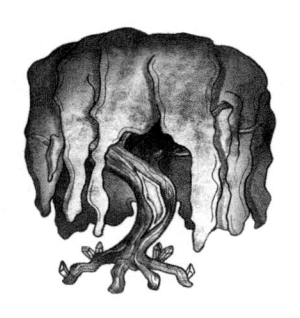

CHAPTER 15

My arm remained firmly in Arenn's grasp as he guided me towards the throne room. The faery palace was so different from how I'd expected it to be. The walls were made from a mixture of quartz and what appeared to be some kind of clay, while thick willow tree roots weaved throughout the walls and occasionally streamed across the floor. To my relief, the lingering dizziness from the spell was fading, leaving only the odd wave of unsteadiness to roll over my body, though the random tree roots were not helping. Quite a few times, Arenn had to catch me mid-fall when a root unexpectedly jutted out of the marble ground.

The clothing here was also very different from the human world. Faery women wore much shorter gowns that exposed the multicoloured skin of their lower legs and ankles, while some of them even wore flowing breeches.

The fabrics were different, too. Some gowns were almost translucent and others shimmered in different colours depending on the angle of the light, like the wings of a beetle.

Arenn continued to guide me until, eventually, we reached a large, round set of doors with guards posted on either side. When they saw the prince approaching, they dipped their heads and rushed to heave the doors apart. With a soft, elegant creak, the doors swung open to reveal a stunningly grand throne room.

The air in the hall was heavy with what must've been magic. It radiated warmth through my body and once again left my fingertips tingling. Along the edges of the room, tall quartz pillars stretched up to support the vast, shimmering ceiling. Many formally dressed faeries stood around the pillars, socialising and flitting between different groups.

We stopped near the centre of the room, and Arenn bowed deeply. Before us were two thrones that appeared to be carved from giant blush pink crystal formations. Seated on the thrones were a man and a woman, both finely dressed faeries. They paused their conversation as we approached, but the moment the woman's gaze met mine, she gasped, dropping her golden goblet. It clattered against the marble floor, sending a wave of silence through the hall as everyone turned towards the Queen.

"Elowen?" she called out, rising from her seat and stepping closer. Unlike the other fae, she wore a long, elaborate gown, with a skirt that resembled rose petals trailing behind her.

"Dearest Naria," Arenn began, addressing me, "please

allow me to introduce my parents, King Bevan and Queen Amabel."

He then turned to them, sweeping his arm towards where I stood. "And Mother, Father, it is with great pleasure that I introduce to you, the very human, Princess Naria of Corlixir."

Shocked noises echoed throughout the hall as suddenly, I could feel the wide-eyed stares of almost every faery in the room burning onto my skin. With a thick swallow, I prayed they couldn't somehow smell fear. In that moment, I would've reeked of it.

"Great Spirits of the Quartz..." The man, who must have been King Bevan, stood as well. "You look just like your mother." Like the Queen, he too wore an extravagant outfit. A glittering flower crown sat above his dark but greying hair, while midnight blue overcoat embroidered with gold leaf patterns covered his large torso.

With a slow curtsy, I replied in a way that tried to mask my shaking voice. I'd practised this speech so many times on the journey through the forest. Why did the words now stick to my tongue now? "Thank you for agreeing to speak with me, Your Majesties. I'm very glad to be here. Your kingdom is so incredibly beautiful." Their warm smiles steadied my nerves slightly as I carried on, "And it is wonderful to finally meet you both. I... I was told that my parents were good friends of yours?"

"More than good friends, dear," Queen Amabel answered, her voice tinged with sadness.

The Faery King stepped over to his wife's side to take her hand. "Indeed... It was a dark time when we were informed of your parents' passing. They were so young and full of life. Nobody expected it... The realm lost so much more than just a kingdom that day." He passed her a comforting smile before his gaze slowly returned to me. "But alas, as delightful as it is to finally meet you, I'm sure you have not just come here to listen to us reminisce. So please, my dear, you must tell us what brings you to our palace?"

My teeth scraped against my lower lip. This was it, the moment I'd been losing sleep over.

Gripping the fabric of my rumpled skirts, I took a deep breath before announcing, "I have come to propose the idea of an alliance."

Quiet murmurs buzzed around the hall. Some faeries seemed to laugh while others sounded perplexed.

"An alliance?" the King repeated with a curious grin. Stepping backwards, he let his large body sink into his crystal throne as his thick hands gripped the armrests. "Forgive me for being so bold, but isn't your kingdom still lying in ruins? You may be a princess, but without your land, or many people for that matter, what could you possibly offer us?"

Swallowing, I continued, "There might not be many of us left. But those of us who survived are thriving, living together in a small village hidden deep within the forests of Drothmore." I chewed my lip, choosing my next words carefully. "While my people are grateful for the support that King Ikelos has provided, they are desperate to go home – to return to a rebuilt kingdom. And I believed, with Drothmore's support, that this would someday be a possibility... but unfortunately it has been made clear to me that their future king has no intention of helping our cause." I took a breath, casting aside the frustrating glimpses of steel that flooded my vision. "If you can help us by providing the necessary funding, materials, and support, not only will myself and my people be eternally grateful, but we would also happily trade enough medicine for all of your subjects and share our advanced healing knowledge with all of your kingdom's healers. Perhaps we could even help to rekindle the relationship between humans and the fae? Faeries could walk freely through the human kingdoms once again, as friends."

Shocked gasps rippled through the crowds of fae, and a few of them scoffed.

"My dear..." This time it was the Faery Queen who spoke. She too had returned to her crystal throne, letting her rose skirt flare out beneath her. "I admire your confidence, but it would take much more than the desire of a single naive human princess to restore the trust that was lost after your parents' deaths. Not to mention, there are a fair number of fae who are quite happy living underground here and avoiding the – no offence to you, dear – but the trials and tribulations of dealing with humans. Some have even left the realm entirely and are living quite contently above ground elsewhere. If the human rulers do not wish to include us in their petty games and wars... then so be it! We are quite content with not getting involved."

At her response, our audience clapped and cheered, while my stomach took a dive to my feet. I hadn't even considered that they might not want to form relationships with the human kingdoms. If only there was a spell that could make the floor open up and swallow me whole – I would beg Arenn to cast it this instant.

Their deafening cheers continued until the King finally lifted a hand to silence them.

"Calm yourselves!" he ordered, his mouth curling into a frown. "We must remember to be respectful when in the presence of foreign royalty." He swept his hand towards where I stood. "After all, I still remember a time when both our nation and Corlixir thrived together. Many a fae were saved in Corlixin hospitals, and together we discovered many of the life-altering potions that we all still use today." He tilted his chin to meet my gaze, his eyes washed with sorrow. "I must express how truly sorry I am for the loss of your kingdom. Corlixir was one of the few human kingdoms where we fae were not seen as outsiders, but welcomed with open arms. I will forever mourn the loss of both the kingdom and your parents."

A heavy silence fell over the throne room.

I let it sit for a few moments before breaking it with my reply. "Thank you for your understanding," I started, my words measured. "Of course, I never knew my parents, nor did I ever walk the streets of my own kingdom, but I grew up surrounded by other Corlixins." My knees trembled. "Though I must admit, to merely have each other is not enough. We need a real home. We need Corlixir back to what it once was." My gaze glided from the Queen and then to the King. "So now I stand before you to ask, no... to *beg* for your help. Please... Please help me rebuild my kingdom, and in return, I will do anything you desire."

Beside me, a soft sound escaped Arenn, a quiet laughter that only I seemed to catch. The entire time, he'd remained still as a statue with his gaze fixed between the two thrones.

Around us, the other faeries whispered, but there were too many hushed voices to distinguish what any of them were saying.

"Did your human friends not warn you that it is unwise to attempt to make deals with the fae?" The King's aged features seemed to burn with mischief. "We are renowned for always coming out on top, or so they say."

"I care only that my kingdom gets rebuilt," I stated, all traces of fear vanishing from my voice. "Whatever happens to me is meaningless; I only care that my people get to return to their rightful home."

"Brave girl," the King mused. "I must admit, when you first came in here, I saw only the sweet and cautious Elowen. But now, I see your father in you too."

A knot formed in my throat, but I swallowed it down. I'd deal with those tears later.

"This is certainly a lot to think about," the King sighed, tapping his fingers against his bearded chin. "But I'm sure we can work out some sort of *alliance*, as you so eloquently put it." He leaned against the tall crystal back of his throne. "For now, you should enjoy the wonders of our kingdom. Please, stay as long as you'd like." His hand gestured gracefully. "Has my son already informed you of the ball we call Luminessia?"

"Not yet, Father," Arenn responded for me.

"Luminessia," the King explained, "is a grand ball where my son will choose his bride and thus declare the future Queen of Faelanna. I remember your parents once expressed that you and my son should marry when you were both of age, but I am not the sort of king who favours the old-fashioned forced engagements."

My eyebrows shot up. If only King Ikelos were so progressive.

No.

If only Lukas were not such a brat.

I forced myself to take a slow breath to calm the anger that now rocked in my stomach.

"My son will marry whomever he wishes, but still, you should attend the ball. After all, a marriage between royalty is certainly one kind of alliance," the King chuckled to himself.

"Thank you, Your Majesty." I dipped my head in respect, trying to ignore the queasy feeling that settled in my chest. If I could not stand to marry Lukas, could I bring myself to marry Prince Arenn? Deep down, I didn't think I wanted to marry anyone, but if marriage was the only way to save my kingdom then, as I said before, I would happily marry a goblin.

The Faery Queen opened her mouth to announce something to the court but was abruptly cut off by a loud, shrieking giggle coming from just outside the hall. When another even louder, more piercing giggle followed the first, both the King and Queen's heads jerked up to stare over me and towards the open throne room doors.

"Is that... another human?" the Queen muttered to herself. "It's like an invasion."

I thought I recognised that giggle...

Whirling to face the doorway, I watched as Raena half stumbled, half walked through the quartz corridor. She was laughing away, hand in hand with a young green-skinned faery guard. The very same guard who'd handled her so roughly in the faery streets, just hours ago.

Beside me, the prince must've spotted her too, as he leaned in close to whisper, "Perhaps we should go and fetch your friend?"

I nodded before both Arenn and I thanked the King and Queen for their time, and promptly exited the throne room.

Outside, Raena and the guard had stopped by a crystal-framed painting. She was leaning into him, playfully swatting at his arm and chuckling as though he had just told her the funniest joke in the realm.

"Raena!" I called over to her as soon as the huge throne room doors thudded shut behind us. Her bubbling laughter faded as she turned slowly, still leaning against the faery guard. When she noticed me, a smile wider than I'd ever seen before spread across her rosy face.

"Naria," she beamed, "I'm so glad to see you! Dearest Valen here was just giving me a tour of the palace. Isn't he magical?" she sighed, gazing dreamily up at the guard's face.

A crease formed in my brow as she continued to giggle and mutter mindlessly to herself. The words were definitely Raena's, but this behaviour was just bizarre. Something wasn't right.

"Are you alright?" Cautiously, I brought a hand to Raena's arm, rubbing it gently, but she ignored my touch, her glazed-over eyes remaining fixed on the guard.

With clenched fists, I whipped my chin up to address the faery. "What did you do to her?"

"Just a simple charm," he mumbled, his feet shifting in place.

The thought of anyone tampering with Raena's mind made me feel ill, but still, I swallowed down the urge to lunge at him. "I don't know what that means, but whatever you've done, you need to remove it. Now."

The guard glanced up at the prince. "I had no choice, sire. She was hysterical! I had to do something, else she was going to break through the bars!"

A shadow passed over Arenn's lips. Then he smiled, a little too sweetly for my liking. "You should know better, Valen. This is no way to treat our guests." Calmly, he lifted a pale hand and pressed his index finger against Raena's forehead. With a sigh, she nuzzled further into the guard's chest, completely ignoring the prince's touch.

"That should clear the charm," he said, lowering his hand.

After a few moments, the glaze that covered her vision seemed to fade as she blinked frantically. Lifting her body away from the guard, she stood swaying until I steadied her.

"Are you alright, Raena?" I asked quietly.

"I... I feel confused," she replied in a tired voice. "I don't know where..." Her brown skin paled, and for a moment, I thought she might faint. "I think I want to go home and sleep for a bit."

"Of course, we'll go home now," I assured her. Biting back my anger, I shot a glare at the guard. Instead of responding, he just avoided my gaze, keeping his hands in his pockets and staring at the floor.

"Leave us, Valen," the prince commanded, and without needing to be told twice, the guard scurried off down the corridor. Arenn then shifted his attention back to me. With a sincere, apologetic look, he said, "I'm so very sorry for what happened with your friend today. If there was a ritual that could turn back time, I would gladly start this whole night over again."

I shook my head. "It's not your fault. Like you said before, our arrival wasn't exactly peaceful."

He nodded, then glanced at Raena, who was struggling to hold her dozing head up with her hand. "Still, there are ways we could've handled it better."

Guilt gnawed at my insides. I should've never, ever brought her here. The Raena I knew wouldn't squash a fly for fear of it staining her gown, yet just a few hours ago, she was prepared to stab a living, breathing faery to protect me. And only the Ancients know what went on in her cell while I was fast asleep. My chest tightened as dark thoughts crept into my mind. I would never forgive myself if something happened to her.

"We should be leaving now. I need to take her home to Drothmore," I decided, taking Raena's limp arm in mine.

The prince nodded, although his jaw seemed to tense at my words. "That is understandable. I'll escort you both to the gates."

We walked mostly in silence back through the palace and then through the streets of the underground faery kingdom. Even though it was night up above, there were so many different faeries wandering down the winding cobbled roads. I wanted to ask Prince Arenn if perhaps faery magic was more active at night, but instead, I spent most of the walk consoling Raena, who wobbled and groaned with every step. Still, the fact that we were walking rather than frantically sprinting to escape angry guards allowed me to finally appreciate more of the wonder of this place. The gigantic domed ceiling must've been at least fifty metres into the air, and to add to the illusion, the same violet orbs from the hallways were scattered across the muddy sky like stars. The terraced faery houses all seemed to be made of different unusual materials, too. Metals and crystals that I had never seen before were packed together with dirt to form bricks that glistened and sparkled under the light of the violet stars.

When we finally reached the same round gates that Raena and I had crashed through just hours before, Arenn stopped and bowed respectfully towards me.

"It's been an enchanting night meeting you, Princess Naria. And not one I will forget any time soon." He lifted his head to present me with a charming smile.

"Likewise, Prince Arenn." I tilted my chin back at him, hoping that Raena – who was still latched onto my arm – couldn't feel how much my traitorous heart had leapt. When he looked at me like that, it was very easy to forget that our initial introduction had been anything but enchanting.

"Promise me you will return soon? There is so much of our kingdom that I would love to share with you." A flicker of something danced across his amber eyes. It made my knees feel weak.

"I can't say how soon I will return." I steadied my voice. "But I will certainly try to visit here again before your ball in two weeks."

"Ah, I trust you will be busy with your foolish prince?"

"Prince Lukas does not own me," I laughed. "But I have already been avoiding him long enough, and he will certainly start to grow suspicious if my room is empty every night."

Arenn propped himself against the wooden door as his voice slipped into a darker tone. "Do you not fear what he will do if he finds out that you're sneaking away to spend the night with a faery?"

A shudder slipped over me. In truth, I hadn't let myself think about what might happen if Lukas learnt about my secret midnight visit to Faelenna. Then again, considering how he seemed to have no issues tormenting or humiliating me, perhaps I would be doing him a favour by finding a more suitable future husband. Clearly, he was under the impression that there was nothing Corlixir could ever do for Drothmore. And he certainly didn't seem to have any romantic interest in me, unless he had a very funny way of showing it...

"I couldn't care less how he might feel about my visit here tonight," I huffed. "I have already made it clear to him that if he cannot help my kingdom then I will have to seek help elsewhere."

"And how did he take that?" Arenn prompted with a grin, folding his arms across his chest.

"Not very well," I admitted, as visions of roses, furious princes, and copper-haired beauties flooded my mind. "As I said though, he does not own me. I am an orphaned princess of a fallen kingdom, so technically, nobody can tell me what to do."

"Such determination," the prince mused, his smile

widening. "But you should still be careful... Even if you believe he cannot force you to do anything, you should never underestimate what jealousy can do to a man, especially a prince." Another shadow flickered across his lips.

I opened my mouth to reply, but was interrupted when Raena groaned loudly into my shoulder. Wincing, I gave Arenn an apologetic look. "We should be going. I fear if we don't leave now, then Lady Raena might not make it back through the forest."

"She will be fine in the morning," Arenn assured me before he knocked twice on the huge gates. Slowly, they creaked open to reveal the familiar dirt tunnel on the other side.

"Farewell, Prince Arenn." I dipped my head before steering Raena back towards the narrow steps that led to the outside world.

"Until we meet again, little human," the prince replied. Then, with a parting smile, he disappeared into the crowd of faeries I hadn't even noticed had gathered around us.

CHAPTER 16

Outside, the air was much cooler than beneath the willow tree. I cursed under my breath as we stepped through the curtain of low-hanging leaves to see that dawn was fast approaching. I must've been unconscious for much longer than I had anticipated. By the time we reached the clearing, the night sky had faded to a muted blue and birds were beginning to sing amongst the trees.

"We must be quick, Raena," I urged as we rushed through the tall grass.

Erik spotted us first, calling out to Theo, who was resting against a tree.

"Look who finally made it back," he huffed. "We were beginning to suspect that the wolves had eaten you."

"Thank you for waiting." I shuffled closer, still holding onto Raena, who by this point was struggling to stand.

Concern tugged at Erik's lips when he noticed her condition. "What happened?"

"She uh... ate a bad mushroom."

Erik scowled, shaking his head. "I hope this trip was worth it."

Behind him, Theo stepped forward, his tired eyes fixed on the sky. "We need to get you back quickly if you want to be home before sunrise." He glanced at me. "Can she ride?"

Erik scoffed. "Look at her, she can hardly stand." He leaned forward to gently pry Raena off me. "I can take her, my horse is big enough for two." His voice then softened as he addressed the swaying girl. "Listen, Raena, I know you're not feeling very well so you can ride with me, okay? I'll get you home safely."

"Careful, Erik," Theo teased, "it almost sounds like you care."

The golden-haired guard shot Theo a warning look before he guided Raena towards the horses.

"Come on, Princess," Theo said to me with a laugh. "Let's get you back."

When I finally arrived back in my tower room, I had just enough leftover willpower to change out of my travelling dress and into a nightgown before I crashed onto the bed. Erik ended up carrying Raena up the stairs to her room beside mine. I'd made sure she made it into bed safely before thanking Erik profusely and slipping him a few extra gold pieces. He'd declined at first, but changed his mind quickly after I refused to let him leave without taking them.

We all needed to get to bed.

Sleep overcame me faster than my eyes had time to close when my head finally hit the soft pillows. But I'd been sleeping for what only felt like five minutes when I suddenly woke to a loud commotion outside my door.

"This is absurd, do you not know who I am? You must let me see her," a male voice sounded from the hallway. My eyes opened only slightly, still heavy from sleep. I had no idea what time it was, but judging by the intense growling of my stomach and the golden sunlight pouring in from the windows, I guessed it was at least midday.

Three sharp knocks echoed through the room.

"Naria! Are you in there?"

Prince Lukas... It'd been almost a week since I'd spoken to him last, but still, I recognised that low, commanding voice. It was a struggle not to groan as I rolled over, my back now facing the door. He wouldn't come in here, it wouldn't be proper. Besides, I was still in my nightgown, and for him to see me like this would be highly—

The door swung open, and my entire body flinched enough to send me tumbling off the bed and onto the hard wooden floor in front of him.

"Lukas," I gasped, clutching a hand to my chest. The thin white nightgown I was wearing did little to protect my modesty. "You can't be in here. You need to leave, now!"

Before me, the prince stood in the doorway, wearing an unusually plain tunic and breeches. His dark brown hair was a mess of waves that flopped lazily against his forehead, and judging by the way his chest rose and fell and his lips were slightly parted, I supposed he'd run all the way up here. When he noticed my nightgown, a subtle dash of red coloured his cheeks, but he didn't move. Instead, he remained frozen in the doorway.

After a few very long seconds, he cleared his throat before speaking in a serious tone. "I came to check on you. It's been so long since we last spoke, and I was worried something might've happened."

"Well, I can assure you, I am completely fine," I huffed, my hand still covering my chest. "Or at least I was until you came barging in here."

He shifted nervously. "I apologise for my intrusion."

Several breaths passed between us as I waited for him to turn and leave. But instead, my stomach dropped as he stepped further into the room, letting the door click shut behind him.

I opened my mouth to protest, but his next words forced all the air from my chest.

"I'm sorry about what happened in the garden."

I blinked, my mouth falling open.

"And I'm sorry for how I acted on your first day. I realise I may have been a bit... harsh at dinner, and you didn't deserve to be treated like that." He swallowed hard and tensed his jaw.

His confession left me speechless. There were so many things I wanted to say – horrible, angry things. But they all melded together in my mind, along with the few traitorous thoughts that said maybe I should forgive him. Perhaps Raena was right? Perhaps he was just deeply affected by his father's curse, and being an arrogant brat was his odd way of coping.

A few moments passed before I finally found my voice, though it came out softer than I expected. "Thank you for saying that."

He nodded, his gaze meeting mine. In that moment, a sense of something I hadn't felt before washed over me. It felt warm, albeit very, very brief.

"And just so you know," he added with a slight smile, "I didn't barge in here. I knocked, several times actually, loudly enough that even the guards began to worry. But you didn't answer."

"I was asleep."

"It's the middle of the afternoon," he said, raising an eyebrow.

"I..." My thoughts raced as I desperately tried to conjure up a lie. "I had trouble sleeping last night." Technically, that was the truth. It's almost impossible to sleep on the back of a horse. Still, Lukas looked unconvinced as he stared down at me with thinned lips.

"Interesting," he noted. But instead of probing further, *or leaving*, his gaze began to roam around the room. "What's this?" he asked as he moved over to my birchwood dresser. On the top, I'd laid out a few glass jars and bottles, each one filled with different rare herbs and wildflower cuttings. The prince peered down at the collection, picking up several of the bottles and studying their labels.

"Just ingredients for making medicine," I said dismissively. "Though I really must insist that you give me some privacy to get dressed before you start poking around my room." I rose from the floor, my arms instinctively wrapping around my chest.

He chuckled then turned back to face me. "Forgive me for intruding. It's just that your room is so different from the bedchambers in my family's wing."

I forced out a polite smile. "It's alright. Just give me a moment to call the servants."

He nodded, but instead of heading towards the door, he chose to remain exactly where he was. There was a heated silence as his gaze lingered on my nightgown. "Actually, I think I'm quite content with this view. Perhaps I'll stay here and watch while they undress you."

My heart almost stopped.

"Why do you look so offended?" He leaned against the dresser, a smile pulling at his lips. "We're to be married soon anyway."

"Even if we were... which we are not! That doesn't make it right for you to..." My cheeks burned.

"For me to what?" His smile grew wider, clearly enjoying this.

I scowled. "For you to look at me like that!"

"You know, I will be doing plenty more than looking once we are married, fiancée." My heart stuttered as Lukas pushed himself away from the dresser. "But of course, how could I forget? You said you were searching for another suitor. How is that going, by the way?" He stepped forward, closing the distance between us. "Have you found your mysterious prince yet? One who is willing to help with your little kingdom problem?"

It was so difficult to remain quiet. So difficult to not rub in his smug face that yes, I had found a 'mysterious prince', and from what occurred last night, he was very likely willing to help rebuild Corlixir. It took everything within me to not explain, in great detail, what happened in the faery kingdom – how I was carried into a foreign palace, how I woke up in someone else's bed, how I was invited to a ball where this 'mysterious prince' would choose his bride.

Instead of the words just pouring out of me, I clenched my jaw and glared at the prince.

"I see..." he taunted. "You know, Naria, I would offer to help with your quest, but the only other unmarried prince I know is Prince Colyn from Hallshire, and from what I've heard, he is unmarried for a reason."

Hallshire, the kingdom of farming and textiles. Surely they would have enough wealth to help rebuild a kingdom, but I'd never heard of Prince Colyn. Which meant he was probably much too old to consider, especially since Raena and I had limited our search to a certain age bracket. Still, a prince was a prince, and if it meant Corlixir would be rebuilt...

When I didn't respond, Lukas spun away and returned to his snooping. For once, I was grateful that he did, as it was only when his back was turned that I felt like I could finally breathe. It didn't help that this nightgown was far too thin and slightly too small. If he didn't leave soon, I would have to resort to bundling myself in the blankets that were still a mess on top of my unmade bed.

The prince wandered past my open wardrobe, letting his fingers run over the different fabrics. Then, he paused when he reached the window. With a heavy sigh, he turned again to face me, leaning against the window sill.

"I have to admit, I didn't just come here to apologise," he started in a serious tone.

'Or torment me?' I thought bitterly, but kept my lips sealed. "I wanted to thank you too."

Oh?

He shifted nervously as this time, I drew closer. "Whatever for?" I questioned.

"I heard that you had an... encounter with my mother," he explained. "I don't know how you managed it, but whatever powder you made for her has helped her immensely. The servants say she hasn't been this calm in months. And she's finally sleeping through the night." He dragged a hand through his hair. "I know that she can be a ahh... difficult woman. But thank you for doing this. You've done her a great kindness and if there is anything I can... or we can do, my father and I, to repay you for this. Then please, all you have to do is ask." He swallowed thickly before lowering his gaze to the floor. Something like pain wavered in his stormy expression, and for the first time ever, he looked almost exactly like the sad prince from the portrait that hung above the grand staircase.

Without thinking, my hand reached forward to take his. Beneath my gown and title, I was a healer, and before me stood someone in pain, someone who needed healing, even if he didn't quite know it himself yet. His lips parted as our eyes met. Then, the faint pleasant smell of some kind of sweet fruit with undertones of salt found my nose. But before I could get lost in it, I stepped away – suddenly very aware of just whose hand I was holding.

"You're welcome," I finally replied, but the words came out a little sharper than I had intended. "It was the least I could do. I only wish I could help your father too, but I'm afraid I don't know of any powders that can cure curses."

Lukas cleared his throat again before shaking his head. "No one can help him. He's spoken to nearly every healer in the kingdom. There's no one who can fix magic like that."

"But what if he needs more than a healer?" My thoughts sailed to Arenn and how he cleared Raena's charm with a mere touch of his finger. "What if we need to speak with people who understand magic better than any of us? What about the fae—"

"Stop!" His sudden shout made my whole body flinch. "You need to stop right there. Whatever you're thinking, stop thinking it!"

The sad prince from the portrait was long gone, and I almost didn't recognise the furious man in front of me. When I didn't say anything, a hint of regret flashed across his features as he dragged another hand through his hair.

"I'm sorry for shouting like that," he said, flustered. "It's just that you don't know what the faeries are like. There's a reason we don't see any living amongst humans anymore, they're not to be trusted." He sighed. "I don't know what your teachers told you, but my father has never hidden the truth from me. I know all about their scheming ways and their betrayals." His words were laced with venom as he turned to the window, his hands grasping the frame with an iron grip. "It wouldn't even surprise me if they're somehow responsible for the King's curse."

A breath caught in my throat. The faeries couldn't have cursed the King, surely Seraphina would've said something if that was a possibility. But then again, who else would do this? If the faeries felt like the humans were effectively banishing them from the realm, would they curse King Ikelos out of spite? Thoughts raced through my mind, overwhelming me until a warm hand came to rest on my shoulder.

I shuddered at the touch. *His* touch.

"Are you alright?" Lukas's tone softened as he slowly removed his hand. "I truly am sorry for shouting. It just surprised me to hear you, of all people, bringing them up."

"What do you mean?" I asked in a quiet voice.

He studied me for a moment, his lips parting as if to speak. But then he stopped himself. "No... I've already frightened you enough today." His hand found the back of his neck. "I'll leave you to get dressed. Like you said, it's not right for me to be in here with you like this." He gestured towards my thin nightgown as heat spread across my cheeks.

I'd completely forgotten how exposed I was.

"Do come and find me in the gardens if you need me." He tipped his chin respectfully and began marching towards the door. Just before he reached it, he looked over his shoulder and caught my gaze one last time. "It was good to see you."

I dipped my head. "It was good to see you too." Was I lying? In that moment, I really wasn't sure.

"Also, may I request that you please not hide from me anymore?" He shot me a taunting smile, and suddenly the smug prince I knew was back. "Ever since ending things with Giselle... and the others, I've been terribly lonely."

My heart leapt. Surely he's not serious. But before I had a chance to ask any more questions, he slipped out the door, letting it click shut behind him.

CHAPTER 17

Lady Raena was nowhere to be found.

After the prince had left and the servants had helped me into a simple gown, I entered Raena's room, assuming she'd still be asleep. Though, the empty bed and yesterday's dress thrown messily over a chair proved otherwise. After that, I'd searched around the palace, and even poked my head into the forbidden library. It was as if she'd disappeared off the face of the realm.

Eventually, as the fear that somehow the faeries had taken her crept into my throat, I decided to wander through the gardens. It was a beautiful summer afternoon, and maybe she needed to walk outside to clear her head, especially after the chaos of last night.

My heart stopped when I finally found her.

Lying sprawled across a stone bench, wearing a lavish red gown that was much too revealing for the occasion, was a rather dazed-looking Lady Raena. Her cheeks were rosy, and she appeared to be giggling softly to herself as she held a small lilac flower suspended in the air above her lovely face. One by one, she plucked the petals from the stem, letting them float gently to the ground. A few landed in her curled hair, which was spread out across the seat of the bench. All the while, a dozen nobles who had gathered around her only watched and giggled at what they were seeing.

"Raena?" I called out to her, shoving through the crowd. As I approached, a thick, sickly-sweet smell filled my nose, almost making me gag. It was so cloying, I couldn't understand how she, or the others standing so close, could stand it.

Reluctantly, Raena's head turned away from the flower, but when she noticed me, a wide smile lit up her face just as it had done in the faery kingdom. The moment I caught her eyes, my heart sank.

Glazed over. Once again.

"Naria!" she almost sang. "I'm so happy to see you! I tried to wake you up this morning, but you were still fast asleep. And I would've waited for you, but oh, my heart was just bursting! I had to step outside to breathe, but then I saw the flowers and..." She sighed dreamily. "I'm just so in love."

So, Arenn hadn't cleared the charm then. But why would he lie? None of this made any sense.

I went to respond and try to find out more, but someone nearby stole my attention away.

"I wouldn't bother talking with her, Your Highness," a familiar voice sneered. "She's been like that all morning – babbling about some man with green skin."

Ignoring their tittering laughter, I glanced up to see the owner of the voice.

Giselle, with her pretty copper hair, smirked back at me.

"She's probably just not feeling well," I responded, hiding my panic behind a blank expression. Raena completely ignored me as I tried to pry her off the bench, too focused on pulling petals from the flower. Finally, after a minute of pointless coaxing, I leaned in closer and spoke in a low tone. "Come on, now. Let's get you inside and figure out what's going on."

"I really wouldn't bother. We all suspect she's gone mad," Giselle snorted. "What did you give her?"

"Excuse me?" I swung my head to face the sneering girl.

"You're from Corlixir, aren't you? We've all heard the stories about Corlixin healers giving special 'herbs' to their friends. You know, the ones that make you feel a certain... *type of way?*" Hushed laughter rippled through the group. "If you give us some, we won't run and tell the prince about Lady Raena's current condition."

My lips flattened. Was this some kind of tragic attempt at blackmail?

"I haven't given her anything," I stated firmly, shooting a glare at Giselle and her friends. "Lady Raena just isn't feeling well."

"Oh, I'm perfectly fine," she chimed, continuing to pluck petals from the flower. "I've never felt lighter."

Giselle tossed me a look before she and her friends burst into laughter.

"Come on, Raena," I hissed, taking her limp hand in mine. "As Princess, I am ordering you to come with me."

The dazed girl sighed, but still eventually swung her legs off the bench. "As you wish, Your Highness."

I went to help steady her as she rose to her feet, when my hand brushed against something hard on her wrist. The moment it touched my skin, a bolt of intense warmth buzzed through me. Gasping, I staggered backwards, almost falling to the grass.

"What... was that?" I stammered.

Raena just smiled at me, seemingly unaffected. "What was what?" she asked innocently.

Stepping forward, I reached for her hand again and pulled it closer. Wrapped tightly around her wrist was some kind of wooden bracelet, and carved into the wood were strange markings. Oddly, there was no obvious clasp or way to remove the bracelet. It was as though it had always been there, bound forever to her wrist.

"I've never seen you wear this before," I thought out loud while studying the bracelet.

"Oh, Valen gave it to me. Isn't it lovely?" she replied with a proud grin.

Hesitantly, I brushed my finger against the bracelet again – this time bracing myself for the warm feeling. Once again, it pulsed through me, and I immediately yanked my hand away. Clearly, it seemed that the love charm wasn't the only gift from that guard.

"We need to get this off of you," I decided, leading Raena away from the whispering onlookers. She protested at first, completely oblivious to the odd looks from the people who passed us by. But it didn't take long for her complaints to turn into pure excited babbling about the green-skinned guard.

"Oh, you should meet him properly," Raena insisted as we arrived back inside the palace. "He's so wonderful and really strong too!"

"I'm sure he is..." I brushed off her comments, trying to focus on what to do. Surely a healer wouldn't be enough – they didn't know magic. So, perhaps a bookkeeper from the library? Then again, I'd have to reveal that we visited the faery kingdom, and I was sure that wouldn't go down well.

Come on, think. But it was so hard to focus with that sickly-sweet smell filling my nose. At least now I was certain it was coming from the bracelet and not the flowers outside.

I knew I couldn't go back to the faeries. After my conversation with Lukas and now this bracelet, I honestly wasn't sure if I could trust them anymore. And I couldn't exactly wander off through the forest in the middle of the day. We'd be spotted by the guards or a hunting party. It would be far too risky.

"You're not taking me back to the library are you?" Raena whined behind me. "Seraphina creeps me out."

Seraphina... She might not be able to remove the bracelet, but still, she seemed to know an awful lot about the fae. Maybe she would know what to do.

"That's a great idea!" I beamed, tugging Raena along as she groaned in protest.

Truthfully, I had no idea how to find Seraphina. She wasn't in the forbidden library when I'd searched there for Raena earlier, and I couldn't exactly wander into the King's chambers unless he'd summoned me. I was sure that somewhere within the Steel Palace there would be a medical bay, and perhaps she would be spending some time there, but I didn't want to draw too much suspicion to Raena. In her current state, they would surely at least want to keep her overnight.

My silent prayers were answered, though, when I decided to peek one more time into the forbidden library – as there, curled up in a small armchair, reading a pocket-sized golden book, was the blonde-haired healer.

She peered up from her reading as we entered, giving us a soft smile – the typical pale blue hood concealing part of her face. "Good evening, Naria," she greeted, nodding her head. Then she glanced at Raena, who was still a giddy mess beside me. Her brow instantly furrowed. "What's this?"

"I'm so glad to see you," I said, relieved, steering Raena towards the centre of the room. "She's under some kind of spell. It's this bracelet." Lifting up Raena's arm, I gestured towards the wooden cuff that was still tightly bound around her wrist. "I think it's magic. I can't see a way to take it off."

"Who says I want it off? I think it's charming." Raena pouted. "It makes me feel... fuzzy." Her cheeks were like two red rosebuds, practically glowing.

Seraphina sighed, heaving herself out of the armchair. As she stood, the purple-edged cloak that hung from her shoulders swayed down her back, finishing just off the floor.

"I see you paid a visit to the fae," she noted, taking Raena's hand to study the bracelet. Bringing it close to her face, she sniffed a few times, then stared at the markings. "This is just a simple enchanted cuff, easy to remove and nothing to worry about."

Relief washed over me. "Thank the Ancients... Do you know someone who can remove it?"

The healer nodded once, then moved to the back wall of the library. Propped up against one of the tall bookshelves was a mop and a wooden bucket that appeared to be filled with magical books. Seraphina leaned down to collect the bucket, and promptly emptied all of the books onto the floor. A few of them seemed to cry out in protest as their pages collided with the hard floor.

I'll never get used to magic.

Once the bucket was empty, she returned and placed it on a desk next to Raena.

"This won't hurt," she said gently, lifting Raena's hand again.

"What is she doing, Naria?" Raena panicked, and I moved forward to comfort her, rubbing her arm. "Tell me she's not going to make me forget about Valen!"

"Oh, you won't forget." Seraphina grinned, bringing her own hand up to hover over the bracelet. "Although, once this is off, you might beg for a memory charm." And with that, the healer swished her wrist, and the bracelet tumbled to the ground with a clatter.

Immediately, Raena cried out and grasped her chest. Her once rosy brown cheeks paled to a sickly green as Seraphina thrust the bucket into her arms just quickly enough for Raena to retch deep into it.

"You're a mage," I breathed, trying to comfort Raena while also trying to make sense of exactly what I'd just witnessed.

The healer shrugged. "Not quite, but you may call me that if you'd like."

"But you're so young, I thought mages were supposed to be old and—" I gasped. "Is that why you're here with the King? Are you some kind of magic prodigy? Can you fix his curse?"

"So many questions," Seraphina tutted as Raena retched again. "Age does not define your power. And yes, I came here to help the King, but my magic cannot help fix a curse that strong. He knows there is no cure. I can only make him comfortable now."

"But..." My mind was spinning with so many questions. "You must be part fae then? Is that how you know so much about them? Do you," I lowered my voice, "do you visit them at night too?"

Darkness flickered over her gaze. "The faeries have no business with me," she replied sharply as her tone shifted to one of annoyance. "Now, please, I do not wish to speak of this further. You should let your friend rest here for a few minutes and then take her to bed. Do not tell anyone about the cuff or that I helped you remove it. I must leave now, the King needs me."

I wanted to argue, to ask her more questions, but she'd disappeared up the stairs before I could say another word, her purple-edged cloak billowing behind her.

Beside me, Raena still had her arms wrapped tightly around the wooden bucket. Once Seraphina was gone, she slowly lifted her head to reveal her face, now sweaty and tinged with green.

"Naria," she winced, groaning, "I can't... I never want to go back."

Returning my attention to her, I patted her back softly.

"It's alright, Raena. You don't have to. And after all this. I'm not sure if I want to either."

"You must do what is right for your kingdom." She groaned again before retching into the bucket. "If it is the only way to save Corlixir, then you should go back." Tears formed on her already wet cheeks. "But please, be careful."

"What happened?" I asked delicately. "If he put his hands on you, I swear I will send an army." I didn't have an army, of course I didn't, but I would find one. For her, I would marry Lukas and make him send one; the divine beings only know he already hates the faeries enough to do it.

Raena shook her head. "He didn't hurt me. I remember everything." She shuddered, still gripping the bucket. "He dragged me to the cell, and when I tried to break out, he cornered me and slipped the bracelet on. My memories are strange after that. I can still see everything, but it's like looking through honey." She swayed for a second, and I held my arms out, thinking she might faint. "Oh, Oceans, I am so tired."

"Let's get you to bed," I told her, trying to ignore the growing anger inside me. "It's been a long night – and day – for the both of us."

CHAPTER 18

A few days had passed since our secret visit to the faery kingdom, but, within my mind, conflict still raged like an intense battle. I knew I'd eventually have to go back, even if it was just to confront Arenn about the behaviour of one of his guards. It wasn't his fault, I knew deep down it wasn't, but still, I couldn't help but blame him for giving the order to send Raena away. The poor girl had spent most of her time over these past few days resting and avoiding anyone but the servants who came in to deliver food. Whenever I'd try to go in and comfort her, she'd insist she just needed time alone. But it was so hard to give her that time when I'd lay awake at night listening to her screaming nightmares through the walls.

The sun was just hovering near the mountainous horizon as I returned to my tower after another long dinner with Lukas. Ever since he'd barged into my room, we'd spent our evenings together again in the dining hall. I'd been hesitant at first, but now, I was glad to have something to clear my head – even if that meant only replacing one kind of confusion with another, like the strange yet warm feeling I'd get every time our eyes met.

I turned a corner into another window-lined corridor when suddenly, a sharp cry echoed down the walls. "Healer! We need a healer!" A young woman dressed in a bright green gown was running frantically through the hallway. "Please, somebody help him!"

My heart leapt into my throat, and without thinking, I raced towards her.

"Where is he? Where's the patient?" I demanded through shaky breaths.

"In the palace grounds, by the big fish pond. But we need a healer, now."

"You've got one," I told her while hoisting up my skirts, and before she had a chance to reply, I'd sprinted to the archway that led outside.

A small crowd of people had already gathered by the time I arrived. The sun was just setting, casting a rosy orange hue across the nobles and servants that swarmed around the mystery patient. In truth, I'd never healed a real person before, but I'd passed every single Corlixin healing exam with flying colours and could name over a hundred different illnesses. How hard could this be?

"Step aside!" I commanded as the small crowd parted to make way for me.

In the centre of the mob, a young, finely dressed boy was lying flat on his back against the grass. With his small frame and innocent-looking features, he must've been no older than fourteen. As I studied him, I noticed his clothes were soaking wet and covered with pondweed, while his lips were a ghostly shade of blue. But I didn't need to be a healer to realise what was wrong.

The poor boy had drowned.

"How did this happen?" I asked the crowd urgently, lowering myself to the boy's level.

"Nobody knows," someone answered. "We just found him face down in the water. He must've slipped in."

My fingers desperately searched his neck for a heartbeat. There was no rise and fall of his chest, so he wasn't breathing, but perhaps there would be some life still. When I felt no pulse, my mind raced.

'Think,' I hissed internally. Any other kingdom's healers would've given up at this point. With no heartbeat, that meant the person's soul had already departed. But the Corlixins had a way to bring them back. There was no magic involved, it was pure science – compressions on the chest and air into the mouth. Only it'd been months since I practised heartflow restoration, and even then, I'd never tried it on a real person. But still, I had to *try*.

Bracing my intertwined hands over his ribs just like I'd been taught, I began pumping into his chest. His lifeless body squirmed underneath me as I pumped, sending gasps echoing around us. A few tried to question me, but I remained wholly focused on the patient and the counting I was doing under my breath.

"Twelve, thirteen, fourteen, fifteen." The whispered number increased with each compression. There was no change in the boy, but I didn't stop. I remembered my teachers insisting that sometimes you would need to do this for ten minutes before heartflow would be restored.

"Twenty-eight, twenty-nine, thirty." I leaned forward and pinched his nose tightly, bringing my lips to his. Shocked noises radiated through the mob surrounding us, but I ignored them, forcing air deep into his lungs.

"She's kissing him!" a man gasped. "This is obscene!"

"One, two, three, four," my whispers continued, his comment passing straight over me.

'Come on,' I begged silently, *'You're so young and I don't even know your name, but I need you to breathe.'* How long had it been since I'd started? Surely no more than a minute, but I had no idea how long he'd been in the pond before someone had fished him out. Heartflow restoration was most effective when it was performed immediately after the heart stopped beating.

I leaned down to force more air into his lungs.

"Come on," I growled, out loud this time. He was far too young to die like this, and drowning in a fish pond – of all the ways to die!

I continued compressions for what felt like hours, but it must've only been a few minutes. Around us, time seemed to slow, and all I could focus on was pumping and breathing, pumping and breathing, pumping and—

The boy gasped beneath me. It was strained and waterlogged, but still, a breath was a breath. Green murky water spouted from his mouth as he coughed and sputtered into the grass. Pulling my hands away, I finally noticed how much they were shaking. I'd never felt such overwhelming relief like this before. It was deep and raw and made me want to scream.

"She used magic to bring him back!" someone accused from within the crowd. "The princess gave him a magic kiss of life!"

"She's no princess. That's dark magic! No one can bring someone back from the dead," another voice snarled.

Dismissing their shouts, I remained focused on the boy as I helped him to sit up. His face was pale with shock, and his whole body shivered like a little mouse. "D-did you s-save me?" he wheezed.

I nodded, then tried to speak in the gentlest voice I could muster. "You were found unconscious in the water. I used an advanced healing technique to restart your... to wake you up again."

The boy shuddered, seeming to not notice the arguing mob surrounding us. "Th-thank you." He shivered, pulling his knees to his chest and wrapping his arms around his drenched tunic.

If only everyone else was as grateful. The people that circled us had descended into chaos, their accusations and suspicions swirling around like a dark storm.

"Did you see that? She kissed a dead boy!"

"It's some kind of trick for her to win favour. The boy wasn't even dead."

"The prince will handle this; he'll throw the wicked mage out on the streets!"

Amidst all the commotion, a deafening scream pierced through the crowd, forcing all their mouths to clamp shut in unison.

"Nathan!" A familiar highborn woman shoved through the mass of people. Her frustratingly beautiful face was speckled with tears, and she wasn't wearing her usual smirk, but still, I recognised her immediately.

"My sweet brother," Giselle wailed, almost collapsing to the floor as she pulled the boy's shaking body into a tight hug. Her whole body shook with violent sobs. "Thank the Forges you're alive. Someone told me you'd drowned! What happened to you?"

"The p-princess saved me." It was difficult to hear his voice over Giselle's sniffling, but the moment she realised what he'd just said, her tear-filled gaze flicked over to where I was still sitting on the grass.

"You? You saved my baby brother?" she squeaked through sobs.

Unsure of how to respond, I just nodded.

Something inside her seemed to break then as she leapt towards me, arms outstretched. Her body collided against mine, almost sending us both tumbling against the grass. For a moment, I thought she might be angry, but then her arms wrapped tightly around my shoulders as she pulled me into the most grateful hug.

"Thank you. Thank you so so much, Princess Naria," she cried into my neck.

Around us, a strange hush fell over our audience, broken only by the occasional whisper. Each of them observed our interaction as though they didn't know what to make of it. Perhaps Giselle had more influence than I'd thought.

"I don't care if she saved him. We all just witnessed forbidden magic," a woman's voice shot from behind me. "We all saw it! She kissed a dead boy and now he lives!"

Slowly, Giselle pulled away from me as I stood and turned to face the woman. Her thick black hair was piled high on top of her head, adorned with pearls and beads, while her umber arms sat folded in front of her chest.

"That was not magic," I explained in a calm tone. "I just used a healing technique."

"No amount of healing can bring someone back from the dead," she spat. "And Lady Giselle is a fool to embrace you, who knows what manner of curses you could place on her."

Shocked whispers echoed throughout the mob, and a few servants shot me looks of disgust.

"The duchess is right. We should take her to the prince to see what he makes of this," a gruff voice said as I felt someone grasp my wrist.

"Stop that!" Giselle protested, but her pleas were ignored. Suddenly, bodies piled in on me, shoving Giselle aside and wrestling with my writhing arms. All I could see was furious faces as my chest tightened. This was all too much. Too many hands. I couldn't breathe! Heavy air blocked my throat as I suffocated with fear.

Stop, please. I wanted to cry for help, but no words came out.

"Enough!" A commanding voice sent a wave through the mob, forcing them to drop my arms.

Lukas...

The crowd slowly parted to reveal the tall, steel-eyed prince, standing just metres away. Concern flashed across his features when he saw me. In the chaos, someone had tugged at my hair, leaving a tangle of ringlets haloing my face. Paired with my tear-stained cheeks and heavy breathing, I must've looked a complete mess, but I didn't care. Lukas was here now, and for once, I was glad to see him.

"What is the meaning of this?" he demanded as he surveyed the scene before us.

The lady with the pearl-decorated hair stepped forward first. Her voice was nasally and grating as she dipped her head in respect.

"Your Highness, we found a young boy who had drowned in the pond. Princess Naria here attempted *some kind* of rescue, although we all saw her use dark magic to revive him." Murmurs of agreement trickled through the crowd. "She kissed him at least five times and then, he just woke up. Only a fool would believe that was not magic."

Lukas stiffened as his brow lowered. "Kissed him?"

My eyes wanted to roll back into my skull. "That's not true," I stated, finding my voice. "Yes the boy was dead when I found him, but I was able to restart his heart using heartflow restoration. It is a lifesaving technique that was used in Corlixin hospitals to revive patients. You give compressions to the chest to mimic a beating heart and force air into the lungs to keep the patient breathing. It's really—"

"You use these big words to try and hide the magic." The woman's venom-laced voice cut off my words. "We all saw you, demon! Don't try and deny what you did."

"I would rather you didn't refer to my fiancée as a demon, Lady Vivian." Lukas's tone was light, but by the way his face had darkened, I could tell he was deadly serious. "Are you forgetting that Princess Naria here is your future Queen?"

The people around me shuffled awkwardly, including Lady Vivian.

"I did not mean to offend, Your Highness." Her grating voice remained directed at the prince. "I only wished to inform you of what we *all* witnessed."

"You witnessed science." I whirled to confront her. "I can't believe this is even up for debate! Your healers might know everything about herbs, but the Corlixins, my people, we understand the body. You have to believe me when I say there was nothing magical about any of that."

Her gaze skimmed over me as though I was dirt under her boot. I'd never met her before, but her name seemed somewhat familiar. Just then, my memories flew back to the very first dinner I'd had with Lukas.

Lady Vivian wasn't too happy either at breakfast, when I told her that you were on your way.

Surely she wasn't another lover, unless Lukas liked ladies on the more mature side. Still, by the way she seethed before me, there had to be more to her anger than plain ignorance.

"I believe her... the princess... I believe her," a quiet shaking voice cut through the crowd. As the onlookers parted, the young boy I'd revived stood shivering beside his sister. Giselle had bundled him up in a thick cloak, and was desperately trying to rub some warmth back into him. "I've felt magic before, but this was nothing like that," he said.

"Ignore him, he's delirious," Lady Vivian spat. "The boy was dead five minutes ago."

"Do not speak of my brother in that way," Giselle retorted. Her eyes were glossy with tears as they found mine.

"Princess Naria saved his life, and I will never be able to thank her enough." She then shot a furious look at the duchess. "So, if she insists it was this... sci-ence, or whatever the word was, then it was that! No dark magic here."

Confused murmurs weaved through the crowd, until Lukas's commanding voice broke through the noise.

"I've heard enough arguing for one day." Everyone's heads pivoted to where the prince was standing. "Magic or not, a boy's life was saved, and we should be very grateful to Princess Naria." I shuddered as the countless stares of at least a dozen people fixated on my trembling body. I could almost feel their suspicions gnawing at my gown.

As if sensing my discomfort, Lukas stepped forward and extended a hand to me. "Come now, Naria, let me escort you back to your room."

I nodded, barely hesitating for a second before accepting his waiting hand.

Before we left the gathering, I glanced at the shivering boy, then addressed Giselle, "Take him back to his room, get him into a warm bath and then some dry clothes."

"Of course, Your Highness." She dipped her head in gratitude. "And please understand I wasn't lying when I said I will never be able to thank you enough. Anything you need, please come to me. I will always serve you." She bowed deeply, the last of the evening sun rays dancing off her copper hair.

I thanked her with a light smile, before Lukas began guiding me back towards the palace archway.

Walking back through the palace beside Lukas was an entirely different experience to wandering the palace halls alone. Aside from having to occasionally jog to keep up with his long strides, there were no hushed whispers or scowling looks. Instead, crowds of people dipped their heads like little bobbing ducks as we strolled through the endless stone corridors. The prince seemed to pay them no mind, barely even acknowledging their bows as we passed by – though I suppose after so many years, you would get used to it.

I wondered if I ever could.

"You certainly put on quite a show out there," Lukas finally said while steering me through an archway. His voice was calm, but there was something on his mind – I could almost see it as it tugged on his brow.

The arch led to another familiar window-lined hallway, but we must've been drawing close to the tower as this one was empty of any chattering nobles. Now that the sun had dipped below the mountains, small candles held by iron lamps illuminated the path. They cast a warm glow across the tiled floors.

"I did what I had to do to save a boy's life," I answered plainly. "It's not my fault that most of your people misread the situation."

We continued for a few more steps until Lukas paused and turned suddenly to face me. After a few quiet breaths, he spoke with a tightened jaw. "Is it true that you kissed that boy?"

I wanted to burst with laughter. "Kissed him?"

"Yes, is it true?" the prince demanded.

My mouth fell open. I couldn't believe it. Was he, a crown prince of all people, really jealous of a teenager? Or was there something else behind his bizarre reaction? Either way, to even ask that was simply ridiculous. He was being ridiculous.

"I thought you were supposed to be sensible," I scoffed dismissively.

"Tell me," he spoke again, his tone dark and low. "Did you kiss him?"

"Why would you even ask that?" I threw up my hands. "This is absurd. I saved his life, didn't I? And if you were there, you would've seen that it wasn't a kiss. Far from it! I was simply forcing the water from his chest—"

"By placing your lips onto his?" he cut in. His features were stormed by such an unnecessary fury, I wanted to scream.

"It does not matter how I did it, because I saved his life!" My raised voice echoed down the empty hallway. "And I don't understand why you even care about any of this. You don't own me. Even if I wasn't trying to just save the poor boy's life, I can kiss whoever I like."

"You cannot." He stepped towards me, and instinctively I backed away. But my voice didn't quieten. If anything, I was more determined to shout.

"I am a princess," I fired back. "I don't serve you, or your father. I serve only my people. And since you have no intention of helping them, I have no intention of ever marrying you. That means, if I wanted to run around the palace grounds and kiss every single man who'd have me then I would."

"I would forbid it," Lukas snarled. Fists clenched, he

marched towards me, forcing my body back until the cold stone wall pressed against my spine. "You may be a princess, but my father is the King of Drothmore. And while he is ill, this is my court. Everything in it belongs to me, including my own fiancée. Don't you dare underestimate my power, Naria. I would exile anyone who dared to touch you. I would lock you in your tower if I had to."

"But why?" My voice trembled as he loomed over me. His jaw was still clenched, and he was so close I could feel the warmth of his skin. The heat rushed through me, igniting my bones and pooling in my lower belly as he laid his hand flat against the wall, only inches from my face.

Before I could shove him away, my breath caught as his gaze lowered to my parted lips. Then, it appeared as if something inside of him had broken. A sudden sadness washed away the rage that poured across his face.

"Because, for some unfathomable reason, I cannot stand the thought of anyone else doing what I am about to do," he finally said.

"What?" I muttered, not quite hearing him over the blood rushing through my ears.

A heartbeat passed.

Then another.

And then, his lips crashed into mine.

CHAPTER 19

I'd never been kissed before. Or at least, not really, and certainly never like this. This was intense. Not just a parting kiss on the cheek, or one that was planted softly on the back of your hand by a charming stranger. This was the kind of kiss that led to bedchamber doors being thrown open, the kind of kiss you'd only ever hear about in those silly forbidden books that teachers would scold you for reading.

The moment we collided, my heart almost took flight like a little bird. At first, I wanted to protest, but any words only came out as a soft gasp as Lukas's warm hands cupped the sides of my jaw. Mere seconds ago, his entire body was ravaged by a biting fury, but now, his touch was so gentle it was as if he believed he would break me. And perhaps he did, because the moment my lips parted and I felt him deepen the kiss, I could've sworn something within me shattered.

Suddenly, just this wasn't enough. Suddenly, my hands that were frozen by my sides flew up as I tangled my fingers into his hair. We drew closer, until our bodies pressed together and a low breathy noise sounded from his throat. When his arm dropped to my waist, I felt myself pushed back against the wall, my head cradled by his other hand. I could hardly breathe as his mouth drifted to the corner of my mouth, brushing kisses over my jaw, and then my neck, and then—

"Stop!" I gasped as my eyes flew open.

"What?" Lukas immediately pulled away, blinking his surprised eyes back at me. "What is it? What's wrong?"

"*This*," I replied bitterly. "This is *all* wrong." My breathing was staggered and flustered. I couldn't believe I almost gave in to him. Him! The one person who couldn't care less about the fate of my people. I could've slapped myself across the face.

"What are you talking about?" He laughed in a frustratingly effortless way. "We are engaged, it won't ruin your reputation if someone were to see us here." His gaze lowered to my lips as he leaned in again. Without missing a beat, my finger flew to his mouth, pressing hard enough to block him from drawing any closer. The movement must've caught him off guard as his eyebrows shot up.

"For the last time, we are not getting married," I grumbled, holding my finger against his perfect lips. "And my reputation is exactly what I'm worried about, *Your Highness*. Do not think I haven't heard the stories. I know what you do to noblewomen and I refuse to just become another one of your playthings. How am I supposed to find someone who can help with my kingdom if everyone believes that we're…"

I stuttered and threw my hands down as I furiously tried to think of the right words.

"We're what?" A dangerous smile grew on the prince's face.

"We're..." I wrinkled my nose before meeting his gaze with about as much fierceness as a hissing kitten. "We're doing... unpleasant things together," I finally spat out.

He chuckled, then brushed his fingers gently along my chin. "I don't know what stories you've heard. But I think you'll find that any time spent with me can be quite pleasant." He tried to kiss me again, but this time, I used both hands to boldly shove him off me. He stumbled back a few feet as I huffed and gathered my skirts.

"When a lady says stop, you listen to her the first time," I chided as he choked with surprise. "You can leave now. I know my way back from here."

As I pushed myself away from the wall, the prince just stared with wide eyes. I didn't in fact know the way, but I also didn't trust myself to be around him any longer than absolutely necessary. I'd be requesting that the servants run me the coldest bath when I finally returned to my chambers. Anything to purge those traitorous thoughts from my body.

"You know, Naria," Lukas began, just as I was about to march down the hallway, "while it pains me to hear that you're still considering other men, I'll admit that your dedication to your suitor search is admirable, even if I don't believe it'll last."

I scoffed and pushed past him.

"Wait," he called as I reluctantly turned my head one last time. "Will you at least let me escort you to your bedchamber? The Summer Ball is just a few days away, and I won't have you throwing yourself down the stairs to avoid dancing with me."

The Summer ball... Just the thought of all those people, and then dancing too, made my head spin.

"If you insist," I huffed, picking up my skirts again and stepping ahead of him. "But just so you know, I'm a terrible dancer."

I heard him laughing as he followed me down the hallway. "Luckily for you, I've been told I am a wonderful teacher."

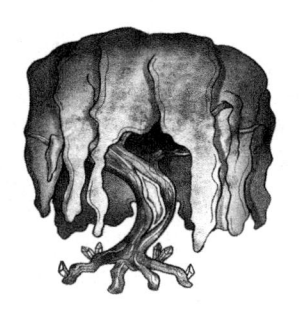

CHAPTER 20

That night I absolutely did not dream of Lukas. Instead, I dreamt of dancing lessons, secret willows, and wicked faery guards. Enough of the green-skinned beasts waltzed through my dreams, along with Raena's screams weaving through the music, that the second the morning sun pried my heavy eyes open, I knew exactly what I had to do.

"You wish to return to the forest?" Theo asked. His eyebrows flew up as we stood together in the dimly lit stables. The fading light of the setting sun was slowly being replaced by candlelight as busy stablehands flitted in and out. I'd been busy that day too, spending all my time planning and preparing for what might be my second and final visit to the faery kingdom. I needed to confront the prince and find out the truth. Were his parents really responsible for cursing the King? Did he choose to ignore the enchanted bracelet bound to Raena's wrist? Every hour, I'd thought of how fragile she looked clutching that bucket in the hidden library. I couldn't bear it any more. Valen needed to be punished.

"We'll return to the willow, but this time not for mushrooms," I told him calmly. "In fact, what I'm about to tell you could land both Raena and I in a whole realm of trouble. So I need to know that I can trust you."

Theo studied me for a moment before answering in a serious tone. "Erik and I owe our lives to Lady Raena. Without her, we'd still be working in her family's fishing yards in Ryntook." He exhaled slowly. "You can explain everything on the way. Just tell me what I need to do."

As we rode through the dark forest, his horse once again leading mine, I let the entire story and all its tiny details pour out of me – everything from my first awkward meeting with Lukas, to discovering the forbidden library, and then our arrival in Faelenna. Interestingly, I chose to leave out the part where I awoke to find myself tied up in a faery bedchamber. And the part where the faery prince was inches away from my flustered face in that very same bedchamber. I trusted Theo, but I couldn't trust myself to hide the blush that would inevitably crawl up my cheeks when I shared *that* chapter of the story.

"I can't believe Lady Raena pulled out a dagger!" Theo called out over his shoulder, snatching my attention away from any dangerous thoughts. "And you're right for not asking Erik to join us. He'd throw a fit if he heard what happened."

Originally, I'd considered having both guards accompany me, but the fewer people who knew about my dealings with the fae, the better. Besides, of the two guards, Theo seemed so much calmer, and given how eagerly Erik had cared for Raena, I worried that he'd be the type to let anger outweigh his logic if he heard what happened in the faery dungeons.

Our horses slowed as we reached the forest clearing. This time, I helped Theo secure the horses before we ventured towards the huge willow tree together. While my hand searched against the bark for that same gnarled spot, my heart pounded against my ribs.

"I'm half expecting Erik to jump out and tell me this is all some big joke," Theo said in a failed attempt to lighten the mood.

"This is no joke," I muttered as the bark began to buckle and morph into a doorway. All I could hear were the faint sounds of nighttime crickets and Theo's soft gasps as the overwhelming scent of spring blossoms hit my nose once again.

It wasn't long before we reached the end of the spiral staircase that led down to the official entrance of Faelenna. Theo had stayed silent, closely following my steps as we descended further and further. When we finally headed through the small archway that marked the end of the steps, the two armoured faeries that guarded the gate immediately straightened. Although they appeared to be much less panicked this time, each of them bowed as though they were expecting me.

"His Royal Highness Prince Arenn has been eagerly anticipating your return, Princess," one of the faeries announced, lifting his head. "Please, let us escort you to the palace."

"I would much rather he comes to me," I requested, trying

hard to mask the nervousness in my voice. "Please inform the prince that I have some urgent business to discuss."

The two faeries exchanged worried glances.

"Of course, Your Highness." The other spoke this time. "We will alert the prince of your arrival." Then, with a bow, he slinked off through a small tunnel that I hadn't noticed before.

Minutes passed, but they felt more like hours as the pounding in my chest only grew stronger. I once again hoped that faeries didn't have a secret way of sensing fear, because otherwise my plan to 'bravely' confront the Prince of the Fae would crumble just as quickly as my stomach dropped upon seeing the gate.

With a quiet grunt, the same guard popped out from the tunnel and wordlessly returned to his place by the entrance. Moments later, the giant round doors began to tremble and groan until, slowly, they creaked open towards the faery kingdom.

My heart fluttered when I caught sight of that familiar silver circlet resting upon a perfect heap of black waves. Just as before, the prince was finely dressed in an black- and silver-embroidered ensemble that clung tightly to his toned chest. And as I glanced up, his honey-coloured irises immediately found mine.

"Princess Naria," the faery prince called from just beyond the doorway, a perfect smile stretching over his pale face, "I cannot even begin to express how enchanting it is to see you again."

He bowed deeply, sending the butterflies in my stomach into a frenzy.

"Prince Arenn," I returned the greeting and steadied my breath. "I wish I could say the same, but I'm afraid I did not come here just to socialise."

The prince tilted his head, and then shot an amused look at Theo, who was positioned behind me. "Who have you brought with you? Do not tell me this is your foolish prince?"

"This is Theo, a palace guard from Drothmore. He accompanied me here as my chaperone. I would have come with Raena again, except she is too terrified to even leave her room." My fists clenched as the words came out more cutting than I anticipated. "Your *friendly* guard Valen gave her a gift that convinced her she was in love – an enchanted bracelet. Thankfully, there was someone at the palace who could remove it, but—"

"Well, I'm glad the problem was resolved." Arenn grinned, shoving his hands into his pockets and sauntering closer.

"The problem has not been resolved." My eyebrows knitted together. "Poor Lady Raena is beside herself. She has nightmares every night; I can hear her through the walls!"

"Watching you be angry like this is so... heartwarming," he chuckled. "You're like a little dog." He let out a mocking, high-pitched bark that sent the two faery guards into a fit of tinkling laughter.

Rage boiled in my chest. If this prince wasn't my only option for rebuilding Corlixir, I would've spun on my heels then and there, never to return. But I had to try and get through to him, not just for the sake of my people but for Raena too.

"What he did wasn't right. I don't care if he thought she was an assassin, you can't just toy with people like that. I need you to promise me you will punish him." As I spoke, something sparkled like the stars in Arenn's devious gaze.

He paused for a moment, deep in thought. Then, another smile tugged at his sharp faery lips. "I will make sure that Valen answers for his crimes. Just for you, I will have him punished in the middle of Luminessia!" The two faery guards gasped and babbled excitedly, as if he'd just announced the opening of a fantastical new theatre show, but my focus remained on the prince as he moved closer. When he was just inches away, his slender fingers trailed down my arm, gently brushing my skin and making my toes curl in my boots. "I will have him punished in any way you so desire, if you let me take *you* somewhere special tonight."

Behind me, I heard the clinking of armour as Theo stiffened.

Arenn's gaze flew over my head and landed on my palace guard, who'd remained silent throughout the entire conversation. "You, Sir Theo, can remain here. My guards will keep you company."

"I'm not leaving the princess," Theo responded in a low, don't-test-me sort of voice.

Arenn chuckled, and then in one swift motion, he wrapped his arm around my shoulders and spun me to face the guard. The smell of wildflowers and cinnamon crept into my nose as his arm held me tightly against his side. "I can assure you that your precious princess is very safe with me. She doesn't need you as her chaperone, in fact, I shall be her chaperone!"

The two faery guards giggled like schoolchildren, which only made Theo lower his brow further. "I don't think you understand how this works."

"It's alright, Theo," I reassured him. "I can handle myself. Please, just stay here for now."

The guard looked as though he wanted to argue, but through gritted teeth, he held it back. "Very well, I will wait here, but if you're not back by morning, I will have to alert Prince Lukas."

"That won't be necessary," Arenn said, lifting a hand to let his fingers tease the side of my face. "I'll take good care of sweet Naria here, and we'll be back before you know it."

Theo shot the prince a warning look, but made no move to stop us as Arenn whisked me through the open gates and deep into Faelenna.

We passed through the bustling night markets with ease, although Arenn's long steps meant I had to occasionally skip to keep up with him. Around us, dozens of faeries picked through various exotic fruits and vegetables, and I could hear faint sounds of strange instruments playing what must've been faery music from a nearby tavern.

"Why is no one reacting to your presence?" I asked, noticing how the crowds of fae perusing the stalls kept to themselves and didn't even bother bowing as we strolled by.

"I've glamoured us," he answered casually.

"What does that mean?"

He tossed me a wild grin and steered me towards a shop window. At first glance, it looked like an ordinary hat shop, but as we drew closer, I noticed something strange.

"Take a look." He gestured towards our reflection, except

it wasn't our reflection. Before us, mirroring each of our movements was a plain looking faery couple. The girl looked a bit like me, with matching blonde curls and glassy blue eyes, but her face was distinctly fae and her clothing fit right into the busy market streets. Even Arenn's reflection looked like a much more common version of himself. His thick dark waves remained, but his face was nothing special, blending seamlessly into the market crowds.

"How?" I sighed, staring deeply at my faery self.

"It's simple really. All faeries can do it, but most can only perform small glamours, like turning an apple into some coins. I've always been particularly good at it, though... I can even change your clothes." He clicked his fingers, and my reflection shimmered. It blurred for a second and then became crystal clear. The same faery face remained, but on her body, she now wore a stunning midnight blue gown with a low neckline and a skirt that finished just above her knees. The skirt hung around her hips like dark rose petals, and as I tore my gaze away, I realised that the same dress clung tightly to my own skin.

"What?" I breathed, running my hand down the smooth fabric.

"Faery gowns suit you," Arenn commented. "But don't worry, I'll change it back before I return you to your grumpy guard. I fear I might meet the end of his sword if he knew I was parading you around in this." He cast a sweeping look over my body, leaving a lingering heat on my exposed skin.

"So, have I actually ever seen the real you?" I asked, trying to distract myself from the way my heart was beating.

"Or have you been glamoured this entire time?"

"What you see before you is the real me," he answered, taking my hand again. "Although, if you don't like how I look, I'll happily change." He winked, then shifted into a completely different faery man. His once ebony hair had morphed into a golden-blonde shade, and his skin now was warm-toned, similar to Lukas's. I gasped, but then he changed again – this time into a pale blue-skinned faery with hair that resembled ice shards. Each second thereafter, he transformed over and over again, every new appearance just as attractive as the last.

"The real you is fine!" I insisted, swinging a hand up to hide my open mouth. I couldn't take it anymore. This conversation had done nothing to steady my racing heart.

Arenn promptly shifted back into his usual charming self, a low laugh radiating from his chest. "I must say, you look exquisite when you're flustered."

I blinked. There was no hiding the burning blush that crept up my cheeks now.

"Come on, we should resume our walk." He tugged my hand, leading me away from the window. "If we don't leave now, I fear that your foolish prince will send an army before we reach the Crystal Caverns."

The Crystal Caverns were even grander than I ever could've imagined. The prince led me through the cobbled faery streets and past a heavily-guarded entrance into a massive underground chamber. Despite its dark stone walls, the cavern shone brighter than any stars in the night sky.

Thousands of crystals were embedded in the walls, each one sending the light dancing into a hundred different colours. Even the air was so thick with magic I could almost taste it – like sweet flowers and sugar on my tongue.

"I've never seen anything so wondrous," I sighed as my gaze caught on a huge crystal formation, almost as big as my bedchamber, hanging from the ceiling. We'd headed deeper into the caves, but despite the dazzling beauty around us, Arenn's gaze was fixed only on me.

"These caverns are the original source of our magic. All faery blood is infused with these crystals, granting us our power," the prince drawled. "But I didn't come here to give you a lesson in crystallography." He tossed me a playful smile. "Let me show you the real reason I brought you here."

Taking my hand, he guided me towards another guarded entrance hidden within the cavern.

"Welcome to my private chamber," he announced, gesturing for me to pass through the small doorway.

My heart stuttered when I saw what was inside. This cavern was like an oasis of pure enchantment. It wasn't anywhere near as large as the caves behind us, but what caught my eye first was the impressive waterfall. Its shimmering waters fell gracefully against the back wall from the ceiling high above, glistening like liquid diamond as it tumbled into a pool that covered most of the chamber's floor. And while the pool itself was clear as glass, the surrounding crystals turned it into a kaleidoscope of different ethereal colours.

Arenn strolled confidently up to the pool, kicking off his boots and slipping his feet into the water. He sighed as the water lapped around his feet. "It's quite warm," he called over his shoulder. "Care to join me?"

I swallowed. Dipping your feet into water was innocent enough, and besides, if he was relaxed it might be easier to confront him on the possibility of his parent's cursing King Ikelos. With a slow breath, I stepped over to the edge of the pool and gently slipped out of my boots. The stone floor of the cave was surprisingly pleasant under my feet, and it thrummed as though it was alive and breathing softly.

"This way," Arenn said, curling his fingers in a come-closer motion. He wasn't lying about the water being warm. Entering the pool felt just like stepping into a bath, but somehow the water seemed smoother against my skin.

"It really is lovely." I smiled up at him.

The prince's gaze locked onto mine. He grinned for a moment as something dangerous flashed across his smile. Then, he began to slowly unbutton his embroidered doublet, each movement deliberate and taunting.

"What are you doing?" I drew away from him. Water splashed up my bare legs as I stumbled back a few feet.

"Do not fear me, Princess," he teased, continuing to tug at his buttons. "I just fancy a quick swim. You are most welcome to join me, though."

My heart raced. Part of me wanted to run – back through the woods and straight up the stairs to my tower bedroom, until I was nestled deeply under my bed covers and no one could witness the crimson blush on my face. The other part of me, the more devious part, wanted to keep watching as the faery prince unhooked the last of his buttons.

Despite my rushing thoughts, my feet remained firmly rooted to the wet stone floor. Then, without realising I was doing it, I gasped as the prince shrugged off his dark shirt and tossed it to the shore.

Ancients, save me.

I'd never seen a boy in this state of undress before. Although, in that moment, it felt wrong to call him a mere boy. His incredible height, broad shoulders, and toned abdomen suggested he was much more than that. I tried so hard to pull my gaze away, but my hungry eyes betrayed me as they continued to feast on all the exposed pale skin of his chest. There was so much skin. And I wanted nothing more than to run my fingers down each perfect line of muscle.

"Something caught your eye?" Arenn asked in a mockingly innocent tone.

I swallowed, wanting to speak, but no words would come out. It was like my throat was full of thick and sticky honey.

The prince laughed deviously. "Are all human girls this easy to torment?"

A warmth rushed through me that had nothing to do with the temperature of the water around my feet. But before I had a chance to answer for my silence, Arenn shot me a playful grin, turned his back on the deeper area of the pool, and let his body fall backwards into the water. My eyes squeezed shut as water droplets splashed high into the air, wetting my cheeks. Finally, when the water settled, I wiped my face and let my eyes fall open.

The prince was gone.

"Arenn!" I cried out, panic washing over me. The water

of the pool was mostly clear, apart from near the centre, where the colour deepened to a murky blue. It was so cloudy down there I couldn't make out anything below a few metres. Ice-cold fear gripped my thoughts. Had he sunk to the bottom? What if he'd hit a rock on the way down and was now drowning? Would I be held responsible for the death of a prince?

Chest tightening, I forced my legs through the water, racing to the deeper section. Warm water soaked through my midnight gown and onto my skin as my panicked movements sent waves splashing all around me.

"Arenn, please, I don't know if I can save you – I can't swim!" I yelled towards the waterfall. The water had now reached my shoulders, and I was struggling to move quickly. How long had he been under for? It'd been barely a minute, so maybe if I turned back and sprinted to the guards outside, they could help him.

Suddenly, something hidden by the depths of the pool brushed by my thigh, and I let out a piercing scream that echoed through the cavern. Then, two familiar arms hooked under my legs and back, and a short moment later, I was lifted out of the water. Droplets cascaded into the pool around us. My shaking body was swiftly pressed against a bare, hard chest – the same bare, hard chest I had so desperately wanted to run my fingers down just a few minutes ago.

Deep laughter rumbled from his body into mine as Arenn held me firmly. "Did you miss me, little human?"

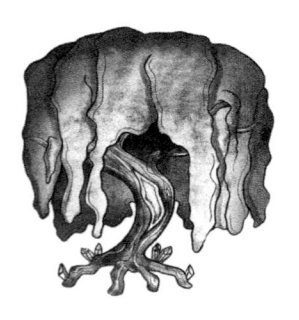

CHAPTER 21

Water dripped from the prince's soaking wet hair and onto my chest as I remained scooped up in his arms. I wanted to smack his smug face. Clearly, this was all some kind of trick to get me into the pool with him, and like a fool, I had run straight into his stunning faery arms.

"Please put me down," I told him. My words were short, and I made no effort to hide the anger storming across my face.

"Are you sure?" Arenn taunted, turning us both towards the centre of the pool. "I thought I heard you shout that you couldn't swim." Slowly, he began to loosen his hold on my body as we approached the deeper water just ahead of us.

He wouldn't... Would he?

"Wait!" I thrust my arms up and wrapped them around his wide shoulders. "At least take me back to the shore first."

"Relax, Princess. I'd never let you drown." His thumb brushed against the skin of my thigh, sending a shiver down my body. My heart was pounding, but it was beating in a way that was different to how it raced around Lukas. With the Prince of Drothmore, it fluttered nervously like a little butterfly. But here, in this cave, with my body pressed against Arenn's chest, the pounding was so intense it almost hurt.

With all the care in the realm, the faery prince lowered me into the water, keeping his hands on me at all times. Carefully, he moved backwards towards the centre of the pool, and I drifted with him, my arms wrapped around his bare shoulders. My feet couldn't touch the stone floor anymore, but somehow I trusted him not to let me dip under the surface.

"Isn't this nice?" he breathed, letting his hands rest confidently on my waist. Our bodies were positioned as though we were dancing, and the echoes of our voices against the crystal-filled walls were our music. It should've been romantic, but I couldn't forget how I'd ended up here, entangled in his arms.

"Do you use that trick often to get innocent ladies to enter the pool with you?" I questioned with a scowl.

Arenn snorted. "You know most *innocent ladies* in your situation would be too busy thinking about how to kiss me." A smile tugged at his lips, and I felt his grip around my waist tighten. "But not you, little human. Would you rather I apologised for rescuing you?"

"Rescuing me?" I blurted out. "I only came over here because I thought you were drowning."

The prince chuckled and spun us around in the water.

The waves lapped gently against my shoulders. "I've been swimming in these caves for as long as I can remember. You needn't worry about me drowning. And to answer your question, only royals are permitted to enter these caverns, so... no. I have never brought another lady, human or fae, into this pool."

I blinked a few times. His words sounded sincere, but still, there was something at the back of my mind that seemed unsure.

Arenn must've picked up on this because he tilted his head to the side, studying me. "I fear you do not trust me... How can I fix that? I can assure you I have shared nothing but the truth from the moment we met."

A twinge of guilt tugged at my heart. Perhaps he was right. Maybe I was letting my past knowledge of faeries sway my thoughts. After all, I came here to help my kingdom, and so far, everything on that front seemed promising.

"I think I just need to know more about you," I answered after a moment of pondering.

"And what would you like to know?" The prince grinned. "For you, I am an open book."

What did I want to know? Other than the fact that he was a prince, I hadn't really learnt anything about him.

"How old are you?" I decided to ask first.

"I was born in 1327, which would make me about twenty in human years."

"Human years?" I repeated. "Do faeries age differently then?"

Arenn's eyes sparkled. "You may have noticed that my mother and father look remarkably young despite having held the throne for over thirty years. Faeries age like humans do until twenty-five, and then, after that, we age very slowly. It's the magic that keeps us looking youthful."

"Right... So if we married, I would eventually be old and wrinkled while you'd remain young until you died?"

The prince chuckled, causing small waves to form in the pool. "There are rituals that can be performed to slow a human's ageing. You wouldn't need to worry about wrinkles while I'm around."

Faery magic was truly amazing. Of course science was wonderful too, but I'd never heard of a herb or powdered mineral that could slow ageing. My breath caught as Lukas's theory crept back into my mind. If faeries could slow ageing, could they also speed it up? Were they responsible for causing an otherwise healthy, middle-aged king's body to waste away with sudden ageing? My chest tightened, and I knew I probably shouldn't ask him this here. If it went badly, we were dangerously close to the deeper water, and I wasn't lying when I said I couldn't swim.

"You have another question for me?" Arenn mused as I felt his fingers stroke my waist.

I took a deep breath before speaking. "You said that there are rituals that can be done to slow someone's ageing... What about a ritual that does the opposite?"

The prince raised an eyebrow. "And what good would a ritual like that be?"

"Well, I..." I chewed my lip, puzzling how best to ask this. "A friend told me that someone they know has started growing old out of nowhere. One morning they were fine, and now they're like an old man."

"Are you sure they're not just ageing naturally? People always say it creeps up on us," Arenn replied casually, with no obvious sign of any hidden knowledge.

"There's nothing natural about this."

The prince shrugged. "There are many sources of magic in this world – and then there are the merfolk and the goblins, too. But if this person is in Drothmore, then it definitely wasn't from us. Not unless someone managed to sneak out past the guards. You can't project a ritual onto someone that isn't here, and you're the first human who's visited in decades." He brought up a hand and lazily threaded one of my curls through his fingers. "Now, do you have any other questions for me? Perhaps something a little more... interesting?" He smiled darkly.

So it wasn't the fae... I wanted to sigh in relief, but that would've drawn too much attention to the question, so instead, I asked the first 'interesting' thing that popped into my head.

"What's your favourite colour?"

The prince laughed. "Why, the perfect ocean blue of your eyes, of course, Princess." My 'perfect ocean blue' eyes wanted to roll back into my skull. He was absolutely shameless.

"What's your real favourite colour?" I insisted with a smile. No matter how much I thought I hated his constant flirting, I couldn't deny how much my body lapped it up.

He winked, leaning closer. "Like I said, I've never lied to you."

We spoke for another hour or so, until I began to shiver – the warm water no longer feeling so warm against my skin. Arenn took my hand as he led me out of the pool. With every step, my soaked dress dripped puddles onto the stone floor. Twisting the fabric in my hands, I attempted to wring out some of the dampness from the skirt, but it didn't do much.

"Need some help with that?" the prince asked tauntingly. Before I could respond, a gust of hot air swept up from the ground, catching my skirt. I could've sworn I heard Arenn huff as I slapped my hands down against it, stopping it just moments before it lifted and put my undergarments on show. "Nearly," he grinned wolfishly.

"If Theo were here, you'd be bleeding out on the floor," I joked as I ran my hands along the now very warm and dry fabric of my dress. "But thank you for fixing my gown."

"You're so welcome," Arenn said graciously before casting another wave of hot air to dry himself.

While he reached for his shirt hanging from one of the rocks, I reluctantly tore my gaze away from his perfect chest to explore the walls of the cavern. The countless multicoloured crystals almost seemed to sing with life as I stepped closer, letting my fingertips brush their smooth surfaces.

"This place is so beautiful," I said, my voice barely above a whisper.

Behind me, I heard footsteps against the stone floor as Arenn paced over to my side. Without speaking, he pressed his hand against the rock wall and then slowly dragged his palm away. In the place where his hand had been, dozens of midnight blue roses suddenly sprouted from the cracks in the rock.

A soft gasp escaped my lips. The mysterious roses continued to grow, their stems weaving around each other until they reached the same size as the roses in the grounds of the Steel Palace. Once the flowers had fully bloomed, Arenn leaned forward to pluck several from the miniature shrub. He held them for a moment in his open palm. Then, the stems began to wind around each other, weaving and changing until they formed a perfect, thornless circle.

"A crown fit for a princess," he announced, proudly presenting me with his final work. In his hands was an enchantingly beautiful flower crown. Delicate streaks of silver ran between the blue roses, partially hidden by the near-black stems.

"Thank you," I said breathily. My head dipped as he raised the crown to place it on my head. Of course, it fit perfectly and was so light I could forget it was even there. "You've shown me so much today, so many things I never even thought were possible... I'd love to learn more about your magic." I lifted my head to stare up at him.

A playful glint flashed across his features as he answered in a low voice. "Faery magic can do many things, although I'd prefer to keep the true extent of my powers a secret for now."

"I thought you said you'd be an open book today," I reminded him with narrowed eyes.

The prince laughed softly before leaning closer. I felt like a tiny mouse as he towered over me. "My dearest Naria," he murmured. "How pretty you look dressed in my gifts."

A smile tugged at his lips while his fingers delicately traced the curve of my chin, tilting my face towards his. "Almost too pretty for me to allow you to return to your foolish prince."

I laughed nervously, the sound echoing through the cavern. He didn't join in; instead, he swiped his thumb across my lower lip, his smile fading into something more serious.

My stomach dipped. "What is it...?" I managed to whisper, but I barely had enough breath to speak as he drew even closer, then pressed his lips against mine.

A whimper caught in my throat.

My eyes fluttered shut, and at first, I couldn't move, couldn't believe that this was even real. Inside my chest, my heart pounded with a strange rhythm of both fear and excitement. The feeling made my knees tremble under the dark rose petals of my skirt.

As if sensing my hesitation, Arenn slipped his hand around my waist, pulling me closer.

"Is this all too much for you, little human?" he whispered, his lips still pressed against mine.

"Not at all," I replied, almost too quickly, just as guilt began to squeeze my racing heart. Visions of deep brown hair and steel eyes danced through my mind.

Silently, I cursed my thoughts. Lukas didn't matter. I didn't want to think about him anymore. And as if to prove a point to nobody but myself, I wrapped my arms around the faery prince's shoulders and deepened the kiss.

The second I parted my lips, Arenn's tongue invaded my mouth. It was as though he was hungry to explore every inch of me. Everything slowed in the now too-heavy air around us, until all I could feel and all I could taste was *him*. The wildest of flowers and the sweetest dustings of cinnamon overwhelmed my senses. Everything about him was pure magic. His tongue continued to stroke mine as his grip tightened almost possessively around my waist. Then, his hands slid along the fabric of my bodice, slipping dangerously low to my hips. A gasp escaped my swollen lips when one of his roaming hands gently squeezed my backside.

"Humans are so much softer than fae," he said in a silky tone. He pulled his lips away for just a second before ending our kiss with a final brush of his lips on mine. "But we should stop now... I must return you to your grumpy guard before we do something you might regret later."

My breath was heavy, and I knew he was right, but tearing myself away from him felt like waking up in a cold room after the most wonderful dream.

"Don't look so sad," he teased. "You know, there are only a few more nights until Luminessia. I trust you will be attending?" His hands slipped back to my waist as he waited for an answer.

"It depends."

The prince's eyebrows shot up.

"It depends on how many other ladies will be there with pretty flower crowns made by charming faery princes." My arms dropped from his shoulders, but before I could step away, his hand snatched my wrist. Gently, he brought it to his face and placed a shy kiss on my palm.

"There will be only one, dear princess." He lowered my

wrist before tucking it around his waiting arm. "Now, you must let me return you to your silly guard. If we don't leave soon, I might not be able to stop myself from kissing you again."

With a smile, I nodded. After taking one final glance at the shimmering crystal pool, I allowed Arenn to lead me out of the chamber.

CHAPTER 22

I awoke the following morning to three gentle knocks on the door of my tower bedroom.

"Princess Naria?" A timid woman's voice called from outside. "There's a delivery of some gowns for yourself."

My body was still heavy with tiredness. Theo and I had arrived back only a few hours before dawn, and the little sleep I did get was tainted with dreams of crystal chambers and secret kisses.

"Thank you, please bring them in," I croaked, reluctantly heaving myself up from the warm pillows.

As my vision adjusted to the bright mid-morning sun, the servant hurried into the room, carrying two large boxes which she promptly placed at the end of my bed. I barely even had time to thank her before she dipped her head and excused herself.

Slipping out of my floral bed sheets, I threw on a plain

gown and raked a comb through my hair – the Summer Ball was tonight, so there was no point in making any effort now. Then, after feeling like I was mostly presentable, I scooped up the boxes, skipped over to my bedside, and knocked quietly on the door that connected Raena's room to mine.

"Raena?" I tried my best to keep my voice gentle and soft. When there was no response, I carefully pushed open the door and stepped inside.

Our rooms, while separated by a crisp ivory wall, were almost identical. The same birch vanity had been placed by her window, and the same wide dressers stood proud by the walls, except, instead of being covered in medicine bottles and herbs, Raena's dressers were practically bursting with colourful gowns and countless accessories. In the centre of the room was a grand silk bed, just like the one I'd woken up in, although on this bed was a giant nest of what appeared to be several layers of thick blankets. As I paced closer, the heap stirred, seemingly alive as rustling sounds came from beneath it.

"Naria?" A muffled cry crept out from the heap. "Is that you?" The voice was weak and very croaky, but still undeniably Raena's.

"It's me," I reassured her. "Would you be able to come out from there? I have a surprise for you."

The heap shuffled for a few moments. "I'd rather not... My face is terribly puffy, and I probably wouldn't stand so close if I were you, it's been a while since I last bathed."

My heart broke for her. All I wanted to do was throw my arms around her shoulders and tell her over and over again that everything would be okay, that the faeries were far from here, and that she was safe, but she needed space and I had to respect that.

Taking a seat in a nearby plush armchair, I sighed loudly enough for her to hear. "That's a shame, because you are the only person I know who would fit into this gorgeous new gown I've had custom-made."

The heap stirred. *That certainly got her attention.*

Two dainty hands slipped out from below the pile of bed sheets. "You bought a new gown?" she questioned suspiciously. A head of midnight-black curls followed the hands, popping up from under the blankets, while two narrowed brown eyes stared back at me.

I nodded, trying to hide the excitement on my face. "About a week ago, I received a letter from that designer you've told me so much about. What was his name... Seh-something?" I knew exactly what his name was. Cedrelei was only the most popular clothing designer in all of Nythinia. Even my friends back in Honeymeade dreamt about someday being able to touch one of his dresses. And of course, with everyone believing I was about to marry Prince Lukas, the designer was very eager to provide two gowns for the future Queen of Drothmore and her closest friend.

Raena's mouth fell open. "*Naria.*" She sprang up from the blankets, shoving them aside dramatically. "Tell me you're not hiding Cedrelei gowns in those boxes." Her gaze locked hungrily onto my lap as though she was seeing the world's most delicious cake, instead of the two rather plain-looking boxes that sat there.

"Was it Cedrelei? Now I actually can't remember," I said, innocently tapping my chin. "Why don't you check for me? I believe this one is yours." I held out one of the boxes towards her, and she snatched it from me, her fingers turning pale as she gripped the sides.

"Naria, if this is Cedrelei, I will scream! I will actually scream!"

Biting down on a smile, I watched as she peeled away the ribbon that held the box shut. Her hands were shaking. And for me, watching her excitement was better than every birthday rolled into one. I could almost hear her heart pounding as she lifted the lid and buried her fingers into the shimmering fabric inside.

"Blessed Oceans..." she breathed. Without waiting a moment longer, she rose from the bed, dragging the dress out of the box with her. The thick fabric of the skirt cascaded to the floor as a deafeningly loud shriek bounced off the walls. "I don't know what to say, Naria. It's... it's—"

"The most beautiful gown I've ever seen," I answered for her.

It truly was. I hadn't provided much of a brief for the designer, other than Raena's sizing and a few details about her family, but apparently Cedrelei had done his own research because somehow the turquoise gown captured every essence of Lady Raena and her birth kingdom of Ryntook. The entire gown shimmered in a gradient of ocean blues, while the bottom of the skirt was a much deeper turquoise, with small golden fish and corals embroidered around the hem. Similar ocean-themed patterns lined the bodice and the thin, flowing off-the-shoulder sleeves. I had never in my life seen something so spectacular and ornate. It would look stunning on her at the Summer Ball.

That's if she still wanted to go. My chest tightened at the thought.

"I was thinking you could wear it for the ball tonight?" I spoke quietly, not wanting to upset her. "But if you don't think you can manage it, that's fine. There will be other balls." I studied her face for any kind of reaction.

"Oh," she breathed, suddenly appearing to shrink behind the gown. "I don't know... Somehow I'd forgotten all about that."

"There's no pressure at all," I insisted. "Don't feel like you have to put yourself out there just because I bought you a new gown."

Her fingers continued exploring the fabric of the bodice as she thought.

"No," she finally decided, her voice taking on a more assertive tone. "I've been in here for far too long now anyway. A ball will be a good distraction. And it would be such a waste to let this dress sit in my wardrobe for a whole season."

"Are you sure?"

She nodded confidently. "Absolutely." A glimmer of excitement sparkled in her smile, and despite the dark circles under her lower lashes, she already looked so much more alive. "Now please, you must show me yours. It should be illegal to have a Cedrelei gown delivered and not try it on at once!"

We burst into a fit of excited giggles as I reached for the other unopened dress box.

Many, many hours later, both Raena and I were finally ready. There must've been magic in the rose-scented bubbles of her bath water as all traces of this morning seemed to have washed away, leaving her looking absolutely stunning. Her turquoise gown fit perfectly, with the glittering corset top emphasising the soft curves of her waist and chest. Even her hair had been detangled and fashionably shaped into a dainty halo around her head before being decorated with gold hair jewellery. She looked radiant, and it was impossible to not feel a twinge of jealousy.

"I should go," she said, fluttering her hand fan as we stepped into the hallway. "The prince will be here soon to escort you, and I don't want to *interfere*." She giggled.

Nerves chewed at my stomach. I hadn't yet told her about last night's visit to the faeries. While we were dressing, I'd spoken about how Lukas and I had grown closer – but of course, it would be hard not to if you have dinner with someone every day. Still, there was no denying that I found him attractive, and clearly, the feeling was mutual. But at the end of the day, it wouldn't matter if we loved each other to the stars and back; if he couldn't help my kingdom, he couldn't have me.

And after that kiss from Arenn, I wasn't sure if I even wanted him at all anymore.

"You wouldn't be interfering with anything," I told her plainly. "There's nothing between us."

Raena's smile fell, and I could've sworn a cold wind brushed past my exposed shoulders.

"Nothing between us?" a low voice repeated from behind me, sending my stomach diving for the floor. "Then perhaps

I should've invited another court lady instead to—"

The prince's mouth fell open as I whirled to face him. He was dressed in a formal grey and gold doublet, while his dark brown hair was styled in such an effortless way – I had to swallow down a heart flutter. Glancing at his face, his stormy eyes must've been too busy tracing the semi-sheer fabric of my gown to remember what he was going to say next, because his mouth quickly clamped shut and his jaw tightened.

His reaction didn't surprise me, my gown was certainly unusual. Unlike the typical flared skirt style that was so popular amongst the other ladies here, the shimmering violet fabric slinked down my body, tightly wrapping around my curves and finishing just off the floor. There was also a long slit that travelled up to my thigh, and although it was completely scandalous, it at least made walking a little easier. Small silver stars were embroidered into the bodice that hugged my waist and chest. And while the low-cut neckline showed a little more maturity than I would have liked, Raena's shower of compliments on how gorgeous I looked convinced me to not rip it off and shove myself into something more plain.

That being said, by the way Lukas couldn't keep his eyes off me, I was beginning to think I might regret that decision.

"I'll see you both at the ball," Lady Raena whispered, dipping her head in parting.

Before she hurried off, I slipped a small vial of anxiety powder into her hand. "If you start feeling afraid again, mix that in with some wine. It will calm your nerves."

She nodded, giving me a thankful smile before she disappeared down the marble stairs.

"What was that about?" Lukas asked, finally tearing his gaze away from my gown.

"None of your concern," I said dismissively. "It's just a mixture of herbs I threw together to help her at the party."

"And why would she need help at the party?" His eyebrows lowered. "If something bad has happened to one of my future subjects, I need to know."

"Like I said, that's none of your concern," I insisted. "This is a private matter between Lady Raena and me, and the issue is being resolved." At least I hoped it was. While I hadn't yet seen Arenn make good on his promise, I hoped that by the time I next visited, that green guard along with his smug smile would be thrown straight into a prison cell.

My firm answer seemed to satisfy the prince, though. With one last suspicious look, he held out his arm for me to take. "Shall we?"

CHAPTER 23

We arrived at the Grand Hall far too quickly. With every step towards it, the blaring music and raging cheers grew more and more intense until, by the time we reached the entrance to the ball, my grip on Lukas's arm was tighter than my corsetlacing. The sounds, the lights, the people – it was all turning my mind in vicious circles, and suddenly the world was moving much faster than I could handle.

Noticing my obvious discomfort, Lukas leaned closer. "Everything alright?" he asked quietly.

"I'm fine," I shot back, my tone perhaps a little too cutting. Glancing around, I tried my hardest to steady my breathing. Really, all I needed was a distraction. I'd be alright if I could just focus on something else.

As I stepped forward to grasp the balcony railing, my gaze scanned the impressive scene before us. We were stood near the top of a wide open staircase that led down to a huge ballroom. In the far corner, several musicians with violins, harps, and other instruments I'd never seen before played jaunty music that could just about be heard over the constant chatter. Below us, couples twirled impressively, dancing in time to the music, and above them, hanging from the ceiling on a golden chain, was a grand chandelier. Just like everything else in the palace, it was brushed with gold and dripping in diamonds that shined so brightly, they made my eyes sting.

"We should start by addressing the other royals in attendance," Lukas suggested as he also approached the balcony. "News of our engagement has reached as far as Ryntook, so I'm sure they'll all be eager to meet you – the mysterious Corlixin princess." Turning away from the dancers, he extended a hand. "Are you ready?"

I wanted to take it, but my mind was still buzzing from the overwhelming scene in front of us. So instead, my fingers dropped from the railing to bury themselves into the fabric of my skirt, rubbing against it in repetitive calming circles.

"I think... I think I need a drink first." Wine would surely distract me, especially since I was really starting to regret not saving some of Raena's anxiety powder for myself.

A concerned smile covered Lukas's face. "I can help with that. Wait here." He then rushed down the stairs and vanished into the crowds, only to return less than a minute later with two goblets filled with shimmering red wine.

"For you," he said as he handed me one of the goblets.

Without any hesitation, I brought the goblet to my

lips and tossed the wine to the back of my throat, scowling at the taste. Red wine was disgusting, but I craved how it would take the edge off any overwhelming sounds and give everything in the room a soft, rosy hue.

"Thirsty?" The prince raised an eyebrow. "You can have mine too, if you'd like?"

I didn't need to be told twice. Within seconds, his wine goblet was also emptied.

"That's so much better," I sighed, already beginning to feel the wine warming my body and dulling my senses. *Perhaps I might actually enjoy this ball now.*

With a half-enthralled, half-concerned expression, Lukas removed the goblets from my hands and placed them on a nearby servant's tray. "Who'd have thought, the brave princess who grew up as a commoner in the woods and had no hesitation when it came to saving a young boy's life, would be scared of a simple party?"

"I'm not sscaredd," I attempted to correct him, but the alcohol was already slurring my words. Apparently Drothmore's wine was much stronger than the watered-down bottles we used to sneak from the village mother's cupboards.

Lukas tilted his head, smiling in amusement. "It seems I shall have to keep a close eye on you tonight. So much for you making a good impression on the other royals..."

"I caan be good," I told him with far too much confidence as my gaze caught on his perfect nose. How had I not noticed how beautiful his nose was before? And his toned arms too... *Ancients.*

"I'm sure you can be," he chuckled, taking my arm to

carefully lead me down the steps. "And please, stop staring at me like that, or I might start to think you were lying when you said there's nothing between us."

We spent the next half-hour arm in arm, greeting the various royals who had visited for the ball. I tried my best to keep my mouth shut, only curtsying politely to greet the other guests – though occasionally, Lukas would have to help me back up again as I wobbled on my feet. While the visiting royals were mostly lovely, I doubted I would remember their names in the morning. Every time a servant wandered past with a tray of wine goblets, I'd snatch one up and finish it before Lukas had a chance to stop me. After the fourth glass, I even started to enjoy the taste of the scarlet liquid as it pooled in my throat.

"Fantastic soirée, dear princeling!"

Lukas spun us around to face a snooty-looking, middle-aged lady. She was plump, her extravagant low-cut gown straining against her ample figure, while her powdered face and rouged lips made her appear as if she'd dunked her head into a sack of flour before kissing a tomato. Standing beside her was her equally portly husband. He was dressed in a lavish velvet suit that looked more like it belonged in a carnival than at a royal ball.

"Queen Marigold and King Thorian of Hallshire," Lukas introduced them to me. It was difficult to remember much about Hallshire with my wine-dampened mind, but I could just about recall the basic facts that Lukas had shared with me over our dinners. Hallshire was the kingdom that specialised in farming and textiles. They traded their produce for other resources across the three other kingdoms, but there had always been tension. Apparently, Hallshire had a habit of being unfair with their trades, claiming every year was a poor harvest, while their people never seemed to go hungry.

"How delightful it is to be invited to your humble palace." The woman forced her lips into a smile, her tone dripping with insincere sweetness. "And who is this?" She glanced at me. Her eyes swept from my head to my slippers in a manner that made me feel more like a piece of meat than a human being. "I don't think we've met this one before," she purred while gripping her husband's arm.

"Allow me to introduce Princess Naria of Corlixir," Lukas answered, his voice unwavering, "my betrothed."

"How quaint," Queen Marigold cooed before turning to her husband. "I didn't realise there were any Corlixins left, did you, dear? I thought they'd all been reduced to cinders."

Her husband grunted in response, clearly more focused on the buffet than any conversation.

Ignoring him, she twisted to face Lukas again. "You needn't bother with this one." She flicked her wrist in my direction. "What use is a Corlixin girl to a future king? If you want a real princess, one a bit more," her gaze swept over me again, catching on my bodice, "substantial, then do ask your father to have a discussion with me. As you know, I have plenty of lovely daughters."

"Thank you for the offer, but that won't be necessary." For once, I was glad that Lukas spoke for me because, at that moment, I wanted nothing more than to snap something cruel right back and then slap the powder off her plump cheeks. Though the feel of a strong arm wrapping around my waist pulled me back to the present. Lukas pressed me tightly against his side, a silent plea to remain calm and unaffected – as much as it might pain me to do so.

Although, what if I had smacked her? Would that have started a war? In my wine-tainted state, I couldn't help but feel that a war would've been worth it just to see the look on her smug face.

"I must ask, though," Queen Marigold carried on casually, "where is King Ikelos? I know your mother is always 'ill', or something of the sort, but I don't think we've had the pleasure of meeting dear Ikelos tonight."

"At this moment, the King is preoccupied with important matters of state. As Crown Prince, I represent him in his absence," Lukas informed her, just as he'd told all the other royals who'd questioned the King's whereabouts. It seemed his curse was not yet common knowledge.

"Interesting..." The Hallshire Queen's expression gleamed with curiosity. She looked as though she wanted to probe further, but then the music in the Grand Hall flowed into a pompous waltz. Her round face lit up with excitement as she shook her husband's arm. "This is our wedding song, dearest! We must show the others how a real dance is done." Ignoring me, she tipped her chin dismissively at Lukas before whisking her husband off towards the dance floor.

Once they'd disappeared, Lukas drew closer until I felt his lips brushing against my ear. "I appreciate that the Hallshire royalty can be difficult, so thank you for handling that in an appropriate manner."

I wanted to come back with some witty retort, but the wine was really starting to swirl my thoughts. When I opened my mouth to speak, only an incomprehensible mess came out.

'No more drinks tonight,' I voiced internally.

With a sigh, Lukas squeezed his hand around my waist. "I'm going to have the servants fetch you some water. Don't go running off. Stay here until I get back."

I nodded obediently, then watched him vanish into the crowd.

A few moments passed as I remained still until, with the wine sloshing rather intensely in my mind, my gaze slowly drifted over to the couples waltzing on the dance floor. They glided around with such elegance that I couldn't help but close my eyes as my body swayed absentmindedly along with them.

It was only when another pair of hands clasped around my waist that my eyes snapped open, and I whirled around. To my surprise, though, instead of the steel-eyed prince I'd expected to see, I found myself face-to-face with a tall, dark-haired stranger.

"What is a beautiful young lady doing dancing alone in a place like this?" the stranger mused. He was certainly handsome, if perhaps in more of a rugged way, but there was something uncomfortable about the way his gaze lingered on my skin – and in his nearly black irises, there was something almost familiar.

"I'm, umm..." *What was I doing?* "I'm waiting... I think... I have to stay here." The words came out in a slurred mess, and the room spinning around me certainly wasn't helping the situation.

At my response, the stranger chuckled gleefully before

tugging me closer to his chest. "Oh my darling, you sound like you need more wine. That can be remedied, but first, let me have this dance?"

Without waiting for me to respond, he took my hand and whisked me towards the dancefloor. All I could focus on was not stumbling as he led me towards the other waltzing couples. When we reached the floor, he spun me forcefully and gripped me so tight I could feel his fingers marking my skin. Beneath my skirts, my knees wobbled as he twirled me in his arms, leaving me struggling to keep my balance. Everything was happening so fast, I barely even noticed when his hand ventured down to my backside.

"Your gown is beautiful, but you know, it would look much more beautiful on the floor of my chambers," he murmured, unease creeping up my throat. Panic welled up inside me as I tried to break free from his grasp. Dropping my arms from his shoulders, I attempted to pull away, but he only chuckled in response as he tightened his hold on me. "It's been so long since I've sampled the goods outside of Hallshire. Give me what I want and I'll make sure you're rewarded handsomely."

"Stop!" I tried to squirm out of his too-strong arms.

"That's not an acceptable answer, darling," he purred, then twirled me forcefully again. His intentions were crystal clear, and I wanted nothing to do with this, but all my attempts to escape only seemed to amuse him. It was only when another hand clamped down on my shoulder that his grip suddenly loosened, and he jumped back.

"May I cut in here?" A familiar deep voice spoke from behind me.

"Prince Lukas," the stranger acknowledged him with a forced smile. He then bowed respectfully. "Forgive me, I did not realise this one was yours."

"I belong to no one but myself," I spat at him. The fear clawing at my heart was replaced by an intense rage.

Lukas drew me back into his chest, wrapping his arms around mine in an annoyingly comforting way. "I suggest you make yourself scarce, Prince Colyn. While the King isn't here, the guards answer only to me, and I've dealt with enough Hallshires tonight for at least the rest of the season."

Prince Colyn's cheeks flushed an angry shade of rouge. Really, I should've known he was royalty. His clothes were so regal, and he looked almost exactly like King Thorian, albeit much leaner and at least twenty years younger.

"Have it your way, *Your Highness.*" He then tilted his chin down to face me. "If you change your mind, darling, do come and find me."

With a filthy wink, he sauntered off into the sea of waltzing dancers, leaving Lukas and I alone once again. I let myself remain pressed against him, perhaps longer than I should have. The violet fabric of my gown was so thin, and his chest was so warm. Around us, the dancers relentlessly twirled along to the music. Everything was still far too loud, but for some reason, with the wine settling in my bones and Lukas's arms wrapped around me, I didn't feel so overwhelmed anymore.

"Are you alright, Naria?"

Was that my heart pounding against my spine, or his? It didn't matter. Suddenly feeling too hot, I spun to face him.

"I'm fine," I said, lifting my chin and steadying my voice.

"Thank you for stepping in. It wasn't necessary, though, I had the situation under control."

The prince lowered his brow. "Certainly looked like it."

I was lying, and he knew it, but I persisted. The way he made me feel just then was dangerous – maybe even more dangerous than Colyn's unwanted advances. I had an entire kingdom resting on my shoulders, and so far, the fae were the only ones who could help. Though I certainly wasn't thinking of any ruined kingdoms or amber-eyed faery princes a few moments ago. Only how the curve of my back fit so perfectly against Lukas's toned chest. I couldn't let myself fall for him. I wouldn't. Not when the entire population of my home village depended on me marrying the right prince.

And Lukas wasn't the right prince.

"I don't need you to protect me," I seethed.

A muscle tensed in Lukas's jaw. Then, from the corner of the ballroom, the same musicians that once played the gaudy Hallshire waltz transitioned their song into a much slower, more inviting tune. Music weaved through the thick air until all I could focus on were Lukas's darkened eyes, and how they were fixed on me.

Without uttering a word, he extended a hand out in front of him. I shouldn't have accepted it, but instinct took over. As soon as my fingers were intertwined with his, he drew me into his chest, and before I knew it, I was dancing again.

Except he wasn't rough like the way Prince Colyn had been. The fabric of my skirt flowed as he led me in a circle, gently pressing his hand to the small of my back. Around us, I could feel the stares of other couples judging every movement. I didn't know this dance. We'd never thrown parties like this in the village, but somehow, this all felt so natural. With him guiding me, it was as though I'd danced this waltz a thousand times before.

"I told you I'm a good teacher," he said in a voice low enough that only I could hear.

I couldn't deny that. We spun together, and then his hands clamped around my waist, lifting me with such ease. I felt like I was flying as he twirled me around, my feet suspended in the air beneath me. Suddenly, it was like the rest of the ball had faded away. There was only myself, the smooth music, and Lukas's hands feeling entirely too warm against the thin fabric of my gown. When he finally lowered me, our faces now dangerously close, my gaze met his. There was something so hungry storming across his features.

And deep inside me, I could feel something equally ravenous.

The music grew faint as his mouth moved towards mine. Heart racing, my eyes fluttered shut. It was only when I felt his breath on my already parted lips that I realised just what was happening.

Cursing internally, I stumbled back. Instantly, I was stone-cold sober.

"I'm sorry," I stammered, bringing a hand up to conceal the heat on my cheeks. "I can't do this with you."

Something like hurt flashed across the prince's face, but before he could open his mouth to speak, I spun on my heels and shoved through the dancing crowds.

"Naria!" I heard him calling after me. Part of me wanted

so desperately to run back, to return to his warm embrace and melt into that kiss. But I couldn't let myself. I couldn't, because I knew if I did, I'd never be able to return to the fae and marry another – ruined kingdom or not.

CHAPTER 24

Without Lukas at my side, the ballroom quickly felt far too intense. The obnoxious chatter paired with the blaring music felt like a hundred nails scratching my skin. I needed air – nice, cold, sobering, outside air – and fast. Barging through the crowds, I searched for the nearest open door, then barreled towards it. The cool evening air immediately soothed my racing heart and scalding skin as I rushed outside.

"Ancients, save me," I sighed through heavy breaths. Confusion swam in the wine that still sloshed around my mind. If it weren't for the transparent glass doors, I'd strip off my gown and collapse in just my undergarments onto the dewey grass. Maybe then, while staring up at the stars, would I finally find some answers.

Taking a few steps out onto the grass, I inhaled deeply. The night air was working wonders on my exhausted senses.

Though I was only engulfed in the bliss for a few precious moments before a familiar male voice sent all the unease rushing back to my stomach.

"Fancy seeing you here, darling."

I bristled at the sound of him. Following the voice, my body whipped around to face Prince Colyn. At first glance, he might've appeared somewhat innocent, his tall frame leaning against a narrow fruit tree as he threw a small orange up and down in his hand. But there was a poisonous desire burning in his gaze, and immediately I stepped a few feet back, ready to dart straight back into the ballroom.

"Don't even think about running, sweet one. We both know you came out here for a reason... Are you bored of your little princeling already?" He tossed the orange up into the air again, catching it quickly in his open palm. "I can show you what a real man feels like." A dark shadow flickered across his face, churning the unease in my stomach into a heavy dread. Though my obvious fear seemed to only entice him further as he pushed away from the tree with a grin and prowled closer, dropping the orange onto the grass.

"Don't be afraid now, I can be gentle."

Absolutely not.

My heart leapt, sending my once-frozen feet springing into action. I bolted towards the ballroom door, but before I'd made it more than a metre, my arms were suddenly pinned behind me as a loud, piercing scream flew from my lips.

"Let me go!" I yelled, thrashing wildly. Oblivious to my protests, the man wrenched my body away from the doors.

"Hush now," he chided. The golden light of the ballroom

faded with every step as he hauled me deeper into the palace grounds. "If you didn't want this you should've worn something other than this damned gown. I've seen the way your prince has been watching you all evening, only unlike him, I *take* what I *want*."

"No, please, stop!" I begged, tears welling in my eyes.

He chuckled, his breath heavy with the stench of alcohol. Then, keeping my hands pinned, he threw me roughly against a tree. The bark felt like daggers scraping my back as I collided against it, the pressure forcing all the air from my lungs – so much that when I tried to scream again, it came out barely louder than a whimper.

"Stop squirming!" he spat before smearing his lips over mine.

I couldn't move. Couldn't breathe. All I could think about was how foul he tasted until, like a whisper in my ear, I recalled the calming words of the village mother.

'Even the strongest of menfolk have a weakness, dear child.'

A weakness...

Thanking the Ancients for anatomy classes, I swung my knee up. Hard. Aiming directly between his legs. Immediately, he stumbled to the side, doubling over to clutch his lower body.

"Little wretch," he cursed.

Finally, I saw my chance. Shoving away from the tree, I dove past the hedgerows and sprinted back through the grounds. My legs ran until they ached, and then they ran even more. We hadn't gone far from the ballroom, but I didn't know these grounds well. The panic, mixed with the dark of night, transformed the pretty flower beds and neatly trimmed hedges into a dense, wild maze. I wasn't sure how much time had passed. My sprinting only stopped when my body painfully thudded against hard metal armour.

"Gotcha!" Behind the cold chestplate, a man called out to someone nearby, "We found her, sire."

A thousand butterflies burst from my heart when I saw just who he was calling out to.

"Naria!" Lukas rushed towards me. My exhausted knees buckled at the sight of him, the relief turning all my limbs to jelly. I hadn't realised that I'd collapsed until he was kneeling beneath me, his warm arms supporting my wilting upper body as I landed in a heap upon his lap. "Where were you? Someone heard a scream from outside. Are you hurt?" His expression was heavy with concern and dark anger.

"I needed some air." My words spilled out between ragged breaths. "Colyn found me... I tried to get away but—" A sob forced its way up my throat before I had a chance to finish, and any remaining dignity was washed away with the relentless tears that followed.

"Shh, you're safe now," he murmured in a gentle yet reassuring tone. Not moving from the grass floor, he jerked his chin towards a nearby guard. "Search the grounds! Search the entire damned palace if you have to! Find Prince Colyn. And when you have him, lock him away in the dungeons." His commands were strong and powerful, almost as if I was laying across the lap of a king rather than a young prince. "Whatever happens, do not let him leave this palace tonight."

"Yes, Your Highness." The guard bowed then swiftly scurried off to alert the others of the urgent new plan.

When we were alone, the tears only fell harder, as if for some reason I'd been holding them back before. Beneath all the blubbering, I hated how pathetic I must've looked. I don't know how Lukas was able to keep me in his arms while I crumbled to pieces, but he did. He held me close, the rise and fall of his chest grounding me as I tried my hardest to steady my breathing.

"Thank you for searching for me," I said in a quiet voice, eventually finding a moment between sobs.

"You needn't thank me." Lukas brushed a stray hair away from my face. "What kind of prince would I be if I left my fiancée to wander the grounds all night long?"

A strange feeling gnawed at my toes, and I wasn't sure if it was guilt or just a chill in the night air. This moment felt far too intimate. Glancing up, all I could see was his perfect bronze face, surrounded by a halo of stars against the inky black sky above. He was so close, it would be so easy, so natural, for our lips to meet.

No. I couldn't do this.

Clearing my throat, I changed the subject. "Won't the King and Queen of Hallshire be furious if they hear their son is in the dungeon?"

Lukas's jaw tightened. "I will deal with the two of them in the morning. They likely won't be pleased, but in Drothmore, it is a crime to lay hands on anyone who is unwilling. Royalty or not, he will be given a trial as anyone else would."

"And if his parents threaten a war?"

He took a slow breath. "I will not let him get away with whatever he did to you. Perhaps I can negotiate with the

King or Queen. He might not be executed, but if he hurt you?"

"He didn't," I told him truthfully. "He just scared me a bit. The mental wounds will heal with time."

"Still..." The hand supporting my arm trailed up to cup the side of my face. With his thumb, he brushed away a tear from my cheek, the closeness making my skin feel warm. "In a few months, maybe even less, we shall marry. And even if you won't accept me as your future husband right now, I cannot – will not – under any circumstances, let any harm come to you. You're my future wife, Naria. No one harms you, even if they are only 'mental wounds.'"

It would be so easy to melt into him, and part of me desperately wanted to. But I cast those alcohol-fueled feelings aside as tears glazed my eyes once again, this time more from frustration than fear.

"Lukas, I—" A finger pressing over my lips interrupted anything else I was about to say.

"You don't need to explain yourself," he told me. "I know what you're going to say, and you're right – we barely know each other. This is all happening so fast... My head is such a mess, and with my father passing away so slowly, I've not been myself." He paused, his jaw tensing. "In time, I hope you can learn to love the real me."

Why was he making this so difficult? Where was this tenderness when I told him about my people living in the forests? How can he promise protection for me but not for all those who need me as their queen? Confusion pounded in my head as another sob lodged itself in my throat. It was hard to breathe through the tears that followed.

"Hush, please," he brushed away the tears that streamed down my cheeks, "it's getting cold, and you're shivering." He was right. In the mess of my tears, I hadn't noticed how much the summer night air had cooled. "Let me get you inside. I'll take you to my chambers and you can sleep there tonight. It's much closer than your tower."

I began to protest, but he silenced me with another finger. "Do not fear me, Naria. Nothing will happen. You can take my bed, and I will sleep elsewhere. I'll send for your servants to help you undress before bed and then again in the morning. Please," he said, his gaze meeting mine, "please let me keep you safe for tonight. At least until the guards have caught Colyn."

I shuddered at the sound of his name. But now that he'd suggested it, I would feel much safer sleeping somewhere other than my isolated tower bedroom, and there were plenty more guards around Lukas's chambers. The extra protection would be very reassuring. Also, the thought of being surrounded by sheets that smelled like him was certainly tempting... Forcing that last thought aside, I took a deep breath.

Focus, Naria, this is only for your safety. Don't let it mean anything else.

Clearing my head of any more dangerous ideas, I accepted his offer. Instantly, his shoulders relaxed, and he smiled in a way that would put angels to shame.

"Let me help you up," he offered, scooping me up from the floor and propping me onto my wobbling feet as if I weighed no more than a feather. My knees were still trembling from all the running, and as he began to lead me back towards the golden light of the palace, I almost collapsed back onto the ground.

"I'm sorry," I sighed, my exhausted body leaning into his open arms.

"It's quite alright," he chuckled quietly. "It's been a long evening for us all. Let me help."

Before my mind could process what was happening, I was swept off my feet and lying back in his outstretched arms. His chest felt so warm pressed against my side, it was almost impossible to keep my eyes open. Everything about the way he carried me was so gentle yet also so secure. There was such grace in the way he walked too, it was like I was floating on an endless lake.

Sleep overcame me long before we reached his chambers. The last thing I remember after my eyes finally closed was the sweet scent of exotic fruits and the strange sense of how I imagined stepping into the warm ocean would feel after a relentless tropical storm.

Peaceful.

CHAPTER 25

When I finally awoke the following morning, Lukas was nowhere to be found. Just like he'd promised, I'd slept alone in his bed, and as dawn broke over the horizon, servants arrived to help me dress. They'd selected a low-cut, flowing red gown adorned with gold trim, and while it certainly wasn't my usual style, I couldn't bear the thought of sending a servant all the way to my chambers to fetch another, so I allowed them to help lace me in.

Catching sight of myself in the mirror, a silent gasp escaped my throat. Just a few weeks ago, I felt like nothing more than a child who'd wandered into a grand palace after losing her way. But now, with the lavish red gown hugging me in all the right places and my blonde hair still curled from the ball last night, I finally felt like royalty.

"You look lovely today, Your Highness," an older servant

remarked after she finished lacing my gown.

"Thank you." I smiled back at her. Warmth pooled in my chest as my gaze wandered from the mirror to explore the prince's chambers. Near the back wall, sunlight filtered through a large, ornate stained-glass window, casting hundreds of different coloured rays onto the polished wooden floors. It was so beautiful. Just standing there, I felt so beautiful. With a quiet laugh, I wondered if everything had always been this beautiful and I'd just never noticed it before?

"Let us know if you need anything else, Your Highness," the same servant told me, dipping her head. Before she left, she shot a knowing smile to the other handmaidens, and one of them whispered something that sent hushed giggles rippling through the group. If this had been any other day, perhaps I would've demanded they share the joke that was clearly made at my expense, but for some reason, I didn't care. Even I laughed after they left. Everything around me seemed so pleasant and bright, it was hard not to.

In the centre of Lukas's chambers stood a grand four-poster bed draped with plush velvet sheets, while the walls were lined with several bookshelves. I'd never pictured Lukas as the sort who liked to read, but the sheer amount of books clearly suggested otherwise. As I moved towards them and ran my fingers over the spines, I wondered what else I would soon learn about him.

It was only when a faint knocking sounded at the door that I finally emerged from my daydream.

"Naria, are you in there?" a sweet voice chimed from the hallway outside.

"Do come in, Raena," I answered, beaming as the door swung open to reveal my friend dressed in a typically lovely peony-coloured gown.

As usual, her face was stunningly made up in golden-brown tones, but for some reason, there was worry behind her rosy cheeks. "Are you alright?" She rushed towards me, clasping my hands. "When you didn't come back to your chambers last night, I went looking for you. Erik told me something bad happened in the palace grounds and that the prince brought you here. What was it? What happened?"

I sniffed with laughter, shaking my head. "Oh, Raena, you mustn't worry, everything is fine. I had a scare in the garden with the Prince of Hallshire, but then Lukas found me and, well..." Imaginary roses bloomed in my chest. "Everything is fine now."

For a moment, Raena's lips thinned as she studied me. Then her gaze flew over my shoulder to the unmade bed in the centre of the room. As her mouth formed a small 'o', I could almost hear the gears turning in her mind.

"Did you?" Heat flooded to her cheeks. "Naria, tell me you didn't... last night?" Her eyes darted around the room. "Or this morning?"

I gasped at her bizarre conclusion. The surprise sent me into a coughing fit as I struggled to catch my breath. "No!" I blurted out between gasps. "No, we didn't. He slept somewhere else!"

Raena cocked an eyebrow, a devious smirk landing on her smug face. "That never stopped anyone."

"I promise, nothing like that happened!" My hands

flapped wildly. "We just shared a nice moment in the gardens, and then he carried me up here. That's all!"

Raena's whole body shook with laughter. "Oh, sweet innocent Naria." She patted my arm in a jokingly condescending way. "I'm glad you enjoyed your *moment*, and I'm really happy you're making progress with the prince." A sincere smile warmed her face. "Does this mean you're not going back to the fae? You seem so happy this morning. Has Prince Lukas finally agreed to help with your kingdom?"

All the golden light vanished from the room, my body stiffened, and suddenly his bedchamber felt ice cold. With a shiver, goosebumps covered my tense arms. Where had all the warmth gone?

Raena chewed her lower lip, as if sensing the change in the air, too. "I see." Reassuringly, she squeezed my arm. "If you feel like you're growing closer, then perhaps he will change his mind about your kingdom?" Hope, or something equally as foolish, danced in her brown eyes. "Confess to visiting the faeries. Tell him that they are offering to help your people. Maybe then he'll understand the importance of this situation." She drew closer, lowering her voice. "I saw you dancing together last night. The way he looked at you… Naria, I know that look. He won't want to let you go."

I wanted to believe her, but deep down, I knew this was all so silly. Love, or whatever this strange thing between us might be, shouldn't be affecting my decision. I was a princess. It was my duty to marry for the good of my own kingdom. Lukas was offering nothing, so no matter how I felt during the ball when he spun me in the air in that enchanting way, I couldn't marry him. Not when I had faeries offering me – offering Corlixir – so much more.

"You might be right," I finally answered. "He may have feelings for me, but," I paused, my heart aching, "that doesn't change the fact that he doesn't care for my kingdom."

"You don't know that!" she protested. "Please, just try one more time to get through to him."

I'd tried so many times to extinguish the small flame of hope that flickered away in my chest, but there Raena was, reigniting it while my foolish heart only stoked the flames.

"Fine," I decided gruffly, mentally preparing myself for the inevitable hurt and rejection. "I don't even know where he is though. He must've left long before I woke up."

A glimmer of excitement flashed across Raena's smile. "I think I know where he might be. Come on, Princess." She took my hand. "Let's go and save Corlixir."

※

The sun was high in the sky by the time we'd tracked down the location of this week's duelling club. Due to the warm weather, the nobles had commandeered a small stage nestled in a far corner of the palace grounds. Surrounding the cobblestone stage were dense clusters of royal blue and ivory hydrangeas, while the thick canopies of oak trees provided shade. The audience was smaller this time too, and a fair number of the people watching were seated on the lush grass, fanning their pert highborn faces and gasping every time a sword came close to hitting someone's tunic.

"There he is," I whispered to Raena, pointing towards one of the masked duellers who was sitting on a patch of grass off to the side.

From our spot near the back of the small crowd, she squinted at the gaggle of duellers. "How can you tell? They all look the same to me."

Before I had a chance to gush about his unmistakable broad shoulders or the cascade of dark brown waves that sat atop his head, Raena cut me off.

"Actually, don't answer that. I believe you." She laughed knowingly. "Let's wait here until they're finished, then you can catch him before he leaves." Flicking open her hand fan, she fluttered it against her face in a mockingly seductive way. "Try not to blush too hard when he wins."

"Stop it!" I swatted her playfully.

A few metres ahead, wooden swords clashed away as the duel continued on the stage. The nearest dueller, a taller man with a thickset build, swung his sword with a deliberate force, while his opponent, a much smaller, more nimble boy, parried each blow with graceful finesse. Every time the broader man swung, the boy darted to the side, and as the duel progressed, it became clear that the smaller one was the crowd favourite. Another lightning-fast dodge, another cheer from the crowd. Though, this only seemed to anger the larger man, as each attack became more and more fuelled by the raging fire within him.

Eventually, after avoiding another lumbering blow, the smaller dueller bolted forward and sliced his wooden sword against the man's tunic. Had that been a real sword, the larger man would be in two pieces.

"We have a winner!" the announcer cried as the crowd erupted into cheers. The smaller dueller grinned triumphantly and took a sweeping bow. Then, he slipped off his thin black mask to reveal a familiar youthful face. There was no hiding the joy that overcame my cheeks when I realised who he was.

"Bravo, Nathan! Winning again!" a young woman called from the crowd. Glancing over, I caught sight of Giselle's copper hair as she squealed with happiness. The victor was her younger brother, the boy who, just a few days ago, had been brought back from the dead with heartflow restoration performed by myself in the palace grounds. It was so relieving to see him well again, and despite our past differences, I couldn't help but cheer along with his sister.

"Bravo!" I clapped my hands together delightedly.

Noticing our cheers, the taller opponent whipped off his mask and huffed as he slapped dust from his tunic. He was red-faced, likely both from the humiliation of losing and the intense exercise. After a few ragged breaths, he glared in my direction, his brow furrowing as he spotted me.

"Well, well," he sneered, loud enough for the rest of the audience to hear, "if it isn't Princess Naria." My name and title slid off his tongue laced with disgust. "Coming to check on your little patient, are we? Why don't you come up here and kiss him again? Certainly got his heart pumping last time."

My jaw tightened as I felt Raena's hand rest on my shoulder. I knew she wanted me to leave it, but I couldn't help myself. Squaring my shoulders, I met his taunt with my own fiery gaze. "You know nothing, sir. I did what I had to do to save a life."

"Absolute Goblinspit!" A collective gasp sounded from

the crowd at his bold retort. "You are a shameless harlot. That boy would've lived whether you slathered yourself onto him or not. Say, if I were the prince I would—"

"That's enough, Lord Webster." Lukas's voice rang out like thunder, silencing the furious oaf. Still masked, he rose from where he was resting on the soft grass. "You will not speak to my fiancée in that way." He then stepped forward, his tone rivalling the dueller's. "And unless you wish to spend a night in the dungeons, see to it that you never use such abhorrent words in reference to any of the good ladies of my court. Do I make myself clear?"

Lord Webster shook with rage, his face turning a ghastly shade of beetroot. The swirling anger within him simmered, and for a moment, it seemed like he might comply with Lukas's demands. But then my stomach flipped as he lunged forward, swinging a wild punch aimed right at the prince's jaw. It landed with a painful crack, sending Lukas stumbling backwards.

Gasps and shouts erupted from the crowd, and suddenly there was a flurry of motion. Lord Webster's face twisted with rage, but before he could strike again, several men leapt up from the grass to force his lumbering body down. Curses and threats spewed from his lips as he was pinned to the stone floor.

With my heart in my throat, I couldn't stand by and watch for a second longer. Rushing forward, I shoved through the panicking crowd and found Lukas. Both anger and surprise clouded his stormy eyes as he held his cheek, breathing heavily.

"Are you alright?" I blurted out. A trickle of blood was

dripping down the hand that covered the side of his jaw. "Please, let me see."

"I'll be fine," he said through gritted teeth, barely even acknowledging me. Twisting his body to face Lord Webster, he snarled, "You, sir, will regret this!"

Above us, thick clouds that I could've sworn weren't there before began to drizzle us in a light rain, while thunder rumbled in the distance. Nobody else seemed to notice it, though, as Lord Webster still writhed with fury against the men who restrained him.

"At least if I am exiled, I won't be ruled by a weak boy king and his harlot bride!" he spat.

Lukas charged towards him, roaring with anger, just as lightning struck nearby, forcing more panic into the already flustered crowd around us.

"Stop!" I cried, lunging forward to throw myself between them. "Stop this, please!"

"Naria, step aside," Lukas growled. "I don't want to hurt you." His burning glare was fixed on the writhing man.

Reaching for his shoulders, I squeezed gently. "Please." I stared up at him, waiting until his thunderous gaze met mine. "Please do not waste another second on this imbecile. He's not worth it." My tone was soothing, or at least as soothing as it could be with the roaring man behind us. My words seemed to help, though. The hurricane of anger that was raging across Lukas's face calmed slightly. Even the rain, which had for a moment turned torrential, slowed too. The Latesummer heat certainly seemed to be wreaking havoc on the weather here.

Glancing back over my shoulder, I addressed the tall

man who had his boot planted down onto Lord Webster's arm. "Do you know where to take him?"

He nodded. "Straight to the dungeons, Your Highness."

"Good." I swallowed, steading my voice. "Take him there now, and if he misbehaves," I cast a heavy look at the pitiful excuse for a man on the floor, "don't be afraid to beat him."

CHAPTER 26

"Hold still." My fingers were gentle as I carefully rubbed a foul-smelling poultice onto Lukas's bruised jawbone.

"You know you don't need to do this," he complained, wrinkling his nose at the smell. "There are plenty of perfectly competent healers in the infirmary."

"Perfectly competent healers that would insist on leeches sucking your blood and rubbing snail guts on your face?"

He shrugged. "At least snail guts would smell more pleasant."

A shy smile tugged at my lips as I continued to rub in the thick paste. It hadn't been easy to convince him to come to my bedchamber, especially after insisting we stop at the kitchens first so I could gather the ingredients I needed for the poultice. He claimed he didn't need any 'Corlixin magic potions' to help him heal. Thankfully, he changed his mind after I reminded him of the bloodsucking alternatives he would find in his own kingdom's infirmary.

"This poultice will help heal you faster and reduce the risk of infection. It's a mixture of crushed garlic and honey, both natural antiseptics." I explained, scooping more of the paste onto my fingers.

"Anti-what?"

"Don't worry." I sniffed with laughter. "Just trust me when I say this will help. Now stop moving."

After a few more grumbles, he finally settled into a more cooperative position as my fingers worked quickly to apply the paste. It was strange being so close to him. Even with the scarlet bruise that was slowly forming at the base of his jaw, I couldn't deny that he was still devastatingly handsome. It would take a thousand bruises to even begin to mar a face like his. But of course, if I were his queen, I'd never let anyone else touch him again.

"All done." I cleared my throat, suddenly desperate to put some distance between us. Just as I started to pull away, his hand reached for mine, and of course, my traitorous heart fluttered at the touch. Bringing my sticky fingers closer, he grabbed a nearby cloth and casually began to wipe the paste off, as if this were a perfectly normal way for a prince to thank a healer.

"I've never known a person of nobility to have any skills other than engaging in court gossip and spending copious amounts of coin." He delicately wiped each of my fingers like a servant would polish a prized cutlery set. "And yet here you are, able to bring people back to life and mix up healing potions in your bedchamber."

"I'm nothing special," I assured him, pulling my hand away to finish cleaning up myself. "You should meet some of the others from my village. They put my medical knowledge to shame."

"You're humble too, I see." He then shot me a glance, leaning back slightly. "And very brave."

I almost choked with laughter. "I am not brave."

"Not many princesses would throw themselves between two angry duellers," he sighed, relaxing further into my bed and spreading his toned arms against the sheets.

Eyes rolling, I retorted, "You'd probably be surprised. I'm sure plenty of women would be happy to throw themselves at you."

That was a mistake.

Propping himself up on his elbows, he asked in a tone that some might almost believe was innocent, "And why would that be?"

"Well..." My cheeks flushed as a wolfish grin appeared on his face. "You know you are a prince after all and—"

"Do you think I'm attractive, fiancée?" Mischief danced in his gaze.

Yes, incredibly so. But I'd rather throw myself out of my tower window than admit that to his frustratingly charming face. So instead, I shrugged, trying my best to ignore the way my heart was racing, and replied in a dry tone, "Looks don't matter to me."

"Oh?" He moved closer. "And what does? Would it impress you if I said I have the biggest sword in the duelling club."

I scoffed in confusion. "Why would that matter?" Maybe

it was a Drothmore thing? As far as I was aware, nobody compared weapon sizes in Corlixir. "Besides, I care about what's up here more." Without missing a beat, I tapped twice against my head. "And as a princess, I care about who can provide the best future for my kingdom."

The amused grin that was covering the prince's face slipped away. "So you're still certain about rebuilding Corlixir?"

Our eyes met, mine turning glossy with desperation. "I can't let my people down, Lukas. As a soon-to-be king, I hoped you would understand that."

Silence hung between us. There was no reason for him to change his mind. Raena was a fool for suggesting that any feelings he had for me might change what he planned for my kingdom, and I was an even bigger fool for holding out any kind of hope that she was right.

But then, something unexpected flashed across his features as he spoke in a light tone. "How about this?"

A breath caught in my throat. Could it be that we weren't so foolish after all?

"I've seen how much you love healing, and the more I hear about how you saved that poor boy's life... Naria, you are spectacular."

My knees began to tremble.

Please, just say it. Say you'll help me.

"So I was thinking, last night..."

Oh Ancients.

"I think I would love for you to have your own hospital, here in Drothmore."

My heart sank like a bucket being dropped in a well.

"It's perfect, don't you think?" he went on with a proud grin. "You can invite all of your friends to work there. I'll happily supply the funding so your scholars can continue the research they never got to finish after the Great Blaze. I'll even let you take time away from your duties here to help out every once in a while. Just think, it'll be the talk of the realm!"

Moments ago, the air was like a summer's day, but in that minute, the air felt more like when you first slip out of bed on a winter's morning. Cold. Stark. Reality.

"Oh, Lukas..." My voice wobbled as a tear rolled down my face. "That's very thoughtful but—"

"What? What is it?" Confusion swirled across his features, and it made my head hurt. How could he not see that this was so far from what I wanted – what I needed – for my people?

"I appreciate the thought, I really do, but the Corlixins in the woods... They don't just want a hospital." I swallowed and steadied my voice. "They want several hospitals, and schools, and libraries, and hundreds of market stalls, where they can buy food and ingredients for medicines. They want streets of houses with bedrooms and kitchens. They want gardens where they can grow their herbs and raise animals. They deserve all of this and more, just like your people do. Don't you see? They don't want to travel to work in a Drothmore hospital, helping Drothmore people only to then go back to a tiny village in the woods. They want their real home. They want Corlixir."

When I was finished, Lukas just stared blankly back at me, blinking several times as if I was speaking another language. After a few painfully long moments, he added, "You know they could live here too? They wouldn't have to walk back to the woods."

"Did you not listen to a word I said?" My voice was deathly low. "This isn't about the woods!"

Lukas rolled his eyes, the motion making me want to slam my fist against the bed sheets. "You're being absurd. I'm making a very generous offer, and you are doing a disservice to your people by not grovelling at my feet."

"Hah!" My head fell back with mocking laughter. "You think you're being generous by offering a mere hospital that I can visit every 'once in a while'? What about when we have children? Are you going to forbid me from going to 'help out' so I can focus only on them? Like a good, obedient queen?"

"You'd do well to remember you are speaking to a future king." Lukas shot me a glare that could melt steel. "As I said before, I'd be happy to let you continue with your hobbies, which is why I suggested we build a hospital. But this whole idea of rebuilding Corlixir is just ridiculous. You cannot expect me to let you spend all your time fighting for a dead kingdom. Drothmore deserves a queen who is willing to give everything to our people."

"Well then, don't let me stop you from finding her." Blonde ringlets swished past his face as I twisted my whole body away from him. I needed something else to focus on. Anything but him. Tears were clawing at the back of my throat and I couldn't bear to let slip any kind of weakness.

His hand reached for my shoulder, but I shrugged him away. "Naria, please... Enough with all this foolish talk."

He sighed as his tone softened slightly. "My father has ordered for us to marry, and therefore we shall. Even if I have to force you down the aisle, you will become my wife, and then Queen."

A laugh caught in my throat. *I'd like to see him try.* With one letter to Honeymeade, I could summon an army of potion-wielding Corlixins with a furious village mother at the helm. Then he'd see what would happen when someone tries to force me to do anything.

"Naria?" he said again.

Turning back slowly, I held my chin high. "Listen to me when I say, if you cannot help me rebuild my kingdom, I will find someone else who can. And if a marriage is required, I will marry him long before you get a chance to try and drag me down any wedding aisles."

"Who? Colyn?" He scowled. "That man is a pig, you wouldn't dare."

I scoffed at his suggestion. "Of course not Colyn, but I will find someone. Perhaps I already have."

The prince's jaw tightened. "Well, you can tell your mysterious saviour that I would love to meet him," he muttered with a glare. "It would be fascinating to hear how he's able to fund the rebuilding of an entire kingdom while also managing the finances of his own. He must be incredibly wealthy."

"Wealthier than you could possibly know," I assured him in a breathy voice.

Unfortunately, he made a fair point, but I didn't dare show it, even as he marched out of the room and slammed the door shut behind him. All that mattered was that the fae might be willing to help. How they would actually do it would be a concern for another day. And with Luminessia falling in two nights' time, that day might come sooner than I expected. After all, just as the Faery King had declared in his throne room, *'a marriage is certainly one kind of alliance'* – and if Prince Arenn could promise a future for Corlixir, then I would marry him in a heartbeat.

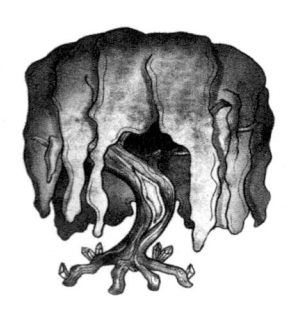

CHAPTER 27

My body felt suspended in ice as I fidgeted with my skirts outside the gates of the faery kingdom. Two days had passed since I last spoke with Lukas – two full days of exchanging silent curses as I'd catch his glare in the hallways, and two very, *very* long evenings of avoiding anywhere his princely presence might be. After our heated conversation in my bedroom, he'd insisted on taking dinner each night in his chambers. That left me to either dine alone in the royal dining hall or do the same in my own tower bedchamber. Thankfully, Raena was quick to offer me company.

After I'd told her about the upcoming faery ball where Arenn would choose his bride, she'd tried everything in her power to change my mind. It was no use, though. Lukas had all but confirmed that he would never help my kingdom, so the fae were my last chance. Still, that did little to calm the unease I felt as I trembled behind the round wooden gates, waiting for Arenn to arrive.

Theo had accompanied me here, just as he did last time. He stood tall beside me, one hand on his sword as he closely monitored the remaining faery guard. Apparently, last time they'd played cards while Arenn and I visited the Crystal Caverns. I recalled him telling me on the journey back that it would've been a fun game, had the two faery guards not taken every opportunity to cheat. When he called them out, they claimed it was 'in their nature'.

I didn't have any more time to consider if I should take that as a warning sign, though, because the wooden gates swung open to reveal a familiar, tall, and darkly handsome figure.

"Good evening, Prince Arenn." I smiled politely, curtsying in greeting.

He grinned and stalked closer. "Good evening, little human." He was dressed more finely than usual – in a blue tunic and breeches set so dark it would match the night sky, while a long black cape with silver flecks hung from his broad shoulders. Even his circlet, which was normally a plain silver band, had been replaced by an ornate flower crown that featured weaving silver vines.

When he was mere inches away, he reached forward to plant a soft kiss on my hand. As his lips touched my skin, it felt as though butterflies had darted out from the vines and fluttered through my body.

"I trust you have come for Luminessia?" he said, rising from the kiss. "My sisters have been pestering me all week, asking about when you would arrive."

"You have sisters?" I asked eagerly before clearing my throat and quickly regaining composure. "And oh, yes, I'm here for Luminessia."

Arenn chuckled. "Such a funny human... But yes, I have sisters. Two, unfortunately. They're twins." His face twisted with annoyance. "I apologise in advance for their behaviour. They're quite... excitable. Especially today. They have requested to help you dress, though, so I'll take you to them now and then we shall meet at the ball."

My head tilted to one side. "Is my gown not acceptable for your party?" Raena and I had worked together to select the most 'fae' gown for the ball. Of course, despite her reservations about Arenn, she couldn't resist giving me fashion advice. After an hour of back-and-forth, we'd decided on a forest green strapless gown. It would've been declared scandalous in the halls of the Steel Palace, but here, where the fae have no issues showing off as much multicoloured skin as they please, it would probably be considered modest.

"No, no, please do not take any offence. You, as always, look divine, Princess." Arenn studied my gown, his gaze lingering a little too long on the low-cut bodice before returning to my face. "But Luminessia is such an extravagant event." His lips pulled into another grin. "And you want to look your best, especially if you'd like to be chosen for a dance."

"What happens if I am chosen for a dance?"

He drew closer, his lips brushing my ear. "Come with me now, let my sisters dress you, and you will find out soon enough."

Our fingers were interlocked as he escorted me through the quartz-walled faery palace. Unlike last time, there were hardly any other faeries wandering the halls. The only sounds I could hear were our footsteps echoing off the white marble flooring and the occasional grunt of greeting from a servant that would scurry by. But despite the lack of fae, the palace seemed more alive than ever. All the colours seemed brighter, and a thick sweetness hung in the air. It fizzled on my tongue every time I opened my mouth to speak, tasting like sugared fruits and sweet berries.

"Everyone is gathered in the ballroom waiting for Luminessia to start," Arenn informed me when I brought up the quietness. Even he seemed affected by the syrupy air. His pale skin glowed under the violet orb lights, and I could feel something powerful thrumming from where his hand held mine.

Eventually, he guided me down a grand corridor, and together we halted before an oddly charming wooden door. Intricate flowers and leaves were carved into the wood, while the handle was sculpted from polished rose quartz.

The prince knocked twice then, with a deep sigh, said, "I do apologise."

"For what?"

But before he could answer, the door flew open. Two young girls with matching auburn waves, identical lavender eyes, and distinctly fae features stared back at me. They blinked for a few moments, seeming to take in every inch of my appearance. Their hungry gazes swallowed my gown, my hair, my face until, in unison, wild grins overwhelmed them and the door slammed shut. I could just about hear the sounds of muffled laughter and squeals as I waited, my chest tight with embarrassment.

"This is where we will part for now," Arenn announced, pulling my attention away from the giggling. "My sisters will take care of you and accompany you to Luminessia."

I folded my arms across my chest. "I'm not sure how mocking me behind closed doors will help me prepare for the ball."

"Do not worry yourself, human," he teased. "My sisters are impulsive, and they can both wield fire. If they didn't like you, you'd be a pile of ashes by now."

"How reassuring?"

"I jest, of course." He drew back with a grin. "But only about the pile of ashes. They do both wield fire, so perhaps don't go pulling out any daggers around them." He winked playfully before stooping into a bow and sauntering down the corridor. "Farewell, dear human. I am so looking forward to our dance tonight."

My focus snapped to the door as it swung open again. The same two girls smiled back at me in an almost feline way. Their synchronised movements were slightly unsettling, but at least now they had stopped giggling.

"Do come in, Princess Naria, our brother has told us so much about you," the one on the left said. Her tone was sweet and lilting.

"Yes, please enter. We have so many questions." The one on the right spoke in a breathier voice, curling her fingers in a come hither motion.

Absolutely no part of me wanted to enter an enclosed space with two seemingly unhinged, fire-wielding faeries. But the alternative was to sprint back through the palace with an imaginary tail between my legs and possibly never know what might've happened if I'd attended Luminessia.

I didn't want to marry Arenn, did I? He was handsome, but there was something dark about the way he looked at me – closer to obsession than love. But if that obsession meant that he would help me with Corlixir, then maybe in time, I would learn to love his roguish ways.

Swallowing down any fear, I smiled. "It's lovely to meet you—" I paused. Of course, I didn't know their names.

"Elsie," the girl on the left chimed, "and my sister here is Elara."

"Enchanting to meet you too, Princess." Elara dipped her head. "Now please, do come in. We have so much to discuss and such little time before Luminessia."

The twins moved aside to allow me to enter, and my trembling feet obeyed – ignoring the pounding in my chest and every warning bell ringing in my mind. The moment I had crossed the threshold, the door creaked ominously shut behind me.

"You can start by stripping off that gown. We have much work to do," Elsie tutted.

Elara echoed her sister's tutting. "Much work indeed."

"When I heard that someone had caught dear Arenn's eye, I almost ignited the banquet hall!" the twin, who was weaving intricate plaits into my hair, babbled excitedly. She was probably Elara, but I'd already been wrong twice. "You know, Papa was beginning to suspect that he was cursed. Twenty years without showing any interest in anyone, man or woman!" She continued twisting the strands of my hair, occasionally threading in a small flower or bud.

I'd been with them for almost an hour, and despite their insistence that they had many questions for me, I'd maybe uttered five words in between their chattering. First, they'd insisted that I bathe. Although it took five minutes of arguing before they decided on which scented lotion to use – nevermind that I detested the scent of jasmine. After that, I was slipped into a silky robe and plopped in front of a wide, willow-framed vanity. The girls then conjured heat from their fingers to dry and style my hair into stunning spirals. Once they were satisfied, one twin remained to braid parts of my hair while the other had spent the past fifteen minutes digging through the wardrobe.

"What do you think, Naria?" The other twin, possibly Elsie, popped out from a rack of dresses. In her hands were two glittering faery gowns. "This one reminds me of lavender, innocent and timid. But this one," her teeth glinted as she grinned, "is like dark amethyst."

"Amethyst, definitely amethyst," Elara answered for me.

"Good choice." She tossed the lavender gown aside and swayed the chosen dress in her arms, swinging it around as though it was a dance partner. "Gosh, Elara, doesn't she look magical?" the girl commented when she caught my gaze in the mirror. "And her human features look so cute! Such precious little round ears and a sweet button nose."

I opened my mouth to remind her that those precious

round ears were perfectly capable of listening, but the other twin chimed out first, "Our nieces and nephews will be so adorable!"

I almost choked.

"Are you alright, Naria?" Elara stopped tugging at my hair for just a moment to lean over my shoulder.

"Oh, she's fine, just nervous probably," Elsie answered for me this time. "Some of our wine will help. We'll get her some when we arrive."

Elara smiled, satisfied with her sister's answer. Her nimble fingers returned to my hair, and for a brief moment, there was peace in the dressing room – until a sudden gasp from Elsie made us both flinch.

"Sister! Haven't you been keeping an eye on the time? We need to leave, now! Luminessia starts in just a few minutes!" She rushed towards us with the amethyst gown, slipping off my robe and helping me into the dress while Elara finished the braids.

"Have you eaten, dear?" the girl working on my hair asked quickly.

I shook my head, but of course before I could answer properly, Elsie took the pleasure instead. "It doesn't matter, our wine is strong. Give her some blushberries."

Elara quickly obeyed, dropping the braid to reach for a small bowl of berries that they'd been feasting on while helping me dress.

"Open wide." She smiled sweetly before shoving a handful of pink berries into my mouth. While they tasted quite pleasant, I wasn't sure I appreciated the forced feeding. "If you feel the wine is making your head spin, you should try to eat something. Otherwise, you'll be too busy dancing around the room naked to try and convince Arenn to choose you."

"Don't give her any ideas! You know how desperate some girls get around our brother."

The pair of them tittered with laughter.

A few minutes later, Elsie was smoothing my gown while Elara applied the finishing touches of a strange pink substance to my lips. There was no denying that the twins were talented. They hadn't changed or glamoured anything, only used pretty fabrics, creamy ointments, and hair twists to enhance what was already there. The backless purple gown clung to my curves in a way that was even more scandalous than the Cedrelei dress I'd worn three nights prior. If Lukas were seeing this, he'd probably throw a fit and then demand I marry him immediately.

Not that it mattered what he thought.

Of course.

"Remember, don't drink too much wine." One of them waggled her slender finger at me, hauling me out from my daydream.

"And don't go skulking off with another faery and breaking our dear brother's heart!" the other one huffed. I wasn't given a chance to reply as more pink paste was smeared onto my lips.

Then finally, after smoothing out my skirts for the fifth time and triple-checking that there wasn't a single blonde curl out of place, the girls both grinned at each other as they sang in unison, "She's ready!"

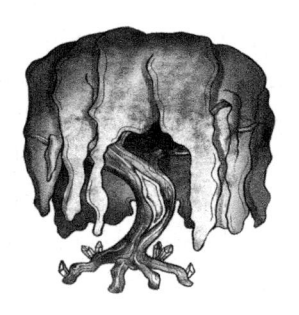

CHAPTER 28

While the magic in the palace halls might've been thick enough to taste, it was there – at Luminessia – that enchantment seemed to touch everything. Everything from the gilded tables loaded with glistening, steaming food, to the hundreds of faeries that socialised around us, their unusually coloured hair and skin shimmering in the light. Even the servants were well-dressed for the occasion, wearing ruffled shirts and velvet waistcoats.

There were no windows in the ballroom, but it didn't seem to matter as the dark-walled chamber was spectacularly lit up by thousands of glowing faery lights. They floated around the ceiling as though they were fireflies, casting shadows against the black, glittering floor. Glancing down, it was like floating over the night sky as my feet padded against it.

"This way, Princess." The twins led the way in their matching ruby gowns. There was no music playing yet; the only sounds being the excited whispers from the surrounding fae.

"Any minute now Arenn will make his appearance, then the fun begins!" Elsie shot me a grin. Thankfully, before we'd left, the girls had fussed with their own outfits, taking a full minute to decide who would get to wear their mother's emerald necklace. Eventually, Elara had emerged victorious, and Elsie settled for a sapphire choker. I was just grateful for a way to tell them apart.

The twins ushered me towards a quieter area on the dancefloor, with a good view of an empty balcony near the back of the ballroom. They babbled eagerly, but I was too focused on the faery lights that were now a little too bright and the sheer amount of fae bustling in the hall.

I was really going to need some of that faery wine soon.

"Dearest guests!" a booming voice bellowed from the balcony.

My head snapped up. Dressed in a black, gold-embroidered overcoat was King Bevan. He peered down upon us from his position on the balcony, leaning over the railing. An extravagant flower crown sat proudly on his greying hair, while golden jewellery set with gemstones as big as my fists adorned the rest of his body.

"I stand before you here tonight to announce the beginnings of Luminessia, the highly anticipated celebration where my dear son, Prince Arenn, will choose his bride."

His speech continued, but it didn't take long before my attention was snatched away by someone making loud gobbling sounds nearby. Elsie had pinched a bowl of candied fruits from the buffet and was wolfing each one down, ignoring the glares from the surrounding fae and the burning disdain from her sister.

As I watched her, a sniffle of laughter breached my throat. Her distraction was a welcome one.

"Soon, we will invite all eligible ladies to the dance floor." My hearing shifted back to the King, who was gesturing broadly at the floor below him. "But first, please welcome my beloved son, and the reason for our celebration tonight, Prince Arenn."

Starlight cape billowing behind him, the prince marched out from behind his father. As he reached the balcony, a roar of intense claps and cheers erupted over the ballroom. Even Elsie paused her chomping for a brief moment to whoop in her brother's direction. Lifting a hand, the prince waved to the crowds, and as he flashed a dazzling smile, I could've sworn a faery girl fainted nearby. It was difficult, but I resisted the urge to check on her. Nobody can die from swooning, right?

"Cherished citizens," Arenn announced, his velvety voice silencing the crowd. "I am so honoured that you have all gathered here today to celebrate my enchanting night. For so many years, I have dreamt of what this evening would bring, and now as I look out upon a sea of captivating faces, I cannot wait to finally meet my bride."

Thunderous applause rippled through the fae, and a few brave young ladies squealed with excitement, jumping and flailing their arms, desperate for even a trickle of attention. The adoration seemed to make the prince's skin glow as he basked in their awe.

"Now please, enjoy the festivities, and may you all be blessed with true love tonight." Arenn ended his speech with a bold flourish as rose petals began to rain down from the ceiling. The audience went wild trying to catch them, each wanting to touch a little piece of him, even if it was a mere conjured rose petal.

But the second he'd disappeared from the balcony, my focus wasn't on the falling roses. Instead, I searched around for the one thing I needed most.

Wine.

The growing excitement in the room had done nothing to slow the anxiety that was now in full bloom in my chest. Everything around me felt like it was racing. I needed something to dull my senses. So, when a servant pushed by with a tray of crystal goblets, I snatched one and immediately swept it up to my lips. Whatever warnings the twins had given me were long forgotten by the time the sweet liquid pooled in my throat. It was so delicious, I couldn't stop tipping the goblet more and more. The taste reminded me of sugary fruits...

Fresh plums.

Honey syrup.

Sweet—oh. It was all gone.

As I dragged the goblet slowly away from my lips, any nearby fae swirled into a mishmash of brilliant colours. Breathing in deep, my body began to twirl in place. I didn't know at what point the faery music started, but by the time it did, I was already dancing. Before I knew it, two other faeries took my hands, or maybe I took theirs – who knows? The memory was foggy. Either way, I was swept into a vast, endlessly spinning dance circle. Uncontrollable giggles bounced off my chest as we danced and danced and danced, only stopping when a pair of strong, familiar hands found my waist and rudely plucked me out from the circle.

"You've had some wine, little human," a male voice tutted as I spun around to face him.

Before me stood a tall, devastatingly handsome faery. But not just any faery – a prince. The same prince I'd kissed in the Crystal Caverns less than a week ago. As the wine swirled my thoughts, all I could think about was the way his mouth had explored mine, and how I desperately wanted him to do it again – right here in the middle of this ballroom.

"I've done nothing wrong!" I teased back with a pout. "I was just innocently enjoying myself, dancing with my new friends."

"Your new friends?" He tilted his head, replying in an amused tone. "I'll have to remind my sisters to keep a closer eye on you."

"I'm having fun!"

"I'm not denying that," he chuckled. My breath stilled as his hands trailed down from my exposed shoulders to my fingertips. Once he reached them, he interlocked my fingers in his and tugged me towards his chest. "But the wine is blinding you, sweet princess. You don't see what I see."

"And what is that?"

His lips brushed my ear, voice dropping to a low whisper. "Every faery's eyes on you."

Before I could protest, he lifted a slender finger to my chin and tilted it slowly to the side. In a wine-soaked blend of colours, I could just about make out the hazy figures of several faeries. I couldn't tell if he was right – if they were even watching me – but either way, I could feel stares burning into my neck.

"Shall we give them a show?" His voice vibrated in my ear, sending a shiver down my spine. Then, his lips were on mine again, but only for a short beautiful moment before they pulled away. The hand that was by my chin dropped to my waist while the other lifted my unsuspecting arm as I was whisked into a slow waltz.

Like two swans on a misty lake, we glided around the dance floor. With every minute Arenn held me in his arms, more space cleared for us. And the moment my gaze flicked from him to the hundreds of fae now in awe of our dance, his velvety voice lured me back.

"Dance for them, Princess. But keep your eyes on me. Only me." Then, he lifted me high into the air, my skirts flowing in a wide spectacular circle around us. Gasps echoed from the surrounding crowd, and once again, Arenn seemed to bask in their adoration as he flashed our audience a glowing smile. This was supposed to be a special moment, just for the two of us, so why did I feel like I was merely a prop while he played the starring role?

When he finally lowered my body, he tucked me close to his chest as we continued waltzing. I couldn't deny that he was an excellent dancer. And with his effortless way of speaking and charming faery features, it was no wonder that he was so popular here. Still, even with our limbs entangled in this way, I couldn't shake the gnawing feeling that something wasn't right. Our bodies fit together so perfectly, but did our minds? He was handsome, but what else?

I needed more.

"So, Prince Arenn," I began, trying my hardest to keep the wine from slurring my words.

He tilted his chin down to smile upon me. "Yes, little human?"

"I've been thinking—"

"Beware of thinking too deeply. Sometimes simple thoughts develop into dangerous ideas," he warned, patting my waist with his fingers before returning his gaze to the audience.

My eyes narrowed, but ignoring his dismissal, I pressed on anyway, "I was going to ask..." His attention snapped back to me. "What do faery children study at school?"

A silky laugh caught in his throat. "Are my dancing skills so bad that you would rather speak of my education?" He lifted my arm to twirl me in place.

"Not at all," I answered when I flew back to his chest. "I just want to learn more about you."

"Curious human."

A few moments passed before I realised that he had absolutely no intention of answering my question. So, with a huff, I tried again, "How about this? What's your favourite thing to do? You know, when you're not being a prince?"

Give me something. I need something more than just this fiery attraction between us.

Sighing defeatedly, he drawled, "I have a garden. I like to visit and tend to the flowers sometimes. Perhaps I'll show it to you if you stop with the relentless questions."

"I only asked you two!"

Something devious flickered across his face as he paused our dance. "You know I can use magic to silence you?"

An odd tingle settled upon my lips, making my tongue feel tired and heavy. But thankfully, the feeling vanished just as quickly as it appeared as a loud shriek pierced through the ballroom. The sound cast a heavy silence over the entire dance floor.

"Oh, Elsie, stop this at once!" I heard Elara's familiar chime following the scream. "You're being disgusting, spit it out!" Despite her lilting voice, she sounded furious.

Whipping my head towards the source, I noticed the two auburn-haired girls bickering near a buffet table. Arenn groaned as he spotted them too, signalling the musicians to resume their song with a frustrated flick of his wrist.

"Ignore my sisters," he muttered while holding me close. "They've always been overly fond of the dramatics."

Letting out a relieved sigh, I went to pull my gaze away from the pair, but then I noticed something that made me freeze. Elsie was gripping her throat, stooping over the buffet table in an awkward, unnatural way. Eyes wide as the moon, she panicked and flapped her hands as if she wanted to speak, but no words would come out. It was only when I caught her fingers shifting to a deathly shade of blue that a fire lit within me as I pieced together just what was happening to her.

"She's choking," I gasped, using both hands to shove myself away from the prince. Arenn barely had a chance to understand what I'd said before I sprung into action, rushing over to the panicking girl. Even Elara looked like she might faint as I shared her sister's condition and urged her to step aside, but I ignored her sudden paling. She was not my patient right now.

Aiming the heel of my palm between Elsie's shaking shoulder blades, I tried desperately to recall my lessons.

In my head, my teacher's voice rang out loud and clear: *'While supporting the body, deliver five sharp blows to the upper back.'*

Sending a silent prayer to the Ancients that I was remembering correctly, I swung down my hand, hard and fast.

WHACK

WHACK

WHACK

WHACK

WHACK

Five sharp blows were delivered to the back, but Elsie continued clutching at her throat, turning an even more alarming shade of teal.

"Come on, Elsie, work with me. Cough it out!" I ordered, but it was no use. My arm strained as her body grew heavier beneath me, and her knees began to buckle. If I didn't help her soon, this ball would take an incredibly dark turn.

'If back blows fail to clear the obstruction, give the patient five abdominal thrusts.'

"Please let this work," I whispered, positioning myself behind her and wrapping my arms tightly around her waist. Placing my fist just above her navel, I took a deep breath. Then, using all my force, I thrusted my fist upwards five times. Each time, I moved with a more intense, more fierce determination.

"Come on, Elsie!" I begged.

Finally, with one last desperate thrust, a soaking wet candied plum flew across the ballroom. A collective gasp echoed from the faeries who'd gathered around us, and as Elsie erupted into a fit of coughs and wheezes, relief washed over me like a sudden, cleansing rain.

"Dearest sister!" Elara sobbed, swooping in to hug her twin the second I stepped back. "Oh, you foolish, stupid, greedy thing! You could have died!" A sharp crack sounded as she slapped her sister clean across the cheek, then shook her furiously.

Definitely unhinged.

"I could've lost you... over a plum!" she cried. "Never do that to me again!" The fury turned to tears as she sobbed again, this time embracing her sister in a tight hug.

There was a brief quiet as they held each other, until a few faeries who had witnessed the whole ordeal began to clap. Those few claps quickly morphed into cheers, and soon enough, there was a thunderous applause that echoed through the entire ballroom.

Twisting away from the girls, my gaze was filled with wide-eyed fae, all clapping and cheering wildly. A few even had thankful tears, which they quickly swiped away before continuing their raucous applause. Their reaction seemed extreme, but I supposed it made sense. I had just saved their Princess.

At the forefront of the applause, Prince Arenn clapped his hands along with the rest of the fae, his starlight cape still draped from his broad shoulders. His amber eyes were glossy with shock and something else...

Whatever it was, it faded in moments as held up his

hand high in the air, signalling for the applause to stop. "To all the fae who have gathered here tonight, I would like to make an announcement."

Silence drowned out their cheers. Even Elara ceased her sobbing to stare expectantly at her brother.

"Princess Naria." He stepped forward, his entire body focused on me as if I was a single glowing light in a room filled with never-ending darkness. "Ever since I first laid my eyes upon you, strange as the circumstances may have been, I've known that you would be someone special. A gift sent straight from the Spirits, right into my waiting arms. There has never been anyone more beautiful, more kind, more noble, and now that I have just witnessed you save my dear sister's life," he paused, looking long and hard at Elsie then back to me, "there has never been anyone more perfect to be my bride."

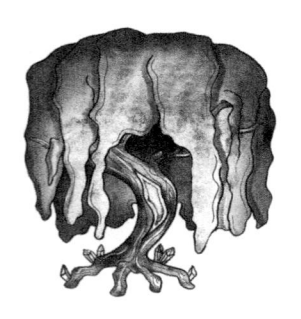

CHAPTER 29

Staggered gasps sounded like crashing waves from around the crowd. Everyone in the room was staring at me, waiting patiently for my reaction. Of course, I wanted to react, but I didn't know what to say. I couldn't move, completely frozen in a cold mixture of fear and surprise.

"Please, sweet Naria." The prince drew closer before dropping to his knees. Desperation ravaged his sharp features. "Ever since we shared our first kiss, I have been consumed by thoughts of you," he continued. "You have invaded my very soul! Anything you want, I will provide for you. If you want a kingdom, I will build it for you. Together, we can restore what your parents lost."

A knot formed in my throat. This was what I'd always wanted. I should've jumped in excitement and screamed immediately 'yes'! Corlixir had the chance to rise again, and I had someone who cared about me, even if he had an overly bold way of showing it. But standing there, in the middle of Luminessia, even as a handsome prince knelt before me offering the very thing I needed, for some strange reason, everything within me was screaming 'no'.

In a dramatic sweeping motion, he extended his pale hand up to me. "Dear Naria, please take my hand. Accept my proposal, and together we can rule both the fae and Corlixir. To say no would be to deny your people a kingdom and to break my heart into a thousand pieces. So please, I beg you, Naria, take my hand."

Did I even have a choice? As Princess, I needed to do what was best for my people, and surely, this was it. My parents trusted the fae, so I should too.

I should say yes. I needed to say yes. I...

"Yes."

Time stopped. *What have I done?*

The moment my hand slipped into his, blinding light flooded the room and I yelped. Searing pain burned down my arm like a raging fire. I tried desperately to pull away, but the prince's grip held me firmly in place.

"Accept the bond, Naria!" I heard Arenn hiss through the chaos. "It will sting for a moment, but then I'll be forever yours, and you, forever mine."

Whatever twisted magic this was, there was no escaping it now. I writhed in pain until, after a few more dreadful seconds, the intense light faded, and slowly, I blinked my eyes open. Embedded into the skin of my forearm, as if they'd always been there, were two glowing crystals, each one smaller than a penny. A quick glance at Arenn's wrist showed he had a matching pair burnt into his arm, just like mine.

"A faery tradition," he noted with a wink, "to mark the proposal."

Then, snatching up my hand, he raised our markings high to the wide circle of fae that had gathered around us. "To my new bride!" he announced, beaming wider than I'd ever seen before. The ballroom erupted into cheers and cries.

"To the happy couple!" a familiar male voice boomed from the balcony. Up above, the Faery King smiled and tipped his goblet in our direction.

"To a successful Luminessia!" Queen Amabel called out from beside him, tipping her goblet too. Just like her husband, she was dressed lavishly and practically dripping with jewels. "And to our dear Naria, may this union bring you the peace that your kingdom deserves."

After lowering our arms, Arenn squeezed me so tightly against his side that it almost hurt. For a moment, I wanted to push him away, and I almost did, but then I stopped myself. What would my parents say if they knew I was being so ridiculously ungrateful? This man, this *prince*, holding me so closely was not only terribly handsome, but he was also young and perfectly willing to help my people. This was everything I should have wanted – everything any princess who grew up in a tiny forest village could ever wish for.

So why was there such an awful sinking feeling in my chest?

"And now," Arenn continued, addressing the crowd with a wild grin, "it is time for me to present a gift to my new bride!" He tossed me a quick glance. "I think you'll like this one, human."

Judging by the sinister glint in his eyes, I doubted that very much.

"Guards!" he barked, making me flinch. Nearby, I heard the sounds of armour clinking as a few well-dressed soldiers straightened to attention. "Please deliver my betrothed's gift, as we discussed."

The surrounding fae cleared a path for the marching guards, and a new dark excitement buzzed through the ballroom. The excitement spread to Arenn's lips as he grinned gleefully.

It wasn't long before the two guards returned, each dragging the limp arms of a thin, green-skinned faery. His face was hidden by a scruffy brown sack, but I could still hear his pained moans as he was hauled across the floor. Once they were less than a few metres away, they tossed the prisoner roughly to the ground and snatched the bag away from his head. My mouth fell open the moment his terrified emerald irises met mine.

"Valen," I snarled, rage curling at the back of my throat. Visions of Raena's terrified face flooded my mind.

Arenn chuckled. "A joyous reunion!" He then leaned in close until his lips tickled my ear – the feeling sending a surprisingly warm shiver down my spine. "Remember when you asked to see more of my magic? Enjoy the show, little human." He pulled away with a smirk.

I barely had a chance to process what he'd said before he lifted his arms and a deafeningly loud crack echoed over the ballroom. Instantly, my hands flew to my ears, and I stumbled back. Several colossal black vines burst from the floor, shooting high up to the ceiling – the sheer sight of them sending our audience into an excited frenzy.

Gasping, I watched in horror as one of the vines coiled tightly around Valen's leg and whipped him fifty feet into the air. With a painful crunch, he crashed against the shimmering ceiling before plunging back to the ground in a blur of screaming green. Just as he was inches away from colliding with the floor, another vine gripped his foot and tossed him back up into the air, only for him to crash painfully against the ceiling once again.

On and on, this tortuous game continued, his screams turning less faery and more animalistic with every throw. A painful crunch, then an awful scream followed by another, and then another. The noise sent my heart plummeting into my chest. I knew I had said I wanted for the guard to be punished, but this wasn't punishment. This was torture – evil, humiliating torture. And it terrified me to see Arenn's eyes glistening hungrily with every horrifying crunch of Valen's broken bones.

"Stop," I whimpered, my chest heaving in fear. "This isn't right!"

"Such compassion," Arenn murmured. "But what kind of prince would I be if I stole the show away from my adoring fans now?" He swept his hand over the buzzing crowd. To my dismay, there were no fearful looks from any of the fae. All their attention was fixed hungrily on the flailing faery as if he was just another part of the night's entertainment. The sight made my stomach churn. Suddenly, I felt a lot less like a princess in a glittering faery ball and more like a tiny mouse surrounded by hundreds of cats – horrible, sharp-toothed faery cats who hadn't eaten in days.

"What do you think, Princess?" Arenn tossed me an excited grin, clearly oblivious to the intense pounding fear in my chest. "Shall I kill him now?" With a flick of his wrist, each vine sprouted an uncountable number of dagger-sized thorns. I winced as one of the deadly vines caught Valen mid-fall, piercing his skin as a blood curdling scream filled the ballroom. "His death is at your command, sweet human. Say the word, and I will end his pathetic life."

I whimpered again just as another thorny vine coiled round his arm, slicing his skin. His blood fell like crimson rain onto the sparkling floor below.

I screwed my eyes shut, desperate to clear my head of the tortuous scene before me.

"Please," I begged, "punish him, but not like this."

A cruel laugh sounded from the prince's lips. "Sweet, innocent, Naria," he mused. "Your merciful nature is charming. Unfortunately, I must give my people what they want. I'm sure, as a princess, you understand."

No...

Then there was a nightmarish crunch, followed by an awful squelch and raucous cheers. Around us, the faeries erupted into an endless wild applause.

My breath stilled as my eyes refused to open. Everything was moving far too fast. I tried desperately to clear my mind, to steady my breathing, but all I could hear were his screams and that same squelch over and over again, as if my mind were caught in a whirlwind.

When I felt Arenn's hand rest on my shoulder, dread slowly crept in with the fear. If Arenn and I were to marry, not only would Corlixir rise again, but he would be *King*.

And I would be unleashing a monster on my people.

I'd seen just how violent his power could be and how he relished every second of pain he inflicted on that faery. Of course, Valen was not exactly innocent, but that didn't change how Arenn toyed with him so cruelly and without a moment's hesitation. Seraphina was wrong. Faeries *were* monsters, and like a fool, I'd just agreed to marry one. It was one thing to refuse a proposal arranged by the very human King Ikelos, but could I break a proposal bound by the magic crystals now embedded into my arm? If the pain was intense from the bond being forged, what would it be like if it were broken?

My breath was racing faster than my thoughts when suddenly everything felt incredibly heavy. My eyelids dropped. Then my knees buckled. Arenn only just about managed to catch me before everything faded to night.

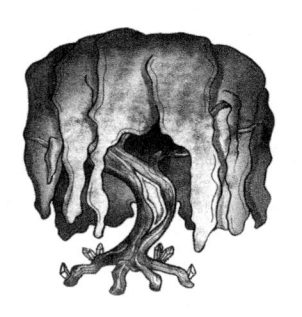

CHAPTER 30

It hadn't been easy to get away from there. After I'd collapsed, Luminessia erupted into a frenzy of panic. Everyone was concerned for the safety of the crown prince's new bride, and although I'd been unconscious for mere seconds, Arenn had insisted on personally escorting me to the infirmary. Thankfully, this turned out to be a blessing in disguise as the second I was left alone, I darted out of the unguarded entrance and barreled out of the palace.

I needed time to think. I needed time away from all of this. Besides, surely Raena would know what to do. Together, we'd fix this.

Surely.

Loyal Theo was exactly where I'd left him, standing outside the entrance gates to the faery kingdom. Concern flashed across his features as he noticed me approaching, though his reaction was hardly surprising. After running all the way from the palace, my breathing was ragged and my pink cheeks dripped with sweat.

"Princess?" he muttered. "What happened to you?"

I was in no mood for stories.

"Please take me home, Theo. I want to go now." Desperate tears were blurring my vision, but I swiped them aside.

"Of course." He nodded. Theo wasn't nosy. Or at least he knew when to not ask questions. Either way, thanks to his calm demeanour, I was able to hold it together as he led the way back to the spiral staircase, with me stumbling closely behind.

Outside, the cool air hit me like a calming wave, along with a welcome sprinkling of light rain. There hadn't been a cloud in the sky when we'd left, but after such a long night, I didn't mind the drizzle. Tipping my head back, I closed my eyes and let the rain rinse the sweat from my face. Perhaps if I stood there long enough, it might wash away all the mistakes of the evening too, although I doubted the crystals embedded in my arm could be flushed out with a few drops of rainwater.

Beside me, Theo stiffened as he cursed something obscene under his breath. I'll admit the chosen curse was a bit of an overreaction to the change in weather, but I assumed he just didn't like getting wet.

It was only when he hissed my name in a panicked tone that I tilted my chin down and blinked the rain from my eyes. Then, the curse that flew from my lips was equally obscene.

"Prince Lukas and Lady Raena," Theo said, bowing deeply. Suddenly, running back to my wicked faery prince didn't seem like such a bad idea.

Just beyond the forest clearing, leaning against a tree with his arms folded, was my *beloved* fiancé. A thick cloak of green covered his shoulders, while his dark wavy hair stuck to his face, dripping with rainwater. He was completely soaked, but I doubted that was the reason for his stormy expression. Beside him, Raena trembled as she sniffled into her sleeve. When she noticed us approaching, her body shook with violent sobs.

"I'm so sorry, Naria!" she squeaked. "I tried to hide! When I heard he was searching for us, I hid in the library. But then he found me, and I couldn't lie to him. He's the Crown Prince! I'm so sorry! If you never forgive me, I'll understand, please I—" Choking sobs overcame her and she fell to her knees.

My heart crumbled, and I almost sank with her. This was all my fault.

"Oh Raena." I rushed over, throwing myself down to where she'd fallen. "Please don't cry, you've done nothing wrong. This was all me!" I cupped her cheek, wiping away some of the wet mud that had dirtied her face. "It's me who should be asking for your forgiveness. I never should've brought you into all this madness. If either you or Theo get punished because of me, I'll—"

"Enough with this pitiful behaviour. No one is being punished." Lukas's cold voice sliced between us. He was so silent, I'd almost forgotten he was there. "Now get up, both of you."

Hesitantly, Raena rose from the ground, and I soon followed. The mud had stained her skirts in a filthy brown hue, but for once, the dirt didn't seem to bother her.

"Theo, escort Lady Raena back to the palace," Lukas ordered with a scowl, "and see to it that she gets a bath. We've been waiting here a while, and I'd rather not be responsible for someone catching their death."

"Of course, Your Highness." Theo didn't spare a moment before whisking Raena away. She tried to protest at first, but one stern look from Lukas sent her scurrying off to the horses.

Soon enough, the sound of galloping hooves faded into the distance, leaving just the furious prince and me alone amongst the trees. Though 'furious' wouldn't even begin to describe the hurricane of anger sweeping across his face.

"I cannot believe what you've done." He spoke first, each word thick with disdain. "Do you even understand the consequences of your actions? You have deliberately defied the orders of your king. You—"

"Your father is not my king," I spat, already tired of this conversation. "I am the Princess of Corlixir, I answer only to myself."

"You are a guest of his palace. You owe him," he seethed as thunder rumbled in the distance. "He built the damned village your people live in! And now you conspire with his enemies – the fae. Of all the beasts in this world, Naria... Why them?"

"You left me with no choice."

"You cannot blame this on me!"

"Can't I?" The clouds above us darkened as rain began

pouring down in buckets, soaking me to the bone. "If you'd just agreed that you'd help me with my kingdom, then I never would've come here. My people need a home, a permanent one! They can't live in the woods forever, relying on food deliveries sent by Drothmore. What about when your father dies, hmm? Will that food stop? Will they starve because you do not care for them? I won't let that happen. Ever. So yes, I visited the fae. Only to try and strike up some kind of alliance between us. And when they offered to help, you cannot blame me for accepting it."

"You are a fool to trust them."

"Maybe." I shrugged. "But I've heard the stories. I know that my parents were once allied with them. Am I really a fool for wanting to rebuild that connection?"

Lukas shook his head. "You really don't know, do you?" The rain had lightened slightly, so I could just about make out his perplexed features. "I can't believe my father never told you."

"What are you talking about?" I huffed.

The prince paused for a moment, then took a deep breath. "Naria, you know that the fae..." His jaw tensed. "They were the reason for the Great Blaze. My father never hid the truth from me. It wasn't an accident. It was them. They started the fire."

The rain had stopped, but it was as though my ears were still full of water.

"What?" I could barely hear myself over the pounding of my heart.

"You heard me," he snapped back. "It was the fae. I don't know why they did it, only they know that. But I do know that they are the reason your parents are dead. So please, listen to me when I say you cannot trust them to help you."

"No... You're wrong..." Desperate confusion poured over my soaked face. "That doesn't make any sense. You're lying to me!"

"I'm not! I'll swear to you, I swear on the Forges that I'm telling the truth," Lukas insisted. "The faeries are liars; they always have been. Why do you think they're stuck out here, forced to live underground, away from everyone else? After the Great Blaze, the rulers effectively banished them from the human kingdoms. The only reason this was all kept quiet from the people was because otherwise there would be a war. But that fire..." He blinked, straightening his shoulders. "I don't know what the faeries have told you, but it was no accident. The fae killed your parents, Naria. Your kingdom is dead because of them, and now you run straight into their prison expecting them to help you?" He shook his head, laughing cruelly while my stomach sank to the forest floor.

His words seemed so sincere, but he had to be wrong. This couldn't be true. Why would the fae be so willing to help my cause if they are the reason my kingdom doesn't exist? Why would Arenn propose? A pounding headache threatened to overwhelm me as I tried to understand any of this at all.

"Listen to me, Naria. Come back to the palace, and I'll take you to my father. I'm sure he'll tell you himself. He can give you more information than he gave me." He stepped closer, his hands squeezing my shoulders. "Just please, promise me that you won't go back to the fae. They're dangerous and you can't trust them." His voice wavered. "Please... please promise me that you won't visit them again."

Something lodged in my throat as his gaze searched mine. My thoughts were a swirling mess, but for some reason, when he looked at me like that, I had the strangest feeling that everything would be okay.

"I—" My breath caught. A sudden rustling stole my attention. "Wait... Did you hear that?"

Lukas tilted his head. "What?"

The rustling sounded again. This time it sounded like small footsteps, and they were closer. Much closer.

"That!" I hissed. Something – or someone – was definitely out there.

"I hear it too," he whispered. Slowly, he lowered his hand to the sword sheathed at his belt. "Get behind me."

In one smooth movement, Lukas spun away, tucking me safely behind his tall frame as he drew his sword. Now that the clouds had cleared, the metal blade glinted in the moonlight as he turned it naturally in his hands.

"I know you're there!" he called out in a strong voice. "Come out now, and I give you my word that I won't harm you."

The footsteps quickened, drawing closer every second until suddenly, they stopped. All I could hear was our combined heavy breathing and the faint whisper of the wind in the trees. Except, when the whisper morphed into a cackle, I realised it wasn't the wind at all.

Just then, a tiny figure darted out from the bushes and raced towards us. Its quick pace was a blur of movement, almost graceful, until it tripped on a twig and landed face-down in the dirt.

At first, I thought it might've been a child – a very peculiar green-skinned child. But when it scrambled to its feet and snarled, revealing a row of pointed yellow teeth, instead of feeling scared, I found myself gasping in bewilderment. Old rags covered the strange creature's body, and although its petite arms seemed to be packed with muscle, the fact that he was barely two feet tall made it difficult to feel intimidated.

"What is a goblin doing this far from the mountains?" Lukas wondered out loud.

"That's a goblin?" I'd never seen one before, only ever heard about them in history lessons.

The creature snarled again. "Ekka woo naga, o'oman!" In his hand, he held a sharpened stick and waved it around menacingly, as though warning us back.

"Woah there, calm down." Lukas lowered his sword and raised his free hand. "It's alright. We won't hurt you."

"Is it dangerous?" My fingers tightened around his sleeve.

Lukas shook his head with a soft chuckle. "Look at him. Even if I didn't have a sword, he'd be no threat."

Letting out a sigh of relief, I peered down at the snarling goblin from behind Lukas's arm. He was right. This creature was no threat. A swift kick would send him flying into the trees.

Not that I would condone that sort of behaviour. He was harmless, after all.

"Let's go home," Lukas said, sheathing his sword. But the moment he did, more rustling sounded from the trees. Then, a dozen more footsteps followed by at least twenty cackles. Before we knew it, strange green creatures were popping out from every bush and swinging down from the tree branches above us.

"Stay behind me!" Lukas growled, holding me back. Whipping my head around, there were green-skinned creatures everywhere I looked. One goblin might be harmless, but what about thirty?

"Still no threat? Wumbah o'oman!" A goblin to our left howled, shaking his staff high in the air. The rest of the mob erupted into roaring cheers of stamping feet and high-pitched screeches.

As their cheering settled, the original goblin prowled closer, jabbing his stick towards us. "You come with us!"

"We're not going anywhere with you," Lukas snapped, keeping me tucked behind him.

"Wumbah o'oman," the original goblin snarled. "You no come with us, we use grobba-bacci!" At those words, the mob turned into a wild frenzy.

I screamed as a goblin leapt onto me, his tiny claws piercing my skin as he scampered up my body. When I shoved him off, another two jumped onto my shoulders, yanking my hair. Even Lukas was struggling as I noticed five goblins clambering up his cloak.

I yelped again when a goblin with a particularly crooked nose jumped up to my face, gripping me by my hair. I tried to swat him off, but two other goblins were swinging from my arms. All I could do was watch as the crooked-nosed beast scooped some grey powder from a pouch, then brought his hand to his face. With a vicious smile, he blew. Hard. A thick puff of grey powder hit my cheeks as my chest broke into a coughing fit. When I could finally breathe, my eyes fluttered open. But for some reason, all I could see were stars and the goblin at my face seeming to shrink further and further away.

"Night night, o'oman," he cackled.

And then, there was nothing.

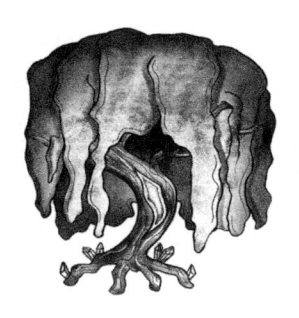

CHAPTER 31

There was nothing for what felt like decades.

Until, suddenly, there was something. A voice. Calling my name, or at least I thought it was my name. "Naria!" He called it over and over again. It was a nice voice, a deep voice, a prince's voice.

Lukas's voice.

Gasping, my eyes shot open and I immediately retched, still tasting the foul grey powder on my tongue. Harsh reality slapped me across the face as I doubled over, except my body didn't move. Something tight around my chest held me in place.

As my vision cleared, I noticed a wetness under my backside. I was sitting on the soggy forest floor, and unfortunately, we were still encircled by bloodthirsty goblins. Although this time, we were also surrounded by lopsided tents and poorly-made campfires that crackled in the cool night air. In the centre of the forest clearing was a large cauldron set over a fire. Three goblins worked together, stirring whatever festered in the pot with a large wooden spoon.

I hoped the strange substance bubbling away inside wasn't for us. It smelled foul.

Glancing down, I took note of at least a dozen muddy ropes wrapped around my arms and chest. With my upper body bound against a large tree, and the intense pounding in my head, it appeared I wouldn't be heading back to the Steel Palace anytime soon.

"Are you alright?"

I whipped my head towards the voice to see Lukas sitting beside me, bound just as tightly to the same tree. Apart from a few light scrapes on his face, he looked fine. *Thank the Ancients*.

"I'm okay," I croaked. Leaning forward, I tried to wriggle out of the ropes.

"It's no use," he huffed. "I've been trying for the past ten minutes. They've tied these ropes so tight; the only way out is if they cut us free."

A gulp bobbed in my throat.

"You've really gone and done it now," he grumbled.

"What?"

"This is your fault, you know. None of this would've happened if you hadn't been sneaking around with the fae."

My mouth fell open. He couldn't be serious. "Well, if you hadn't insisted on having our conversation in the middle of the woods, then the goblins never would've found us. I just wanted to go home. I could be in bed right now, but instead, I'm here – probably about to get murdered by one of those little beasts."

Lukas snorted, but then a half-smile tugged at his lips.

"What?" I growled.

"You called the Steel Palace home," he remarked, glowing as if he'd just had a moment of revelation.

I scoffed. Did I really call it that? My tower definitely now felt more comfortable than my single bed in the shared girls' dorm ever did. But still, Corlixir was my home. Or at least it will be when it's rebuilt. Someday.

"So?" I scowled at him. There was no need to get caught up in these pointless details. "I live there, don't I?"

"You do," he mused playfully. "But I like to think that by saying things like that, you're adjusting to the idea of becoming my wife. Drothmore would be your home for sure when you are Queen."

His words were so absurd, I almost choked. Shaking my head so hard it hurt, I replied in a cutting tone, "May I just remind you of our current situation? Whether you think I am 'adjusting' to that idea or not, which I absolutely am not, you seem to be forgetting that we are tied up in the middle of a goblin camp – with no way of escaping! We'll probably both die here, and all you want to do is play the blame game and make up stupid points that suggest I would ever want to marry you."

"Relax, fiancée, I know what goblins are like." He tipped his head back so it rested against the tree bark. "I know they'll do anything for gold. They won't harm us once they realise my father is the richest man in the realm."

Despite how much I hated it when he was right, I prayed that this time he was. After an already disastrous day, getting murdered by a mob of deranged creatures was the last thing I needed.

"It's odd though," he said in a relaxed voice. "I've never known goblins to be this far from the mountains, let alone to have a camp out here. There must be something else going on. This isn't normal."

"No chat chat!" Out of nowhere, a goblin pounced onto Lukas's lap, jabbing at his arm with his pointed staff.

"Back off," Lukas growled, his calm demeanour vanishing just as quickly as the goblin had appeared.

The snarling creature launched some spit at his face. "Prisoners no chat chat! You wait for Grimlurd, then we feast!"

"Feast?" I echoed, startled by my own voice.

The beady-eyed goblin shot me a look, then cackled. Vicious laughter shook his entire tiny frame. "Yes, yes! We feast! Been much time since we had last o'oman. Tasty tasty o'omans. O'omans go in de pot!"

My stomach churned. Was that why their cauldron smelled so putrid?

"O'omans in de pot! O'omans in de pot!" The goblin chanted repeatedly, as if his next meal wasn't still breathing right in front of him. Around us, other goblins heard his chorus and began to join in with their own scratchy voices. Together, they sang the chant, waving their staffs wildly in the air. A few adventurous ones even scampered up the sides of their tents to balance on the roof poles and perform some bizarre kind of dance.

"O'omans in de pot! O'omans in de pot!" It was a complete frenzy of unified screeching and flailing arms.

"This is mayhem," I said breathily.

Lukas squirmed beneath the ropes. "They may be disgusting creatures, but we'll get out of this alive. You have my word."

Before I could argue how unlikely that was, especially considering we were surrounded by more than fifty chanting maniacs, a roaring voice boomed across the forest. The explosion of sound sent a dozen birds fleeing from their trees, and all the goblins' tiny green mouths clamped shut.

"ORDA GOBLINS!"

All heads collectively snapped up towards the voice.

Across the camp, a broad, ominous figure loomed behind the cooking pot. While he was taller than the rest of the goblins, his head would still barely reach my shoulders. A thick, black fur-lined cape hung from his shoulders, while a long, crooked nose dominated his muddy green face. Lying across his chest was a necklace of miniature skulls – no, not miniature skulls. Goblin skulls.

"Grimlurd!" the goblins yelped, all doubling over to plant their faces into the ground. Even the ones who were balanced on the tent poles leapt down to throw themselves against the forest floor, mimicking the others. Some form of bow, perhaps?

"Rise, gobbas," the figure instructed with a proud wave of his hand. The goblins quickly obeyed, scrabbling to their feet. I didn't speak a word of goblintongue, but judging by their respect for the figure, it was clear that 'Grimlurd' was some kind of king.

"Well, well, well…" His yellow irises homed in on Lukas and me, sending a chill down my spine. "What have my gobbas found for me today?"

The goblins jumped ecstatically and pointed their stubby fingers towards us. A few barked out some phrases in goblintongue, while others just cackled with glee.

As he listened to their squawks, Grimlurd's lips stretched into a hideous smile. "O'omans, you say?" Then he stalked towards us, skulls jangling with each step. When his boots were mere inches from our feet, he lowered himself to a squat, the hideous grin still plastered on his face. "Tell me... What's a couple of o'omans doing out at this time, wandering in the woods?"

Even from a metre away, I could still smell his putrid breath.

Lukas scowled. "Go on, tell him, Naria. You are the reason we are out here, after all."

Seriously?

"We... Um..." My tongue felt heavy, as if it was covered in sticky honey. "We were just—" A breath caught in my throat as Grimlurd swooped his head in closer.

"Scared, o'oman?"

"No." But my voice was trembling. And so were my knees.

Grimlurd laughed in a horrible, scratchy way. "Scared ones are the tastiest. I will enjoy eating you first." He then jabbed his finger towards a nearby goblin. "You! Untie her. Get her ready for cooking. Tomorrow, we feast!"

Without waiting a second, the goblin he'd pointed to grabbed a sharp, curved blade and leapt towards me. I whimpered, but the sound was immediately drowned out by at least fifty goblin cheers. Clumsily, the beast with the blade sliced through the ropes that bound my chest – almost severing an artery or two in the process. Eventually, my restraints fell away, but before I could stand, a dozen tiny clawed hands grabbed each of my limbs as I was hauled away from the tree.

"Stop, please!" I squealed, struggling desperately to wriggle out of their grasp. While one goblin might not be a threat, a dozen had the strength of at least two large humans.

After leaving it for far too long, Lukas finally piped up, his strong voice cutting through my screams. "Enough of this," he said in a tone that was still much too calm for my liking. "Don't you know who we are? My father will have you executed if he hears how you're treating royalty."

Grimlurd tensed. "What was that, o'oman?" He lifted a hand, signalling the goblins around me to stop. They obeyed quickly, letting my limbs drop to the forest floor.

"I said, don't you know who we are?" Lukas repeated as though he was growing bored. "I am Prince Lukas of Drothmore, and that," he jerked his chin towards my limp body, "is my fiancée. So unless you want to meet an army of soldiers this time tomorrow, I suggest you let us go."

Grimlurd howled with laughter, the rest of the goblins joining in with their own cackling hysterics. "You think I care about that, o'oman? You are wumbah!"

So 'wumbah' meant fool? Noted.

Ignoring their laughter, Lukas persisted, "Surely you know who my father is? He's the King. He owns all the mines in Drothmore. That's more gold than you could possibly ever comprehend." At the mention of gold, the goblins immediately ceased their laughter and twisted their little bodies towards Lukas, all their beady eyes fixing onto him. "If you let us go, he will make sure that you are rewarded handsomely for your kindness."

The goblin leader seemed to consider the offer for a moment. He tilted his head, hummed softly, and brought a clawed hand up to scratch his chin.

After some contemplation, Grimlurd answered in a gruff voice, "I no longer have any need for gold... but! Because I am an honourable goblin, I will spare you." He jabbed a green finger towards Lukas. "But not you." He then swung his finger towards me.

"No," Lukas barked. "The King will be furious if you hurt her. She's a princess. She's royalty too."

Grimlurd shook with laughter again. "If she is a princess, then I am a pretty, pretty mermaid!" The other goblins cackled while jumping up and down with vicious glee. "Look at her." He stomped over and grabbed my arm, plucking me off the floor like I weighed nothing at all. "Look at what she wears." My muddy cheeks reddened. In the panic, I'd completely forgotten about my revealing faery gown. "She is no princess... You bought her off the streets. That is why you were in the woods, eh?"

I'll admit the dress was scandalous, but to assume *that* was a bit of a stretch.

Still gripping my arm, Grimlurd sneered, "A prince sneaking off to have his way with a street lady. Too embarrassed to take her to the palace, hmm?"

"He's telling the truth. I am a princess," I growled, trying to break free from his grasp.

"Quiet, street lady. My gobbas are hungry, and you will make a fine dinner." He dropped my arm without a care, and I landed with a thud on the leaves below us. Once again, before I even had a chance to stand, goblins swarmed over me, hauling me towards the fire.

"Wait a minute!" Lukas shouted, panic settling into his voice. Clearly, this was not going how he planned. "You want dinner? Take me instead."

"You are wumbah," Grimlurd chuckled, pausing the goblins who were dragging me away with another lift of his hand. "I do not care who your papa is, but lucky for you, I made a deal with someone who would not be happy if I killed you before she had her chance, so you live... for now."

Deal? What deal? And who was 'she'? Even Lukas looked confused.

"Strip her first," Grimlurd ordered, as my heart nearly leapt from my chest. "No point in cooking the dress when we can use it for rags."

"No!" I yelled, but my desperate protests were ignored. Goblins leapt onto me. There were so many tiny hands touching me everywhere. It was relentless. Panic surged from my chest, bubbling out as I screamed and slapped the beasts away, but they kept coming. First, the deep purple skirt was torn away in long ribbons. Then, a horrendous rip sounded down my back as the dress tore in half.

"Stop!" Was the last word I heard before a tremendously loud crack boomed from the sky.

A fierce streak of lightning. Followed by the most deafening roll of thunder.

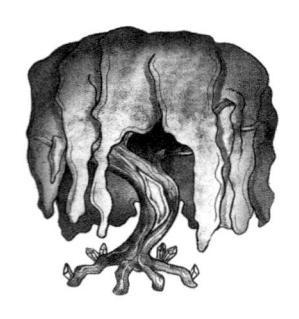

CHAPTER 32

Blinding light filled my vision. So blinding, it was as if the Ancients themselves had decided that I'd suffered enough. Suddenly, all the little goblin hands vanished from my skin, and when I finally opened my eyes, all I could see was an endless white void. My hearing was gone, too, replaced by a constant whistling. Though I knew I was still in the forest. I could feel the wet leaves under my bare legs and the scraps of my gown falling away, leaving me in just my corset and bloomers.

"Run!" a nearby goblin screeched, piercing through the whistling. Then, there were the pitter-patter sounds of tiny feet scrambling away as I continued fumbling blindly on the forest floor.

"Grimlurd's dead," another goblin squealed. In the distance, I could hear the sawing noise of a rope being hacked apart.

"He's fae!" That squeal made me flinch. Was Arenn here? Frantically, I blinked, desperate to clear the imprint from the lightning. Someone must've summoned a storm. It couldn't have been natural. The weather was so calm until the second my gown was in pieces. Arenn's sisters wielded fire, and he clearly could manipulate nature – so maybe he could summon lightning, too? He must've come for me after noticing I'd run away. Imagine chasing your bride into the woods and finding her with her gown being torn away by goblins. You'd be furious. Furious enough to conjure up a storm and strike down the goblin leader then and there.

Just then, a pair of strong arms lifted me from the ground.

"Arenn?" I questioned as my vision finally cleared.

"Who's Arenn?" Lukas loomed over me. With a halo of brown hair circling his striking face, he appeared almost angelic against the backdrop of the night sky. And in that moment, something about him smelled sweeter too, like citrus fruits from the warmest parts of the realm.

As I continued to stare, his concerned eyes searched over my exposed arms and legs. "Did the lightning hit you? Are you confused?"

Confused didn't even begin to describe the mess that scrambled my mind. But it wasn't because I'd been struck by any bizarre lightning. Glancing past him, the sky was completely clear again. No trace of even a single wispy rain cloud. There was definitely magic at work here.

"What happened?" I stuttered. "What was that?"

"Nothing," Lukas said dismissively as he hauled me to my feet. "Just a freak storm. We've had a lot of those recently."

"But, the lightning... it came out of nowhere."

"Like I said, a freak storm," he repeated, frustration growing in his tone. "Now let's go before the goblins realise that too."

Surrounding us were hundreds of panicking goblins. They squealed and scampered around the camp in all different directions, a few bumping into each other and tumbling backwards. It was utter mayhem. A few metres away, lying on the ground in a smoking heap, was the charred body of Grimlurd. It must've been a direct hit from the lightning, as a horrific scar traversed down his mossy skin.

Suddenly, a crazed goblin slammed against my leg, and I yelped. But just as the little beast steadied himself, his gaze swung to Lukas, and all the green drained from his face. "It's him!" he screeched. "He's no o'oman, he's fae!" The goblin collapsed backwards in fear, his chest heaving dramatically as if he were inches away from a horrific monster instead of two scared humans.

"It's time to go." Lukas tugged on my hand. In the chaos, I hadn't even realised he'd taken it.

"But what does he mean?" I stammered, my gaze darting between Lukas and the petrified goblin. "Why do they keep saying you're fae? What are you hiding?"

The prince's jaw tightened as he turned away, his lips remaining sealed.

"Are you human?" I wasn't even sure why I asked that question. He had to be. His ears were round, and there was nothing supernatural about his perfect face. Still, with his hand in mine, I could feel a strange sensation, as though something powerful was crackling beneath his skin.

"Was it you?" I insisted, louder this time. "Did you summon the lightning?"

"I don't know!" He whipped around to face me. "Maybe... It just happens sometimes. I can't control it, I can't explain it, and there's absolutely not enough time to try and figure it all out here. So let's go." Before I could ask any more questions, he stormed off towards the trees, dragging my hand and then my body along with him. I didn't bother arguing. He was right; the goblins would probably come to their senses any minute now, and we needed to be long gone by then. But still, who was he really? Because the longer I felt the buzzing power radiating from his skin, the less I believed he was merely an ordinary human prince.

***

The goblin camp was much larger than both Lukas and I had anticipated. When we were bound to that tree, it was hard to see past the first ten or so tents, but standing, the ugly canvas tents and flickering campfires seemed to stretch on for miles. As we marched through the camp, Lukas used a stolen goblin blade to force aside any goblins that dared to cross our path. Though most of them bolted at the sight of him, screaming that the fae had come to strike them down with lightning just like he'd done with their precious Grimlurd.

After passing what felt like a hundred tents, we stumbled across a tall black horse secured to a tree. Spiky metal goblin armour protected its front and sides, while a long saddle was fastened to its back. With its broad, strong legs, it could probably carry at least five goblins into battle.

"We'll get back to the palace faster with this," Lukas noted, urging me towards the steed. Before I could protest, his hands found my waist, and he lifted me swiftly onto the horse's saddle.

"But there's only one horse, and I can't ride without someone leading me," I shot back, trying to ignore the tingling feeling that his touch had left on my skin.

Lukas untied the reins from the tree and moved to the horse's side. "He's big enough for both of us," he said, casually vaulting himself up and sliding close behind me. My breath hitched. That tingling sensation was nothing compared to the way my skin now burned, especially when his hand brushed my bare thigh as he reached for the reins. I hadn't realised until then, but my bloomers must've ridden up while I settled in the saddle. The snowy white fabric bunched around my upper thighs, leaving far too little to the imagination. Cheeks reddening, I shuffled in place, quickly smoothing out the fabric to cover as much skin as possible.

"There's no need to be embarrassed, fiancée," Lukas whispered. "We both know I'll see much more than that when you're my wife." His lips brushed my ear as he kicked the horse into motion.

Scoffing, I opened my mouth to retort, but the horse's sudden movement sent my backside sliding down the saddle. I squealed until my shoulders collided with his hard chest. A gasp slipped from my lips as one of Lukas's arms wrapped around my waist, the other maintaining control of the horse. With my entire back tucked safely against his torso, it was almost impossible to hide my shaking breath.

Silently, I prayed that he wouldn't notice how much he affected me. Otherwise, this would be a very long journey home.

It was much easier to see the end of the goblin camp on horseback. Once we'd cleared it, Lukas used the position of the rising sun in the sky to figure out which direction led us towards the palace. I hadn't realised how quickly the night had slipped away from us. We'd only just set off into the woods before the stars had twinkled out completely, and the once coal-black sky gave way to a hazy blue.

While we rode at a slow pace through the forest, a million questions kicked around my mind. There were so many, I didn't know where to begin. And it certainly didn't help that after a few minutes of holding the reins, Lukas's arm had slipped down and now rested across my left thigh. After such an eventful night, it was already difficult enough to think without the distraction of his arm constantly brushing against such a sensitive area of my body.

His other distracting arm remained securely around my waist. Even though there was no risk of me falling now, I couldn't bring myself to request that he let go. So instead, in my sleep-deprived state, I just let myself lean further into him. We were both filthy from the mud, but somehow he still smelled so pleasant. Letting my eyes flutter shut, I breathed in deeply then exhaled. There would be plenty of time for questions later. For once, I just wanted to enjoy the moment.

"Comfortable?" he murmured. His voice vibrated in my ear as I nuzzled against his chest. How was it possible for something so firm to also feel so warm and safe?

"Wake me up when we get to the palace," I replied, not moving from my position.

"I thought you'd be bombarding me with questions right now," he continued calmly. "You had quite a lot to say in the goblin camp."

"I'm too tired for questions and besides, I don't feel like arguing with you, I just want to sleep," I answered with a sigh. "Sleep and pretend."

"Pretend?" he mused.

What was I even saying? I must've been more exhausted than I thought.

Keeping my eyes closed, I explained, "Sometimes when everything gets too much, I close my eyes and pretend that I'm someone else, somewhere far away. Right now, I want to forget about Corlixir, and Drothmore, and the fae, and anything else that comes with a thousand responsibilities. I want to just pretend that we're two ordinary people, taking an ordinary ride, and maybe we're on our way back to your cottage – not a palace, or anything fancy. Just for a moment, I want to be only myself. Not a princess. Not a future queen or anything like that. Only Naria. And you can be just Lukas."

I stayed pressed against him, listening to the rise and fall of his chest as he breathed. He probably thought I'd lost my mind along with my gown back in the goblin camp, but I didn't care. As long as he let me stay leaning into him, nothing else mattered.

Ancients, I really was tired.

"I understand," he said finally after a minute of silence. "We don't have to talk or argue about anything important."

His tone was soft, almost tender. Then, the arm that was around my waist tightened as he squeezed gently. "You can sleep now, forest princess. I'll wake you when we're back at the... *cottage*."

A smile warmed my cheeks. Just for a moment, I'd never felt happier. And as I drifted off, the horse's movements rocking me to sleep, I imagined the two of us were on a boat staring out at a vast endless ocean. Realms away from any ruined kingdoms and wicked faeries.

Only us.

CHAPTER 33

It felt like I'd barely slept for minutes before I was rudely awoken by the abrupt shouts of Drothmore stablehands and the whinnying of horses. Scowling, I nuzzled deeper into my pillow. I had no idea why there were stablehands or horses in my bedchamber, but they'd be fools if they thought I'd be leaving this terribly comfortable bed anytime soon. It was so warm and firm, albeit a little bit squirmy.

Wait... Squirmy? Beds shouldn't be squirmy.

"Welcome home, Naria." The bed spoke to me in a voice that was smoother than syrup as I felt something thick drag across my waist.

My eyes sprang open. This certainly wasn't my bedchamber. Surrounding me were the bright stone walls of the Steel Palace stables, along with a dozen busy stablehands. They buzzed around like flies as they busied themselves with the huge black horse I was sitting on. Nervous whispers fluttered between them as they shot occasional glances towards me, and someone else. Someone that I was leaning against in a far too intimate way.

Shame flooded my cheeks, and immediately, I straightened up in the saddle. I couldn't believe it. I'd actually fallen asleep on him. We'd never be able to look at each other in the same way again.

"You're finally awake," Lukas commented as he slipped out of the saddle, taking all the warmth with him.

"Sorry," I croaked sheepishly. I hadn't noticed until then, but someone had draped a white cotton shirt across my shoulders. Beneath it, I was still scarcely dressed in my corset and bloomers, my destroyed faery gown left in tatters on the forest floor. I supposed that was probably what the stablehands were gossiping about. Of course, they'd be wondering why the strange Corlixin girl had arrived back at the palace in the early morning hours, accompanied by the prince, half-dressed and covered in mud. You didn't need to be creative to come up with a few scandalous reasons. And my cheeks burned at the possibilities.

"Let me help you down," I heard Lukas say from the cobbled floor. But when my head turned to face him—

Oh Ancients.

The shirt that had been kindly draped across my chest clearly once belonged to him, as he was now standing on the ground with his perfectly toned chest completely bare. He was also completely filthy. We both were. But still, even covered in tiny cuts, caked in mud, and with his dark brown hair tousled from the ride, I found myself unable to look away. Everything about him was so beautiful, he was almost divine.

"Are you alright?" he questioned innocently. Immediately, my eyes tore away from his chest.

"Sorry," I said again. "I'm just tired. Exhausted, actually." As if to prove my point, the biggest yawn heaved its way up my throat. There was no lie there. Even the horse was starting to look like an attractive bed, but the impatient twitch in his black-tipped ears suggested otherwise. I'd probably be thrown to the ground before I got any sleep at all.

I heard a few servants giggle as Lukas helped me down from the horse. I'd slipped his shirt over my head to give me a small ounce of modesty, but still, a girl in her bloomers, arm-in-arm with a half-naked prince wasn't the most innocent of pictures. The news would be all over the palace before noon.

"Ignore them," Lukas whispered as he draped a plain cloak over my shoulders. "I'll make sure any rumours are dealt with. I won't have anyone questioning your virtue before we're married."

I chewed my lip, remaining doubtful as to how he could possibly explain our situation in an innocent way without letting everyone know about the goblin army waiting in the woods. Mass panic or a few disapproving looks – we'd have to choose one.

"I'll also be speaking with my father today about what we encountered in the forest. He'll likely want us to send a few small forces out there to deal with them before things get out of hand," Lukas explained, keeping his voice low to avoid the eavesdropping servants. "For now, please just get some rest." He accepted another cloak from a servant and fastened it around his own bare shoulders. "I can arrange a meeting between the two of you later if you'd like to discuss... other things with him. But only when you're dressed and well-rested."

There were so many *other things* that needed to be discussed, my mind felt ready to burst. For once, though, I didn't argue. Lukas was right. I needed sleep more than anything. Sleep first, then deal with all the real problems later.

By the time I finally reached my bedchamber, my heavy eyelids were threatening a mutiny against the rest of my body. It was torture. My silk bed was so close, but I knew I needed a bath more than I needed to collapse onto those soft sheets. Thankfully, the servants were quick to help me peel off the few layers of clothing I had left on. And before I knew it, I'd been plopped into a bath, and mud was being scrubbed off every inch of my body. Though no amount of scrubbing could wash away the feel of a dozen goblin hands tearing at my skin. Only time would clear that memory.

While soaking in the lavender-scented bathwater, I caught a glimpse of the two tiny crystals still embedded in my arm. The one closest to my wrist was slightly larger than the other, but otherwise, they were hardly noticeable. Letting my head rest against the rim of the steel tub, I prayed that Lukas hadn't yet spotted them. Surely, even if he had, he wouldn't know what they meant, but still, I'd rather not inform him that I was now engaged to two princes. I doubted that conversation would go over well.

I'd fallen asleep in the tub when the servants reappeared to help me dress. The sun was still high in the sky, but at the prince's insistence, I'd been dressed in nightwear rather than a typical regal gown. Once the servants were finally finished, I'd practically leapt into the warm embrace of my bed sheets, and with my eyes finally shut, I drifted off before the metal bath had even been carried out of my chambers.

CHAPTER 34

Tall pond reeds swayed around me like dancers in a moonlit ballet while fireflies buzzed through the dreamy night. Breathing in, the air was thick with magic and tasted like a forbidden lover's kiss – dangerous yet still so sweet. Even the cloudless sky above was so lovely as I lay flat on my back in an open patch of grass. Occasionally, a shooting star would twinkle across the swirling purple sky, leaving behind a shimmering blue trail. It seemed to happen so often in this nighttime world, but every time it took my breath away.

"Why did you run from me, little human?" a male voice echoed from beyond the reeds. Like a serpent, I could've sworn I felt it wrap around my neck for a few moments, just long enough to make me gasp before it vanished into the long grass.

Fear settled in the back of my throat. This was *my*

beautiful dream, so what was *he* doing here?

Pushing myself to my feet, I peered over the pond reeds to see a tall, looming figure staring back at me. His black clothes were plainer than usual, and his hair was a mess of midnight waves, but it was still undeniably him – the charming, and yet terrifyingly violent Prince Arenn of the Fae.

"You need to leave," I called over to him dismissively. He might be powerful in the real world, but here, as a mere figment of my imagination, I could say and do whatever I wanted.

A devious smile tugged at his lips. "But you haven't answered my question." He began pacing closer. Behind him was a vast lake, surrounded by the same swaying pond weeds that separated us now. Pure white swans drifted across the water, causing ripples in the constellations that reflected from above. Everything about this place was so enchanting. Even Arenn's pale faery skin seemed to shimmer slightly as if he'd been crafted from stardust.

Though no amount of stardust could fix a monster.

"You tortured and killed that faery, even after I begged you to stop," I accused when he was just a few steps away. "And, I have it on good authority that your parents were responsible for the death of my kingdom." My fists clenched. "So forgive me for not wanting to share my dream with any more murderous faeries right now."

Arenn paused, and he swept a heavy look over my trembling body. I was wearing the same nightgown I'd fallen asleep in. It was fairly modest, but by the hungry way he was staring, I could've been wearing nothing at all.

"I know nothing about the true cause of the Great Blaze,

and I seriously doubt my parents do either," he replied, clearly unphased by my tone. "But I must say, if your so-called 'good authority' is your foolish prince, then I suggest you consider whose heart he may eventually win by keeping us apart. Don't underestimate the extent a man will go to – and the lies he would spin – to keep the one he loves, sweet human."

My lips flattened. Lukas didn't love me, and he certainly wouldn't lie – especially not about something as important as this. With a confused sigh, I shook my head. This conversation didn't matter. None of this was real, anyway.

"And in regards to Valen, I did what I had to do," Arenn carried on nonchalantly. "Aren't you forgetting? He gave your friend an enchanted bracelet. Would you rather I let him walk free? Unpunished?"

"That doesn't mean he deserved… that." I shuddered. His screams still echoed in my mind. "You were cruel… And besides, I saw it in your eyes. You enjoyed sucking the life out of him. You're a monster. So you can't blame me for leaving the second I got the chance."

"A monster?" he repeated with a thin smile, something feral dancing across his lips.

Again, this was just a dream, and he couldn't hurt me here, could he?

"Do you fear me, human?"

My chest tightened. "No."

Grinning, he stepped closer until he was mere inches away. Then, bringing his hand to my face, he swept his fingers under my chin and tilted my head up. While everything else seemed so hazy, his touch felt so real on my skin. It almost burned.

"You're lying to me," he chided. "And I don't like it when people lie to me." His words were strict, but there was a dark enjoyment hidden in his sharp features, as if every tremble from me only fed him more. "So I'll ask you again, little human, do you fear me?"

This isn't real.

Exhaling a ragged breath, I maintained eye contact. "No."

"Wrong. Answer." Arenn's fingers crept up from my chin as he swiped his thumb over my lower lip. When his other arm found my waist, he wrapped it tightly around me, forcing me closer. I gasped as our chests collided – the very real scent of wildflowers and cinnamon filling my nose. "Whatever shall I do with this naughty lying mouth of yours?" he pondered out loud. My breath shuddered as the hand that was caressing my face dropped to my hips. "I know..."

Before I could push him away, he scooped me off the ground and tucked my legs securely around his waist. With him carrying me like this, our lips were so close I could imagine his taste on my tongue. It was just like when he held me in the crystal pool, except there was no water to soften my landing if I fell...

Swallowing hard, my arms quickly wrapped around his shoulders.

"You mustn't tell lies, Princess," he chastised me in a low, warning tone.

"Or what?" The words slipped off my tongue almost instinctively.

He flashed a wild smile, then pressed his lips against mine.

Instantly, my heart leapt. *I didn't want this.* But then a strange feeling washed over me and I resisted for barely a second before my lips parted and I welcomed him in. The moment I did, everything else faded away into a dreamy, foggy void. There was only me, him, and the irresistible taste of wildflowers on my tongue. I hadn't realised how desperately I'd been craving that taste until now.

As his tongue explored my mouth, fear danced with the passion in my heart. This was so incredibly dangerous. After seeing what he was capable of, I could barely stand to be in the same room as him – just meeting his poisonous gaze was enough to transform me into a trembling mess. Yet, there I was, shamelessly dragging my fingers through his thick black waves while we claimed each other's mouths.

"This *is* a dream, isn't it?" I asked, keeping our lips a mere heartbeat apart.

"Of course it is." He gnawed my lower lip, smiling deviously. "We're miles away from each other right now, and there are no lakes like this in Nythinia."

"But you taste so real," I said breathily.

A low laugh rumbled in his chest. "How peculiar... I suppose the next time we cross paths you will just have to kiss me again. Then you can tell me how real this feels."

My head pulled back in surprise. "We won't be seeing each other again," I assured him, but without his lips on mine, my mouth felt uncomfortably cold.

"Is that so?" He ran his tongue over his teeth. "That's quite a shame, and will be terribly inconvenient since we are now engaged." I tensed at his words, and as if to drive the point further, the crystals on my wrist began to ache.

"You know, it is very difficult to break a faery engagement... It's almost impossible and very painful. You'd also need to find someone else who'd be willing to break it. And of course, their desire for you must be stronger than our bond or they'll die trying." His eyes sparkled as his lips curled into a sinister grin. "Does your foolish human prince fancy a go? Does he finally see the beauty that I see? How I'd love to see him dead at our feet. I'd so enjoy watching his torture."

"Don't say that," I snarled. Furious, I shoved my hands against his chest, suddenly desperate to be as far away from him as I possibly could. "Put me down. Now."

His smile faded like someone snuffing out a candle. Then, something else burned brighter in his gaze. Rage? Betrayal? Jealousy? It was so hard to tell.

He didn't drop me, though. Instead, his grip on my legs only tightened.

"You have feelings for him," he growled. Around us, the once-enchanting scene seemed to drain of colour. It was all so bizarre. With each passing moment, I felt less like this was my dream and more like I had somehow invaded Arenn's.

"Feelings for Lukas?" I snorted, but I could've sworn I felt Arenn stiffen at the mention of his name. "Don't be ridiculous." The idea was completely absurd. I could never love anyone who didn't love my kingdom. "Now please, put me down."

"You're lying again, human," he grumbled. This time there was no dark amusement in his tone, only fury. "You know how I feel about liars."

"Stop this." My heart pounded just as my fists did as I beat them against his chest. "Put me down."

To my surprise, his grip on my thighs loosened, and slowly I slipped down his tall form. I thought, naively, for a moment that he might've calmed down, but when my eyes caught his, there was a burning rage like I'd never seen before. It made my blood turn to ice.

In one swift and very sudden movement, his leg hooked behind mine, and we both tumbled to the grassy floor. He cradled my body as we fell, one hand behind my head and the other protecting my back. The moment we hit the grass, he straddled my hips with his strong legs. Then, without giving me a chance to wriggle away, he grabbed both of my wrists and pinned them over my head.

Drawing his lips to my ear, he said in a low, venomous whisper, "I don't share my toys, Naria." I shuddered at the sound of my name on his tongue. "Especially not with other princes." My breath caught. There was no way I could escape now, not with the full weight of him pressing down over me.

"I promise you," I began in a mousy voice, "there's nothing between Lukas and I."

"Stop saying his name!" he roared, his grip on my wrists tightening.

A nervous whimper slipped from my lips. At the sound, Arenn's expression softened, and the hand that was holding my wrists drifted to cup my face. "Please forgive me, Princess, I didn't mean to frighten you." His fingers gently stroked my cheek. "You know I'd never hurt you, don't you?"

I nodded quickly, while praying he wouldn't see through this lie.

"Good," he sighed. "I just cannot bear the thought of

another man messing with your pretty little mind. It... It consumes me." He shook his head before lowering his face to plant a line of soft kisses at the base of my jaw. "You're mine... My Luminessia bride. My future wife. My little human." He punctuated each phrase with another gentle kiss.

This was all just a bizarre dream. It had to be. Just my own fears of our new engagement messing with my head. I'd wake up soon, and I'd be fine. But then, why did this all feel so real?

Once Arenn was satisfied, he lifted his head away from my jaw. He seemed much calmer now, but it was still hard for me to relax with his body pressed so close against mine. A tiny, traitorous part of me even seemed to like the closeness.

"I'm afraid I'm still going to have to punish you for lying to me, little human." His gaze drifted past my chin.

"Oh?" I said innocently, trying to mask my racing heart.

"Don't be afraid, though," he murmured, his face lowering to my neck. "You might even enjoy this."

My stomach dipped. But before I could speak another word, his lips attached to my skin and he gnawed while sucking gently. I gasped at the feeling. It wasn't painful; wasn't pleasant either. Maybe somewhere devious in the middle. I resisted the urge to knot my fingers through his beautifully messy hair.

After a few more seconds, he pulled his now slightly swollen lips away.

"Now everyone will know that you're mine, sweet princess." His fingers brushed gently down my cheek.

I was going to ask what he'd done, but before I had a chance to, another low voice cut through the dreamscape.

"Naria!"

I knew that voice. It was Lukas. But hearing it only made me want to groan. It was already bad enough to have one prince invade a perfectly nice dream.

"Who's that?" Arenn asked, a shadow passing over his features. "Is that *him*?" I knew full well who 'him' was referring to.

"Naria, please wake up!" the voice called again, louder this time.

"What's he doing in your bedchamber?" he growled. "Tell me, human!"

"I-I don't know," I answered breathlessly.

Arenn studied me. "You speak the truth... for once." Then he straightened up, but still remained straddling my hips. "You tell your foolish prince that if he dares to touch you, I'll kill him." Around us, the world began crumbling, fizzling out into a blur of candlelight and floral bed sheets. Before Arenn disappeared too, he took my hand and planted a soft kiss on my open palm.

"I'll see you soon, Princess." And then he leaned forward, his lips meeting mine again, but this time he didn't taste anywhere near as sweet. Only the faintest hints of wildflowers and dustings of cinnamon rested on my tongue, along with something else; something far more sinister.

And the worst part was, I didn't mind the taste.

CHAPTER 35

The blurred bed sheets and hazy candlelight became crystal clear as I was roughly shaken awake. Lukas knelt on the bed beside me, one hand on each of my shoulders. His tawny hair was a choppy sea of waves, while only a thin nightshirt covered his bronze chest. It was as though he'd just woken up and run all the way here in the middle of the night. But I supposed, judging by the candle that flickered away beside us and his heavy panting breath, he probably had.

"What is it?" I croaked. As I blinked away the sleep, I noticed a strange phantom ache lightening in my hips. It almost felt as if someone really had been sitting there, pinning me down to that swaying grass and placing soft kisses along my jaw.

No. Impossible. That was a dream.

"Sorry for waking you," Lukas began, his voice wavering.

"But I had to come. Something's wrong." Behind him, moonlight poured in from the window. I must've slept for the entire day and most of the night. Somehow, though, I still felt exhausted.

Pushing myself up to lean against the headboard, I met his worried eyes. "What happened?"

"I... I don't know," he stammered. "I went to speak to the King. I needed to tell him about the goblin camp in the woods. But when I arrived at his chambers, I was told that he was resting. So I gave him time. I let him have his rest. But when I came back after a few hours, I was just told the same thing—"

"You know he's ill," I cut in. "I'm sure he's fine, probably just resting."

Lukas shook his head as he dragged a sweaty hand through his hair. "I tried to get some sleep, but I couldn't. I just... I couldn't shake the feeling that something was wrong. That's when I decided I would just force my way into his room. But when I made it past the guards, his bed was empty... I can't find him anywhere, Naria." His breath quickened. "He's been taken by someone, I'm sure of it."

"Wait, wait." My heart stuttered. "How do you know he hasn't just left the palace for some perfectly innocent reason? Maybe his healer needed to take him somewhere for more treatment?"

It was silly to even suggest that. The last time I saw the King, he was in such a poor state that leaving his bed would've only caused him more suffering, but still, I couldn't accept that someone had just taken him. Why would they do it? If this was an assassination attempt, why not just kill him where he slept?

"I've searched the entire palace. Nobody knows where he is," Lukas carried on, his cheeks paling. "And then I searched for my mother... She's gone too. I checked her bedchamber. None of her servants were there and her bed was empty."

My stomach churned. Erissa wasn't responsible for the King's disappearance, was she? She certainly seemed to hate him enough, but could she really be capable of stealing away a king? The woman's mind was barely even there. She couldn't have done this. Whoever had the King surely has the Queen too. After all, a kingdom without either of its rulers is a kingdom ready for invasion.

Exhaling, I steadied myself. I knew I had to stay calm. Drothmore could be hours away from a war, but a panicking prince and a trembling princess would be no good to anyone. And there was still time to fix this. There had to be.

"Okay," I said finally, my voice calm and precise. "What about your armies? Did your father ever tell you what to do in the case of an incoming invasion?"

Lukas's shoulders tensed. "I've already spoken to the generals. Apparently, a few days ago, the King requested that our largest armies be sent to patrol the northern borders of the realm."

"But that would mean—"

"We're completely unprotected," he confirmed, his words making my chest seize. "The generals have just sent their fastest riders to tell the armies to come home. But it'll take days before they reach the northern border, and even longer for our armies to return."

"How many soldiers do we have left?" I asked, dreading the answer.

Lukas sighed, sliding a hand over his face. "Only the guards that patrol the palace and a few other small forces."

In other words, Drothmore was doomed.

"How could this happen?" The room began to blur as tears threatened to overcome me. Then Lukas drew closer, and the storm inside my mind settled for a brief moment, until he spoke again.

"Everyone is telling me that you might be able to answer that question."

His accusation sent all the air rushing out of my chest.

"What?" I almost choked. "You can't possibly think I would have anything to do with this. I wouldn't even know where to start with ordering armies about, or... kidnapping people. I—"

"Listen to me." Lukas grabbed my hand, grasping it tightly. "I trust you. And I know you never would've gotten involved in this willingly, but... the timings, Naria." He winced, conflict raging across his features. "You move into the palace, have secret meetings with the fae – my father's greatest enemies – and now there are goblins in the woods? I want to believe you're innocent, but the generals certainly don't."

The tears broke free then, streaming down my face while deep in my chest, my heart pounded. Each intense beat forced more and more air in and out of my lungs. This couldn't be happening. This was just another awful dream.

"I swear on my parents' graves, Lukas," I insisted between sobs, "I had no idea that any of this was going on. I didn't know there was a goblin camp in the woods until we were *both* captured. And even when I visited the fae, there was never any mention of *any* invasion! If I knew that they were planning this, I promise you I would've reported it back here immediately." I took a breath to steady my shaking voice. "Trust me, I know what it's like to lose a kingdom. I would never wish that fate on anyone." I met his steel gaze. "Not even on my greatest enemy."

A deafening silence fell between us. After what felt like hours, Lukas swallowed hard, nodded, then ran a hand through his messy hair.

"I believe you," he admitted in a calmer voice. "The generals might want you thrown in the dungeons, but I'm going to tell them you're to remain in your tower with Lady Raena. It's safer up here, and I'll make sure to leave you both with a guard that I can trust to get you out of the palace if things take a turn for the worse."

"But what about you?" I asked, fear settling in my stomach.

Lukas hesitated for a moment before answering. "I'll be travelling back to the goblin camp with a few of our remaining soldiers."

"What? No!" Something cracked within my chest. "It's too dangerous!"

"I don't have a choice, Naria." He breathed heavily. "I'd bet my life that the fae are behind all this and that they've sent the goblins to do their dirty work. My mother and father could be being tortured in that camp as we speak. I have to try and rescue them – for the sake of my kingdom."

Another sob forced its way up my throat, but I swallowed it down. I knew he was right. What kind of future king would he be if he didn't try?

"Then let me help you," I suggested while wiping away a tear. "When you find the King and Queen, they'll probably need healing. I can help with that! Or if any of your soldiers get injured, or if you do?" I cast aside the painful image of Lukas bleeding out on the forest floor. That would never happen. I would never let him die.

To my immense frustration, Lukas shook his head. "No, like you said, this is an incredibly dangerous mission. I can't risk you being hurt in the crossfire."

"But I can heal—"

"I said no!" Lukas cut me off with a fierce glare. "I can't risk it. I won't." Then the glare faded to a softer look as he sighed. "Besides, you've seen the... *tricks* that I can do. If the situation calls for it, then I'm sure I can repeat what happened in the woods, and the little beasts will scatter, just like last time."

I'd almost forgotten about the bizarre weather. Making a mental note to force him to spill *all* of these dirty secrets when we weren't on the cusp of invasion, I leaned forward to remind him of the one thing he seemed to be forgetting. "But you said you can't control it yet."

Whatever the strange magic was that lurked under his skin, it was useless if he couldn't wield it on command. And it wouldn't take long for the goblins to realise that too.

"What if you try to use it and nothing happens?" I pressed. "I know we have our differences, Lukas, but I still can't bear to think of you getting hurt."

He stiffened, glancing away almost sheepishly. "If it reassures you, I'll make sure to bring a few healers from the infirmary," he offered. "And I'll try again to locate my father's healer. I've heard her skills are unmatched in the realm. I was actually hoping to question her on what happened in the King's bedchamber, since she always seems to be right by his side, but she seems to have vanished too, along with my parents."

"Seraphina is gone as well?" I pondered out loud. The more I learned, the more confusing this situation was proving to be. Wherever she was, though, I hoped she was safe.

Shaking my head, I focused on what was really important. My gaze locked onto Lukas. "Promise me you'll come back from this unharmed?"

"I promise you." His jaw tensed. "Naria, I—" There was a brief silence, and he chewed his lip, as if there was more he wanted to say but he couldn't bring himself to say it yet.

"What is it?" I asked softly.

He shook his head, rising from the bed. "I'll tell you when I return."

I wanted to argue, but I knew if I opened my mouth, a sob would force its way out instead of any useful words.

When he reached the door, he paused for a moment, glancing over his shoulder one final time. "Stay safe... forest princess," he said, then he smiled in a way that made my heart ache the second the door clicked shut behind him.

Please, please stay safe too.

I lasted all of two hours before I began throwing on a lightweight travelling gown, our heated conversation still ringing clearly in my mind:

'But I can heal—'

'I said no!'

It didn't matter what he'd said. Every time I blinked, I could only see him flashing across my vision – lying there helplessly against the bloodstained leaves of the forest floor. It made me feel ill. Of course, I couldn't fight, and if someone tried giving me a sword, I'd probably end up stabbing myself. But I wasn't lying when I said I could heal. I knew I could help them. Without me, Lukas and his soldiers would be defenceless against the hundreds of savage goblins.

So I was going to help. And there was nothing that could possibly change my mind.

Just then, a soft knock sounded at the door.

"Who is it?" I asked hesitantly, but any fear faded instantly when the door slowly opened and Raena's kind face blinked back at me.

First, she smiled, clearly relieved that I was alright after my ordeal yesterday, but then her gaze dropped to the travelling gown that swung around my calves, and then to the healing supplies on my hips. The colour drained from her cheeks as she pieced it all together.

"Don't tell me you're leaving too?" Raena squeaked, using her body to shut the door behind her.

"I have to," I insisted. "I can't just let him ride out to his death. You haven't seen the goblin camps, Raena. There are so many of the little monsters! He'll die!" Another sob lodged in my throat but I swallowed it down. I had to stop with the crying. These pesky tears weren't helping anyone. Especially not Lukas. Wiping a hand across my face, I turned to continue packing up my medical supplies.

Behind me, Raena stepped closer. "Erik told me everything that happened," she said in a gentle tone. "I heard about the goblins and how the Drothmore armies have left us. It's not safe out there anymore. You should stay here and wait for news. I'm sure the prince will be fine."

"You don't know that," I shot back, hurriedly stuffing crushed flowers into little potion bottles. "He could be dying right now, and no one would be there to save him!"

"There would be healers amongst the soldiers. This isn't your fight, Naria." I felt her place a hand on my shoulder.

"But what if it is?" I spun around, tears streaming down my cheeks. "This is all my fault. I should've never visited the fae. What if it's Arenn who called for the army? What if I've made him jealous and this is all because of me?"

Raena shook her head, making the tight curls around her face bounce. "You're being silly. None of this is your fault," she soothed. "From what you've told me, it wouldn't make sense for the faeries to do this. Not unless there's something else going on, and whatever it might be, it would be much bigger than any of us." She wiped the tears from my cheeks. "Now please, let's just try to relax. How about we read a book together? I can fetch that naughty romance you liked? Remember how it made us fall about in laughter?" She just about managed to tease out a weak smile from me before I forced my lips to flatten.

Another blink, another flashing image of a bloodied prince.

"There's no time for reading." I returned to my herbs, making sure to pack an extra few nightbriar leaves for dressing wounds.

Over my shoulder, I heard Raena let out a frustrated huff. "Naria, stop this madness." Her soothing tone was long gone. "If you go out into those woods, you will surely die. Do you want to have a quick sparring match with Erik outside? You wouldn't even last a minute. You—"

"Erik's our guard?" My face lit up like the morning sun. "That's fantastic!" I whirled back to an open-mouthed Raena. "He'll take me into the woods for sure. You can persuade him!" This was perfect. I'd be by Lukas's side in no time. We'd be together and—

"STOP!" Raena's scream pierced through my racing thoughts as if she'd thrown a dagger right at my head. Even Erik peeked his head around the door to check if everything was okay. Though a quick glare from Raena sent the door slamming shut again. My seemingly innocent friend was actually quite scary when angry. Perhaps she should come along too – one scream and the goblins would scatter.

"You will stop these ridiculous thoughts at once! I will not have you dying on me," she seethed, her face burning with rage. "I will never forgive myself if anything happens to you while you were supposed to be safe here, with me. I know you want to help, but you *can't* fight them. And no amount of healing herbs or potions will ever kill a goblin."

Kill a goblin? Could I make a poison perhaps? I did know a few recipes...

Despite my wandering mind, Raena went on, "You don't know how to wield a sword or use a bow. You'd only get in the way during a fight. Prince Lukas would probably kill me himself if he came back here and you were still out there."

A poison wouldn't work. There's too many goblins, and I'd have to feed it to them somehow. I needed something bigger. Brighter. Something more... explosive. My mouth fell open.

"Are you even listening to me?" Raena huffed.

"Yes, well... I was." But how could I convince her that this would work? "I'm sorry... you're right."

"I'm right?" She raised an eyebrow.

"Yes." I took a breath and closed the gap between us. "Of course, you are. I can't fight and I'd only get in the way if I tried to." My fingers crumpled the fabric of my skirts. "I wouldn't ever be able to help with just my herbs but... I might know another way."

Raena studied my face. "Go on?"

I took another deep breath. *Please let this work.* "A few years ago, back in my village, there was a storage cupboard where our teachers would keep all of the different healing ingredients. Sometimes, my friends and I used to sneak in late at night, and, well... mix some of the powders together."

"So you were a bit naughty?" she interrupted. "What's this got to do with the goblins?"

"Just listen," I persisted. "One night, we mixed together a few ingredients and something strange happened. There was a big, loud flash. Then the cupboard began to fill with smoke, and it glowed too!"

"The cupboard glowed?" Raena's brow furrowed, unconvinced.

"No! Not the cupboard, the smoke!"

She shook her head. "I don't see how that's possible. That just sounds like magic."

"Exactly! And the goblins are terrified of magic." I grinned, praying that she'd piece it all together. "If I can use the same ingredients to recreate the sparks and the smoke, I can convince them that I'm a faery. And if they think I have magic, they'll run for the hills. I can give Lukas the time he needs to find the King and Queen. It's perfect!" My heart thrummed in my chest. Surely she would understand now.

Raena blinked a few times, her pretty face completely blank. "I don't know, Naria. There were a lot of 'ifs' in your plan. What if something goes wrong?"

"It won't," I assured her, snatching up her hand in mine. "And if you don't believe me, then at least let me show you the smoke. I have all the ingredients here. I packed almost an entire healer's chest when I left the village. Just let me show you. Then you'll see how it could work." I stared back at her with glossy, desperate eyes.

After a few tense moments, she relented with a sigh. "Fine. Show me."

I almost squealed.

"At least if you're busy mixing up potions, you won't be strolling through any goblin-filled woods."

CHAPTER 36

"Are you certain this is safe?" Raena asked, cowering against the back wall of my bedchamber, specifically the corner that was furthest from the mysterious mound of silver- and honey-coloured powder on the floor.

"Absolutely," I lied. In my hand was a goblet of water, ready to be thrown onto the mound. If I was being honest, I was about eighty-five percent certain that I was remembering the recipe correctly. Maybe closer to eighty, actually. Although, even if I was misremembering, that didn't necessarily mean this would end in disaster. Only once did our cupboard experiments go completely wrong, and on that occasion, we only needed about a week with the healers before we could properly breathe again.

"We'll be fine," I assured her, though my hand trembled as it gripped the goblet. "All I need to do now is add the final ingredient."

"Wait!" Raena squeaked, but she was too late. I jerked the cup forward and water splashed onto the powder. The moment it hit the mound, a huge purple flame roared up to the ceiling, filling the room with intense heat. Raena screamed. Then, barely a second passed before the door swung open and Erik barrelled in.

Face-to-face with the blaze, his jaw almost hit the floor. "What in the name of the Oceans..." he gasped.

In the centre of the room, the tall violet flame soon fizzled out, leaving only a monstrous smog behind. It glowed ominously as swirls of purple and green explored my bedchamber. Through the thick smoke cloud, I could just about make out Raena's faint whimpers. Her chest heaved as she remained pressed against the wall.

"It's alright," I called over to her, relieved that my memory hadn't failed me. "The smoke is harmless. It just looks scary."

"This is magic!" Erik spat.

"Sci-ence," I corrected, enunciating each syllable.

The guard dragged a nervous hand through his blonde waves. "Raena, you stay there. Don't move. I'm alerting the generals." He shot me a glare. "I always knew we couldn't trust you. Faery scum!"

I resisted the urge to roll my eyes back into my skull. On the bright side, at least his reaction proved the goblins would fall for it.

"Don't, Erik. Please. It's not magic." Raena spluttered while arching away from a glowing smog tendril. "I don't really understand it, but I know it's not magic. I saw her mix the powders."

"What you're seeing is just a natural reaction between

aethernite, powdered sulphur, and water," I explained. Lifting my hand, I let the coloured smoke snake around my fingers. "I can make it even more exciting by adding some iron filings, if you'd like to see that too?"

"No!" Raena cried.

"Absolutely not!" Erik echoed.

I shrugged. "I'll save it for the goblins then."

Raena groaned, a thin layer of sweat forming on her forehead. "Please, can you just make it stop?"

"It'll fade on its own after ten minutes or so. But I promise you, this smoke is harmless." As I spoke, a thick tendril of green smog curled around my face. I coughed as it went up my nose, suddenly feeling unusually queasy. "Ah, perhaps not completely harmless."

"What?" Panic flared across Raena's face.

Quickly, I swatted the smog away with my hand. "It's fine, we're all fine," I insisted. "Just hide in your chambers until the smoke clears. Meanwhile, Erik and I will leave for the woods. I've already made enough of this mixture to put on a good show. The goblins won't know what hit them." I grinned, swishing away another curious smog tendril with a flick of my hand.

"I am not going into the woods with her!" Erik thundered.

"Oh please, Erik, just do whatever she says," Raena called back to him, her tone edging on desperation. "I fear if we let her mix up any more of these powders, she'll kill us all."

He looked at her with worry tugging at his brow. "But what about you? What if invaders come and I'm not here to protect you?"

"I'll be fine. I have my dagger."

"You have a what?" Erik's eyes almost popped out of their sockets.

I chuckled. Beneath all the pretty dresses and perfect hair was a whole new side of Raena that he'd clearly never seen before – cunning, chess champion, and mighty quick with a dagger.

"Trust me, your lady will be fine," I cut in.

Erik shot a scowl my way. "You know we'll have to ride quickly if you want to catch up with the prince?"

I nodded.

"And since you're not my princess, if there's any trouble, I won't hesitate to leave you."

"Erik!" Raena coughed.

"I understand." My focus remained on him, the smog making it easier to ignore Raena's protests.

"Then fine. I'll take you to him," he conceded.

I could've screamed with joy.

"But once we find His Highness, I'm coming back here to watch over Lady Raena." He turned towards Raena, searching for her through the wall of smoke. "I promised your father I would keep you safe. And I don't break my promises." There was something almost tender in his voice, and the way it coated each word made it sound like a random past promise wasn't the only reason he didn't want to leave her.

"Thank you, Erik." Surprisingly, her tone was just as wistful as his. How could I have been so blind before? I'd definitely be asking her about this later – that's assuming I return here alive and with Lukas.

A shudder ran through me. As much as I loved to play matchmaker, there was no time for this now.

Clearing my throat, I interrupted their exchange of longing looks. "Pardon my intrusion, but I really believe we ought to leave sooner rather than later."

Erik grunted, shooting me another scowl. How Raena could stand him, I'd never understand. If she was like gold dust, he was no more than a frowning gargoyle.

"Right," he grumbled, after the scowl had well and truly settled onto his face, "we'll leave now, before I come to my senses and change my mind."

This was going to be a long journey.

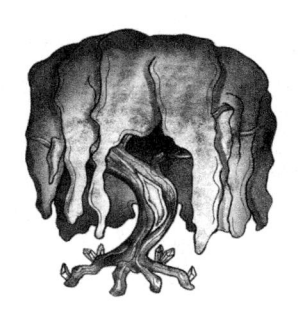

CHAPTER 37

Erik wasn't lying when he said he rode fast. Dawn was just peeking its head over the horizon by the time we'd reached the stables and acquired two horses. After that, it'd taken us less than an hour to follow the hoof marks through the woods and reach the outskirts of the goblin camp. But once we were actually there, peering out from behind a shrub as the familiar view of lopsided tents and rushed campfires stood before me, a gnawing feeling of worry nipped at my heels.

Despite the four pouches of aethernite and sulphur that hung from my hips, I only had one chance to get this right. One chance to convince the goblins that I actually had immense power. One chance to prove to them that I wouldn't hesitate to fill their entire camp with noxious smog unless they return to whatever disgusting mountain crevice they'd crawled out from. And of course, I knew it was an ambitious plan, but I had to try. Only I'd forgotten just how many goblins there were that scurried around the camp, and how easily their horrible little claws had pierced my skin...

"So, what now, Princess?" Erik spoke under his breath whilst kneeling beside me. Somehow he was still scowling – he hadn't stopped since the moment we'd left Raena in the tower. I was tempted to order him to return to her just so I had a break from his glares.

"Now, I have to run in there," I jabbed my finger towards the camp, keeping my voice low, "pretend I'm a faery, create a huge distraction with my smoke, and then hope that wherever Lukas is, he's already found the King and Queen so he can get them out of here without getting caught."

Erik raised an eyebrow. "I thought the plan was that I delivered you to the prince and then I went home?"

"That was your plan." I said, my scowl matching his. "My plan is this."

"Your plan is ridiculous," he scoffed. "So what if they're scared of a bit of fog. There's hundreds of them, if not thousands. You go in there, you die."

"I suppose we'll see, won't we." I flashed him a grin, trying my best to mask my thundering heartbeat. "If something goes wrong, don't be afraid to run back to Raena. She needs you more than I do."

Erik blinked several times as if he didn't recognise the girl staring back at him. Honestly, I couldn't blame his reaction, as neither did I. The plan was completely reckless, completely unlike me. I was careful, cautious – sometimes a little too cautious – and yet, at that moment, I felt brave enough to run through a raging fire. When Lukas left early that morning, something deep in my chest shattered. And now all I could see was him dead, bleeding out, and the very thought made me want to scream into my pillow. So I had to help. Even if it was ridiculous and reckless.

"Wish me luck." I shot Erik a wink as I leapt up from the hedges.

Thankfully, he didn't try to stop me.

"GOBLINS!" I bellowed at the top of my lungs, shoving through the shrubs to march into the camp. Instantly, the dozen goblins that were babbling around the campfire all spun their little green heads towards me.

"O'oman?" A few of them hissed out. But their expressions were blank, as if they had no idea what to make of this bizarre woman who'd just strolled so confidently into a den of beasts.

"You've taken something from me!" I started, shooting my hand high into the air. The moment I had their attention, I began chanting something nonsensical and waving my hand in mysterious, completely made-up patterns. In hindsight, I really should've done a bit more research into what casting a spell actually looked like – if Arenn had seen me then, he'd probably take offence. Still, this whole thing was a distraction, something for them to gawk at while my other hand subtly emptied out two leather pouches onto the forest floor.

"O'oman no use magic!" One of the goblins jerked his spindly finger at my insane dance, but I could see him trembling slightly. This was going to work, it had to.

My hand hovered over the waterskin that hung from my belt. *Any second now, there'll be chaos.*

"You are all foolish goblins!" I roared, continuing my performance. "Now you will feel my wrath!"

Then, I poured the water. A huge violet flame exploded from the ground, reaching almost as high as the treeline; even I jumped back in surprise at the sheer scale of it. Though, the small jolt of panic that I felt was nothing compared to the sudden terror that overwhelmed the camp. Goblins leapt from their log seats, squealing and yelping in fear.

"A fae! A fae!" one screamed. Another tumbled to the ground after bumping into five other panicking goblins. It was pure chaos, and thankfully, exactly what I'd hoped for. Squealing, they plunged in and out of their tents, gathering their belongings and the hands of other goblins to whisk them away from the danger. A few brave souls even dared to scamper off further into the camp, to warn their goblin friends of their impending doom.

Soon, glowing smoke began to billow out from the dying flame. Just like in my bedchamber, it roamed around the camp, swirling in tendrils of ghastly purple and ominous green. Any goblins that had remained either collapsed to the ground in fear or found their courage and darted off into the woods. Terrified screams sounded off in the distance as word quickly spread around the entire camp. If they were smart, they'd send a swarm of goblin soldiers to overwhelm me, but they weren't smart – they were goblins. And this was just science.

I steadied my racing breath as only myself and the smog remained in this corner of the camp. A part of me couldn't believe it'd actually worked. Although I knew I'd still need to march further in and do it all over again if I wanted this to be a proper distraction.

Swallowing down any residual fear, I pushed my way through the smog and wandered deeper into the goblin camp. Eventually, I'd find another good clearing – somewhere where they could all see my 'power'. I couldn't help the nervous chuckle that flew out of me as I walked. Now that the fear had faded from my rocking stomach, this could almost be considered fun. The Ancients know that the little beasts deserve it.

"Naria?"

My chest tightened. I recognised the voice, but it wasn't Lukas's. This voice was soft, like a little bell. Turning around, a feminine figure stood before me. Long, slightly curled blonde hair and a pinched nose sat in the centre of her pale, delicate face. The long sea blue robe that covered her shoulders was edged in purple ribbon, and with her familiar blue hood resting on her head, she looked no different to how she'd appeared when I saw her last in the forbidden library.

"Seraphina?" I breathed, relief flooding through me. "Oh, thank goodness! I'm looking for Lukas. Do you know where he is? Is he alright? Are you alright?" The desperate questions spilled out of my mouth faster than fifty galloping horses. "Sorry," I blurted out, "I just... I need to know that he's safe."

Seraphina tilted her head. "The prince is fine." Her tone was calm as ever, despite our strange situation. "I'm more confused as to why you're here, and why the goblins are screaming that there's a faery who's terrorising the camp."

She narrowed her sharp eyes. "You didn't tell me you could use magic."

"Oh, I can't," I laughed, but for some reason, it came out as more of a nervous giggle. "I combined aethernite and sulphur to make the smog. It's science, not magic at all."

My knees trembled. This was strange, and I knew I should be feeling relaxed by now. If Seraphina was there, that would mean that Lukas and his fellow soldiers were nearby and they could use my distraction to escape the camp. But oddly, there was no sign of him or any soldiers, and for some reason, all the fear had returned to my stomach.

"You should go home, Naria," she cautioned, glancing around nervously. "Or take a horse to the willow and hide with the faeries, at least until this all settles over. It's not safe here, and this isn't your fight."

Confusion tugged at my brow. "What? Why would you say that? I need to help Lukas. Didn't you hear? Someone has sent his armies away? Drothmore is probably hours away from an invasion. I can't just hide until this all finishes. There might not be a kingdom to go back to!"

"And the realm would be much better for it." There was a quiet seething anger in her tone. Her annoyance caught me completely off guard, but before I had a chance to question it, she continued in a droning voice, "You're right though... Or at least you were. In a few hours, there *would have* been an invasion on Drothmore, although now that will have to be postponed until tomorrow morning at least, considering the goblins will need to be rounded up again. Such pesky skittish things." A frustrated sigh escaped her lips.

"What are you talking about?" I demanded, heartbeat

quickening. "You're the King's healer."

Her gaze snapped to mine. "That man is no king. He's barely even a man." The words were dripping in such intense venom that it made me flinch, but the second she noticed me bristling, her tone softened. "I'm sorry, I shouldn't be angry at you. Corlixir is just as much a victim as the rest of us. And you... you've suffered just as much as I have, if not more." She paused, then something like determination blazed across her features. "But mark my words, Princess, once Drothmore has fallen, I will make sure the last thing that disgusting man sees is his kingdom in ruins before we drag a knife through his coal heart, together."

Seraphina was insane. That was the only possible explanation for all this. Maybe finding a cure for the King's curse had driven her to the point of madness? Or maybe something dark and twisted had crept out from these woods and slowly consumed her instead. Either way, I wasn't safe there anymore.

Gulping down any fear, I spoke in the calmest voice I could muster, "Thank you for finding me. This has been an... enlightening conversation, but I think I'll be on my way now." My lips forced themselves into an uncomfortable smile. "Though before I go, I really would like to check on Lukas. Do you happen to know where he is?"

Find Lukas. Warn him about the crazed healer. We both run back to Drothmore. That was the new plan.

Seraphina rolled her eyes. "I told you before, the prince is fine. I'm keeping him safe."

"What do you mean – keeping him safe?" Fear rose to my throat, making my voice tremble. "Where is he, Seraphina?"

If she or her goblin 'friends' had hurt him...

Ignoring my question, she grunted and twisted her body away, moving to pace around the forest clearing. "Arenn will be furious... You being here wasn't at all part of the plan."

"What plan?" I asked nervously.

Seraphina huffed. "Well, while the goblins were swarming the Steel Palace, he was going to swoop in, find you cowering away in your bedchamber, and rescue you himself, all while fighting off a horde of angry goblins. He claimed it would be sure to make you fall in love with him at once. I said it was a ridiculous idea. If I'd known my father had raised such a dramatic son, I would've thought twice about coming home."

My head was spinning. What was she talking about? I'll admit the idea did sound like something Prince Arenn would come up with... But Seraphina was human, undeniably so. Her ears were round, her cheekbones were flat, and while her nose was a little sharp, she was clearly still completely, undeniably human.

"King Bevan can't be your father," I told her. "You're not a faery."

Seraphina took a step towards me. "I'm afraid I haven't been completely honest with you, Naria," she confessed as her small hands reached up to remove her hood. The moment the fabric slipped away from her head, so did any belief I held that she was actually just an insane human.

First, her ears grew to be long and pointed. Then, the softness of her face hardened into typical faery-like features, her jawline sharpening and her cheekbones becoming more pronounced. Even her eyes, once a pale blue, shifted to a more intense shade of sapphire. By the time the hood had been fully pulled back, any blonde in her long hair had completely faded away as her curls cascaded past her narrow shoulders in unnatural hues of lilac, green, and blue. There was something else too, something I couldn't quite put my finger on. It was clear now that she was fae, but there was an unusual shimmer to her pale, creamy skin, and I could've sworn I saw a few scales on her neck before she swished an emerald lock over them.

"It's such a relief to remove a glamour," she sighed, tilting her sharp chin up to the sky. "I made it easier on myself by enchanting the hood, but still, it's like taking off a tight gown after a long night of dancing. So freeing."

After all this time, the King who hated faeries was being treated by one. My mouth fell open. So many thoughts were swirling in my mind.

"So it was you who cursed the King then?"

"Clever girl," Seraphina chuckled.

"Why?" I asked breathlessly.

"All your questions will be answered in time, dear Naria." She smiled, excitement brimming on her lips. "For now, I believe your fiancé has come to rescue you. Of course, it's not exactly how he planned, but he'll have to take what he can get."

"What? Lukas is here?"

Seraphina chuckled again. "Your *other* fiancé."

Any flicker of hope in my heart was immediately snuffed out by her tinkling laughter and the sound of dry leaves being crunched under someone's boots behind me.

"Hello again, little human."

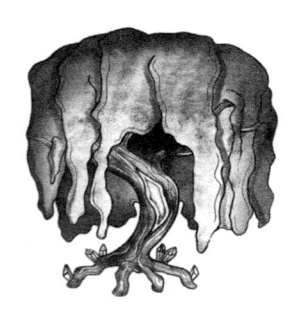

CHAPTER 38

My heart stilled as the scent of wildflowers hit my nose.

"I hope you have a good explanation for why my betrothed is standing in the middle of a goblin camp. Or did you bring her here just to torment me, *dear sister*?" The deep voice spoke again, his tone heavy with warning. "Surely you can tell you've frightened her. She's trembling."

An arm slipped around my waist and pulled me tightly towards a familiar, hard chest, the motion doing absolutely nothing to steady my shaking limbs. Glancing up, my eyes caught on Arenn's sharp jawline. I wanted to feel angry, but the heat of his body pressed against mine only stirred up memories of last night.

My cheeks warmed. Thankfully, that was *still* just a dream. Nothing more.

"You should stop with the dramatic entrances, then maybe she wouldn't tremble so much," Seraphina sneered. "Though I can assure you, brother, I had nothing to do with her being here," she carried on nonchalantly, as if I wasn't standing right between them. "Apparently, she came here to help the Prince of Drothmore. And you can see by casting a look at the state of my poor goblins that she had more of an effect than he did – or the twenty or so soldiers he brought with him, if you could even call them that," she scoffed.

"Naughty little human," Arenn tutted with a playful grin. He tilted his chin down towards me, running a hand along my cheek. "Close your eyes now. Let me take you away from here."

My stomach dipped. Finding some courage, I yanked myself out of his grasp and whirled around to face him. "I'm not going anywhere with you," I stated boldly.

Seraphina shook with laughter. "So much for a chivalrous rescue!"

Beneath his midnight waves, Arenn glared at his sister. "You stay out of this," he growled before returning his gaze to me. "Now please, don't be difficult. You must close your eyes, or else you'll be sick, and I'd rather not have to call the servants into my bedchamber at this time in the morning." He spoke as though he was addressing a small child. It made me feel so small. I hated it.

"I said, I'm not going anywhere with you," I repeated, anger rising in my chest. "I came here to help Prince Lukas, so unless you can take me to him, I'm not leaving this forest."

Arenn's shoulders tensed. "You would be wise not to mention his name again, Princess." He stalked closer, snatching my wrist with one pale hand. "Like I said last night, I don't share."

My chest tightened. *No, but that would mean...*

Before I had a chance to ponder just how many of my dreams he'd been watching, or how that was even possible, Arenn commanded in a husky, pressuring voice, "Close your eyes."

No. I didn't want to. But his voice echoed in my mind. I resisted for barely a second before the compulsion overwhelmed my senses and my eyelids forcibly closed.

The moment they did, a woosh of cool air hit my face, and suddenly there were no more distant goblin screams. The smoky scent of dying campfires vanished, too, replaced by the soothing smell of pine and jasmine. Under my boots, even the forest floor felt suspiciously soft, as though I was standing on a plush rug instead of dried, crunchy leaves.

It was only when Arenn allowed me to open my eyes that I realised we were not in the forest anymore at all. Instead, I found myself in the middle of a familiar quartz-walled bedchamber. Thick willow roots weaved through the ceiling over a large silk bed – the very same bed I'd woken up in on my first visit to the faery kingdom. In the corner of the room was the same ornate chair from which Arenn had interrogated me, although this time there was a black nightshirt and some loose breeches draped over it. The silk bed was also unmade, as if someone had left in a hurry. Then it hit me: the regal engravings that wrapped around the bed posts, the circlet that rested upon the dresser...

This wasn't just any spare bedroom in the faery palace. This was Arenn's bedchamber.

My mouth fell open. "You interrogated me, a complete stranger, in your own bed?"

His grip on my wrist loosened as he chuckled. "Would you have preferred a cell? You know, it's not everyday I get to apprehend a mysterious human girl." He sauntered over to the chair, collapsed into it, then propped his elbows against the wooden armrests. "Besides, if you actually were an assassin, maybe you'd have begged for your life by attempting to seduce me." He smiled in a way that was almost feline. "I wouldn't have said no. I've never bedded a human before."

I almost choked. "You're disgusting!"

"And yet you still accepted my proposal?" he mused, tilting his head playfully as his silver earrings glinted in the golden light of the room. "You do know what will happen once we marry, don't you? We will be expected to consummate."

Warmth flooded my cheeks and I quickly avoided his gaze. I couldn't let him see what his words did to me, but this room was so small and there was nowhere to hide. If that silk bed wasn't his, I'd bury my burning face in the sheets and never leave again.

A low laugh sounded from where he was sitting and judging my reaction.

"I was worried that I might've been too late," he started, lifting his hand to prop his chin against it. "I thought that maybe your foolish prince would've already had his way with you, maybe even several times. But I can see it clearly now... You're as innocent as a little flower."

My knees trembled. "My private life is none of your concern."

"It will be when we are married."

"I am not marrying you," I snapped, my hands balling up into fists beside me. "We were engaged under false pretences. This was clearly all some scheme. You send your sister into the Steel Palace to pose as the King's healer, who by some coincidental reason seems to be suffering from a faery curse, have her manipulate the generals into sending our armies away, and oh, also have her convince me to pay you a visit, too?" My heart pounded against my ribs as I pieced it all together. "I'm not a fool, Arenn. Did you not think I would work it all out? Now she will have Drothmore and you can have Corlixir. But I'd rather die than ever marry you. Drothmore may have already fallen, but you will never rule *my* kingdom."

Arenn's smile faded. Rising from the chair, he stepped closer until he towered over me. My chest heaved with my quickened breath. He wouldn't actually hurt me, would he?

"Do not for a second believe that I am on the same side as *her*."

I blinked, confusion stuffing up my throat. That was not what I expected.

"I'll be honest with you," he continued coolly, "I didn't even know I had another sister until a few hours after Luminessia."

"What?" I breathed.

"When she stormed into the palace shortly after you... departed, I assumed she was just some lost faery who'd gone insane after spending too much time outside the realm. But when my mother and father found out she was here, they became hysterical." A distant scowl crossed his face. "Suddenly all the attention was on precious darling Lyssi. Let's just all forget that was supposed to be *my* special night. It's only the Crown Prince's Luminsessia," he scoffed.

"Lyssi?" I questioned.

"That's her name. Or at least what my mother kept screaming over and over again when she fell to her knees in the middle of the ballroom," he drawled. "Rather embarrassing, really."

"But why would they never mention you had another sister?" My fists loosened from where they were clenched as I ran a few fingers through my hair. "How do you know this isn't some elaborate trick?"

Arenn shrugged, moving to lean against his dresser. "It's possible... But my father has the power to manipulate people's thoughts and memories. I'm sure he'd be able to tell if someone else was using his own tricks against him. And in my mother's case, her reaction seemed genuine, albeit a little dramatic." He sighed, rolling his shoulders. "These are strange times for all of us, Princess. My mysterious long-lost sister arrives with a secret goblin army, desperate to invade Drothmore. And while she's not a threat to Faelenna at present, who knows what will happen when she's bored of her new kingdom." He picked up his circlet, running his fingers along the woven strands of silver. "I'm still the eldest, so eventually, when my parents retire, this kingdom will fall to me. I trust Elsie and Elara to never challenge me for the throne, but I cannot trust *her*."

I studied him carefully. "Would you stop the invasion then? Kill Seraphina to protect your throne?"

His amber irises flicked up to meet mine as he returned

the circlet to its place. "I thought you didn't approve of murder?" he mused gleefully. "You told me yourself last night that you thought I enjoyed sucking the life out of that poor faery." He prowled closer, my heartbeat quickening with every step. "You called me a monster."

"How?" I asked breathily. "How is that possible? That was a dream."

A wild grin dominated his jaw. "It was a dream, of some kind..." He snatched my wrist, running a slender finger down the two crystals that glittered in my forearm. "Ever since you agreed to my proposal, we have been connected. You can enter my dreams. I can enter yours." He traced around the crystals as I shivered. "Our connection is growing stronger now, too. That's how I found you in the forest today. Last night, I could barely feel your presence, but this morning I could sense you were close and that you were scared. That's why I came for you."

"How romantic," I replied, the words dripping in sarcasm, "but please don't enter my dreams anymore."

"Why?" He grinned. "Are you scared we might do more than share a kiss next time? You know there are no real-life consequences from making love in a dream?" I choked back a gasp. "I know it's not proper before we are married, but no one will ever know."

When I shot him a furious scowl, he finally released my wrist. Still, he drew closer, his voice darkening. "You know this connection between us will only grow stronger. Haven't you felt it already? The pull to always be closer? It will keep drawing you to me... Soon, you won't be able to stay away."

"I think I'll manage," I retorted.

"We'll see."

He held my gaze for a few more heated moments before pulling away and heading towards the door.

"Where are you going?" The words just slipped out.

"Miss me already?" he chuckled. "Do not fear, I won't be long, little human. There is some business I must attend to before I retire today. For now, though, you should rest. I'm sure you've gathered by now that fae tend to be most active at night. You'd be wise to try adjusting to our schedule, especially since you'll probably be staying with us for a while."

A knot formed in my throat. I was a prisoner here, even if Arenn danced around the words.

"I can't sleep in your bed," I protested, glancing at the sheets that probably smelled exactly like him – so dangerous, yet the butterflies in my stomach seemed to crave those wildflowers.

"Then sleep on the floor." He laughed cruelly while reaching for the door handle. "Although, you may wake up to me carrying you into bed. The servants will gossip if they believe I am mistreating my betrothed." Before I could argue that he was doing exactly that, the door locked shut behind him.

And I'd never hated myself more for immediately wishing he'd come back.

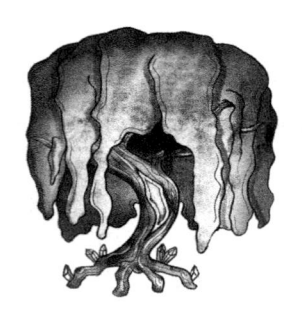

CHAPTER 39

Arenn wasn't there when I woke up the following evening, nor was he present when a faery servant briefly unlocked the door to deliver a tray of breakfast. The food looked delicious, and I couldn't hide the rumbling in my stomach as the servant lifted the silver plate coverings. But still, I couldn't bring myself to eat – not when all I could think about was Lukas. Was he trapped here too? Were they at least feeding him? Or was he locked away, hidden deep in a cell somewhere, being tortured by a wicked faery prince?

I shivered, the smell of the food suddenly making me feel queasy.

Yesterday, or shortly after whenever Arenn had left me in his chambers – it was so hard to tell the time in a windowless underground palace – half a dozen faery servants had filtered into the room. They'd helped me prepare for bed and replaced the travelling gown I was wearing with a shimmering nightdress. The fabric was so thin I could see the outline of my fingers when I dipped them beneath the skirt. I wasn't sure if Arenn had joined me in bed after that since I fell asleep so quickly, but if he had, I hoped he'd been gentlemanly enough to at least keep his eyes, and his hands, to himself.

An hour or so after breakfast had been delivered, I heard the door unlock again. The same servants hurried into the room, this time with a floor-length faery gown in their pastel-coloured arms. Not wanting to spend any longer in my almost translucent nightgown, I allowed them to lace me into it. Though I probably should've taken a closer look at the gown first. The midnight blue fabric was barely opaque and the skirt was more of a thin panel that exposed the sides of my legs up to my hips. The neckline was also scandalous, swooping low as it barely covered my chest, leaving far too little to the imagination. Even for a faery, this outfit would be improper, and I dreaded to think why Arenn had chosen for me to wear this – of all the gowns in the kingdom.

Just as the faery servants were finishing threading tiny blue flowers into the curls of my hair, the door swung open. The sound made me stiffen, but I recognised the sound of his heavy boot steps long before my glare caught him in the vanity mirror.

"You shine brighter than the caverns today, dear human," Arenn announced, shooing the servants away with a few flicks of his wrists. "How did you sleep?"

I didn't answer, choosing instead to remain silent as I

sat rigidly on the small stool by his vanity station. He might control where I go and how I dress, but he did not control my words.

The prince sauntered closer, clearly not bothered by my lack of response. His hands brushed my exposed arms in slow, sweeping motions as he stood behind me, admiring the servants' work.

"You really do look exquisite," he murmured while continuing to stroke my arms. "But something is missing... hidden away behind your pretty hair."

Forcing down a shiver, I felt his fingers hook around my hair, sweeping it away from my neck and resting it all on one shoulder.

"There." He smiled, stooping until his face was beside mine in the mirror. "Now everyone can see that you belong to me."

A deep wave of shame hit me as I noticed just what he was referring to. Marring the side of my neck, blooming softly on my skin, was a small rosebud-sized bruise. It didn't hurt, but clearly that was not Arenn's intention when he put it there two sleeps ago. It was a visible reminder of my biggest mistake yet, second only to agreeing to marry him. Just looking at it made me feel ill.

I'd never let him kiss me like that again.

"Don't look so displeased," Arenn said, drawing back from the mirror. "You'll be delighted to hear I have a surprise for you." A devious smile pulled at his lips. "He's waiting in the royal dining hall."

My heart fluttered for the briefest moment before immediately sinking in my chest.

Lukas.

I whipped around to face the faery prince.

"What have you done?" My lower lip trembled both with rage and fear. So many horrible, awful visions flooded my mind. "If you've killed him, I swear, Arenn, I'll never forgive you!"

"Relax, Princess." He grinned. "Your precious prince is alive and well. My new sister is taking very, very good care of him." He laughed lazily. "In fact, she's arranged for us all to have lunch together in the dining hall. We'll leave as soon as you're ready." His slender fingers swiped the bottom of my chin, tilting my face up to meet his gaze. "Do take your time, though. I want you to look your best when he sees you. I want him to know exactly what he's missing, and what I now possess." He smiled, then planted a cold kiss against my lips.

The scandalous gown, the love bite on my neck – it all made sense now. I was merely a trophy. A toy for a jealous prince to show off and prove to the world that he had won. I almost refused. If it weren't for the chance of seeing Lukas again, I never would've gone.

But I had to see him again, even if it was for one last time.

"I'm ready," I said flatly.

I could hear his screams long before the guards had even opened the huge doors that led to the royal dining room. Each roar of pain shattered my heart over and over again, while Arenn only chuckled.

"Sounds like it's playtime! I hope she saves a piece for

me." He grinned hungrily, as though we were about to feast our eyes on a slice of vanilla cake rather than a tortured human prince.

It made me feel ill.

When the guards finally heaved the giant wooden doors apart, my gaze found him immediately. His limp body was sprawled across a long dark quartz dining table, surrounded by at least a dozen chairs. Every few seconds, he was tossed up into the air and then slammed down again by invisible hands. Each impact, another cry, followed by the awful sounds of bones breaking.

"STOP!" I screamed, racing towards him. There were other guests there too, sitting around the table, but I barely even spared them a glance. In that moment, it was only the two of us, and all I could focus on was how lifeless he looked and how his once-perfect skin was covered with layers upon layers of fresh bruises. Were it not for the yelps of pain, I'd be searching for a heartbeat.

"Lukas?" I pleaded, holding either side of his face. "Lukas, can you hear me? Please answer me."

My own tears hit his cheeks as he struggled to form a reply. "Naria?" he wheezed in a strained voice. "You shouldn't be here." He coughed, wincing at the movement.

"It's alright." I spoke softly, breathing through relieved sobs while stroking his cheek. "I followed you into the woods to help. I'll heal you, I'll—"

"Arenn, could you please control your beloved? She's interrupting our entertainment." A frustrated woman's voice made me flinch. Glancing up, I noticed Seraphina – or Lyssi, as I'd recently discovered – sitting at the head of the table. She wore a deep red faery gown with a plunging neckline. The typical pale blue hood was nowhere to be seen, so her faery features were on full display, and her sharp eyes glared daggers at Arenn who hadn't yet left the doorway.

"You've injured him so badly, he's barely conscious," Arenn complained, crossing his arms across his chest. "That wasn't part of the deal, Lyssi."

She stiffened at the sound of her name. "It's Lyssandra," she corrected. "Lyssi died eighteen years ago, thanks to that scum." She jabbed her finger across the dining table, and it was only then that I realised just how many people there were.

Sitting on either side of Lyssandra were the Faery King and Queen, both looking equally uncomfortable. The Queen fidgeted nervously with her wine goblet, and even the King was sitting far too rigidly in his seat. Next to Queen Amabel was Erissa. Her gown was dirty, and she'd been stripped of any jewels, but still, she didn't seem too concerned with the situation. She watched Lukas with a bored expression, twirling her fork in circles on her empty silver plate. Opposite her was Ikelos. His entire body was so thin and frail, he could barely keep upright in his seat. The cream tunic he wore had been ruined by thick streaks of mud, as if he'd been dragged straight from his bedchamber and then all the way through the forest to get here. And his eyes, though heavy with cobwebs, darted around anxiously as Lyssandra aimed her slender finger directly at him.

"You're the real reason for all of this, aren't you, *Ikelos*?" she hissed viciously. "Actually, don't answer that. I've already decided if I hear another word from you, I'll cut out your tongue!" She laughed, her high pitched cackle sending a visible ripple of fear through the guests around the table – everyone except for Erissa who was still absent-mindedly twirling her fork.

"A deal was a deal though, brother. You'll get your moment." Lyssandra pushed up from her seat, letting it scrape loudly across the marble floor. She marched over to where Ikelos was hunched, placing one hand on his forehead and the other on Lukas's chest. A breath of silence passed before she scrunched up her face and began muttering foreign words. Then, Ikelos groaned in pain while Lukas gasped, arching his back and writhing.

"What are you doing?" I demanded. "Stop it! You're hurting them!"

She ignored me, continuing to mutter the strange phrases. Tears clouded my vision. This couldn't be the end. There had to be a way to stop this. I was debating smashing a plate against Lyssandra's head when I noticed the strangest thing – the red and purple blemishes on Lukas's skin were beginning to fade.

My mouth fell open. Any scrapes sealed themselves, and his skin returned to a healthy glow. Even the dark circles under his lashes were fading, too.

"You're healing him?" I breathed.

"Not healing, just transferring some of Ikelos's lifeforce," Lyssandra grumbled. "It's not as if he'll have much use for it later anyway." She then stepped back, swaying a little as Lukas's eyes snapped open. He sat bolt upright on the table, gasping for breath, and immediately I reached for him.

"Lukas?" I panicked. "How do you feel? Please tell me you're alright."

He struggled to catch his breath as he turned to face me. "Naria, I-I thought you were a dream."

My hands cupped his jaw again, and for a few small moments, there was peace – until I noticed his gaze catch on something else as his entire body stiffened.

"You!" he snarled, glaring at Lyssandra. "You're a traitor! You betrayed us." Twisting away from her, he grabbed my shoulders urgently. "You need to get out of here now, Naria. That woman, that... thing, whatever she is, she's insane."

Suddenly, I was yanked away when another, much colder hand clamped down on my wrist.

"And *she's* also the least of your problems now, princeling," Arenn threatened, forcing me close to his chest. I tried to break free, but his grip was too strong. "If you touch my betrothed again, I won't hesitate to kill you."

Lukas was speechless. But only for a few heartbeats. "Betrothed?" he echoed, as if he hadn't quite heard him correctly.

Tears made rivers in my cheeks while I quietly mouthed the words, "I'm sorry."

"Yes, little princeling," Arenn purred, running his fingers down my exposed arms. "Now you know you should've married her when you had the chance." He gripped my cheeks, nuzzling his face into my hair. "I'm so looking forward to our wedding night. Although, now she's here, it'll be hard to wait. She smells so... sweet."

"Don't you dare touch her!" Lukas roared, slamming his fist down onto the table. He leapt at Arenn. And was barely inches away when suddenly he was forced backwards, landing roughly in the chair beside Ikelos. Desperately, he fought against the invisible chains, but they were too strong. No amount of thrashing let him move even a little from the chair he was pinned to.

"There'll be no fighting at the dinner table, boys," Lyssandra chided, waggling her finger as though they were just two misbehaving children. "And you," she shot a glare at Arenn, "stop causing trouble and sit down. Don't make me use magic on my own family."

"Of course, dear sister." Arenn smiled sweetly, leading me over to a chair opposite Lukas. I went to reach for the chair, but he smoothly sat down first and pulled me into his lap instead. "You can sit right here, *fiancée*." The faery prince's arm curled around my waist before I even had a chance to push myself away.

"Now we're all seated, we should eat!" Lyssandra announced with an excited grin, clapping her hands together as though this was a perfectly normal family dinner.

While the servants poured in with plates of steaming food, I risked a glance at Lukas. His steel eyes were fixed on Arenn, with a burning rage like I'd never seen before.

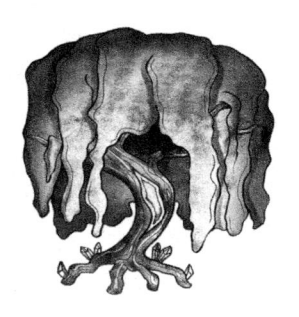

CHAPTER 40

An hour later, most of the food still remained uneaten in the centre of the dining table. Huge stacks of bread rolls, plates piled high with meat slices, and bowls filled with brightly coloured fruits and vegetables were all left untouched, as if someone had dipped one of the carrots in poison and none of us were brave enough to take the first bite. Only Arenn and Lyssandra seemed to enjoy the meal. They eagerly helped themselves to several slices of meat and sauces, while the rest of us sat in silence... All except for Erissa, who spent at least fifteen minutes lazily chewing on a dry bread roll.

"Aren't you hungry, little human?" Arenn lips hovered by my ear, the fabric of his tunic feeling rough against the exposed skin on my back. "You should eat something."

He plucked a strawberry from a nearby bowl and waved it in front of my lips.

"Open wide," he commanded, his voice echoing in my ears. I tensed my jaw, but my resistance was no match for his compulsion. The second my lips parted, he slipped the strawberry in, using his other fingers to push up on my jaw, forcing me to bite.

"Good girl," he praised as the fruit juices trickled down my chin, "but you're so messy." Shamelessly, he gripped my face in his hands and leaned closer. At first, I thought he was going to kiss me, until his tongue stroked up from the bottom of my chin. Immediately I flinched and tried to break free of his grasp, but his hand kept my wrists pinned behind my back. Slowly and repeatedly, as if my skin was covered in the sweetest sugar, he licked up to the corners of my mouth – while I just accepted it, helplessly trapped.

Humiliation burned on my cheeks. Everyone was watching us, but the fury of Lukas's glare would've rivalled the strongest hurricane.

After a few more awful licks, Lyssandra's frustrated voice stole everyone's attention away. "Blessed Oceans, could you save this behaviour for your bedchamber?" she scoffed. "I'm trying to eat."

"Agreed," Erissa added, not bothering to look up from her bread roll.

"A thousand apologies." Arenn lifted his head, turning to face his sister dramatically. "Though if there's nothing more to be said here, I would quite like to retire to my chambers so that Naria and I can continue our... conversation."

My insides curled.

"I'm afraid you'll have to wait," Lyssandra shot back. "We still have much more to discuss."

Arenn rolled his eyes, then leaned back in his seat, pulling me along with him. "Get on with it then. Some of us actually have duties to attend to."

The look Lyssandra flashed at him was verging on murderous, but it didn't take long for her to compose herself.

After taking a deep breath, she addressed the table, "I'm sure that some of you might be wondering why I've gathered us all here today. As you know, it is not common for we fae to dine with our human friends." She swirled her goblet in her pale hand. "But today is not a common day... Today, dear friends and *beloved* family, marks the day that the foul, the disgusting, the wicked... Ikelos Forgeborn will be brought to justice." Her goblet slammed against the table as she cast a long look at Ikelos. The frail king didn't seem to notice, though. Over the course of the meal, he'd weakened to the point where he was barely able to hold his head up.

"On my journey here I was considering the best way to expose his crimes. I could just tell you, but I feel that I could not even come close to describing the horrors that this man has subjected both humans and faeries to," Lyssandra continued, her words dripping with venom. "So, I will ask everyone now to hold hands, and I will show you exactly why we are all here and why Ikelos deserves to rot in the darkest pits of the underrealm for all eternity." From under the table, she lifted her hands, holding them out for her parents to take.

The Faery King and Queen exchanged worried glances, but each took a hand, extending their own to Ikelos and Erissa. Hesitantly, they accepted too as Arenn took Erissa's other hand and then held mine, squeezing it a few times. I wanted to reach for Lukas, but Arenn held me far too tightly to move.

"Now please, close your eyes," Lyssandra instructed once we were all mostly connected. "And I will show you a story of love." She glanced at Erissa. "And betrayal." She glared at Ikelos.

Forcing down the fear that rose in my chest, I closed my eyes.

Fresh, salty air overwhelmed my nose as I heard the strange, rolling sounds of water. My eyes flew open, immediately squinting from the bright sun that warmed my face. It was hot, so much hotter than the more temperate forests of Drothmore. An intense breeze whipped hair across my face, but after I wiped it away, I gasped at the view before me. Stretching out to the distant horizon, was a perfect, endless line of blue. The sapphire water seemed to go on forever, only meeting the land as it crashed across the golden sand, metres away from where I stood. I'd always dreamt of seeing the ocean, but no amount of dreaming could ever compare to seeing it like this. The view took my breath away.

"Welcome to the beaches of Ryntook," Lyssandra announced from behind me. Whipping my body around, I noticed tall cliffs that reached up to the sky and strange trees with huge, long, jagged leaves. Most of the dinner party was there, too. Everyone, except for Erissa and Ikelos, was gathered on the sand, all looking equally bemused by our new surroundings.

"Pay attention now, because this is where our story begins." Lyssandra swept her hand towards the shoreline.

Hesitantly, I returned my gaze to the ocean, then almost jumped out of my skin when a young man walked right by me, passing inches away from my face. He was tall, with dark brown hair and copper skin, while his face and the confident way he held himself appeared oddly familiar – so familiar that had I not seen him so close, I would've assumed it was Lukas.

"The star of our story," Lyssandra narrated as the pieces clicked together in my head.

Ikelos wasn't gathered with the others on the sand because that was him. This was *his* memory.

In silence, we all watched as young Ikelos marched towards a large rock that jutted out from the water. He waited there for a few moments before a young lady appeared, too. She pushed herself up from behind the boulder as water dripped down the seashells that daintily decorated her chest. Just like Lyssandra, her hair was an unusual mix of lilac, blue, and green tones, while her face was something else entirely. With her full lips and bright eyes, I'd never seen someone so beautiful and so full of life.

It didn't take long for my breath to catch as I glanced down and realised that this was no ordinary young woman. Instead of legs, a long, blue, shimmering fishtail swung delicately over the side of the rock. I'd never seen a mermaid before, but I'd heard the stories. Their beauty was supposed to be so breathtaking that it would send sailors diving off ships and plummeting straight to their deaths, just for the chance of a kiss from one. If all merfolk looked like her, then those stories had to be true. Even my heart fluttered as I studied her perfect features.

The mermaid smiled down at Ikelos, then lowered herself so that their lips met. They held each other in a passionate embrace as Lyssandra's voice cut through the sound of the nearby waves crashing.

"How beautiful Erissa was," she sighed.

No. That couldn't be Erissa. I refused to believe it. While the young woman did seem somewhat familiar, her face was too radiant, too glowing with flawless beauty to even be compared to Erissa's dull and lifeless features.

But before I could argue, the world around us dimmed. The light disappeared for only a few heartbeats before the sun shone brightly once again. When I glanced back at the rock, both Ikelos and the mermaid had disappeared, though the sound of quiet sobbing turned my head in another direction.

A few feet away, young Ikelos stood facing the ocean, while the same woman stood opposite him. Her fishtail had disappeared, replaced by two slender legs. As she sobbed quietly, she clutched Ikelos's tunic with one hand and draped the other across her swollen belly.

"There's no need to cry, my love," young Ikelos consoled her as she wept. "The healers said you'll be home long before the baby arrives. Just use this time to rest and gather your strength. I will be here the moment you resurface."

My gaze paused upon her belly. If that *was* Erissa then that meant...

"I love you," she whispered back between cries, "and I'm so sorry it has to be this way, but I will think of you every moment I am gone." They held each other in a tight embrace until Erissa's legs slowly morphed into a long, blue fishtail. She gasped at the transformation, while Ikelos just held her for what felt like an eternity, neither one wanting to let go first. Eventually, he lowered her gently into the water. Then, they shared one final kiss before she dipped her head beneath the waves and vanished in a shimmer of blue.

"There is a ritual that the merfolk can perform to give themselves human form, but unfortunately, the effects are only temporary." Lyssandra's steady voice pulled me back from the scene once again. I turned away to find her, but my attention instead found Lukas. His bronze skin paled as his gaze remained fixed on where his mother had been.

Did he know? Was that where his magic came from?

"Every few seasons, Erissa would have to return to the ocean to rest and recover her abilities," Lyssandra drawled, forcing my attention away from Lukas. "This time away was brief, but of course, any time away was far too long for Ikelos. Three seasons each year with his love were not enough. He wanted more..."

Our surroundings dimmed once again, but this time, when the light returned, we were in a small, dusty-smelling, windowless room. Tall bookshelves extended up to the ceiling as Arenn, Lukas, and Lyssandra stood on either side of me. Gathered in the centre of the room, huddled around a large bubbling cauldron, were both Arenn and Lukas's parents, each one a perfect younger copy of themselves.

"The ritual is not a difficult one," the young Faery Queen explained, swirling her hand over the cauldron's mysterious purple liquid, "but be careful, dear, and remember what I said." She shot a nervous glance at Erissa. "If you accept the potion, you will change drastically. You will be completely human. There's no going back from this."

Erissa swallowed, shaking her head. "Thank you, but I'm afraid this has been a waste of your time." With trembling lips, she turned to Ikelos. "I'm so sorry, my love, but I cannot do this. If I become human, I will have to say goodbye to my sisters forever. I know both yourself and dear Lukas miss me terribly every time I leave, I miss you both too! But I can't give up this part of me, not even for our son. I'm so, so sorry." She clutched his hands as her quivering features brimmed with heartbreak.

"I don't wish to see anymore of this!" Lukas's voice stole my focus away from the gathering. "This is all a trick anyway. That woman is not my mother."

"Isn't she?" Lyssandra grinned. "Then I suggest you stay for a little longer, or you'll miss the best part. Let me show you what our heroic king does next." Her smile faded as the world dimmed for a final time.

When our vision returned, the scene had changed again. We were back in the Steel Palace, this time standing by the fireplace in the King's bedchamber. It was late at night, the dying embers of the fire casting an orange glow over the huge darkwood bed in the centre of the room. Resting on top of the pure white sheets was Erissa. Even while fast asleep, she still looked just as radiant as she had on the beach. The soft colourful waves of her hair pooled effortlessly around her shoulders.

"I'm so sorry, my love..." A whisper cut through the darkness. Out from the shadows, Ikelos stepped forward, holding a vial of shimmering purple liquid in his trembling hands. "I have to do this. You can't keep leaving us." He drew closer to where Erissa slept. "For the sake of our son. I love you."

The King used his fingers to force her lips apart as he tipped the vial into her mouth. My heart shuddered. I could feel the cold shift in the air the moment the violet liquid touched her tongue.

"No," I muttered, smacking my hands over my wide-open mouth.

And then the screams started.

It was as if Ikelos had just dragged a spear through her heart. She arched her back, writhing and twisting her body in such intense pain while her screams tore along the walls of the bedchamber. Ikelos stumbled backwards, collapsing to the floor. He shouted the words 'I'm sorry' over and over again, but his panicked shouts could've been whispers as they were drowned out by her wretched screams. As she continued to wail, the warm glow faded from her hollowing cheeks. All her otherworldly beauty drained away along with the bright colours in her hair, leaving behind a lifeless, white-haired wraith of a woman.

"Do you recognise her now, boy?" Lyssandra hissed over the awful sounds of Erissa's wails. Her glare landed on Lukas, who stood frozen by the dying fire. His face was completely blank. Just like his mother, all the colour had drained from his skin too, and I almost didn't recognise him. His jaw was clenched so tightly to stop it trembling. I'd never seen him look so conflicted, so... afraid. It made my heart ache.

Without caring about the consequences, I rushed towards him.

"Not so fast, Princess." Arenn's hands caught my wrists before I could move any further.

I screamed with rage. "I swear to the Ancients, Arenn – if you don't let me go!"

"Are we done here?" he called out to his sister, ignoring me as I struggled in his unrelenting grasp. "Surely by now we've seen enough of this spectacle?" He jerked his chin towards Erissa, who still wailed in between pained, sobbing gasps.

"How could you—" But the world began to fade away before I could finish my sentence.

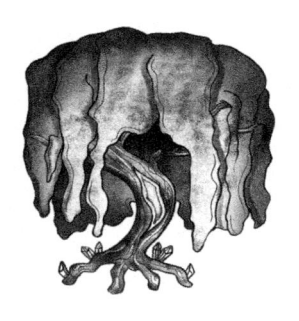

CHAPTER 41

There was nothing until, with a gasp, I blinked my eyes open.

We were back in the very real faery palace. All of us had returned to our seats, my back still pressed against Arenn's chest as I was held securely on his lap. Across the table, Lukas glared at his father, but the intensity of his gaze was so fierce it could've burnt the frail man's skin.

"Is it true?" he demanded. "Did all of that really happen?"

The King's chest heaved as he croaked out a weak response, "Yes."

Lukas slammed his fist against the quartz table. "All this time, Father! All this time, you told me she was ill! Never thought to mention why? Never thought to mention that she... my own mother wasn't even born human?" He slammed his fist down again. "You lied when you told me she was ill. And then you lied again every time you told me she would get better!"

"I did it for you," Ikelos replied in a strained voice. "I just wanted you to have a mother. Ryntook is so far away, and she'd be gone for an entire season. The servants told me you cried for days the first time she left and that you never really stopped until she came back. I couldn't bear to put you through that again. I—"

"You could have been there for me! I was a baby and you were my father. When I cried, you should have held me!"

"I had a kingdom to run," Ikelos scoffed, sending a cloud of dust onto his tunic. "I didn't have time for children. That was precisely why I married your mother. You were her responsibility, but she was too busy frolicking in the ocean. So that's why, when the faeries presented us with a way to fix all this, I made the decision for her. And I made the right choice."

Lukas's jaw tightened as a heavy silence fell over the table.

"You may as well have murdered her," he seethed. "I will never forgive you."

Lyssandra cleared her throat, then tapped a spoon lightly on the side of her goblet. "I hate to interrupt your conversation, boys, but we do actually have other important matters to discuss."

"Why do you even care about this?" Lukas spat, whipping his head up to face her. "You're no friend of my mother's. Why are you punishing us all for his cruel actions?"

"Calm yourself, princeling. I'm not finished with my story." She leaned back in her chair as our attention returned to her. "In our world, magic cannot be created nor destroyed. So when your father gave your dear mother the potion that stripped her of her merfolk abilities, those powers transferred to the one who created the potion."

"Well, that's just wrong," Arenn argued while Queen Amabel nervously sipped from her goblet. "Clearly our mother isn't a mermaid."

"Such a clever observation," Lyssandra shot back, her voice dripping in sarcasm. But she ignored Arenn's scowl as she continued, "Unbeknownst to our innocent mother at the time, she was actually pregnant with yours truly, me! So when Erissa lost her mermaid essence, it flowed right back to my mother and straight into her womb. Can anyone guess what happened eight months later? What about you, dear brother? Since you are feeling so clever tonight?"

Arenn's arm around my waist tightened. "You were born with a freakish little fishtail," he answered coolly.

"That's right. Sweet baby Lyssi was born equal parts mer and fae. How shocked my parents were when the healers had to dunk their newborn baby into a bath full of water just so she could take her first breath." Lyssandra scowled as Queen Amabel's lower lip trembled.

I was glad Lyssandra didn't insist on showing us that particular memory. I'd assisted with more births than I could count as part of my education, so I had no issue with that, but to see a mother who could barely recognise a baby as her own child? The thought of it made my blood run cold.

"Of course, I couldn't stay here either," Lyssandra went on. "Merfolk need saltwater to thrive. So, as a mere babe, I was shipped off to the coasts of Ryntook, to live with the others like me, until my parents could find some kind of solution to fix this whole situation. Or clearly, in my case, until I was strong enough to trade away the damned tail myself." A flicker of fear passed over her features, but I barely had time to notice it before she carried on in a more relaxed tone. "And then, when my parents went to visit their beloved friend Ikelos to come to some arrangement, because surely he and his wife would want to help remove these wayward powers from an innocent baby, even if it meant Erissa somehow claiming them back... What did you tell them, Ikelos?" Lyssandra waved her pale hand towards him.

He grumbled a response that was barely audible.

"What was that?" she insisted, raising an eyebrow.

"A deal was a deal," he grumbled again, louder this time. "They could've come up with a spell on their own to fix the baby. I'd already paid for the potion. Our deal was done."

"But you weren't done, were you, Ikelos?" Lyssandra said as her voice darkened. "You grew scared and paranoid that the faeries would come after you. That they'd steal your wife and force her to take her essence back. And by that point, you knew she'd agree, that your wife would do *anything* to return to the ocean." She paused for a moment, then let her chin rest in her palm as a smile crept over her lips. "Why don't you tell dear Naria what happened when you paid your Corlixin friends a visit?"

A breath caught in my throat. Instantly, my eyes locked onto Ikelos.

"What's she talking about?" I demanded. "What happened?"

The King stiffened, his already pale face turning whiter than his bed sheets. "Nothing. Happened."

My heart thundered in my chest. He was lying, clearly he was, so I whipped my head to face Lyssandra.

"Tell me!" I demanded again. "Tell me what happened in my kingdom."

Lyssandra's smile grew further, stretching up her sharp cheekbones. The silence was killing me until finally, she broke it with her lilting voice. "Do you remember when I told you of the mages that used to reside in your kingdom?"

I nodded. "The human descendants of the fae."

"That's right," she confirmed. "Your darling king here decided to pay their school a visit, after my parents begged him to help them fix me. He wanted the mages to use their magic to banish the faeries from human soil. Of course, they refused. Ikelos's idea was mad. But he didn't take no for an answer. So what did you do, Ikelos, when they told you no?" she prompted him. "Tell her."

"I..." The frail king tried desperately to keep his mouth clamped shut, but it didn't take long for the compulsion to overthrow any resistance. "I... I burned down their s-school."

Burned?

No...

"And when was this?" Lyssandra encouraged him. "Did this happen to be only hours before the famous fire that destroyed poor Corlixir? Do tell us, Ikelos."

His body shuddered as he feebly attempted to resist the compulsion again. "Y-yes."

"Father..." Lukas gasped, but I could barely hear him

over the thundering in my ears. Suddenly, I felt incredibly dizzy, as if the dining room was spinning in endless circles around me. Too fast. Too much.

"It was you," I muttered, "it was always you... You started the fire!" My chest seized. Every breath I took felt entirely too short as little stars filled my tear-blurred vision.

"You... You destroyed my kingdom." The words got stuck behind a choking gasp. In the distance, I could've sworn I heard Lyssandra's cackling laughter.

"YOU KILLED MY PARENTS!"

Ikelos froze. Even Erissa flinched at the sound of my scream, letting the bread roll she was nibbling on clatter against her plate.

Heavy sobs began to work their way up my throat, but I forced them down. Slamming my palms down on the table, I shoved myself off Arenn's lap. For once, he was smart enough not to try to stop me as I marched over to the other side of the table where Ikelos was trembling. Roughly, I grabbed the back of his chair and yanked it backwards, my knuckles white from the force. It slid across the floor with a deafening scrape until I was towering over the weak, shivering king as he cowered away in his chair.

"Naria, be careful before you do something you regret," Lukas warned, slowly rising from his chair.

"Ignore him," Lyssandra snarled, also pushing herself up from the table. She glided to my side, her long crimson ball gown trailing behind her. "Here. I have something to make the job easier." Lifting her skirt, she plucked a thin silver dagger from her boot. It glinted in the golden light of the room as she placed the hilt in my palm.

"Wait, no!" Ikelos whimpered. "Please!"

"Don't do this, Naria. He might be a monster, but you're not. Let the other rulers punish him for his crimes," I heard Lukas beg.

My knees trembled with both rage and fear. The dagger felt so heavy in my palms. I wasn't a killer, and I knew I'd regret this, but every time I looked at the snivelling man before me, all I could imagine were my parents' screams as they burned alive in the flames *he* started.

"Do it, Naria," Lyssandra hissed into my ear. She leaned against my side, placing a cold hand on my shoulder. "Do it for me and do it for your kingdom."

"Wait!" Ikelos protested. He was too weak to leave his chair. Too weak to put up a fight. And thanks to the teachers he'd found for me, I knew exactly where to strike to make this a slow and painful death. Sucking in a deep breath, I raised the dagger.

"Yes," Lyssandra hissed.

"No!" Lukas pleaded.

"Seeing you with a weapon is so alluring, little human," Arenn purred.

My jaw tightened. I'd be sure to kill him next.

"Wait!" Ikelos begged with tears streaming down his cheeks. All I needed to do was swing down, but my arms were frozen above me. Why was this so impossibly hard? Squeezing my eyes shut, I finally thrust the dagger towards him. "You're forgetting about the treaty!"

Something hard caught my wrist seconds before I pierced his chest.

"What did you say?" Lyssandra snarled. Slowly, my eyes

opened to see her fingers curling around my wrist. With a shuddering breath, I dropped the dagger, letting it clatter to the floor. Disbelief washed over me as all my rage was replaced by horror.

I almost killed a man.

"You should ask your parents," Ikelos's dry voice answered her, but I could barely hear him over the pounding of blood in my ears.

Huffing, Lyssandra shoved herself off my shoulder as she glared at the Faery King and Queen. "What's he talking about? What's this treaty?"

Queen Amabel almost dropped her goblet. "Oh, don't worry about that," she stammered.

"It's nothing you should concern yourself with. It's a mere trivial political deal," the Faery King added, a humourless laugh following his words.

Ikelos cackled. "Look inside my head, girl. Like you did with the rest of my memories. I'll show you what they're hiding from you."

Lyssandra furrowed her brow but still reluctantly obeyed, placing a hand against his wrinkled forehead. After a few tense seconds, she gasped and quickly drew her hand away.

"You lied to me!" Her head snapped up to where her parents were still sitting at the table.

"No, no." Her father rose out of his seat, waving his hands frantically. "I can assure you it was merely a political deal!"

After he spoke, the temperature in the room plummeted, as if someone had just cracked open a window on a brisk winter's morning. I would've questioned it, had my hands not already been shivering so much from another, even colder feeling that weighed on my chest. If the village mother were here, she'd tell me it was probably shock. I did almost kill a man.

Ancients... Could I even still call myself a healer?

"Gold for a daughter," Ikelos cackled again, forcing my attention away from my trembling palms. "I give you gold, and you stay out of the human kingdoms and far from my wife. Though I'll admit, I never thought you'd actually accept it! You faeries are no better than the goblins." He threw his head back as he shook with laughter.

"Quiet!" Lyssandra snapped at him.

The Faery Queen fiddled with her auburn hair. "We always knew you'd come back home eventually, and the gold was very useful to us!"

"More useful than a daughter?" Lyssandra spat.

"Well, they did already have an heir, little sister," Arenn pointed out with a flourish of his arms, while Ikelos fell apart with dry laughter.

"I said be quiet!" Lyssandra snapped again at Ikelos.

Just then, the strange coldness shifted to a damp feeling, making the ends of my hair feel wet. I glanced at Lukas, who looked equally confused as water droplets formed on the tips of his fingers. No one else seemed to notice, though. Ikelos continued to shake with roaring laughter while Lyssandra's parents desperately tried to justify their decision.

"You did come back to us in the end," the Faery Queen reminded her.

"Ask them how much gold they have stored away because of you." Ikelos spoke between choking laughs.

Lyssandra growled with anger, her head whipping between a cackling Ikelos and her babbling parents. Beneath my feet, the floor seemed to tremble. Then, the water that had soaked my hair and clothes suddenly disconnected itself from my body and rushed towards Lyssandra in a violent, horrifying wave of blue.

"I SAID BE QUIET!" she screamed, as a huge crystal-blue serpent made entirely of water gushed up from her raised arms. As it soared into the air, my mouth swung open and I stumbled backwards. I'd never seen magic like this before. Power thrummed from its swirling blue body – intense power, so full of rage, I could almost taste it.

Without a breath of pause, it barreled towards Ikelos, the sheer force immediately splitting his chair to pieces. One moment he was laughing, and the next, he was being torn apart in a blur of crashing and foaming waves. His cursed body didn't stand a chance as he crashed against the back wall of the dining room. Then, just as quickly as it had appeared, the water serpent vanished, evaporating into nothing but a small puddle around the King's lifeless body.

Heart pounding, I sprinted over to him before I even realised I'd moved. Everyone was silent as I fell to my knees to roll him over. But I knew what I'd see before I saw it. Glazed over eyes. Parted lips. Quickly, I padded my fingers along his neck, feeling for a heartbeat. Nothing.

"King Ikelos is dead," I announced coldly.

Behind me, someone cheered.

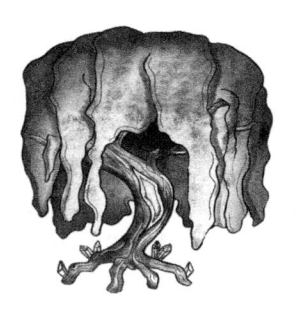

CHAPTER 42

"A toast to my dead husband!" Erissa cheered, raising her glass.

The last few minutes were a foggy mess in my mind. At Lyssandra's insistence, everyone had returned to their seats at the dining table – of course, everyone but Ikelos, whose body had been left untouched on the floor. I then vaguely remembered Arenn scooping me up from where I was kneeling and placing me into a chair beside him at the table. And then someone else, possibly Erissa, filling my goblet with wine. But I barely recalled lifting the glass to my lips – only how much my hands shook as I gripped the stem of the goblet.

I couldn't explain the feeling. Every time I caught sight of the dead king's body, a cold dread crept up from my toes. I'd seen death before, many times. We used to have cadavers delivered to my home village so we could study them, but they were just tools for learning. This was a human being. A king. He'd been alive just minutes ago, and now he was dead.

I downed the wine. Then I snatched Arenn's glass and downed that too.

"That's the spirit, Naria!" Erissa grinned. "You know, I think we should throw a ball." She glanced at the Faery Queen. "You'll help me plan it, won't you, Amie? Let the whole realm celebrate with us! Everyone shall be invited. It's been years since—"

"The King is dead, Mother," Lukas growled, his knuckles turning white as he gripped the head of his wine goblet. "Your *husband* is dead. Show some respect."

Silence fell over the table, and I risked a glance at Lyssandra. She'd been oddly quiet since Ikelos's death, her focus remaining fixed on her goblet as she sipped her wine slowly.

"Is the wine not to your liking?" Erissa asked, twisting to face her.

"It's fine," Lyssandra shot back in a raspy voice. "I just—" She cleared her throat. "I think we should drink something a bit stronger."

Without a moment's hesitation, Erissa signalled to a nearby trembling faery servant. "Fetch us the strongest wine. Quickly!" She spoke with such confidence, as if this were her own kingdom. I'd never seen her like this before. Perhaps the King's death had restored some of her sanity.

Although any hope of that soon faded when the servant hurried back with a black bottle of faery wine. After the servant placed the bottle on the table, Erissa swiped

Lyssandra's goblet and promptly tossed the leftovers over her shoulder, as if this were the usual way to deal with unwanted wine. We all watched in surprise as the red liquid splashed against the sparkling white floor, some of it landing on the poor servant's apron.

"Ugh, clean that up, won't you?" Erissa groaned, as if the entire deliberate act was an accident. The trembling servant didn't hesitate to obey, falling to her knees to wipe up the stain.

"Clumsy thing," Erissa scoffed as she poured the wine, filling both hers and Lyssandra's goblets to the brim. With an innocent smile, she handed Lyssandra her goblet back. "To my dead husband, and to our future friendship!" She raised her glass high.

"Indeed," Lyssandra grumbled, before downing the entire glass in a few deep swigs. After lowering her goblet, she paused for a moment, then added, "You do realise that now Ikelos is dead, I will be taking your kingdom?"

Erissa nodded with a light chuckle. "Of course! It's no good to me anyway, dear."

Lyssandra's lips thinned. "And I will be killing your son." Gasping, my heart lurched as if someone had just punched me in the chest. "I thought about keeping him as a pet," she yawned, "but he looks far too similar to Ikelos for my liking."

"Do whatever you'd like to him." Erissa shrugged as my heart raced. "He was always more of my husband's son than my own. I never wanted children, but the King had to have his heir."

"How could you say that?" I spat.

Erissa shot me a warning look. "Quiet, girl."

All this time, Lukas said nothing, choosing instead to stare blankly at his goblet, as if he'd heard all this before. It took everything within me to not reach for his hand across the table, but Arenn's heavy palm pressing into my thigh served as a reminder for what would happen if I tried.

"It's strange," Lyssandra mused as she rested her chin in her palm. "I thought I'd feel happy once Ikelos was dead... But instead, I feel—" She yawned again. "Empty and..." Her eyes flickered shut for a moment before they snapped open. "What?" she gasped, snatching her goblet. "What isss in this w-wine?" But I could hardly understand the slurry mess of words that fell out of her mouth.

Erissa grinned wildly. "Special Corlixin sleeping powder. Courtesy of dear Naria's medicine collection." She tossed me a wink.

"You poisoned me?" Lyssandra whimpered, clutching at her throat.

"Oh no, dear," Erissa chuckled. "I take some every night to help me sleep. I just gave you about five nights' worth."

Five nights wouldn't kill her, though she'd probably spend the next few days in bed.

I blinked as the realisation in my mind washed away some of the rage. So that was why she poured the wine onto the floor... A distraction?

"I truly am grateful that you murdered my husband," Erissa carried on. "It feels like a weight the size of the realm has lifted off my shoulders. But I'm afraid I can't have you killing my son. As much as he's always reminded me of *him*, my son is innocent, and so is Princess Naria."

"I was never... going to... hurt her." Lyssandra's head lolled with sleep.

"Oh Lyssi," the Faery Queen wept. "Whatever happened to my sweet baby girl?"

When her eyelids finally fluttered shut and her body slumped back in her chair, a silence fell over us all. But it lasted for barely a moment before King Bevan shot out of his seat.

"Guards!" he barked, as several faery men rushed into the room. "Take Lyssandra to a spare bedchamber. Bind her with iron chains – make sure they are iron!" he insisted. "And then lock the door. I want at least two guards outside her room at all times."

"Yes, sir!" The guards obeyed, swiftly lifting the sleeping faery out of her chair.

The King then swept his gaze over to his son, who was lounging lazily in his seat beside me.

"Arenn, go with them," King Bevan ordered. "See to it that they bind her in the correct chains. We can't risk her using any of her abilities again."

"Can't you just trust your own guards?" Arenn complained, reluctantly heaving himself out of the dining chair.

The King shook his head. "We can't let there be any more mistakes. Your mother and I didn't know how strong she was before. But we've all seen it now. She has the Divine Gift, and more power than any of us. The whole realm will suffer if she overwhelms us for a second time."

I didn't have a chance to ask what he possibly meant by 'Divine Gift' as Arenn huffed and then offered his hand out to me. "Let's go, human."

At his words, Lukas shot up, now free of the chains that had bound him before. "She's not going anywhere with you," he stated, anger biting at his tone.

"I suggest you sit back down, princeling," Arenn growled.

"My father is dead," Lukas answered coldly, "therefore I am no longer a prince."

Arenn scoffed. "Prince or not, Naria and I are still engaged. By faery law, that means I *own* her." I opened my mouth to protest, but one sharp look from the faery prince forced my lips to clamp shut.

Lukas was silent for a few breaths before he turned to glare at King Bevan. "Today your daughter murdered a king," he started, his voice strong. "When the other rulers find out – and they will find out – they will send their armies. You might be fae, but there are at least ten times more humans. Your strength is no match for our numbers." His eyes narrowed. "So let me offer you a deal, from one king to another." Pausing, he marched over to the Faery King, only stopping when he was mere inches away. Despite being at least half his age, Lukas towered over him. "I will tell the rulers that Ikelos died from his curse. I will tell them that we travelled here to search for a cure and that you all tried your very best, but there was nothing you could do. You can keep Lyssandra. Forges know you're probably the only ones who can contain her anyway. But in return, I need your army to help dispose of the goblins, and," Lukas paused, his jaw tightening, "Naria will return home to Drothmore, with me."

"Absolutely not!" Arenn thundered.

Ignoring his son's protests, the Faery King stroked his

beard in thought. "How long will you require our army for?"

"No more than a day," Lukas replied. "The goblins are cowards. They'll flee at the slightest whiff of faery magic."

King Bevan nodded as my heart raced so fast it could've burst from my chest. "Then we have a deal."

"Father!" Arenn's jaw almost hit the floor. "You can't let him take her from me! I am your son and she is *my* betrothed, does that mean nothing to you?"

"Quiet, boy." The Faery King flashed him a glare. "The new King of Drothmore is being very generous to us. We should be grateful that this is all he wants."

"But Father—" Arenn attempted to argue more, but was interrupted when Queen Amabel pushed up from her seat. Quickly, she hurried over to his side and tugged his ear towards her lips. She spoke to him for only a few moments, in a hushed whisper, until eventually, with a sweet smile, she pulled away and returned to her place at the table.

I didn't hear what she'd whispered, but whatever it was, it must've been very convincing. Arenn scowled at Lukas before lowering his gaze to where I was still seated.

Leaning in close until his lips brushed my ear, he dropped his voice to a low whisper. "You can run back to Drothmore with your princeling. You can even run to the other side of the realm. But remember what I told you in my bedchamber, little human... Soon, you won't be able to stay away." Delicately, he scooped up my hand and planted a soft kiss onto my skin.

"Until we meet again, dear princess." Then, with a reluctant smile, he sauntered out of the dining room.

CHAPTER 43

"Where are you taking me?" I asked with a giggle. Below, the horse rocked with movement as I leaned back against Lukas's warm chest. Everything around me was shrouded in darkness, but when I went to subtly tug down the rim of my satin blindfold, Lukas's hand closed around mine.

"So impatient," he teased, guiding my hand back to my lap, "though I promise you'll find out soon enough. We're almost there."

I let out a mocking groan. "You said that half an hour ago."

While the world around me remained a mystery, I was certain we were still travelling through the same forests we'd entered into this morning. It'd been weeks since the failed goblin invasion on Drothmore, and by now, the crisp autumn air had wrapped itself around us like a gentle chill.

Tugging my cloak closer, the faint earthy smell of mushrooms hit my nose as leaves crunched beneath us.

Thankfully, despite all the chaos following the King's passing, it hadn't taken long for Lukas to settle into his father's position. Since you can't exactly run a kingdom from your bedchamber, the crown prince had already taken over most of the King's duties long before his death. Still, ever since the day of his coronation, we'd hardly spent any time together at all. He'd been so busy with this one particular project. So many times I'd offered to help, or at least asked to know what he was working on, but each time I was given a different excuse for why I absolutely could not be involved. At first, it was because it was just a highly secret matter. Later, it was because it actually involved another kingdom entirely. So, this morning, when he'd arrived at my chambers to tell me that he was finally ready to share it, my heart almost burst from my chest.

"We're here," Lukas murmured into my ear. Tiny bumps formed on my skin as the autumn wind picked up. In the distance, I could hear faint laughter and chatter. We must've reached the edge of the forest. Perhaps we'd even gone as far as Dalking.

I went to slip off the blindfold, but Lukas did it for me. The second the fabric fell away from my face, I gasped, and my hands smacked over my wide-open mouth. We were certainly not in Dalking.

"Welcome home, Princess Naria."

Stretching out to the horizon was a vast plain of ruins and half-crumbled buildings. In the distance, lavender spires punctured the skyline, while thick, destroyed walls and towers sprawled between them. In a cleared grassy patch before us, were several very familiar buildings and a scruffily built schoolhouse. Dozens of people ran in and out of the houses, gathering resources and supplies, all helping the fifty or so uniformed Drothmore soldiers who were reassembling other small homes. It almost looked just like it did in the forest, except it was here – in the plains of Corlixir.

Tears formed in the corners of my vision. "You moved my village," I stuttered breathily.

"Soon, it'll be much more than just a village," Lukas added. Then, with a smile, he slipped out of the saddle and helped me down too, holding my waist to steady me as I felt my boots touch the soft grass. "All the Honeymeade buildings are due to be completed by the end of next week," he explained, tilting his chin towards the village. "Then we will begin reconstructing the schools, libraries, research towers, and anything else your people need to thrive here." His gaze returned to me as my heart thundered in my chest.

"I... I don't know what to say," I stammered, wiping away a stray tear.

"Do not think you need to thank me." He drew closer, taking my hands in his. "It may take time, and we may still need to seek the help of other rulers if we run out of funding, but I promise you this, Naria." Our eyes met as his jaw tensed. "Even if it takes decades... Even if there is a war because the other rulers do not wish to see Corlixir rise again, or even if I have to personally scrape every gram of gold off of every damned gilded dresser in Drothmore to pay for it all, I am committed to restoring the kingdom that my father stole from you."

My lower lip trembled. "From the hearts of all my people, thank you, Lukas." The words came out barely louder than a whisper, but he still heard me, clutching my hands tightly in response. When my lips slipped apart to say more, a loud shout stole my attention away.

"Naria!" a girl screamed from the village. "You're back!"

Whirling around, I was met head-on by a familiar, young, brown-haired woman – her arms outstretched, charging at full speed towards me.

"Ivy!" I squealed, throwing my arms around her as our bodies collided with a heavy thud. "Oh, how I've missed you!" The moment her long hair brushed past my nose, the scent of medicinal herbs overwhelmed my senses. I took a deep breath, inhaling the smell. It was so good to be home.

"You have to tell me everything," Ivy said, beaming as she stepped out of the hug. "So much has happened since you've been gone. They finally let us start our research projects, Clare's had her baby, and, oh! Terrence and Marius are a couple now!"

"Terr and Marius are a couple?" I repeated, swinging up a hand to hide my grin.

"I know, it's about time, isn't it?" she giggled. "Really should've happened years ago. But enough about the village, I can't believe you're back!" She squeezed my arm. "You must tell me, how was Drothmore? Did you get to go to any balls? Did they give you a tiara? Did you meet any princes?" Her gaze then flew over my shoulder, landing on Lukas, who was still standing rather awkwardly behind me. "Oh, Naria..." She drew closer, dropping her voice to a low whisper. "Who is this handsome stranger you've brought with you? Please tell me you'll be leaving him with us."

Quickly, I stifled a giggle before stepping back to introduce the pair. With a smile, I turned to Lukas first. "Lukas, please allow me to introduce you to the lovely Ivanya Brightlock, one of my closest friends."

Ivy dipped her head gracefully as Lukas took her hand and bowed in formal greeting. "It is delightful to meet you, Miss Brightlock."

"Oh please," she laughed, her voice like a bell, "just Ivy is fine."

"And Ivy," I addressed my friend, "this is Lukas. Or more specifically, His Royal Majesty King Lukas Forgeborn of Drothmore."

Immediately, the colour in Ivy's face drained to a pale cream as she doubled herself over into a panicked bow.

"Your Majesty?" she blurted out, her cheeks flushing pink. "Please forgive me for acting so informally, I did not realise—"

"It's quite alright," Lukas chuckled, gesturing for her to rise. "There's no need for any formalities while I am here." Then his voice took on a more lilting tone. "I'm just glad that I was able to meet the one friend that Naria has spoken so highly of."

I shot Lukas a look, which he met with a subtle wink. *Lying charmer.*

"Spoken so highly of?" Ivy passed me a shy grin. "Oh, Naria, and here I was thinking Marius was your favourite."

Innocently, I shrugged, "You've always been the best at medicine mixing."

That was no lie. Ivy was one of the most talented medicine crafters in Honeymeade – possibly even the realm.

"You're too flattering." She swatted my arm playfully. With a quick glance back at the village, she added, "Shall we introduce your handsome royal friend to the rest of the group? Everyone is taking a break in the schoolhouse. If we leave now, we can catch them all together. They'll all be so happy to see you." She grinned, taking my hand again.

"If I may," Lukas cut in before I could reply, "I'd quite like to steal Naria for just a minute. There is one small matter we must discuss, but then afterwards I'd be honoured to meet the rest of her Corlixin friends."

Ivy blinked up at him. "Of course." She smiled, before her gaze landed on me. "Enjoy your *discussion*." With a playful wave of her fingers, she turned to hurry back towards the village.

The moment she was gone, I tilted my head towards Lukas. "Is something wrong?" I asked.

"It's nothing to be concerned about," he reassured me, "but first, let me show you something."

Guiding me up a gentle slope, away from the village, he stopped us by a small section of grass, hidden partially by some trees. As I peeked around them, my breath caught. I could see it all from up here – my old dormitory, the herb supply, even Ivy running back to the schoolhouse. Nothing could have wiped the grin off my face. *This was my home.*

"Naria?"

My heart fluttered like a little butterfly at the sound of my name. Then, that butterfly bloomed into a thousand roses when I spun around and saw *him*.

Lukas was once again before me, but this time he was down on one knee. In his hands, he held a stunningly-crafted ring. The golden band glimmered in the light, while the precious stone centrepiece reflected a rainbow of glittering colours.

"Princess Naria," he began softly, "I know that we are technically already engaged, but I wanted to do this properly and give you this ring with a promise." He took a breath as my heart caught in my throat. "Like I said before, it might not happen overnight. We might run into problems. And it may even take years to find the funding, but, if you accept this ring and willingly become my wife, I assure you we will rebuild your kingdom. Together."

Sunlight pierced through the thick clouds above, making his bronze skin appear to glow. I almost couldn't breathe. This had to be a dream.

When I didn't answer, he continued, his voice stuttering slightly, "I know this probably feels like a lot, and I'm not asking you to love me. This is really more so I can justify all the spending to the court council. We can keep our... relationship completely political. At least until you're comfortable." The tips of his ears flushed red. "I'll never force you to do anything. We wouldn't have to—"

"Oh hush," I finally replied as the happy tears broke through. Falling to my knees, I collapsed onto the ground in front of him. "You have done so much for me. So much that I feel I can never say thank you enough." I held his face with my hands. We were so close I could hear his breath shudder.

"You..." I wanted to say more, but then my gaze caught on the ring. Up close, it was even more impressive, with delicate engravings in swirling patterns etched around the band. I could've studied it for hours. "This ring is... I've never seen anything so beautiful."

"Thank you." Lukas grinned. "It wasn't easy to make."

My eyebrows shot up. "You made this?"

"Of course, metalwork is one of my many talents," he said as his grin straightened into a proud smirk.

"I can't believe it," I breathed. "You're so—"

"Talented?" he offered. "Charming? Any maiden would be lucky to have my heart?"

"Modest," I decided with a laugh.

Our eyes locked, but only for a moment until my gaze found his lips. Then, that was all I could focus on as I felt myself being drawn slowly towards him, closer and closer before finally, without letting myself think anymore, I pulled his lips into mine.

He froze. A few heartbeats passed. And then my back was against the soft grass as he kissed me endlessly. With the two of us so close, all I could taste were summer fruits, salted caramel, and the sweetest daydreams. But if this was just a daydream, I never wanted it to end.

My fingers tangled in the soft waves of his hair as one of his hands slipped down my waist.

"Your Majesty?" someone, probably one of his soldiers, called abruptly from beyond the clearing.

Above me, Lukas growled. He kissed me once more in a parting way, then again, then again, and then again! Until I pushed him off me with a giggle.

"Do you need to deal with that, *Your Majesty*?" I teased.

"Probably," he murmured, running his hand down my thigh, "but you never answered my question."

"Hmm?" I answered dreamily.

He left a trail of soft kisses down my neck. "Do you accept my proposal?"

"Is this not enough of an answer for you?" I whispered back. "Yes, of course I accept!"

With a smile brighter than I'd ever seen before, he propped himself up with his hands in the grass. "You're absolutely radiant," he breathed. Then he kissed me one last time before finally pushing himself up and heading towards where the soldier called from.

Before he left the clearing, he called back to me over his shoulder. "You stay right there," he commanded, pointing his finger at me. "We're not finished."

I laughed, letting myself flop back onto the grass. It was still slightly damp from last night's rain, but I didn't care. Everywhere he'd touched felt so warm, and everywhere he hadn't only burned for him. I took a deep breath, closing my eyes to inhale in the cool autumn air. The scent of fresh leaves and wildflowers filled my nose. Even with him gone, I could still taste him on my lips, still feel his touch on my waist.

When I eventually opened my eyes, the smell of wildflowers growing oddly stronger, I almost jumped out of my skin as a large black cat stared down at me.

"Ancients!" I gasped before scrabbling to prop myself up onto my elbows. "What is a cat doing all the way out here? Do you belong to someone in the village?"

The animal meowed, then smoothly rubbed its side along my arm. A soft purr sounded from its belly, and as I lifted a hand to absentmindedly run my fingers through its thick dark fur, two amber irises blinked slowly up at me.

"Aren't you a lovely thing?" I smiled. "If no one here claims you, I might have to take you back to the palace myself. Though Lukas might be a little jealous." A light chuckle bounced from my throat.

The cat rubbed his fur along my arm again, then flopped onto his side. Without thinking, I went to stroke him again when my gaze caught something glittering behind his paw.

"What's this?" I mused, gently lifting his front leg. He meowed in a long, lazy sort of way, and as I brushed the fur aside, my fingers caught on something cold.

Embedded in the cat's fur, above its paw, were two tiny crystals, mirroring the ones in my own wrist. Instantly, my breath stilled. The similar smell, those familiar eyes... A shiver colder than winter rushed down my spine.

"Arenn..." The name spilled out of me with a jagged breath. I moved back, suddenly desperate to be as far away from this *creature* as possible.

The faery cat stretched lazily before rolling to his feet. His amber eyes met mine as one narrowed into a slow and deliberate wink. Then, he slinked back towards the treeline, as if nothing had ever happened, his tail swishing casually behind him.

ACKNOWLEDGEMENTS

First of all, a big thank you to YOU, my lovely reader, for making it to the end. I hope that you found at least some joy in reading the first part of Naria's journey and that your own kingdoms are forever prosperous.

Secondly, I need to thank Michael for being my very first reader and for loving me always, even on my goblin days. Without you, I never would've been able to finish writing this first book or share it with anyone other than the plushies on my bed. I love you to the stars that we see at night, and then to the stars beyond.

I'd also love to give a heartfelt thanks to Blu, Marina, Ivana, Tom, Freya, Vlada, and my mum and dad for reading my book even when it was fresh out of Google Docs and full of typos! I deeply appreciate the feedback you gave and all your support.

Finally a special thanks to my cover designer, Krafigs_Creative, for creating such a wonderful cover; you captured the enchanting, fairy-tale vibes perfectly. And to Mariska from Rubre Art for providing me with such beautiful illustrations and book formatting.

WHAT'S NEXT?

Thank you for reading *Of Ashes and Wildflowers*!
If you liked it, please consider leaving a review. As an indie author, every review makes a big difference.

Naria's story continues in *Of Oceans and Broken Princes*.
Available to read now on Kindle Unlimited or as a paperback!

You can find updates on Instagram at @erinfae_author
And on TikTok at @erinthebookfaery
https://erinfaewriting.wordpress.com/

Printed in Dunstable, United Kingdom